I don't ha ... are all laid out in front of me.

The door was locked. The room was comfortable, replete with a well-stocked kitchen and an entertainment system that was so up-to-date it contained movies yet to be released. But the door was locked.

*You're considered a risk. They don't know the extent of my power to influence you.*

Oliver turned in his rotating chair to face Five, whose accommodations were less plush. Behind the carbon alloy mesh that separated them, Five's room was empty except for a water dispensation device that resembled a giant hamster lick. Five was lying flat, his appendages splayed like the spokes of an elephant-sized wheel. His skin had a stony, mottled texture, and there were bristles protruding at evenly spaced intervals across it. The cilia protruding from the tips were as thick as nautical rope, and transparent.

"Because you were able to win over a thirteen-year-old boy, they think you might be able to convince me that I'm fighting on the wrong side? That's absurd."

*But they don't know that,* Five said. *They think you've become too familiar with me. Too friendly.*

## ALSO BY WILL MCINTOSH

Soft Apocalypse
Hitchers
Love Minus Eighty
Defenders

# DEFENDERS

## WILL McINTOSH

www.orbitbooks.net

ORBIT

First published in Great Britain in 2014 by Orbit

A CIP catalogue record for this book
is available from the British Library.

ISBN 978-0-356-50215-1

Printed and bound in Great Britain by Clays Ltd, St Ives plc

Papers used by Orbit are from well-managed forests
and other responsible sources.

MIX
Paper from
responsible sources
FSC® C104740

Orbit
An imprint of
Little, Brown Book Group
100 Victoria Embankment
London EC4Y 0DY

An Hachette UK Company
www.hachette.co.uk

www.orbitbooks.net

*To James Pugh*

# PART I
# INVASION

# Prologue

## *Lieutenant Enrique Quinto*

*June 26, 2029. Morris Run, Pennsylvania.*

It was a quaint Pennsylvania town, many of the buildings well over fifty years old, with green canopies shading narrow doorways. Even the town's name was quaint: Morris Run. If not for the abandoned vehicles, filthy and faded by two years of exposure to the elements, and the trash stacked along the sidewalk, Quinto might have expected someone to step out of the Bullfrog Brewhouse and wave hello.

"Lieutenant Lucky?" Quinto turned to see Macalena, his platoon sergeant, making his way to the front of the carrier. Quinto wished he'd said something the first time someone called him Lucky, but it was far too late now. Most of the troops he was leading today probably didn't know his real name.

"One of the new guys shit his pants," Macalena said when he drew close, his voice low, giving Quinto a whiff of his sour breath.

Quinto sighed heavily. "Oh, hell."

"The kid's scared to death. He hasn't been out of Philadelphia since this started."

"No, I don't blame him." Quinto looked over Macalena's shoulder, saw the kid perched on the side of the carrier, head down. He was about fourteen. The poor kid didn't belong out here. Not that Quinto couldn't use him; they called raw recruits "fish food," but sometimes they were surprisingly effective in a firefight, because they were too scared to think. The starfish could get less of a read on what they were going to do, which way they were going to point their rifles. Usually the newbies didn't shit their pants until the shooting started, though. "Does he have a spare pair?"

Macalena shook his head. "That's the only pair he owns."

Quinto reached into his pack, pulled out a pair of fatigue pants, and handed them to Macalena. "I hope he's got a belt."

Macalena laughed, stuck the pants under his armpit, and headed toward the kid.

What an awful thing, to be out here at fourteen, fifteen. When Quinto was fourteen, he'd spent his days playing video games, shooting bad guys in his room while Mom fetched fruit juice and chocolate chip cookies and told him when to go to bed.

They reached the end of the little downtown, which was composed of that single road, and the landscape opened up, revealing pine forest, the occasional house, mountains rising up on all horizons. There was little reason for any Luyten to be within eight miles of this abandoned backwater town, but they were all out there somewhere, so there was always a chance they'd be detected.

Quinto tried to access his helmet's topographical maps, but the signal still wasn't coming through. He pulled the old hard copy from his pack, unfolded it.

4

The carrier slowed; Quinto looked up from the map to see what was going on. There was a visual-recognition drone stuck in a drainage ditch along the side of the road. As they approached, the VRA drone—little more than a machine gun on treads—spun and trained its gun on each of the soldiers in turn. When it got to Quinto, it paused.

"Human. *Human!*" Quinto shouted, engaging the thing's vocal-recognition failsafe. It went on to the next soldier.

It was always an uncomfortable moment, having a VRA drone point a weapon at you. You'd think it would be hard to mistake a human for a Luyten.

Failing to identify anything that resembled a starfish, the gun spun away.

"Get a few guys to pull it out of the ditch," Quinto said. Four troops hopped out of the transport and wrestled the thing back onto the road. It headed off down the road, continuing on its randomly determined route.

Pleasant Street dead-ended close to the mouth of the mine, about half a mile past an old hotel that should be coming up on their left. When they got to the mine they'd have to unseal it using the critical blast points indicated on the topo map, then a 2.5-mile ride on the maglev flats into the mine, to the storage facility.

If someone had told Quinto two years ago that he'd be going into an abandoned mine to retrieve seventy-year-old weapons and ammo, he would have laughed out loud.

It wasn't funny now.

The locomotive and five boxcars were parked right where they were supposed to be—as close to the mouth of the mine as the track would allow. They were late-twentieth-century vintage, the locomotive orange and shaped like a stretched

Mack truck. Quinto called Macalena and his squad leaders, instructed them to set the big recognition-targeting gun they'd brought along in the weeds on the far side of the road, and place two gunners near the entrance with interlocking fire. When that was done, they got the rest of the squads moving down the tunnel. The quicker they moved, the sooner they'd be out of hostile territory and back in Philly.

Quinto took up the rear of the last carrier for the ride down into the mine. He was not a fan of deep holes with black walls, and when his CO had first laid out the mission Quinto had nearly crapped his own pants.

Macalena climbed in and took the seat beside him.

"So what are we looking for? I cannot for the life of me guess what we're doing in here."

Quinto smiled. It must seem an odd destination to the rest of the men, but they were used to being kept in the dark about missions. The fewer people who knew, the less likely the starfish were to get the information. Or so the logic went.

"The feds have been sealing huge caches of weapons in old mines for the past two centuries, waiting for the day when Argentina or India or whoever took out our more visible weapons depots. They coat them in Cosmoline and pretty much forget about them."

Macalena frowned, sticking out his big lower lip. "You mean, old hand grenades and machine guns and shit?"

"More or less. Flamethrowers with a pathetically limited effectiveness range, eighty-one-millimeter mortars, LAW rockets, fifty-cal MGs." Most were outdated weapons, but simple, easy to operate.

Macalena shook his head. "So we're that desperate."

In the seat in front of them a private who was at least seventy was clinging to the bar in front of her seat. She was tall—at least six feet. The slight jostling of the carrier was clearly causing her old body discomfort. It was true what they said: There were no civilians anymore, only soldiers and children.

"Yup. We're that desperate," Quinto said. "They've destroyed or seized so much of our hardware that we have more soldiers than guns."

"What's Cosmoline?" Macalena asked.

"I didn't know, either; I had to look it up. It's a grease they used back in the day to preserve weapons. Once you chip away the hardened Cosmoline, the weapons are supposed to be like new."

Macalena grunted, spit off the side. "Dusty as hell in here. And cold."

"Let's be glad we're not staying."

Macalena's comm erupted, a panicked voice calling his name.

"What have we got?" Macalena asked.

"Vance is dead. Lightning shot, from the trees to the left of the mine."

"*All stop!*" Macalena shouted. The carrier slowed as Quinto dropped his head, covered his mouth as the implications sunk in.

Lucky no more.

"Where are you now?" Macalena asked the private.

"Inside the mine, about a hundred yards."

"Stay there."

Quinto looked up at Macalena, who raised his eyebrows. "What do you want to do?"

He wanted to get as deep in the mine as he could, and stay there, their backs against the wall, weapons raised until the starfish came to get them. Of course the Luyten would never

7

come down, because they were reading his thoughts right now. Plus it was far easier to blow the mouth of the mine and leave them to suffocate.

Quinto ordered the small caravan to turn around and head toward the mouth.

They barely got moving before they heard the flash-boom of a Luyten explosive. The cave shook; bits of dirt and debris spewed at them, then everything settled into silence, the cave now truly pitch-black, save for the carriers' headlights.

They climbed out of the carriers. Some of the troops cried, and there was no shame in that. One woman went off to the side of the tunnel and knelt in the rubble to pray. Quinto didn't know their names, because he hadn't served with them long. Troops came, and died, and new troops came. Only Lieutenant Lucky went on, mission after mission. Quinto realized he'd begun to believe he really was lucky, or special. Destined to see the war to its end.

It killed him, to think he wouldn't get to see how things turned out, whether the bad guys won, or the good guys pulled something out of their asses at the eleventh hour.

Quinto used the walkie to apprise HQ of their situation, so HQ wouldn't wonder when Quinto's platoon never returned.

"Lieutenant?" Macalena said. He was studying the topo map he'd borrowed from Quinto. "Did you see these?" A few of the enlisted came over to look at the map over Macalena's shoulder as he ran his finger along black lines set perpendicular to the mine. "There are five vertical shafts sunk along the length of the mine. I'm guessing they were escape routes in case of collapse, or ventilation, or both."

Quinto looked up from the map, impotent rage rising in him. "Jesus, Mac, couldn't you have waited a half hour to notice this?"

It took Macalena a second to understand. When he did, he grimaced, curled his hand into a fist, crumpling a section of the map. He turned and walked a dozen paces down the shaft, cursing quietly, viciously.

Even Macalena was too green for this war. He'd been in the infantry for only four months; before that he'd been writing military technical manuals. The army needed fighters more than writers these days.

If Macalena had waited even fifteen, twenty minutes before examining the old map, chances were the Luyten would have been out of range, and they could have climbed out of this hole and gone home.

"We need to move," Quinto said. "The fish are going to find those exits and seal them up. Spread out, find the exits. When I get to the surface I'm going to set off a Tasmanian devil, give us some breathing room. As soon as it's spent, get out there. Understood? Let's move."

"Couldn't we just stay down here? Dig our way out when they're gone?" It was the kid who'd crapped himself, looking absurd in Quinto's big pants. "If we go up there now, they'll kill us. I mean, maybe they'll get distracted by something and leave…" He trailed off.

Everyone stared at the ground, except for the soldier who was praying.

"Let's go," Quinto said.

Quinto grasped the cold rung of the ladder that had dropped down when they unsealed the iron hatch.

"Good luck to you, Lieutenant," one of the troops waiting to follow him called. It was Benneton, the old woman. The kid who'd crapped his pants was there as well, along with four others.

Quinto looked up into darkness. "Here we go." He headed up the ladder. A lot of people who'd been as lucky as Quinto might have been tempted to believe the streak would hold, but Quinto knew his past held no hint of his future. More to the point, he knew he had no future.

It was a forty-foot climb according to the map, but adrenaline made it effortless. When he reached the top, he twisted the seal on the hatch, then pushed with his back and shoulders to force the hatch open. Daylight flooded into the dusty shaft as dirt and moldy leaves rained down on him.

The kid, who was just below him, passed up the Tasmanian devil. Reaching among the big spines jutting from the central carbon-fiber sphere, Quinto activated it, tossed it outside, and pulled the hatch closed.

The buzzing of razor-sharp shrapnel hitting, and then burrowing around inside everything within five hundred yards, would have been reassuring if Quinto weren't absolutely certain the starfish had retreated outside the Tasmanian devil's range as soon as Quinto thought about using it. At least it would back the fish up so they wouldn't be able to pick off Quinto and his troops as they climbed out of their holes.

"Here we go," Quinto said to the boy. "Have your weapon out. Run as fast as you can. Try to take one with you." His guess was that Benneton would stay behind, shoot from the cover of the shaft until the Luyten cooked her. That's what Quinto would do in her situation; it would probably afford her a few more minutes of life. He took a deep breath, trying to grasp that this was the end, this was the moment of his death, but he couldn't.

As soon as the Tasmanian devil went silent, Quinto threw open the hatch, his heart thudding wildly, and ran.

Their carriers were trapped in the mine, so his best chance

would be to make it to the locomotive. Of course the Luyten would have fried the locomotive, so really there was nothing to do but run, and when the fish closed in, turn and fight.

Two hundred yards ahead, he spotted four of his troops running north, into the woods, toward the nearest cover. That probably made more sense than what Quinto was doing, but all of the moves open to them were losers. It was always the same: The fish knew their exact location, but they had no idea where the fish were. If you could catch a fish out in the open, it couldn't dodge automatic weapons fire, but you almost never caught them out in the open.

Quinto glanced back, saw the kid was two steps behind, his dirty cheeks tracked with tearstains.

The locomotive had been melted to a lump. He kept running. Everyone but he and the kid had headed north. Since Quinto wasn't dead yet, it was safe to assume the fish had gone after the larger group first. If he could get outside their range, which meant seven or eight miles, he and the kid might have a chance. Quinto pushed himself to pick up the pace, but when he did the kid started to fall behind, looking panicked. Quinto slowed.

In the distance, Quinto heard the worst sound in the world: the sizzle-crackle of a Luyten lightning stick, a sound as much felt in your body as heard by your ears. Then another. He was spared the pungent, unearthly sweat smell of the weapon. He was too far away.

When he'd made it through the town, Quinto took another glance back. The kid was a hundred yards behind, one hand clutching his side. No way this kid was going to run another four or five miles. Panting, his throat coated in phlegm, Quinto considered leaving him behind. No. No matter how fast he ran, he wasn't going to outrun Luyten on foot. He could try calling HQ and beg for a carrier to come get him, but they'd only tell him what he already knew: They weren't going to feed the fish any more than they had to.

So he stopped, pulled out his comm, and waited for the kid to catch up. The kid stopped beside him, put his hands on his knees.

"You want to call anyone? Your mom or dad alive?"

The kid eyed the comm. "Just my little sister." He swallowed, looked at Quinto. "We're going to die, aren't we?"

"Yeah. We are."

"Maybe they got distracted by something. Maybe the others killed them."

"Maybe," Quinto said. He thought he heard the snap-crackle of something moving through the woods to the north. "Come on." He tugged the kid's jacket and headed into the woods on the opposite side of the road.

Should he call his own mother to say goodbye? He would like that, but he didn't want to risk having her on the line when he died. He didn't want that to be her last memory of him.

Branches whipped his face as he tore through the brush. It was pointless, but he couldn't relinquish that last millimeter of hope that he might get lucky, just one last time. He barreled down a slope as the landscape opened, then splashed through a stream and raced up the bank.

He spotted a flash of crimson ahead, behind a thick cover of green leaves, and stopped short. The kid stopped short beside him, looked at him, questioning, just as a bolt of lightning burst through the foliage.

# 1

## *Oliver Bowen*

*March 9, 2030 (nine months later). The South Pacific.*

The door was locked. The room was comfortable, replete with a well-stocked kitchen and an entertainment system that was so up-to-date it contained movies yet to be released. But the door was locked.

*You're considered a risk. They don't know the extent of my power to influence you.*

Oliver turned in his rotating chair to face Five, whose accommodations were less plush. Behind the carbon alloy mesh that separated them, Five's room was empty except for a water dispensation device that resembled a giant hamster lick. Five was lying flat, his appendages splayed like the spokes of an elephant-sized wheel. His skin had a stony, mottled texture, and there were bristles protruding at evenly spaced intervals across it. The cilia protruding from the tips were as thick as nautical rope, and transparent.

"Because you were able to win over a thirteen-year-old

13

boy, they think you might be able to convince me that I'm fighting on the wrong side? That's absurd."

*But they don't know that*, Five said. *They think you've become too familiar with me. Too friendly.*

The CIA yanks him out of his position at NYU three days after the invasion begins, shifts him from Research to Interrogation as their field agents die off, tells him to figure out how to communicate with Luyten, and when he succeeds, he becomes a suspected sympathizer? Beautiful.

*The next time someone comes, ask them when you'll be informed where we're going.*

Oliver couldn't help laughing. "You mean *you* don't know?" He waved in what he guessed was the direction of the submarine's bridge. "Pluck it out of someone's mind."

*I don't have to pluck. Your minds are all laid out in front of me. No one on this vessel knows.*

"*No one* knows where we're going?" It seemed an absurd notion, though it also made sense. If no one on board knew where they were going, or why, a Luyten who happened to be flying nearby—within their eight-or-so-mile telepathic zone—wouldn't be able to find out, either. The mission must be important. "How are they navigating if they don't know where we're going?"

*They're given a set of coordinates corresponding to a point in the ocean, and when they reach it, they're given another.*

"So where are we?"

Oliver jolted back in his chair as one of Five's mouths opened, revealing a bobbing, twitching hole ringed with teeth that resembled the spines on cacti. Smacking, hissing air and background sounds like water draining came from the hole, the sounds so unearthly and repulsive that at first Oliver didn't register that they were approximating words.

"Find out where we're going," Five said aloud.

The ubiquitous hum of the sub's engine was the only sound in the room as Oliver composed himself. Ultimately it didn't matter whether the Luyten communicated telepathically or using spoken words, but it was still profoundly disturbing to hear the thing speak.

"You're just full of surprises, aren't you?" Oliver said.

"Unlike you." Somehow the creature managed to inject a note of irony, and perhaps contempt, into the awkwardly formed words.

Oliver slid out of the chair, went right up to the nearly invisible net of carbon fiber that separated them. "Don't assume you know my mind just because you can read my thoughts. We may not be as simple as you think."

"Yes, humanity is the pinnacle of evolution. The chosen ones, the purpose for the existence of the entire universe. How could I forget?" Aware that Oliver was having trouble understanding his strangely formed words, Five simultaneously broadcast his words directly into Oliver's mind, giving him the uneasy sensation of hearing the words with an indescribable overlap. "I know your mind better than you."

Oliver grunted, folded his arms across his chest. "Right."

"You're uneasy. You're afraid I might try to prove my claim."

It was pointless to disagree. Oliver had quickly learned how absurd it was to deny what you were thinking or feeling to something who knew precisely what you were thinking and feeling.

"You love your wife now—"

"*Shut up.* I don't want to hear about Vanessa. *Just leave it.*"

Five waited patiently through Oliver's outburst, then continued. "After her affair, her denials, the angry divorce ... now you love her. Before, when you claimed to love her, you also despised her."

Oliver turned, went to the door, and thumped on it with the flat of his palm. "Hey, come on. Unlock this door. *I'm* not the POW."

"There's an irony you're not aware of, in your newfound feelings for your wife. Should I share it with you?"

Oliver turned to face Five, who was running the fine cilia that served Luyten as fingers across the stump of the limb he'd lost. "No. Thanks for the offer, but, no."

"It's something you'd be interested to hear."

When Oliver didn't answer, Five continued. "All right, then why don't I move on? What else can I tell you, to demonstrate you're as simple to read as I think you are? How about your deepest sexual cravings? Some of these you would never admit to yourself. For example, you'd like to be tied up, gagged with your own dirty sock, and spanked by a woman twenty years older than you."

Oliver couldn't care less about his repressed sexual desires. They were what they were; he couldn't control them, only whether he acted on them. But Oliver knew Five was only playing with him now. It had already dropped the bait it knew Oliver couldn't resist.

Five grew quiet, waiting for the question it already knew was coming.

"Fine. What's the irony I'm not aware of?"

All of Five's eyes fixed on Oliver. "The irony is, your instinct to love her is right, because she never had sex with Dr. Paul."

As the words registered, Oliver's vision darkened around the edges, as if he were going to pass out. In some ways, he wished he would. "You told me she had. You gave me specific details."

"I lied."

An icy numbness crept through him. He'd destroyed his marriage on the word of an alien bent on wiping out the human race. He'd taken Five's word as unassailable proof, because Five could reach right in and pluck the truth out of Vanessa's thoughts. Only he'd forgotten Five had abilities beyond reading minds. The ability to lie, for instance.

He'd told Vanessa he knew she was lying, said her unwillingness to admit the affair bothered him more than the infidelity itself. The floor, which was nothing but steel under a thin layer of beige carpeting, lurched beneath him, either because the sub was adjusting course or his knees were wobbling.

"Why would you lie? I didn't even ask you about Vanessa—you volunteered the information."

"I did it to serve as a reminder."

*"A reminder of what?"*

"That I might be lying to you at any time."

It dawned on Oliver that he had no way to contact Vanessa, and had no idea when he would, because he didn't know where he was going, or why. When he did finally contact Vanessa, would an apology make any difference? He'd trusted the word of a Luyten over hers.

This was going to torture him. In all probability that was Five's intention in telling him now. Or maybe he was lying now, simply to distract Oliver at a crucial juncture.

"Maybe," Five said.

# 2

## *Kai Zhou*

*June 29, 2029 (nine months earlier). Washington, D.C.*

Kai knew better than to look up at the old man behind the counter to see if he was watching. That was a dead giveaway. Instead, Kai tracked him through the reflection in the refrigerated display case, which was no longer cold, because it was illegal to waste energy to keep drinks chilled. Not that anyone had the energy to spare on such a luxury anyway.

The old guy had an underbite that made him look vaguely apish; what gray hair he had was combed straight back in thin lines. He was watching Kai, frowning, suspicious. Kai knew he looked like a hungry kid who had no one taking care of him, but he couldn't help it; he couldn't find it in him to relax the scowl, to smile. This was also one time Kai's size was probably a liability. Mom used to say he looked sixteen, not thirteen.

A wave of pain washed over him at the thought of his mom. Right now he didn't even feel thirteen—he felt more like eight. He wanted his mommy, wanted her to rock him

18

while he pressed his face against her long, soft hair. That's all most kids wanted since the invasion began. There were no tough kids left, only scared kids. And desperate kids, like him.

The door to the convenience store creaked open; a chubby woman with a tattoo on her shoulder stepped in and went to the counter. Kai seized the opportunity, snaring three fat pieces of jerky and stuffing them under his jacket, pinning them under his left arm.

He rose, spent a moment looking at the drinks in the nearly empty case, most of them homemade, the corporate logos printed on the bottles partially covered with white handwritten labels. Hurrying was another dead giveaway.

He paused again on his way to the door, watched a news feed playing on the TV above the front counter for a moment.

It was war footage of half a dozen Luyten storming a power plant. You almost never saw so many in one place, in the open. They were guerrilla fighters; they lost some of their advantage when they clustered, so when they attacked in force it usually meant they'd identified a poorly defended target.

Kai was repulsed by the sight of them—giant starfish, faceless, silent. Two were flying in their weird formfitting six- and seven-pointed craft, while the rest were on the ground, galloping on three or four of their limbs, staying behind vehicles and trees for cover, their free arms firing lightning bursts from the skintight battle gear that looked like ornate brass embroidery. A couple of human soldiers were peppering them with machine gun fire, but the Luyten always had a second's warning, always knew which way the soldiers were going to point the weapons. If the soldiers had larger weapons—flamethrowers or tanks—they'd have a chance. Then again, if they had larger weapons the Luyten would have known, and wouldn't have attacked in the first place.

When he couldn't stand to watch anymore, Kai headed toward the door.

The old guy moved from behind the counter with surprising speed, beating Kai to the door, brandishing a stun gun.

"I didn't see it, but I know you've got something." He waved the gun. "Open your jacket."

Kai wanted to tell the man he had no right to search him just because he looked filthy and tired, but it was pointless to argue. He reached into his coat and pulled out the jerky.

The chubby woman with the rose tattoo tsked, shook her head. She'd moved over to watch.

"I'm a good kid. It's just, my parents were killed when Richmond got overrun, and I don't have anywhere to go." In a shrill, childish whine he added, "I'm so hungry."

The old guy plucked the jerky from Kai's outstretched hand. "I don't doubt what you're saying. Times are hard." He gestured toward the road with his chin. "Check with Refugee Services, see if they can give you some food."

"Refugee Services is *closed*. It's been closed since I got here. Please, let me have one?"

The man shook his head brusquely. "I can't hand out food to everyone who's hungry. I got almost nothing to sell as it is." He gestured toward the door.

Kai looked out into the dark, frigid, rainy night. The rain ticked against the storefront window. It was turning to sleet. He turned back. "Can I at least stay in here to keep warm? I won't take anything, I promise."

The man looked pained. "I'm trying to run a *store*. It ain't easy, you know. I let you stay, what about the next kid who wants to stay? Pretty soon I'll have to close for good like the rest of them."

Reluctantly, Kai pushed the door open, tucked his chin against the cold. Empty hands buried in his jacket pockets, he hurried down the street, weaving to find a path through the piles of trash, much of it electronics that didn't work or took too much energy to operate. In the street vehicles whooshed silently past, but only occasionally, nothing like traffic had been before the invasion began.

He wasn't sure where to go. He turned left at the end of the block to get off the main artery, passed mostly dark apartment buildings, eyeing the occasional warm yellow lights inside windows covered with security mesh. Kai longed to be in one of those apartments, in a warm bed, but none sported the green sash that indicated refugees were welcome. They were all full, or, more likely, the families inside were ignoring President Wood's plea to open their homes to people fleeing the Luyten.

The problem was, there were a lot more refugees now. Before Richmond fell, refugees had poured into the city as the starfish seized more and more of the outlying areas, and Kai and his family had done what they could to help them, like they were supposed to. Kai had shared his clothes with the refugees who were his age, brought them along to hang out with him and his friends. He could still remember how proud his mom was, how she smiled whenever he did something nice for one of the scared, shrunken kids who came down the road pulling a suitcase. Now that Kai was a refugee, there were too many for that sort of kindness. Washington was packed with refugees.

It was so hard, getting used to each thing that was taken

away. First, communication, when the Luyten took their satellites out. No way to speak to Grandma, or to Pauly, who'd been his best friend until last year. Then, as the Luyten choked off the routes between cities, no toothpaste, no food that arrived at the table ready to eat. Then the Luyten gained control of most of the solar and wind farms, the coal and nuclear plants, and there wasn't enough power to heat the house, or the water, or to run his handheld.

Now he had no warm bed, no food to eat at all.

He was heading away from the makeshift shanty camp where he'd stayed the past three nights. The camp was too far to reach in the cold and dark; he'd walked too far, trying to find food.

His toes were already numb, his shoes soaked from puddles he couldn't see.

He wished he had someone with him. Anyone. If he could pick one person who was still alive, it wouldn't be one of the cool friends he'd started hanging out with in the past year; it would be Pauly, who he'd known forever. Scrawny, goofy Pauly, whom Kai had pretty much dropped, for no good reason. Mom had been disappointed in Kai when he ditched Pauly. She'd told him you don't throw away friends.

What he wouldn't give to have Pauly beside him. Kai wondered where Pauly was, what he was doing.

There was an old brick and concrete building ahead, three separate dark, open bays of what must have once been an auto body shop, or a fire station. The building must have been fifty years old. It had been a long time since things were built out of red brick.

The first bay was nothing but a concrete floor, providing shelter from the rain but little relief from the cold, gusty wind. There was a door sitting slightly ajar, up three concrete steps along the wall. Even if it was a tiny toilet room, it would be warmer, at least.

The door squealed when Kai nudged it open. The room stank of cigarettes. A woman was curled up in one corner of what had once been an office. She was partially covered by a corner of the wall-to-wall carpet, which she'd peeled up from the floor. In the faint light, Kai took in her swollen face, matted hair, her bulging, empty eyes, wide open and unblinking. He swung the door closed with a cry of disgust.

Skin prickling, he scurried down the steps and out of the bay, back into the biting rain.

There were two more bays. Kai didn't like the thought of being so close to a dead body, but he was shivering uncontrollably from the cold. He couldn't keep going. What were the odds he'd find another abandoned building?

There was a door in the second bay, but it led to a bathroom, not an office. The third and final bay had no inner doors at all, so Kai returned to the second, gathered up what scraps of paper he could find, along with a small cardboard box, and returned to the bathroom.

The room smelled dank, with an undertone of dried urine. Still shivering, Kai pulled a half-used roll of toilet paper off the dispenser and used it to dab his wet clothes. It wasn't much help.

The room was too small for Kai to stretch out, so he curled his legs in, used a wadded-up juice carton as a pillow, and piled the trash over his legs as best he could. It felt strange, not to have Kabuki say good night. He missed Kabuki almost as much as he missed Pauly, though not nearly as much as he missed his mom. He knew Kabuki wasn't real, was nothing but a bunch of chips in his handheld designed to say pleasant things and follow directions, but he'd been a part of Kai's life for as long as he could remember.

Kai was freezing. He couldn't stop shaking; his hissing breath echoed off the half-tiled walls.

An image flashed, of the woman in the next bay. She must have frozen to death, maybe last night. And she had a carpet.

There was a draft whistling through the space where Kai had left the door open a crack. It would be warmer if he closed it, but he would lose the sliver of gray light. He didn't want to be in the pitch dark.

It had all happened so fast. It didn't seem long ago that he'd watched the first newscast of Luyten dropping from the sky. He remembered he'd been surprised when the schools were closed the next day. Only a week ago he'd been in his warm bed in Richmond. His mother had tucked him in, told him not to worry about Dad, who was with his brigade less than forty miles away between Richmond and the Luyten surge. A day later he was on a bus roaring down Interstate 95 packed with kids and old people.

There was no point in crying, but he couldn't help it.

The sound of his own crying made him feel worse. What was he going to do? Why wouldn't anyone tell him what to do, where to go?

*Did you smell?*

Kai cried out, jolted upright. He hadn't thought the words, they'd just come, raking through his head in a voice like steel fingernails on glass, the pronunciations all *off* in a strange and unsettling way.

*She's smoke. Lighter.*

Kai clamped his palms over his ears. His soaked pants were suddenly warm; he was vaguely aware he'd wet himself.

*Build fire.*

It felt like there was something crawling around in his head. Kai sat frozen, trembling, praying it wouldn't happen again.

*Or you die.*

Kai howled in terror. He didn't understand what was happening to him.

*Happening to you. Kai. Freezing.*

His teeth were chattering; his whole body was shaking from the cold, from fear. The voice went on, about the cold, about Kai dying, about fire. There was enough trash around to burn, but he had nothing to start a fire with.

*She's smoker. Lighter.*

A lighter was what he needed.

*You dead this morning. Do you Kai?*

The voice had asked him something. Kai was afraid that if he didn't answer, the voice might get angry, might do something to him. Drive him crazy, pull him down into whatever dark, awful place it came from. Something about the voice was so terribly wrong, so profoundly *off*. It was as if the words were jagged, scraping the inside of his head.

*You do?*

"No, I don't want to be dead," Kai said aloud, the volume of his own voice in the tight space making him flinch.

*She smoked. Lighter.*

Maybe he was already crazy. This was just what it was like, wasn't it? Voices in your head?

*Lighter. Her pocket.*

Kai jolted. Her pocket. Suddenly he understood what the voice was saying. She smoked. The dead woman smoked. He'd smelled stale smoke in there, hadn't he? The voice was telling him there was a lighter in her pocket.

*Yes.*

He didn't want to go back in that room. She was dead; her eyes were bulging—

*Or you die. Go.*

Kai shoved the door open, peered into the bay, half expecting to see something crouching there, waiting for him, but there was nothing but concrete, shadows, the howling wind.

Bent against the wind, Kai marched into the next bay, his heart in his throat. He climbed the steps, put his hand on the knob, twisted it partway.

Maybe the voice lived in the bathroom. Maybe if he didn't go back it couldn't get him, couldn't talk to him—

*Wrong. Go on.*

Kai gripped the handle tighter. It was ice cold. He twisted it, pushed the door open a foot.

There she was. He pushed the door open farther, took a step into the room. She was old, maybe sixty, Hispanic or maybe Indian. The tip of her tongue was jutting from between her blue lips.

He didn't want to do this; he'd rather freeze to death than stick his fingers in her pocket and feel her body. Would it be squishy or stiff?

The voice was silent, but he knew that if he waited it would speak to him again, would tell him to get the lighter. It might even yell at him. That would be awful. He had to do it. Quickly—as quick as he could. Kai's breath was coming in quick, rattling gasps. He took a deep breath and held it, stood paralyzed for a moment.

*Do it.*

The voice was like a shove at his back. Kai scurried to the body, squatted.

*Other one*, the voice said before Kai even had time to lift his left hand. He reached with his right, slipped two fingers into her pocket.

Her hip felt stiff through the denim of her jeans. It didn't feel as bad as he'd feared, but it was still bad. He felt the pointed tip of the lighter, but couldn't reach it.

*Pull her flat.*

That would mean touching her, really touching her. Kai so desperately didn't want to do that.

Whimpering, he scooted back, grasped her feet by her tattered shoes, squeezed his eyes closed. As soon as he pulled, the shoes slipped off. His belly roiling with disgust, he half flung, half dropped them, then grasped her spongy, swollen ankles and *pulled*.

The body slid forward inch by inch, then suddenly her head lolled to the left and she dropped, hard, to the floor. Not thinking, just wanting to get it over with, Kai shoved his hand into her pocket, closed his fingers around the long, thin lighter.

A moment later he was in the bay, running.

*Trash for fire.*

The voice was right—this bay had much more trash than the others. Kai ran around picking up as much as he could carry before returning to the second bay.

Moments later, he had a small fire burning. The heat felt marvelous on his fingers, his cheeks, his nose. The orange light pushed back the shadows and the darkness, made a place that was *his* in a way he couldn't put into words.

*Better. Yes. Collect more trash.*

Kai did as he was told, checking the last bay and returning with another armful of trash, which he set in a pile near the fire.

*Now sleep. I'll watch you for danger.*

The voice was horrible, but the words were reassuring, and they were growing clearer, less grating. Kai lay down, closed his eyes. He was so tired.

It would watch over him. How would it watch? Where were its eyes, Kai wondered?

He was drifting off, his front side warm, his back and feet still stiff with damp cold. The voice would watch over him.

Kai jolted upright, suddenly knowing whose voice it was.

*I won't hurt you.*

They knew what you were thinking. But Kai had never heard of one *speaking* to someone. Never. Not on the news, not from anyone.

*We can if we want.*

It heard everything he thought. There was no way for Kai to stop thinking, no shelter from it. It was in his head. They could read your mind until you were a few miles away. Kai pressed one hand to the cold ground. He had to—

*If you run, I will hurt you.*

Kai froze, a trickle of dread running through him.

"Where are you?" he whispered.

*Close.*

Kai sat utterly frozen, afraid to move, afraid to breathe.

*Sleep.*

# 3

## Lila Easterlin

*June 30, 2029. Savannah, Georgia.*

Lila's toothbrush was wet. She studied the other toothbrushes in the cup, trying to figure out who they might belong to in order to rule out suspects, running through all of the people who now used this bathroom, and trying to decide who was most likely to use someone else's toothbrush.

None of the toothbrushes looked like it belonged to her cousin Alfe, the hick from West Virginia she had met a grand total of twice before he and his family showed up on their doorstep last month. Toothbrush in hand, Lila stormed through the house, skirting bedding and mats, piles of clothes and suitcases, until she found Alfe eating a bowl of Lucky Charms, her favorite cereal, which she'd been rationing for the past six months because it was probably the last box she'd ever have.

Lila held her toothbrush in front of Alfe's nose. His beard looked dopier by the day, all patchy and scraggly on his narrow, hawklike face.

29

"Did you use this?" she asked.

He ate a spoonful of her Lucky Charms, studying the brush. "I might have."

"This is *my* toothbrush." She curled her lip. "I can't think of anything more disgusting than brushing my teeth with a brush you just used to dislodge bits of food from your mouth." She shook the toothbrush for emphasis. "This is mine. Don't use it again."

"But I don't have one," Alfe said, raising his shoulders.

"That's not my problem," she nearly shouted.

Her father appeared in the arch between the kitchen and living room, wearing boxer shorts and a T-shirt. "What's going on?"

Lila folded her arms defensively. "He used my toothbrush."

Her father looked at Alfe, who said nothing, then back to Lila. "Okay. Alfe, I'll find you a toothbrush. You—" He pointed at Lila.

"Don't point at *me*. I didn't do anything."

He kept his finger poised an inch from her nose. "Don't talk like that to Alfe."

Lila sighed heavily, tempted to point out that Alfe was also eating her cereal, but she knew that would go nowhere.

"Is he a starfish?" Dad asked, pointing at Alfe.

Lila closed her eyes, willing herself to be calm. "No." This was her dad's favorite routine. We have to pull together, blah, blah, blah. She got it; she just didn't want her toothbrush in Alfe's mouth.

"Then he's on your side."

Lila nodded, knowing Dad would only belabor the point if she argued.

Dad smiled, satisfied. "I'll find you a toothbrush," he said to Alfe. Lila watched him walk off, disturbed by how skinny he looked, how little he resembled the stocky, jowly man Lila had known all her life.

"I don't know how he can do what he does every day and still be so positive," Alfe said, shaking his head in wonder as he watched Lila's father walk away.

Lila studied Alfe for a moment, deciding whether she wanted to reply. She decided she didn't really have a choice, given that he'd said something nice about her father.

"He's always been like that. Three days after my mother left us to become a Fire Monk, he was helping me make a Halloween costume, and one for himself. Not that your wife leaving you to join a cult compares to disposing of thousands of bodies every day." Lila used to be embarrassed by what her father did for a living, back when being a mortician was about applying eyeliner to corpses. Now that it was about finding locations for mass graves and collecting DNA samples so relatives might one day know where their loved ones were buried, she felt better about it. "Sometimes people ask me why he's not fighting in the war."

Alfe snorted. "That's a pretty stupid question."

"I know." It was the first time she'd said more than hello to Alfe since he arrived, and now she felt shitty for making a big deal out of the toothbrush. He might be okay.

"Did you see your mother much?" Alfe asked.

Before the invasion, he meant. That went without saying. "Now and then. She's too serene for me. Puts me to sleep talking to her." She didn't want to talk about her mother, so she thought of another topic. "Was it hard getting here from Blacksburg?"

Alfe nodded. "We had one really bad moment. We stopped

at a lake to get water, and when we went down to the lake, there were two starfish standing in the water a hundred yards away, filling some of their weird sacks."

Lila felt a crawling sensation. "Holy shit. What did they do?"

Alfe put his hand over his mouth, shook his head. "They turned and stared at us. They seemed as surprised to see us as we were to see them, although we know *that's* not likely."

"What did you do?" Lila whispered, knowing she would have nightmares about this.

"We ran like hell back to our truck."

"They didn't chase you?"

Alfe shook his head. "All I can think is, they decided we weren't worth the trouble. Or maybe it was because it was a mother and three kids. Because, you know, sometimes they leave the kids alone." Lila nodded. She'd heard stories of Luyten letting children go. "But while we were running away, I just kept thinking, I'm about to die. Any second now I'm going to die."

Lila studied Alfe's face for a moment, then held out her toothbrush. "Here."

"Oh, no, that's okay. Your dad said he'd get me one."

She kept the toothbrush out. "If he does, you can give it back to me."

Alfe took it and thanked her. Lila went off to see what her dad was up to.

He was with Uncle Walter, whose burn scars seemed to get worse as he healed, rather than better. His face was nothing but a mottled red and white blur. They'd picked up the local news, which was now the only news, on the antenna her dad had fashioned out of junk car antennae. The picture was snowy, flickering in and out, confined to a small patch on the wall to conserve energy.

The newswoman was broadcasting from what looked to be someone's living room. She was a Clarise Wilde look-alike, from the brief period when it became fashionable to try to look as much as possible like one superstar celebrity or another, using plastic surgery. Now it just seemed embarrassingly old-fashioned and self-centered.

Using a printed map pinned to the wall, she explained that the starfish had seized control of the Bluffton/Beaufort area, so travel between Savannah and Charleston was no longer possible. They also continued to attack and board ships leaving the port, usually coming across from Hilton Head. Sometimes they used their own craft, which resembled colored amniotic sacks spitting bolts of lightning; at other times they were in human boats they'd seized.

The picture flickered and stretched, giving the Clarise Wilde look-alike a thin, otherworldly appearance.

"Man, I miss satellites," Uncle Walter said.

So did Lila. All those channels, so clear you could barely tell the pictures from the real world. Much more than that, though, she missed her direct feed. She missed being connected to a hundred friends at once. It would be easier to cope with the terror that gripped her all day, every day, if she had her friends to lean on.

She also missed being good at something. She'd been such a good VR engineer and navigator, better than any of her friends, anyone in her entire school. The feed had been her world, and then, suddenly, it was gone, and so was everything Lila cared about, everything that made her special.

The TV image flickered and died, along with the overhead light. In a distant room, someone cursed.

Uncle Walter checked the time. "Did we even get an hour that time?" He said it in an even, almost conversational tone.

33

No one complained. Even when they were complaining, they used a tone that made it sound like they weren't. Only Lila complained.

Since it was going to grow stiflingly hot inside rather quickly, Lila went outside. She sat under the crepe myrtle—the only tree in their tiny fenced-in yard—and tried not to think about how close the starfish were. She put in her earbuds, played a song by Park Zero. Usually his voice lifted her spirits. Today, though, she remained tense, uneasy.

They were surrounded now. For the longest time the starfish had kept to the wilderness areas, appearing only to sabotage a rail line, a power station—places Lila would never go, so she was safe. Now they were everywhere.

Lila wandered toward the fence, trying to get her mind off the Luyten, although the knot in her stomach was always there, whether she was thinking of them or not.

There was a truly impressive pile of junk in the alley behind the low stone wall. Someone had cleared all of the crap out of her pack-rat father's garage—probably to make room for refugee friends and relatives—and dumped it in the alley. Lila went to the fence to take a closer look.

Her dad must be heartbroken, to have all of his useless junk evicted after he'd spent thirty years letting it pile up. There were vehicle wheels and doors, engine parts, ancient video screens, busted solar panels from the time before the big solar plant was constructed south of the city. Lila hoped the starfish were enjoying all that power.

The back door slid open. Lila would never get used to the harsh sliding sound it made when it was opened manually. Dad joined her at the fence.

"This might be the only bright side to what's going on. I

finally had a reason to clean out the garage, and help carrying all the junk."

"I was just thinking about how heartbroken you must be. All of this good junk you might need someday."

"Yeah," Dad said laughing. "Someday."

Lila reached over the fence and lifted up a cylindrical object. "What's this?"

Dad shrugged. "I don't know."

Lila dropped it. It clattered off a long-obsolete medical diagnostic fMRI kit and wedged against an old TV screen.

"Find something productive to do," Dad said, not unkindly, shooing with his hands as if she were a puppy. "If there's nothing around here you can think of, go down to Civil Defense and volunteer. They'll find something for you."

Lila didn't want to go to Civil Defense. She didn't want to be around a lot of people, have whispered conversations about which city the starfish had overrun, what human weapon they'd figured out how to convert for their own use. She picked up another piece of junk, an old solar panel, and turned it over, looking for a date. There was none.

If only the war were taking place in the virtual world instead of the real one. She'd probably be in Washington, D.C., right now, designing weapons systems, or sabotaging the enemy's capabilities. She knew VR tech inside and out. This hard tech—Lila turned the panel on its end, ran her thumb along its thin edge. It was a mystery.

"So what's it going to be?" Dad asked.

Lila set the solar panel down, leaned over the fence, and fished an identical panel out of the pile. If she had to do something productive, maybe she should take a crack at this old shit, see if she could make it useful again. There must be similarities between tinkering inside the feed and tinkering with actual chips and circuits. The technology was fifteen years old—how complicated could it be?

Lila spotted a bunch of solar panels, shoved aside a stuffed penguin doll she'd gotten for Christmas when she was six, and started stacking them along the fence. The satellites might be down, but they still had the standard home library downloaded on the handheld. Surely there were all sorts of old tech manuals available.

Her father was waiting for some sort of reply.

"Go away," she said. "I'm working."

Dad walked away, shaking his head.

# 4

## Oliver Bowen

*March 10, 2030 (nine months later). The South Pacific.*

There was nothing to do except read, watch movies, or talk to Five. If Oliver was home, he could at least be working on his comic collection. *Spider-Man* was complete, save for issue fourteen, the first appearance of Green Goblin. It was the early issues of *The Hulk* that were proving most difficult to locate.

It was insane, utterly insane, to be seeking out old comic books with the world on the brink, but it was the only thing in his life that wasn't depressing and seemingly hopeless.

Oliver started when Five began to speak aloud. He still wasn't used to the gurgling, hissing sound of his voice, so unlike the telepathic version.

"All of that effort, just to move paper with colorful pictures into closer proximity to you. That's all you're doing, really."

"I'm not going to argue with you. I honestly don't care what you think of my behavior."

"Of course you do," the Luyten said. "You used to play online poker. You were very good, weren't you?"

"I was very good." Oliver tried to control his rising impatience.

"Now you collect comics. Why is that, do you think?"

"Because poker takes other people, and without satellites I don't have access to other good players." He rubbed his eyes; he was tired, even though he was getting plenty of sleep. "Besides that, it takes energy. It taxes your cognitive resources. When I'm not working, I'm too tired, mentally and emotionally, for poker. There's no thinking involved in collecting comic books."

"No, there's certainly not. A child could do it."

Oliver poked at something caught between his teeth. "A child could do it. Yes. Provided he had a decent income."

The comment made him think of Kai, of the decision awaiting him when he got home. If he adopted Kai, they could collect comics together. He could teach Kai to play poker; that might inject him with fresh enthusiasm for the game.

Was it foolish, to consider adopting a thirteen-year-old boy? He couldn't imagine sitting Kai down to talk about sex, or disciplining him if he did something wrong. How did you even discipline a thirteen-year-old? His own upbringing would be no help on that front; his parents had met at an Asperger's clinic, where they were both undergoing outpatient treatment.

Maybe all of it was moot. How much time did they have left, realistically? A year? He should adopt Kai, and let the kid eat ice cream for dinner every night, if that's what he wanted to do.

"Do you want to know why you really collect comic books?"

Oliver groaned. "I'm not the one who tortured you. I have been nothing but civil to you. Why are you so hostile?

"I'm not being hostile. I'm just passing time."

Until that night, when the people in charge had tired of Oliver's inability to get Five to tell him anything useful, their conversations had been relatively polite. Certainly not warm, but polite. Two emissaries, on opposite sides of their species' struggle to the death, discussing the situation in even tones.

"Do you want to know?" Five asked.

Oliver didn't answer. Five knew he didn't want to know, that he was sick to death of having his mind cut open and pinned to a piece of cardboard, but Oliver knew Five would ignore this, because that was the game.

"You collect comic books because you harbor an infantile desire for the superheroes to be real. You want the Hulk, Spider-Man, and the Silver Surfer to come and save you. To save your kind. Even a cowboy on a white horse would do."

Go ahead, Oliver thought, pluck the name of the cowboy on the white horse out of my head. Only it's not a white horse, it's a silver horse. The hat is white.

"The Lone Ranger," Five said.

"Yes, I'm waiting for the Lone Ranger to save me." Oliver had never actually *watched* that ancient show, but that was beside the point.

"No one is coming to save you."

Oliver looked at his fingernails. Had he remembered to pack nail clippers when the security contingent showed up at his house and told him to pack? Hopefully they'd been in his shaving kit when he packed it. He went to the bathroom to look.

"You have no hope left," Five said. "I respect that. You're realistic, for one of your kind."

He stared into the mirror. Was that true? Did he have no hope?

It was almost true. Not 100 percent true, but it wasn't a lie.

Oliver looked into his own tired, watery eyes and realized he was letting this creature beat him. If he had no hope, if he'd given up in his heart, he was useless. He was betraying President Wood, his country, his kind, who were trusting him with a crucial task. Maybe he was here primarily because all of the men and women more capable of doing this job were dead. Maybe that was true.

*It is true.*

"Shut up!" he shouted.

Even if it was true, he had assets and abilities those people lacked. He needed to better utilize his assets.

Maybe he could turn Five's humiliating insights around to his advantage. Five was good at exposing his weaknesses. Fine, now he knew what his weaknesses were. As any decent psychologist knew, if you're not aware of your weaknesses, they control you; if you're aware of them, if you face up to them, you control them.

Based on Five's attacks, his weaknesses were Vanessa, and his lack of confidence in himself.

*They're just the tip of the iceberg.*

*"Shut up."*

As Five had so aptly observed, he was waiting for super-heroes to show up and save him. Since all the superheroes— all of the CIA's action people—were dead, he needed to get himself a cape. Even if, inside, he didn't feel it, even if he felt like a fraud, it was time to play the part of the big, strong CIA agent. It was time to lock out his doubts and fears, put his head down, and take bullets until he couldn't get up anymore.

"You're wrong," he said aloud, because to humans

speaking something aloud held a certain power, made the words real in a way thinking them did not. "I'm realistic; I recognize that we're losing. Badly. But I still have hope. We haven't lost yet. We're headed somewhere, and I'm pretty sure we're not going there to surrender."

The little speech sounded canned even to his ears; they were the sort of words Batman might speak in a comic book. But Oliver had to admit, it still felt good to say them.

# 5

## *Kai Zhou*

*July 1, 2029 (eight months earlier). Washington, D.C.*

Kai pried the flagstone loose from the walk that meandered through the church's walled garden. The small, square key was underneath, just as the Luyten said it would be. He plucked it from its hiding spot, headed for the back door of the church.

*Not there. Back the other way. Walk along the wall.*

Kai did as he was told, his mouth watering with anticipation despite the wild guilt he felt. A *church.*

There was a small graveyard set inside a low, ornamental fence. Ivy covered the fence and crawled along the ground.

*There. Behind the statue.*

Behind a mold-stricken statue of an angel with spread wings was a raised concrete circle with a steel cover. Looking around first, though it was probably unnecessary, Kai approached the cover, inserted the key into the hole, and pulled the hatch open.

The cover lifted fairly easily, revealing a dark hole, a ladder leading down. Kai climbed to the bottom, a dozen or so feet below the ground. He was surrounded by shelves of food—dried, packaged meals, like the ones soldiers ate.

*Whose are these?* he thought. It was confusing, to speak to it without speaking. There was no line dividing what he wanted to say and what he just wanted to think.

*The pastor. Speak out loud if you prefer, but quietly.*

"Why is this food down here?" Kai whispered, relieved.

*Because he doesn't want to share it. Take six.*

Hands shaking with anticipation, Kai grabbed the meals, struggled up the ladder one-handed, and headed for the gate.

*Not yet. Go toward the church.*

"I don't want to get caught," Kai whispered.

*I know where everyone is. Go.*

Kai went. The voice directed him along the back of the church, to a dirt- and leaf-covered black steel grate in the ground along the back wall.

*Open the grate. Drop four down.*

*Drop* them. Why on Earth would he do that?

Realization swept over him with an icy chill. It was down there. Hiding. Probably hurt.

*I'm in trouble, just like you. I'm alone and afraid, just like you.*

It was difficult for Kai to imagine one of those big, ugly monsters being afraid, and lonely. "Why are you lonely? I thought you could talk to other Luyten in your head."

*They're all too far away.*

They had an eight-mile range. Kai remembered hearing that.

*That's right.*

* * *

As Kai knocked on the door, he told himself he had no choice but to do what the Luyten told him. It hadn't made any threats, but it was huge, and powerful, and he was just a kid.

A woman answered the door. She was Asian like him, a streak of gray running through her long hair. More important, the aroma of fish and rice wafted through the door from a nearby kitchen.

*Her name is Mrs. Boey. Tell her you have a message from her daughter. Valerie.*

"Mrs. Boey? My name is Kai. I have a message from your daughter Valerie."

The woman's expression transformed. "You heard from my baby?" She opened the door, put a hand on Kai's shoulder, and led him inside.

*Valerie is outside Richmond, alive. She helped you escape. She asked you to tell her mother she's sorry about the argument they had before she left.*

Is Valerie alive, Kai thought.

*Probably not.*

With a crippling knot of guilt in his stomach, Kai told Mrs. Boey her daughter was alive and well, as a dozen people sitting elbow to elbow around a kitchen table looked on. Food was already on the table, and after Kai delivered his news the woman had little choice but to invite him to share their meal. The food was delicious; Kai ate voraciously, every chopstick-full sticking in his throat on the way down as he watched Mrs. Boey across the table, smiling, probably eating more easily than she had at any time since her sixteen-year-old daughter left to battle the Luyten four months earlier.

He should tell them, he thought. He should blurt out that there was a Luyten hiding under the church. Once it was out, there was nothing it could do. It was the enemy. It and its kind wanted to wipe out everyone on Earth, and they were *succeeding—*

*If you tell her, you'll go back to being cold and hungry.*

Kai didn't want to be hungry again. More than that, he didn't want to be alone in the dark, stumbling through places where there might be dead bodies.

"Do you have family nearby?" an old, bent woman asked Kai.

"No. I have an aunt and uncle in Connecticut, but it's too far."

*I'm not a soldier. I haven't killed anyone.*

It was not the first time the Luyten had told him this.

It claimed it had been shot out of the sky, part of a small contingent of Luyten on a night reconnaissance mission over D.C. The military knew a Luyten had been shot down in the area and they were hunting for it. For *Five*, he reminded himself. It had asked Kai to call it Five. It must have been injured in the crash, but it wouldn't say.

After the meal, Mrs. Boey said, "I'd ask you to stay, but as you can see, there's just no room." She gestured toward her relatives, most of them young or very old.

Kai told her he understood, and followed her to the door carrying the leftover food she had given him.

As he headed toward the back of the church, Kai wondered if Five had purposely chosen a house where Kai was likely to get food, but not a place to sleep. If someone took Kai in, he would have less incentive to protect Five's secret.

*Yes*, Five said. *I don't want to die. I'm just as afraid to die as you are.*

"Why are you doing this to us?" Kai whispered, although there was no one to hear him—the street was cold and empty, the orange glowlights along the sidewalk his only guide in the darkness. "Can't we share the world? Why do you have to have it all to yourselves?"

*We would have done that gladly, but we know your minds. Do you really think your kind would have taken us in as refugees? They won't even take you in.*

Kai pulled open the grate leading to the church's basement and dropped the food Mrs. Boey had given him into the darkness.

*Wake up.* Five's message was deafening, like an alarm set too loud.

Kai lifted himself from the cold concrete, looked groggily into the street, where mist crawled close to the pavement. "It's the middle of the night."

*Soldiers are coming with spotlights. Hide in the bathroom.*

Still half asleep, Kai gathered the towels and blanket he'd pilfered from an apartment using a key hidden by its owner and hurried into the bathroom.

A few minutes later Kai heard the purr of engines. Two all-terrain crawlers rolled past on fat tires, flashing spotlights as soldiers scanned the buildings with night glasses. Kai pulled the bathroom door closed.

"How do they know where to find you?"

*My heat signature. I have a baffle, but I can't run it all the time.*

"Why not?"

The crawlers purred away. Kai wondered if Five was debating whether to trust him. He wondered if it should.

*I trust you now. But after I leave, or I'm killed, you'll tell your people what you've learned about me. If I'm gone, probably they won't believe you. But if I'm caught, they will.*

Kai immediately thought to lie, to claim he wouldn't tell. Then he caught himself, remembered lying was impossible.

*Talking to you was a betrayal of my kind. I feel deeply ashamed. I was alone, in terrible pain. I was afraid to die.*

Was Kai betraying his kind, by keeping Five's secret? He was sure he was, although it wasn't as if Five was a threat, hiding under a church, cut off.

*To answer your question, I'm almost out of power. That's why I can't run the baffle all of the time.*

Kai had gotten accustomed to the sensation of Five speaking in his head. It wasn't as unpleasant as it had been at first. It reminded him of how he'd grown to like hot sauce on his chili. The first time he'd tried hot sauce it had been awful, burning his tongue and lips, making his eyes water. But the stinging had grown pleasant.

When he pictured where the voice was coming from, though, when he pictured that giant starfish crawling around under the church...

That made him dizzy with fear.

"I don't understand why you don't just sneak out of the city, if you know where everyone is."

*I am large, and a novel sight. I can't evade the eyes of every person who might look out their window.*

That made sense. "So how will you ever escape?"

*Unless one of my kind enters my range so I can contact it, I won't.*

It was morning when Five woke him again.

*They're coming back. More of them. Many more.*

Kai peered out at the rectangle of street visible from his sleeping spot, at the passing vehicles, the faded pod-style apartment complex across the street. "Will they find you?"

*Yes, probably. You should get away now, before they come. Otherwise they might question you about what you've seen or heard. Their eye gear is equipped with vocal stress-detectors, so they'll know you're lying. I don't want you to get in trouble because you were kind to me. Go now, through the back.*

Kai gathered up his bedding and ran out through the back side of the bay, into waist-high milkweeds that choked the space between the garage and the building behind it.

The telltale whisper of an ultralight copter grew louder as Kai pushed onto the sidewalk and turned right, up a hill.

*You should feel proud,* Five said. *We should both feel proud. We were kind to each other, despite everything. I'm not ashamed to call you my friend.*

A line of army crawlers appeared at the top of the hill, the crawlers' legs tucked, their big wheels spinning.

Kai watched them pass, his emotions in a tangle. He would miss Five, would miss its company at night, but he was also relieved to be getting away. He wanted to be free of the terrible guilt that he was betraying his people, although he would probably always feel guilty for consorting with the enemy. What would people think, if they found out?

Kai heard shouted orders. A moment later a squad of soldiers trotted around the corner—men and women, young and old, some in brick-red camo fatigues, others in torn jeans and soiled T-shirts. Head down, he pressed close to the buildings to let them pass. They were young, but not kids. Soldiers in their prime. There weren't many of them left.

What if a soldier asked him directly if he'd seen or heard anything? Would he lie to protect Five? Five probably knew the answer to that better than Kai did.

Maybe that was why Five told Kai to leave: not out of

concern for him, but because Five was afraid Kai would betray it.

*That's not true. I'm trying to protect you.*

Down the hill, Kai could see the church, had a partial view beyond the fence, into the garden. Two soldiers were in there, but they didn't seem to know where to look. Five's baffle must still be working.

*I'm using the last of my power reserve to operate it. It won't last much longer, but maybe long enough.*

One of the soldiers was a woman. Asian. It could be that woman's daughter. What was her name? Valerie. If those two soldiers went into the basement, would Five kill them?

*I'm not a soldier. I'm not a fighter.*

Kai would, if they were Luyten, coming to kill him. In an instant.

He took a step toward the church, then hesitated. What should he do? Both choices seemed wrong.

He closed his eyes, pictured his mom. What would she want him to do? What she would want was what he should do. *You don't throw away friends*, she'd told him once. But wasn't it wrong to be friends with a Luyten in the first place? They'd killed her, and Dad, too.

Opening his eyes, he headed down the hill, toward the church.

*Kai, please. Don't. I just want to go home. I just want to see my mother. Now that I know you, I could never help them.*

As Kai pushed through the gate, the soldiers turned, their weapons pointed at the ground.

"Go back to your home—" the Asian soldier started to say.

"It's in there," Kai said, pointing at the church. "In the cellar."

Both soldiers were suddenly wide-eyed alert.

*They'll kill me. Please. They'll burn me.*

"You *saw* it?" the other soldier, a black man, said.

"I—" Kai struggled to describe how he knew. "I heard it."

*We're friends.*

The Asian soldier was babbling into her comm, repeating what Kai had just said, then giving their location.

"Promise you won't hurt it. It's just a scout—not a soldier."

The two soldiers gawked at Kai like he was nuts, as a dozen others stormed through the gate.

"The cellar?" a gray-haired soldier called as they ran by.

"That's what the kid says."

They surrounded the hatch, one of them holding a flamethrower.

*They're coming. I'm scared, Kai. I'm so scared.*

Kai bolted toward the church. *"Don't hurt it."*

"Hang on," the Asian soldier shouted at the others. They waited as she turned to Kai, one hand on her wrist comm. "Kid, I need the truth from you—this is very serious. Are you saying the starfish actually *spoke* to you? Or do you mean you heard it moving around down there?"

Kai looked her right in the eye. "It spoke to me."

After a short interchange on her comm, she ran over to the others, huddled around the hatch. "We're taking it alive."

"Holy shit," a tall, brown-skinned soldier said.

"CIA is sending people to help."

The Asian soldier sidled over to Kai, wrapped a hand over his shoulder. "Stick around. They want to talk to you." She must have seen that this scared Kai, because she added, "Don't worry, they'll take good care of you. There's lots of food there."

# 6

## *Oliver Bowen*

*July 2, 2029. Washington, D.C.*

His shoes echoing in the big, dank corridor, Oliver picked up his pace. He was late, and he couldn't easily explain why that was, because the truth was he'd been on the toilet, dealing with anxiety-induced diarrhea.

It was one thing to be drafted into the CIA, given the circumstances, but this—this was too much. Maybe his background made him the perfect candidate to attempt communication with this Luyten, but his disposition did not. He was not an action guy; he was a behind-the-scenes guy. He should be in Research, advising someone on how to approach the situation; he should not be approaching the situation himself. But so many of the action guys and gals were dead, and Oliver had to admit, on *paper* he seemed ideal for this assignment. He knew more about how to bend someone to one's will with words and gestures, more about the use of language to gain power, than anyone alive. He just wasn't sure how well that knowledge translated into action.

He watched the room numbers pass on the big steel doors, but it turned out that wasn't necessary. Ariel Aardsma, his supervisor, was waiting in the doorway of the room he was looking for, her arm across the shoulders of Kai, the boy who'd talked to a Luyten. Assuming he was telling the truth.

Kai was big for a thirteen-year-old, but with a baby face, and long-lashed eyes. He was staring into the room where the Luyten was being held.

"Dr. Bowen," Ariel said. "This is Kai."

The boy went on staring into the room. As Oliver reached them, he peered inside the room as well.

The Luyten was unconscious in its cell. It was mustard yellow, its body housed in a thick, ornately ridged exoskeleton. Doctors had sealed the massive wound, injected binders to facilitate healing. Oliver eyed the stump, trying to imagine what it had looked like when the soldiers went under the church to get it. They'd said that after losing the limb in the crash, the thing had sutured the gaping wound closed with electrical wiring it pilfered from an air-conditioning unit under there.

Being so close to it was unnerving.

"Kai has been very helpful," Ariel said. "We've had a good talk with him."

Oliver had watched the interview remotely the day before. Incredible as it was, the boy's story checked out in every detail. The woman's corpse in the bus repair depot, the key under the flagstone, the hidden cache of food, his intimate knowledge of the local woman's relationship with her daughter; all of it had checked out.

Beyond the facts, Kai looked scared to death. He kept swallowing, and he was blinking rapidly, his hands dangling limply at his sides. This was not a kid who craved the attention that came with making wild claims about telepathic conversations with Luyten. Under ordinary circumstances Oliver would have been repulsed by the idea of subjecting this child to any more close contact with the Luyten, but these circumstances were as far from ordinary as they got.

Ariel led them into the room, closer to the Luyten. Kai was staring at it like it might leap from the cell and tear him apart at any moment.

"It can't reach us. Don't worry." It had to have been a kid. Oliver was clueless when it came to kids. He didn't know how to talk to them, was uncomfortable in their presence. When his sister visited with her children, Oliver always found urgent work he needed to do.

"Well," Ariel said, "I'll leave you to it."

Evidently Kai shared Oliver's wish that Ariel stay, because he watched her leave with an expression bordering on panic. Ariel and others would be monitoring remotely, but Oliver was on his own when it came to getting Kai to relax.

"Why don't you sit down?" Oliver gestured toward a chair.

Kai sat on the edge of the chair like a kid in the principal's office. The room didn't help things; it was bland and oppressive, windowless, nothing on the walls but an American flag in a wooden frame, and the ubiquitous population tracker, doggedly ticking back the dwindling world population.

"So it looks like we're going to be working together."

Kai swallowed, nodded.

"Maybe we should discuss procedure and strategies?" When Kai didn't respond, Oliver forged ahead. "Here's what I think might work best: Once the prisoner regains consciousness, repeat anything it says to you out loud. This way we won't have to rely on your memory later. It's important that you repeat word for word…" The boy was looking past Oliver, his lips forming a tight O.

Oliver looked over his shoulder. The Luyten's eyes were open. It was watching them.

"Is it speaking to you?"

Kai shook his head.

Oliver stood, inched closer to the Luyten. "Say something to it. Out loud, like you did when it was under the church."

It was clear Kai had no interest in speaking to the Luyten. He licked his lips and said, "I just wanted to get you help. You were hurt."

Oliver studied the Luyten, then turned and watched Kai. "Anything?"

"No."

Feeling simultaneously foolish and very uneasy, Oliver moved within a few feet of the flimsy-looking mesh that separated them from the creature. "My name is Oliver Bowen. I understand that you can communicate with us. Are you in pain? If you are, I may be able to arrange relief."

He had no idea if the medical people had administered a painkiller. Probably not—they knew next to nothing about the creature's physiology. He'd made the offer more as a generic gesture of concern.

Oliver turned and looked at Kai. "Anything?"

Kai shrugged. "No."

There were a few possibilities. The Luyten might be staying silent because Kai could no longer help it, or because it knew they wanted to communicate with it to seek some advantage in the war. It was also possible the Luyten was communicating with Kai, and Kai was lying because he was on its side. Oliver thought that was unlikely.

"What's that?" Kai asked, eyeing the population counter on the wall. At the moment it read three billion, seven hundred thousand and change. The numbers went on rolling backward, counting down.

"It's an estimate of the world population." The number shrunk by several hundred in the time it took Oliver to answer.

Kai studied it. "How does it know when someone dies?"

"It's just an estimate, based on updates people here receive."

Kai pressed his tongue to his upper lip, stared at the readout, mesmerized.

"Why don't you try talking to the Luyten again?"

"He told me to call him Five."

The idea of it having a name unsettled Oliver in a way he couldn't articulate.

"It's a he?" Oliver asked.

Kai shrugged. "I don't know. It just seems like a he."

"Why Five?"

Looking sheepish, Kai shrugged yet again. "I don't know."

Luyten tended to congregate in groups of three, when they congregated at all, so Five probably didn't correspond to his place in a group or family, although it might. It was a prime number, but Oliver couldn't see how that mattered. Maybe it wasn't his real name, only one he'd chosen for Kai to use.

"Does the number five hold any special meaning for you?" he asked Kai. "Your lucky number? Your birthday?"

Kai couldn't take his eyes off the Luyten. "Not really."

Oliver stared at the Luyten. Looking at it was unpleasant, not only because it was large and terrifying, but because of the wound, the ragged stump.

Oliver folded his arms across his chest, leaned closer, counted its limbs.

Five. There had been six, now there were five.

It was a tiny insight, but it provided a glimpse into how the creature thought.

"Why don't you try talking to Five again?" he said.

"What should I say?"

"I don't know. Anything." Oliver waved his hands, trying to come up with something. Topics of conversation were not his strong suit. "What did you talk about before?"

Kai shrugged. "Where to find food, how scared we were."

That wouldn't work now. What else could you talk about with an alien? Maybe they should try to win it over, with pleasant topics. Small talk. Fall back on standard CIA interrogation procedures.

"Tell it about your hobbies."

"My hobbies?" Kai said it as if he'd never heard the word before.

"Things you liked to do. Before, you know, you couldn't do them anymore."

Haltingly, Kai began to talk about a water park near his house, where you surfed up a stationary fifteen-foot wave.

The Luyten remained silent.

# 7

## *Lila Easterlin*

*July 2, 2029. Savannah, Georgia.*

It had once been an indoor flea market. The battered sign
by the road, hanging from a rusted pole, read KELLER'S FLEA
MARKET. It sported an image of a cartoon flea. Now it was
an enormous morgue, a body factory. Lila hated the place,
dreaded going in there, but her father was too busy to bring
the containers out, and there were too many for Alfe to carry
on his own. Plus, Alfe didn't look any more eager to go inside
than Lila.

"You ready?" He was already holding the balled-up T-shirt
close to his mouth and nose.

"Shit. I'm never ready to go in there." She stepped out of the
two-seat open buggy she'd salvaged and converted to solar.

Inside, she tried to keep her eyes on the concrete floor,
three feet in front of her, but her peripheral vision picked up
a bit of the horror show that was all around, and her imagi-
nation filled in the rest. The bodies were on tables, on the
ground, some literally stacked in piles along the walls. Many

were badly burned; most had gaping wounds. The ones who'd been killed by the Luyten's lightning gun had the soles of their feet blown out.

Even if she were wearing blinders, the rancid stench would have made the place intolerable. Even with the T-shirt covering her mouth and nose, she held her breath as long as possible before taking a quick, gasping breath and holding it again.

Lila wondered if you ever got used to the smell and sight of bodies. Maybe she had, to a degree, only so gradually she hadn't noticed. Wouldn't the sight of hundreds of bodies have sent her screaming and gibbering three years ago? Probably.

She spotted her dad, wearing a transparent mask that covered his whole head. He was collecting DNA samples, moving from body to body with a handheld DNA harvester. He spotted Lila and Alfe a moment later, and pointed toward the back of the immense, low-ceilinged space. Lila waved with her free hand, hurried to the back where she found half a dozen battered, filthy red gasoline canisters.

It was difficult to carry three canisters each while keeping the T-shirts in place, but they managed. As soon as they were outside, Lila let the arm holding the T-shirt and one canister drop to her side. She exhaled heavily, trying to drain every ounce of the rotten air out of her lungs before inhaling the relatively fresh outside air.

"I don't know how he does it," Alfe said, breathless, hands on his knees. "It's like being in a pit of hell."

Lila nodded as she turned and headed for the buggy. The sooner they got downtown, the sooner this hellish errand would be finished. Discovering the taps were not working that morning had shaken Lila, for surely if there was one thing you could count on, it was water.

* * *

For Lila, downtown Savannah had always been an oasis, an ancient, beautiful city of manicured squares and elegant architecture. Today it felt like a moldy, menacing place. All around people were running, shouting. There was a heavy police presence, but the police looked as exhausted and scared as everyone else.

Lila turned right onto Bull Street, anxiety rendering her unable to glean even the slightest satisfaction from the way the buggy she'd rebuilt and retrofitted to run on solar power was performing. Ahead, Chippewa Square was all but empty; there was no water distribution going on like they'd heard on the radio.

She pulled over, looked around for some indication of what might have happened.

Someone whistled. Lila spotted an old woman sitting on a porch.

"You looking for water?" the woman called. She was wearing a pink kerchief tied under her chin, and shelling pecans by hand on a rickety card table.

"Yes!" Alfe shouted.

"They moved it to River Street." The woman pointed east.

Waving thanks, Lila headed toward River Street, wondering why they'd changed the location at the last minute without leaving word at the original site. Things were so uncertain. In the past it was always easy to know who was in charge, where to go for what.

In the seat beside her, Alfe watched the houses roll past while he chewed on his cuticle. In two weeks he'd be sixteen, and he'd go off to fight. Lila would have envied him, would have snuck off and joined him, if going to fight wasn't synonymous with going to die. She'd be going soon enough—ten months, assuming she was alive ten months from now.

She caught movement out of the corner of her eye and flinched, adrenaline washing through her. It was only a tour bus, likely pressed into service to transport refugees. They wouldn't suddenly be marauding through downtown, she reminded herself. There would be warning, the emergency siren at least. Sharpshooters were stationed all around the city; high-def cameras that could focus on objects a mile away were watching in every direction. That there were more of them outside the city than usual didn't mean they were coming.

None of that was the least bit comforting. And if they came, they would kill everyone, except maybe the children.

"You okay?" Alfe asked.

"No."

"Yeah, me neither." He studied his finger, chewed at his cuticle a little more before adding, "I feel like we're all in a room, and the walls move in a little more each day."

"I've never had so many nightmares. I don't want to sleep, but being awake is just as bad."

Pedestrian traffic was growing heavier. Many of them were pushing handcarts, or carrying pails or water skins. Ahead, the crowd was tightly packed. Lila parked on the edge of the cobbled sidewalk, and they followed the crowd down the rough cobblestone to River Street. Between the brick buildings that used to house bars and gift shops for the tourists she caught glimpses of the Savannah River, where hundreds of enormous slate-blue fins jutted from the black water—markers for the portable hydroelectric power generators that filled the river. Along with parking lots filled with solar panels and a few hastily built rooftop windmill farms, it was all that staved off total blackout conditions.

There was no line, only a throng pressing toward an elevated scaffold where half a dozen people were distributing water through spigots that resembled gas pumps. A truck carrying a filtration system was drawing the water out of the river.

There was a rumor circulating that the pumps to Savannah's houses were working fine, but Luyten had contaminated the city's underground water supply, so the water had been turned off. It was difficult to separate the rumors from truth.

The crowd swelled, and soon Lila and Alfe were surrounded by people. It was an unpleasant feeling; those on the outside tended to push forward, eager to get closer, as if the river might run dry before they reached the front.

"There should be police here, getting everyone into lines," Lila said.

"I guess they're all on the perimeter."

The honk of a tugboat made Lila's heart nearly burst through her chest. Several others glanced toward the boat as well, hypersensitized to anything that resembled the emergency siren.

There were shouts from the front of the crowd, jostling that rippled backward until a boot heel sunk down on Lila's toes. Pain coursed through her foot; she was nearly knocked down as people pushed backward.

"Where? Where is it?" someone closer to the river shouted.

"They're coming, oh God, they're coming."

Suddenly people were stampeding. Jostled and pummeled, Lila turned and struggled to stay on her feet. Someone had spotted Luyten. They must have come down the river, maybe underwater.

She heard Alfe calling her name, spotted him ten feet away,

weaving in the tightly packed mob. He shouted something, but she couldn't make it out.

The crowd carried her across River Street, up a steep cobbled road. When they reached Bay Street there was more space to move. Her heart racing, Lila jogged up Whitaker, watching for starfish, expecting one to appear behind her at any moment.

"*Lila!*"

It was Alfe, pressed against the First Citizens Bank building up ahead. Lila ran to join him.

"We have to hide," she said.

"That won't do any good. They'll know right where we are."

She grabbed Alfe's wrist. "Remember when you saw them by that lake? They'll know, but two people aren't worth chasing."

They ran into the bank. It was deserted, save for three or four employees, one of them armed, and an elderly couple. It was less a bank now, more an exchange center, where people swapped gold, gems, ammo, anything that still had value.

"They're coming!" Alfe shouted.

"Why didn't the siren sound?" a woman in a blue and white business tunic asked. She looked to be in charge, was beautiful in a way that made Lila think of mannequins.

"I don't know," Alfe said.

Outside, someone shrieked. Crowds were still running past.

Lila looked around for a place to hide. Somewhere tight, where Luyten couldn't easily reach. An inner room, or better yet, if there were stairs leading down into a cellar... or a vault.

"Does this bank have a vault?" she asked.

"A vault?" the beautiful woman repeated.

"Come on," Lila said. Alfe followed her behind the row of

teller stations, down a wide hallway. It was an old bank—it might have one of those vaults full of safe-deposit boxes.

"There," Alfe said. She'd been looking for a big, round opening, but it was a narrow, heavy door.

They waited by the entrance to see if the others were following. Two of the employees appeared, the old couple a dozen steps behind them. A moment later, the woman in charge followed.

"It won't lock," Alfe said, pointing at the edge of the heavy door, where the bolts had been soldered in place. They pulled the door closed as far as it would go. Despite lacking a lock, being in the small steel room in near darkness gave Lila a sense of safety. She and Alfe sat on the floor with their backs against the far wall. The others sat as well.

They waited, listening.

"Anya, shouldn't we run?" the armed employee, a muscular guy in his thirties, asked the woman in charge. "We can't hide from them."

"They can't hunt down every person in every building," Lila answered. "They kill people as fast as they can, so they'll go after crowds in the streets." If one of the starfish did want to get to them, Lila had no doubt it could. She'd seen them squeeze through smaller spaces than the double doors of this bank.

"But if they're here, they won't ever leave. Once they take over the city they can take their time coming to get us."

Lila hadn't thought beyond the next few hours. "Once they move past us, I guess we head out of the city."

"To where?" the old man asked, trying to control the panic in his voice.

There was a crash, out in the lobby. It sounded like a table of trade goods being upended.

"Shh," Alfe hissed.

All of them looked toward the door. It knew where they were. In a few seconds that door would fly open, and it would kill them all. Lila pulled her legs to her chest. Out of the corner of her eye she saw Alfe's Adam's apple bob.

Muffled shouts erupted outside. The voices sounded surprised, alarmed, angry. Not terrified. They didn't sound like people being killed.

"What's going on?" Anya asked, her voice low.

"Maybe it's more people looking to hide." Alfe got to his feet, opened the door wider. "This way," he called.

"Who is that?" It was a woman's voice. Footsteps clicked down the hall. Alfe stepped back as the door swung open to reveal a small, pudgy woman in her fifties or sixties. "Anya? Carl? What are you doing in here?"

"The starfish are coming," Anya said.

The woman in the doorway shook her head. "It was a false alarm. Evidently porpoises strayed too far up the river, and someone thought they were a starfish."

Lila let out a burst of laughter. Porpoises? That stampede was started by some nearsighted putz who'd spotted porpoises.

"The looters were real, though. I walked right in on them—they ran off with armloads of automatic rifles."

Lila felt incredibly foolish, but compared to what she'd been feeling a few minutes earlier, foolish felt good.

# 8

## Oliver Bowen

*July 12, 2029. Washington, D.C.*

Oliver never tired of looking at her, at her dark eyes, the perfect slope of her jawline. That she was his wife never ceased to astonish him.

Noticing his attention, Vanessa glanced at him. "What?"

"Nothing. I'm just looking at you."

She smiled, dimples forming on either cheek. "Cut it out; it makes me feel self-conscious, like I've got something sticking out of my nose."

Oliver turned, watched the buildings pass outside his window. As they passed through the gate to the CIA compound, Vanessa said, "We did it."

Oliver tried to think of what they'd done. "What did we do?"

She pulled over to the curb in front of his building. "We went a whole morning without once mentioning the war." She held up her palm; Oliver gave her a high-five.

"That's right. I forgot all about it." They'd made the pact

the night before; by morning it had gone out of his head, buried by a thousand thoughts and worries.

"In that case, you're lucky."

"What was the penalty again?" Oliver asked.

"Lip-synch to a song of my choice. In my underwear."

"That's right." Oliver laughed. He leaned in, kissed her goodbye.

"It's nice, getting a break from it. Almost like taking a vacation to the past, before it started."

"It is. We should do it every morning." They needed to come up with ways to hang on to at least some semblance of normal life.

"You're on your own for dinner," Vanessa said as he opened the door.

"Oh?"

Vanessa looked away, over his shoulder. "Paul and I are going to grab a bite after work."

A surge of adrenaline hit him. "Why can't you grab a bite at lunch?"

"Because then we'd have to hurry." That familiar defensive tone leaked into her voice. "It's not like I go out with friends often."

Oliver clutched the door, wanting to think of something to say that would change her mind, but came up blank. "It's not your going out at night that bothers me; it's your going out with Paul. If he's just a friend, why can't I come?" Paul was a charming, handsome, muscular friend, the sort of man Vanessa would look very natural standing beside.

Vanessa leaned back in her seat, closed her eyes, and sighed heavily. "Can we not have this argument now? Why can't you trust me? Have I ever given you the slightest reason not to?"

"No." His voice was low, his tone leaking the defeat he felt. "It's just that—" What could he say, that he hadn't already said a hundred times?

"I'll see you when you get home." Oliver turned and headed for the gate as Vanessa pulled off.

Her friendship with Paul was the one thing their marriage couldn't seem to get past. Oliver wanted to trust her, and he did with anyone else, but she and Paul seemed to share an intimacy that Vanessa didn't share with Oliver. One of these days he was afraid she'd realize she was with the wrong man, and he'd lose her. He didn't think he could handle this without her; she brought out the best in him, gave him courage he wouldn't otherwise possess.

The Luyten was exactly where he'd left it, lying flat in the center of the cell, looking remarkably like a beached starfish.

"Good morning." There were five angry red abrasions on the Luyten's side, just under one of its limbs. Oliver squinted, trying to see them better.

They were almost perfect circles, like burns. Oliver turned, waved the room's comm awake, and connected to Ariel.

"Do you know how the Luyten sustained these injuries?"

"Yes, we took it through a session of enhanced interrogation last night."

The answer threw Oliver. He'd half suspected that was the case, but Ariel's matter-of-fact tone surprised him.

"All right. Can you tell me what happened?"

"Nothing," Ariel said. "It was in obvious pain, but it didn't communicate with anyone. We kept Kai in an adjoining room, in case it would only speak to him."

It surely wasn't the first time they'd tortured a Luyten.

Oliver went back to the cage. "Why did you choose that spot on its body?"

"Autopsies show there's a high concentration of nerve endings there."

Oliver nodded, trying to act as blasé about it as Ariel clearly was, though the thought of torturing the creature made him queasy.

"Hi." Kai was hovering in the doorway.

"Come on in. You doing all right?"

Kai nodded vaguely, looking uncomfortable. Oliver tried to think of something to say to put the kid at ease, one of those snappy things adults said that made kids laugh, let them know you weren't so different from them. His mind was a fat blank.

He went back to studying the Luyten. He wasn't surprised that torture was ineffective. They were tough bastards. Given their telepathic nature, Oliver guessed being cut off from communing with its own kind was more distressing than electric shocks. Maybe it drew some sustenance from tapping into human minds, the way an amphetamine addict might draw meager sustenance from a cup of coffee.

"Kai, when you and Five were communicating, did he seem, I don't know, like he was glad to have you to talk to?"

Kai bit his bottom lip. "I guess. He told me we had a lot in common."

"What did you have in common?"

Kai scrunched his face, thinking. "I don't remember the exact words, but it was how we were both scared and lonely. Or something like that."

"You haven't mentioned that before."

Kai looked at the floor. "I forgot about it until you asked. Sorry."

"No, not a problem. Thank you for remembering."

"You're welcome."

If loneliness was unpleasant for it, what would happen if it was completely isolated? If the Luyten reached out to Kai not only as a means of getting food, but for companionship, it meant it could fulfill some of its social needs through contact with humans.

"I think I may know a way to torture it for real," Oliver said.

# 9

## Lila Easterlin

*July 16, 2029. Savannah, Georgia.*

Lila was in the backyard working on the solar array she hoped would soon power their house, when the emergency siren sounded.

It was a mournful sound, a giant dog who'd been put out on a cold night. Her terror found another gear, one she hadn't known existed. There were no drills; if the siren was sounding, the Luyten were coming.

She raced inside to find out what was going on.

Her father met her inside the door, holding both of their emergency evacuation bags.

"Where are we going?" Lila asked.

Her father handed Lila her bag. "Atlanta."

"*Atlanta?*" Atlanta was hundreds of miles from Savannah, all of it starfish territory. He might as well have said Mars.

Dad headed toward the front door. "They're coming, Lila. Savannah is going to fall. Atlanta's the closest place that's safe."

That couldn't be right. "There's nowhere between here and there?"

"No. There's nothing left but the cities. Let's go."

"Can I—" She was going to ask if she could grab a few more things before they left, since they were never coming back, but the look on his face silenced her. He was terrified, his eyes wild.

She climbed into their Toyota, her knees shaking as her father set the gearshift to emergency, overriding the governor. They sped off.

Interstate 16 was packed, with everything from bicycles to militarized land yachts pressed into the six lanes, crawling along. They'd been on the road four or five hours and had gone maybe fifty miles.

"It's going to take days to get there at this rate." Lila peered out the window at a family of four perched on a scooter, bulky packs strapped across their shoulders, even the kids. "How many miles is it to Atlanta?"

Up ahead, a Luyten stepped out of the trees.

Lila screamed, the sound bursting from her. The Luyten crossed the high grass along the side of the highway, stopped on the shoulder, and pointed the blue-green, mushroom-shaped head of a heater at the nearest vehicles.

Through the sealed window Lila heard shrieks of agony as vehicles cooked, the exteriors warping and bubbling, black smoke pouring out at the seams. The air filled with the stench of burning rubber and steel.

The Luyten swung the heater toward the next cars in line, and the next. Paralyzed, her breath caught like a knot in her throat, Lila stared as the vehicles melted.

"*Run*," Dad howled.

71

His voice broke the spell. Lila burst from the passenger door and instinctively headed across the highway, in the direction everyone else was running.

"This way," Dad called.

Lila stopped and changed directions, following Dad toward the nearer trees, moving *closer* to the Luyten instead of away. Shoulders knotted, she waited for the Luyten to turn the heater on them, but it went on down the row, focusing on the vehicles, but catching most of the fleeing people as well. The people caught in the path of the heater blackened in seconds, their clothes disintegrating without a flame as they dropped to the ground, writhing and twitching, then going still.

Bursting into the tree line, Lila was immediately tangled in thick brush. She dropped to her belly and crawled, squeezing beneath vines and clinging branches.

A few dozen feet to her left, branches snapped and foliage shuddered as a second Luyten pushed toward the highway. Lila froze, head down. It knew she was there—she knew that—but the urge to hide was too powerful to resist. She waited, praying for it not to pause and turn toward her pathetic hiding place.

It crashed out of the trees, toward the cacophony of screams and the stench of burned bodies.

Lila's father called her name, his tone low and urgent. She answered, crawled toward him until she was in his arms, his whiskers scraping her cheek.

She followed him as he wove through the woods, finally breaking through into the back lawn of a housing complex. The grass was waist-high, the complex deserted. No one had lived there for a year, at least. They were in Luyten-controlled territory.

They sprinted around to the side window of one of the

units; Dad pulled a flagstone off the top of a low landscaping wall and used it to smash out the window.

In the distance, Lila still heard screaming.

Her father shimmied inside, then reached out and helped Lila.

"Look for a vehicle password," Dad said, out of breath. "People always write them down somewhere. Check in drawers, the insides of kitchen and bathroom cabinets, in notebooks." He headed into the kitchen.

Lila wanted to find a heavy blanket and curl into a ball beneath it, try to replace the images of those people dying with something, anything else. Instead she headed upstairs to search for a code. She dug through the dresser, tossing some woman's socks and panties on the floor, sweeping her costume jewelry off the bathroom counter.

After ten minutes they gave up and went to try another unit. Across the street, Lila spotted a door standing partially open.

"Dad." She pointed at the door.

"That makes things easier," Dad said. They headed across the street.

Lila stood behind him as he pushed the door open.

The living room walls were draped in thick layers of what looked like brightly colored fabric. Heavier semi-stiff fabric bisected the space, cutting it into a number of chambers at forty-five-degree angles. It was strange, beautiful, and absolutely awful, all rolled together. There was no doubt about what it was.

Her father took two stiff steps backward, out of the doorway. He was pale, the corners of his mouth twitching.

"If it was in there, it would have gotten us by now," Lila whispered, aware of how stupid it was to whisper. If you were close enough to a Luyten that it could hear you, it had known about you for quite some time. Whispering wasn't going to save you.

They headed toward the far end of the complex to continue their search, as Lila digested what she'd just learned. The starfish were living in houses. If the starfish won, they'd fill neighborhoods and cities, as if they'd built it all themselves and had been there all along.

"I didn't know they lived in our houses. I thought they lived underground, in those tunnel systems they dig."

Dad nodded. "I did, too. I'm sure the people in charge know how they live." He shook his head in sad wonder. "We used to know everything as soon as it happened. Now everything outside our neighborhood is a mystery."

Lila's attention was drawn toward a pile of parts squeezed between two of the units. Some were engine parts; the biggest pieces—leaned up against the side of one unit—looked like wings.

Lila stopped short. "Hold on." She trotted over.

It was a solar ultralight—not much more than an adult toy, but it seated two.

"If we could put this together, we could fly it to Atlanta." Silently, her father examined it.

"I can do it," Lila said. "I can build this."

# 10

## *Oliver Bowen*

*July 16, 2029. Washington, D.C.*

As the elevator descended, Oliver felt a tingling in his belly, like he'd just hit the apex on a roller coaster and was headed over the drop. It went on and on. It was hard to conceive that he was dropping eight miles below ground. All that stone and earth pressing down on him. Oliver wasn't particularly claustrophobic, but it was distressing nonetheless.

The elevator opened onto a conference room, with a long, thin black table and a dozen chairs. Framed pictures of President Wood and Premier Abani Chandar, leader of the World Alliance, were the only decorations.

The rest of the facility was set up as an apartment, functional and comfortable, but far from luxurious. It was intended to house a team of strategists who knew things even Wood and Chandar didn't, who communicated with other teams in similar bunkers through sealed, written documents, their minds out of range of any possible Luyten interception. Now it housed Five, whose cage took up half the living room.

Oliver sat on a couch facing the Luyten's cage, crossed his foot over his opposite knee. He'd waited five days, hoping that was enough isolation.

"You know what I'm thinking, so you know I intend to keep you down here until you talk to me. If you do talk, there'll be no reason to keep you down here any longer, and we can move back to the CIA compound." He looked up at the low ceiling. "Personally, I'd prefer to be there."

He waited, not exactly sure what it would feel like if Five did speak to him. Kai said it was unpleasant at first.

When nothing came, Oliver went to the kitchen. He paused in the doorway. "Can I get you something? Maybe some tea?" He waited a beat, then smiled. "I'm a tricky one, aren't I? You'd have to talk if you wanted something. You're not falling for that, eh?"

He didn't really feel like tea, but he made some anyway, brought it back to the couch. Sipping a hot beverage made the place, and this company, seem less creepy. Maybe it was the everydayness of it.

He was all alone down here, with a creature who evidently knew his every thought. If anything went wrong, no one would get here in time to help.

*What could go wrong?*

The mug slipped from his fingers, spilled scalding tea into his lap. Oliver leaped up, jerked open the buttons on his pants, and yanked them down. Gritting his teeth against searing pain he hobbled into the kitchen, turned on the faucet, and splashed cold water across his thighs.

It had spoken to him. There could be no doubt, no mistaking that feeling, which Kai had very accurately described as a scraping.

Oliver found an ice pack in the freezer. After pulling off his shoes and soaked pants, he pressed the ice pack against his right inner thigh, where the skin was the reddest. Then he returned to the living room and sat on the dry side of the couch in his briefs. "Well, that was clumsy of me. Can we pick up where we left off? Nothing could go wrong, absolutely nothing. We're just having a talk."

Five didn't respond. Oliver waited, watching the Luyten expectantly, not sure which of its seven eyes to look at.

When some time had passed, he tried again. "Where do you come from?"

Nothing.

"What harm would it do to tell me where you're from?"

*No harm whatsoever. How does it benefit me to tell you?*

Oliver suppressed an urge to plug his ears, to run to the elevator and get as far away from the Luyten as he could. Instead, he shrugged. "If we only talk about things that benefit you, it's not going to be much of a conversation, is it?"

*What gave you the impression I wanted to have a conversation?*

"You spoke to me."

*I had something to say.*

"This is going to get awfully boring if we don't talk."

*I don't get bored.*

"But you get lonely."

Using its appendages, it raised itself from the floor. *And you made sure I would, didn't you?*

"If you'd just communicated with me, I wouldn't have been forced to take those measures."

Oliver waited patiently, but Five didn't reply.

"I'm sorry I caused you discomfort."

Five only watched him.

Oliver stepped closer to the mesh dividing them. "Is there something you'd prefer to eat? I can arrange to have it sent."

Nothing. Oliver ran a hand through his hair, exhaled audibly. Hundreds of people must be watching the live feed by now. He turned to face the comm link, a silver quarter-sized disk set in the wall, and recounted everything the Luyten had said to him so far. Then he turned to face Five again.

"We don't have to talk about sensitive topics. You choose the topic." Oliver held out his empty hands. "Whatever would interest you."

Still nothing.

Of course the Luyten would be aware that this was standard CIA interrogation procedure. Get the subject talking about anything, learn what makes him tick. Then win him over. The question was, was it possible to win over a Luyten?

# 11

## *Oliver Bowen*

*July 17, 2029. Washington, D.C.*

Sixteen hours later, a text message from President Wood came, encouraging Oliver to try harder, imploring him to find a way to break through. He could imagine what must be happening up there. Some were arguing they pull Oliver, let the Luyten stew a few more days. Others would want to replace him with one of their other experts, who'd tried and failed to get the Luyten talking. Some, at least, were arguing that Oliver needed more time, or else he wouldn't still be down there.

Oliver wasn't sure which argument he agreed with. He didn't want to give up, yet he desperately wanted to escape this stiflingly claustrophobic bunker and see the sky. The bunker was equipped with plenty of outdoorsy VR simulations, but as realistic as they were, they couldn't remove Oliver's awareness of his location.

He wondered what would become of Kai, now that it was clear he wasn't the only one able to communicate with Five. Would they continue to house him at the compound, in case they needed him? Would they try to find a home for him? Surely they wouldn't simply turn him out onto the street. Oliver wouldn't let them. He'd take Kai in himself if it came to that.

Oliver poured himself a glass of milk in the kitchen and returned to the living room. Or should he think of it as the interrogation room? Not that there was much interrogating going on.

It wasn't only claustrophobia that made him want to get back to the world. Oliver wanted to get home to Vanessa. He was worried Vanessa would use his absence as an opportunity to spend time with Paul.

*To spend time with.* What a pathetic euphemism. The truth was, he was afraid Vanessa would use the opportunity to fuck Paul. That was the crux of it, wasn't it? He was afraid she was having an affair.

A few of Five's eyes were tracking Oliver as he paced. He needed to get his mind off his marital problems, focus on the much, much larger problem at hand. How criminally narcissistic was it, to be thinking about his wife's suspected infidelity when he'd been entrusted with a task that could help save the entire human race? He needed to stay focused, to find a way to extract useful information from this Luyten.

"Why Earth, of all the planets in the galaxy?" he asked the Luyten. "Does your kind just enjoy a challenge?"

*You're right, you know. Your wife is having an affair.*

Oliver was so shocked by the words he very nearly cried out. "What did you say?"

*When she dropped you off at work, her mind was close enough that I could hear it. She is having sex with Paul.*

"You can't—" He was going to say 'You can't know that for sure,' but he checked himself. Yes, it could. "You're lying."

*As she was driving off, she was thinking about taking Paul's penis in her mouth while they drove to—*

"*Shut up.*" Oliver could imagine her, breathless, telling Paul the things she wanted to do to him when they got to his house.

A voice message came through the comm, fed directly to the earbud connected to his comm, although they might as well have broadcast it aloud, for all the secrecy it afforded them.

"What's happening down there?" It was Ariel. "Your heart rate is one-twenty. Can it inflict harm psychically?"

"No," Oliver answered. "I'm okay. I'm just adjusting to what Kai described—the unpleasant sensation in my mind when it speaks." He didn't want to air his dirty laundry in front of who knows how many agents and operatives, and didn't want to get pulled out when he was making progress.

*To address your spoken question, it never occurred to us this planet would be inhabited. When we arrived it was too late. Either we settled on Earth, or our kind would die out.*

"We would have given you asylum, if you asked." He dragged a hand down his sweaty face, still not able to banish the image of Vanessa going down on Paul in a car.

*No, you would not have.*

"You don't know that."

*Yes, I do.*

"If you were oblivious of us, why did you take such pains to stay hidden behind various celestial bodies as you approached? For God's sake, you parked behind the moon. You did that so we wouldn't detect your approach."

It felt childishly satisfying to bring up the Luyten mother ship. Humanity's one real victory had been sending a motley collection of weaponized space vehicles and shooting their mother ship out of the lunar sky.

*When I say "when we arrived, it was too late," I don't mean when we arrived in your solar system. We detected your existence well into our trip, through your SETI transmissions, but long before we reached your solar system. We took precautions once we were aware of your existence. Some of the musical compositions included in the SETI transmissions were quite interesting, by the way. We enjoyed Bach.*

Ariel's voice intruded through the comm. "Get to the questions we prepared, before it goes mute again."

"Christ, it knows everything you're saying as soon as I do." Oliver gestured emphatically at the speaker on the wall. "Just speak through the goddamned speaker."

*It doesn't offend me,* Five said. *Though needless to say, I don't intend to answer any of those questions.*

"No, I didn't imagine you would." He glanced at the comm. "That's why I didn't ask."

*Although those questions aren't the real reason your people are so eager for you to open communication with me.*

Oliver froze, slowly canted his head to one side. "What do you mean?"

*There's no point in speaking aloud. I don't have ears, or the capacity to detect sound.*

"It helps me organize my thoughts." Oliver wasn't going to let this creature tell him how to behave. A good interrogator was always in control of the situation. "You said there was another reason they want me to establish contact with you. What's the reason?"

Ariel cut in on the comm. "Oliver, what is it saying? Give us an update."

Oliver ignored her, waited, watching the Luyten groom itself with its cilia.

*Isn't it obvious?*

"Not to me."

"Oliver? What's going on?" Ariel asked.

*They want to discuss terms for surrender.*

Maybe it shouldn't have been a surprise, but the sheer magnitude of the words, the finality of what Five was suggesting, rocked Oliver. He turned to face the comm.

"It says I'm here to discuss terms for surrender."

There was a long delay, then "Hold on."

Surrender? His head spinning, Oliver tried to unpack what that would mean. Would humans lay down their arms, and the Luyten take control of everything—all the territory they didn't already control? In exchange, no more humans would be killed. But how would they be treated?

"President Wood is coming down," Ariel said.

The president of the United States.

Was coming down to speak to him.

Under different circumstances he would have been excited by that prospect.

Oliver headed to the bathroom to check himself in the mirror, to make sure he looked presentable.

Surrender.

How had it possibly gotten to this point?

When the starfish first rained from the sky, spinning like pinwheels, protected as they entered Earth's atmosphere by huge porous bags that bore zero resemblance to any Earth transport, everyone had been terrified. But in every case, they'd dropped into unpopulated wilderness, in groups of three, and at first did little more than hide.

Oliver set his comb back on the sink and headed back into the living room.

When they began to attack, the targets were small, the goal more likely sabotage than occupation. They would hit a

83

railway line, a wind farm, an isolated community, then disappear back into the trees, or underwater in breathable embryos that turned out to be miniatures of their mother ship. People were petrified, but it felt more like some horrible infestation than an invasion.

When it became apparent the Luyten could read human minds at will, people got really scared.

The attacks grew steadily bolder. Satellites. Weapons systems. Nuclear plants. Attacks on people living in the country escalated to the point where most fled to the safety of urban hubs, ceding more and more territory to the Luyten.

It had been a brilliantly executed attack.

The elevator flashed, indicating visitors.

President Wood was short and stocky, with a crooked nose and a curled-down mouth set in a perpetual sneer. Two Secret Service agents hung back near the elevator as Wood crossed the room to shake Oliver's hand.

"You're doing good work," Wood said. "You've succeeded where many others have failed." He held up a hand. "Don't get me wrong, that doesn't surprise me. I've seen your résumé. You have forty IQ points on me, and I'm not as dumb as I sound, and your work on influence techniques at NYU?" He shook his head. "Remarkable."

"Thank you, sir." Oliver motioned toward the little kitchen. "Can I get you something?"

"Nah, I'm good." Wood wandered over to Five's cage, studied the creature. "So why don't the three of us have a talk?" Wood waited a beat, then turned to Oliver. "Did it answer?"

"No."

Wood turned back to Five. "What harm would it do to talk?" He looked at Oliver, eyebrows raised.

Oliver shook his head. "Earlier it asked what it gained by talking to us."

Wood raised one eyebrow. "Awfully cocky attitude."

"I know."

Wood studied Five a moment longer, then sighed and turned away. "I understand it told you we wanted to discuss surrender."

Oliver nodded. "Is it true?"

Wood started to answer, stopped, began again. "It's one option." He rubbed his upper lip for a moment. "Put it this way: If you can get our friend to discuss whether they would accept our surrender, and under what terms, we would be interested to hear what it has to say."

Oliver nodded slowly, digesting this.

"That's not to say there's nothing in the works. There may be."

"But you don't know?"

"If I knew for sure, so would they." Wood jerked a thumb in Five's direction. "Then we'd have nothing in the works."

# 12

## *Lila Easterlin*

*July 17, 2029. Savannah, Georgia.*

As rooftops came into view below them, Lila had second thoughts about the plan. She watched her father, a bead of sweat dangling from his nose, his fingers squeezing the throttle. The plane had automatic stabilizers, but still, it was not exactly safe for someone who'd never flown one to just take off and go.

The breeze kicked up and the plane wobbled, the stabilizers on the wings whirring, trying to compensate. They were above the tall pine trees, the highway visible on Lila's right, a long strip shrinking in the distance.

"You're doing great!" Lila said, having to shout over the wind.

Dad only nodded, his attention glued to the task. He kept going up, up; Lila had imagined clearing the trees and then staying as low as possible.

"How high are you going?" she asked.

"High enough that we're out of range of Luyten weapons.

There's no hiding the fact we're up here. If any Luyten on the ground can just point a heater or lightning rod and cook us, we won't make it far."

Lila hadn't thought of that. Being in the air—away from all the Luyten on the ground—made her feel safe from them, but every Luyten they passed would know they were there.

"How high can we go?" she asked.

"I don't know. How high can you go and still breathe?"

Lila thought about mountain climbers. At the top of tall peaks, climbers could barely breathe, but how high was that? She missed her feed; whenever teachers had wanted her to remember some esoteric detail like the heights of mountains, Lila had rolled her eyes and ignored them. "Like, I don't know, maybe twelve or thirteen thousand feet?"

Dad nodded. "I guess if we're getting too high, we'll know."

When the altimeter read thirteen thousand feet, they were still breathing fine, although Lila felt slightly out of breath, and inhaling deeply didn't make the feeling go away. The cold was worse. Lila was wearing a thin short-sleeved tunic, and she was trembling. Their emergency packs, which included warm clothes, were back in their fried car.

The ground below was a patchwork of black-and-white towns, brown fields, green forest.

"How do we find Atlanta?" Lila asked. The ultralight had a built-in GPS system, but with satellites down it was useless.

"I'm just heading due west."

Was Atlanta due west? It must be, more or less. Certainly they'd spot the downtown skyscrapers if they were anywhere close.

Dad glanced at her. "I can't believe you were able to assemble this. It would've taken me a week."

"You told me to find something productive to do."

"I did. And you did."

Lila studied the airspeed indicator. They were going just over sixty miles per hour, which meant maybe a two-hour trip. She turned to look over her shoulder at Savannah.

Smoke was rising from a thousand places. Some of the larger buildings were visibly on fire, the flames licking the sky. A container ship was sinking on the river.

*"Oh, shit."*

The words jolted Lila awake, set her heart pounding. She looked around and immediately spotted what had caused her father to cry out: seven or eight Luyten were in the air, heading toward them.

They were in modified human Harriers, their massive bodies hanging in harnesses below the craft. Dad was descending, the nose of the ultralight pointed at a steep angle that sent uneasy butterflies through Lila's gut.

It was hard to tell if the Luyten were dropping to intercept them. If they were, Lila and her father were going to die.

"Oh shit, oh shit, oh shit," her father was chanting, clearly in shock. Lila gripped the dash, afraid to look for the Luyten. The ground below was a checker of farmland broken by roads and occasionally buildings.

Lila ventured a look up: The Luyten craft were much closer. They were flying in a circular formation, as Luyten always did, closing on them.

*"They're coming after us!"* Lila screamed.

"I'm gonna ditch us," Dad said, his chin pressed into his neck, his mouth stretched in a grimace. "Find the—"

Suddenly, Lila was burning. She screamed in pain, the

worst of it coming from her fingers, where her rings were searing her skin.

Dad was screaming, too, his fingers sizzling where they gripped the controls. "We lost the engine." He held fast to the controls, as the ultralight plunged and his fingers burned.

The heat was getting intolerable as the Luyten closed on them. Lila scanned the dash, frantically seeking the crash suit indicator. There was nothing she could see that looked like an emergency icon. Surely all aircraft, no matter how small, were equipped with crash suits.

Then she saw it, down by her dad's right foot: a square yellow icon with a fold-up ring. She struggled to read the simple, red-ringed instructions: *Pull ring out, turn clockwise.*

"Wait until we're close to the ground," Dad said. "As close as possible."

"I *know*!" Lila screamed, trying to concentrate. Her shoes were burning her feet. She kicked them off.

Suddenly the heat let up.

Crying with relief, Lila looked up and back, and spotted the Luyten pulling away.

It was deadly silent save for the whistle of the wind. They were close to the ground, quickly growing closer. Pine trees hurtled by just below. Lila realized they were moving much faster than they seemed.

Her skin was throbbing all over. They'd been just on the edge of the heater's range. Besides her ring finger and feet, she felt like she had a very bad sunburn.

They cleared the line of trees; Dad tried to bank so they would drop along the length of a cornfield. Lila hadn't known you could grow corn in Georgia. For some reason the thought made her laugh hysterically. She tried to stifle the laugh, but that only made it worse. They were going down, about to crash, and she couldn't stop laughing.

The ultralight was canted, the left wing lower than the right. When the left wing was about a dozen feet above the corn, Lila twisted the ring to activate the crash suits.

She had the barest instant to see the ultralight burst apart, then the suit inflated around her, pushing her flat, pinning her arms at her sides. She was turning in the air, head over heels, the blue sky framed inside the tight rectangle of vision the suit afforded, then trees, then the startlingly green cornfield, and blue sky again.

Hitting the ground was much worse than Lila had anticipated. It felt like she was being beaten with a steel bar as she slammed into the ground again and again. Then she rolled and skidded, her momentum carrying her farther than she thought possible.

Finally, she stopped rolling and lay still. She stared up at the sky, the clouds drifting by.

High above, a lone Luyten flew by. Although it was high, it was surely not eight miles high, so it was reading her thoughts at this very moment, perhaps considering whether it was worth the trouble to land and finish them.

It continued on, maybe because they were only civilians, weaponless, lying in a field scattered with wreckage.

"Lila?"

She had no idea how to deactivate a crash suit. When she'd seen them on the news, the people inside were always surrounded by concerned medical personnel who knew how to deflate them.

Lila felt around with her fingers, the only part of her body she could move. They came in contact with a bulb. She squeezed it three or four times, and suddenly the suit hissed and settled around her in a plastic puddle. She pushed it off and struggled to her knees.

Dad was heading toward her, limping deeply, a purple bruise rising on his cheek. "Holy shit," he said. "Holy shit, Lila." He looked at his hands: His palms were covered with angry red sores. "Holy shit."

"Do you know how far we are from Atlanta?" Lila asked.

Dad nodded. "It was in sight when the Luyten showed. Maybe ten or fifteen miles to the suburbs?" He pointed to the right. "The interstate is that way. Maybe we can hitch a ride with some of the refugees."

Lila struggled to her feet. She expected to feel lancing pain in one limb or another, but besides her burning skin and a lot of soreness and a few bumps and bruises, she was all right.

# 13

## *Oliver Bowen*

*March 11, 2030 (eight months later). Easter Island.*

As they stepped onto the ramp leading off the submarine, Oliver found the fresh, salty breeze delightful. They'd been on the sub for only four days, but it had felt like a month. At first all Oliver could see were the rocks of a jetty. He climbed a ramp, and as he cleared the rise he saw palm trees scattered on an open, rocky plain sloping upward. A handful of horses were grazing in the shadow of a line of a dozen or more enormous stone figures. Oliver recognized the long heads; the sharp, angular, features; the shelflike brows and unreadable expressions.

"Easter Island. Rapa Nui." He'd always wanted to visit, never found the time.

Off to his left, close to shore, Oliver spotted a group of crisply uniformed officers disappearing down a stairway leading underground. There was no military base on Rapa Nui as far as he knew. It must have been constructed since the invasion. Closer to the water, a large forklift was carrying

Five and his entire enclosure. The forklift set Five on a raised platform, which sank slowly into the ground until Five disappeared.

"Dr. Bowen? This way, please." A woman with gray crew-cut hair, wearing a black suit, sidearm, clearly CIA security, touched his elbow. She steered him toward the staircase that led under the island.

Oliver followed the agent down the steps, stunned as the size and scope of this operation unfolded before him. He was descending into an immense open space. The cavernous room was bisected into dozens of smaller spaces, separated by transparent material that gave the facility an unnerving sense of weightlessness. Hundreds of people were visible, hurrying about, seemingly walking on air.

"What is this place?"

"I'm taking you to a briefing, sir," the agent said.

"It must have cost billions to construct this facility."

"You're only seeing a fraction of it. It covers most of the space under the island."

The far walls were raw stone. Oliver watched as someone stepped onto a small framed platform, grasped the handles jutting from its frame, and shot out of sight. He was led into a room along one wall—one of the few fully enclosed rooms. A thin black woman who looked about sixteen met him at the door.

"Dr. Bowen, I'm Dominique Wiewall. I head up the biological side of the defenders project." She had a lilting Caribbean accent and spoke quickly, breathlessly. "I'll be providing your orientation, which, if you don't mind, I'd like to start straightaway."

Oliver nodded. "Please, I'm dying to know what's going on here."

Wiewall motioned for Oliver to take a seat at a circular meeting table in what looked to be her office. There was a computer station in one corner, a dozen or so small wood carvings of Moai along a single shelf, and a big framed poster of a gorgeous rain forest. Along the bottom of the poster, *Island Rain* was printed in teal cursive lettering.

As they sat at the meeting table, an impressive three-dimensional display of the island materialized above it.

"Rapa Nui is a volcanic island," Wiewall said without any preamble, still speaking rapidly. "The underground is riddled with caves—lave tubes created by three volcanoes that formed the island. The original residents lived in these caves in the years before they died off. The caves, and the incredibly remote location of the island, made it a perfect base of operations."

A red line appeared, surrounding the island.

"Elaborate precautions have been taken to keep the Luyten from becoming aware of this project. *No one* knows the details of the project except those on the island, and anyone who comes to the island, stays."

"You mean, I have to stay here indefinitely?" Oliver thought of Vanessa, then reminded himself: Vanessa was a weakness. No weakness.

Wiewall nodded. "You will. If all goes well, though, that should not be long. Maybe three months. The project is in its final stages." Her head was nearly shaved, leaving only a sheen of tight black curls outlining the elegant shape of her skull. Come to think of it, most of the people Oliver had seen had severe haircuts, as if time was too precious to devote to hair grooming.

He couldn't imagine what they were working on, what sort

of weapon would justify expending such massive resources. For the first time in a year, he felt a flicker of hope.

*It's a desperate, last-ditch effort.*

Oliver had almost forgotten Five was there. *What is?* he thought. Five would already know the details.

Five didn't answer.

The display changed, from Easter Island to an enlarged map of a human neural network, the receptor sites for the various neurotransmitters highlighted with different colors.

"I know you have a background in psychology, so I'll skip the preliminaries," Wiewall said. "We've studied Luyten physiology using corpses salvaged from battles. Based on those examinations, our medical experts think the Luyten's telepathic ability relies on the presence of the neurotransmitter serotonin."

Oliver nodded. That made sense. Serotonin was what made humans feel human, what made them feel love, sexual desire, awareness, and interest in the world.

In the display, the serotonin receptor sites vanished. "If there is no serotonin present, the Luyten can't read the target, and their telepathic advantage is neutralized."

"If you removed people's serotonin receptors, they'd be in a catatonic state, so there'd be no mind to read."

Wiewall nodded. "That's true. But we haven't removed serotonin receptors from human brains; we've designed a brain that functions without serotonin."

"Designed a brain?" All Oliver could think was Wiewall was speaking metaphorically. "You mean some sort of advanced AI?"

The display changed to another neural network. It was organic, but utterly unrecognizable to Oliver.

"The world's superpowers have all had well-funded genetic engineering programs since the beginning of the century. Soon after the Luyten invaded, they began pooling their resources and knowledge."

Oliver leaned forward, examined the display more closely. "But if you excised the entire serotonin system, you'd have a domino effect. You'd have to change everything."

"We did. And more." She stood, motioned Oliver toward the door. As Oliver stood, Wiewall paused, then smiled for the first time. "I have to admit, I'm looking forward to seeing your reaction to this. Most of us have been here the whole time, and we've gotten used to seeing them."

"Them?"

Wiewall's smile broadened. She led him out, down a long transparent hallway, into a lift that took them down six, seven, eight stories.

"I was sure you'd be looking toward AI technology," Oliver said as they dropped. "That seemed the obvious direction; what little success we've had has involved drone and robot technology."

Wiewall shook her head. "That would have been a dead end. Robots are stupid in all the ways that matter in this war. Luyten can't read their minds, sure, but they don't have to, because robots can't develop independent battle plans, can't come up with creative strategies without human assistance. They can't react to anything *new* the Luyten throw their way."

Transparent dividers were suddenly replaced by thick concrete walls.

They'd engineered humans with utterly different neurological functioning? Oliver couldn't quite buy that. It just couldn't be right. He kept expecting Five to weigh in, but Five stayed silent.

They slowed to a stop; the lift door opened.

Oliver clutched the wall, his knees jelly, his heart hammering fiercely.

They couldn't possibly be real.

"They won't hurt you," Wiewall said. Her voice seemed to be coming from a distance, although she was still right beside him.

They were sixteen feet tall at least, walking on three legs, ghost white, their huge faces obviously inspired by the statues ringing the island.

"How is this possible?"

The creatures were engaged in a training exercise in an enormous space that must have been a half mile square. Their movements were fluid, athletic, assured; the third leg allowed them to run incredibly fast—faster than a Luyten.

*It's not a footrace*, Five said. There was something in his voice. It was tentative. Afraid, even. *They wasted their time bringing me here.*

Why *had* they brought Five? Oliver had been too mesmerized by the giant warriors to consider the question until Five brought it up.

*They want to find out if I can read them.*

"Can you?" Oliver asked aloud.

Wiewall glanced at him. "Can I what?"

"Sorry. I was speaking to the Luyten. I don't know why I do it out loud."

"It's speaking to you right now?" Her voice held a tinge of awe.

"That's right."

The giants were carrying standard weapons: bayoneted assault rifles, grenade launchers, all enlarged to match their massive scale. On top of this there were what appeared to be blades running down the sides of their arms and legs for hand-to-hand combat. Other hardware was attached to their skintight black uniforms at their forearms, like it was a part of their anatomy. In that regard, it reminded Oliver of Luyten weaponry.

"The weapons bulging from their forearms…" Oliver began.

"Their arms and legs are artificial, from the joints down. That not only made them simpler to design from a genetic perspective; it makes them stronger and faster. They control their artificial limbs entirely through thought."

Oliver watched them for a moment. "Their movements are so fluid."

Wiewall smiled like a proud parent. Then the smile was gone, and she was all business again.

"Notice they only have three fingers. Our ergonomics team determined that was maximally efficient for handling weapons."

Their fingers looked like powerful claws, thick and long. And they were fleshy—not at all mechanical-looking. "Are these all of them?" Oliver asked. He counted twenty.

"So far we have two thousand. If they're effective against the Luyten, the plan is to produce several million at facilities already being constructed under cities around the world. No one involved in building the facilities has any idea what they're for; they're working from blueprints."

Oliver nodded. It was an incredibly ambitious undertaking. The cities involved must be diverting a substantial percentage of their resources to the construction.

*Do you know what she's thinking about you right now? She thinks you're bizarre. You never make eye contact. You fidget. Just now, you were digging at your scalp with a fingernail while speaking to her.*

Willing himself to ignore the comment, he turned to Wiewall and asked, "How will you convey battle instructions to the—what are they called?"

*She wonders if you're autistic.*

"Defenders. That's the point—humans can't know the defenders' intentions; otherwise the Luyten will as well. They fight independently. They develop their own battle plans."

He gawked at Wiewall. "You're kidding me."

"They don't look it, but they're extremely intelligent. They're epigenetically primed to learn extremely rapidly. They learn to speak in a matter of weeks. Then, when they're not here training, they're in a classroom studying warfare. All they know is military strategy and tactics. They don't sleep, so their training is almost nonstop."

Oliver didn't know what he'd been expecting. An airborne virus that affected Luyten but not humans. A new superweapon. He hadn't expected this. If the Luyten could read the defenders' minds, though, they'd be nothing but bigger targets.

"You said your medical people *think* the Luyten's ability won't work without serotonin present. How confident are they?"

Wiewall paused, then, in a careful, deliberate tone, said, "Some are more confident than others."

*You just scratched inside your nose. Yes, it was just barely inside, but it doesn't matter. Do you know how uncomfortable you just made her? Do you see how she's averting her eyes? It drove Vanessa crazy when you did things like that in public.*

Oliver squeezed his eyes closed, knowing that would only make him seem odder to Wiewall, but needing a moment to regain his composure.

"Five isn't going to help you," he said, opening his eyes. "He understands what the stakes are. He'll die first."

The young scientist's expression did not instill confidence. "I was told that wasn't my concern."

"Whose concern is it? Mine? Because I'm telling you right now, Five may talk to me, but believe me, he doesn't say anything useful."

Dr. Wiewall swallowed. She was blinking rapidly, clearly uneasy. "I'm not sure what to say. If there's a plan, there may be a good reason no one in the Luyten's range is aware of it. Or maybe they're just hoping the Luyten will slip up. I don't know."

Chuckling morosely, Oliver looked at the ceiling. "If that's the plan, they don't know Five very well."

# 14

## *Oliver Bowen*

*March 12, 2030. Easter Island.*

Hands on hips, his breathing slightly labored from the walk up the sloping field, Oliver took in the line of statues. *Moai*, the locals called them. They were watching the horizon, their faces resolute. Waiting. At least that's how it looked to Oliver, now that he'd seen the defenders. The resemblance was uncanny. How the geneticists had engineered that resemblance, Oliver could not imagine.

"What do you know," Oliver said aloud. "Maybe the Hulk and Spider-Man showed up after all."

No response. Oliver thought he knew why Five had gone mute: He didn't want to risk tipping off Oliver about whether he could read the defenders.

So much had changed since Oliver learned of the defenders. Five had been right—before, Oliver had had very little hope. There had seemed no reason for hope. Humanity had been whittled from seven billion to under four in a matter of three years. They were surrounded by the Luyten, crowded

101

into the cities, starved of food and resources. All that seemed left was for the Luyten to wipe out the cities.

"Dr. Bowen." It was Wiewall, on the comm he'd been provided.

"Yes, ma'am?" he replied, then winced as he heard how stupid he sounded calling her ma'am. His attempts at levity usually fell flat.

"You'd better start heading back. They're bringing the Luyten down in a few minutes."

"On my way."

Oliver took one last look at the Moai, and realized some were the same height as the defenders.

Wiewall and a CIA security guy who'd introduced himself as Ski led Oliver into what looked to be a medical bay where a lone defender waited, sitting against the wall, one of its three legs canted. The defender watched them enter but otherwise didn't acknowledge them. Oliver wondered if it had a name, if it would know what to do if Oliver went over and introduced himself. Its expression was as unreadable as the Moai.

As they waited, others filed into the room, including the commander of the operation, Colonel Willis. Oliver had met him earlier, thought he seemed like a bright, decent guy.

The hum of machinery interrupted his thoughts; Oliver turned. The big forklift was bringing Five, still caged, into the room.

The defender's reaction was immediate. It stood, stared at Five, craning its neck to see the Luyten better. Then it began to pace, never taking its eyes off Five, keeping a uniform distance.

"This is the first time it's ever been in the presence of a

Luyten," Wiewall whispered. "They're conditioned to despise them."

The defender looked down, then back up at the Luyten.

"Is the Luyten communicating with you?" Wiewall asked.

"No. Five's giving me the silent treatment." Oliver raised his voice. "Aren't you, Five?"

*I wonder if Vanessa went ahead and fucked Paul after you were so convinced she already had. Maybe they're living together now.*

Oliver did his best to ignore the comment. This was too important; he couldn't allow himself to be distracted.

The defender paused in front of a table built in along the wall. It picked something up, then resumed pacing. Oliver squinted, straining to see what the defender had picked up.

It was a bayonet. Large enough to look formidable in the defender's hand.

"What's it doing?" Oliver asked. He looked around, but no one responded. There were about a dozen people present now. All eyes were on the defender.

Oliver turned, studied Five, who was watching the defender. There was nothing in its manner that might indicate whether it knew what the defender was thinking, although Oliver had always struggled to read the Luyten's body language.

The defender stopped pacing. Its mouth a tight line, it took a deep breath through its nose, exhaled. With shocking speed, it hurled the bayonet at Five.

An instant later, the bayonet was embedded in one of Five's limbs—it had gone right through the eye set in that limb. A cawing filled the room, multiple voices squawking in an eerie harmony. It took Oliver a moment to realize it was Five, screaming in pain and surprise through all of his mouths at once.

He hadn't even *tried* to duck. The attack had caught Five completely by surprise.

Oliver rushed toward the Luyten. Five was gripping the bayonet with the cilia that served as his hand, pulling carefully, trembling from the pain.

"Kill you all," Five said aloud, the pitch of his voice rising and falling. Gasps ran through the small crowd.

Five worked the knife out a half inch. Black blood dribbled from the ruined eye, pooling along the ridge that ran from each limb, spiraling to the center of his body.

"They won't stop us. We'll kill you all." Five pried the bayonet farther.

"Can somebody help it, for God's sake?" Oliver said. He glanced at the people now clustered around Five's prison. "Are any of you medical personnel?"

A man with heavy jowls studied Oliver, then glanced at Five. "Let it bleed awhile."

Oliver pointed into the cage. "That's the only Luyten who has ever communicated with a human being. Do you really want to let it die?"

Drawn out of a stunned stupor by Oliver's raised voice, Colonel Willis said, "He's right. Get the thing patched up."

The man studied Five. "We'll have to sedate it first."

Oliver opened his mouth to argue, then realized it would be foolish to insist Five was not dangerous. Five was very dangerous.

He stepped back, rejoining Wiewall. "So now we know."

Wiewall nodded, clearly unnerved. Whether she was shaken by the attack on Five or Five speaking, Oliver didn't know. "It was an ingenious test. Whoever devised it must have left the island before the Luyten arrived, so it wouldn't be forewarned."

On the far side of the room, the defender had resumed

pacing. Occasionally it lifted its head to look at Five. Oliver wondered just how the test had been arranged. "I'm going to speak to it." He gestured at the defender. "Does it have a name?"

"Robert. They're all male, though they have no genitalia."

As Oliver approached, the size and mass of the thing became more apparent, and more intimidating. It continued pacing, evidently unable to relax in the presence of a Luyten. Oliver could relate to that.

"Excuse me. Robert?"

The defender considered him, snorting air through its long nose, reminding Oliver of a bull.

"Who instructed you to injure the Luyten with the bayonet?"

The defender frowned. "No one. Colonel Willis ordered me to determine whether the Luyten could read my thoughts. It can't."

"No, it can't." Oliver's mind was reeling. The defenders were definitely more intelligent than they looked. Their faces were stiff, didn't express much in the way of emotion, but he shouldn't have been fooled into thinking that reflected their intellectual ability. He thanked Robert and returned to Wiewall, who'd been watching from a distance.

"Robert devised the test himself."

Wiewall tilted her head. "I'm surprised. Pleased, but surprised. They're engineered and trained to be skilled tacticians, but still, that's impressive problem solving."

"What happens now?"

Watching Robert pace, and glower at Five, she said, "Now we make more."

# 15

## *Oliver Bowen*

*May 9, 2030. Washington, D.C.*

Oliver watched the city go by through the limo's one-way glass. He wiped his sweaty palms on his pants. The D.C. area gave you a deceptive perspective on what was happening in the world. It wasn't that D.C. was the same as it had been before the invasion, but the fortifications around the entire D.C.-Alexandria area were so heavy you felt a sense of safety and stability.

The limo pulled to a stop in front of Vanessa's apartment, a walk-up in a luxury complex, and Oliver's heart rate doubled. He had no idea how she would react to him showing up at her door. In the weeks since Five revealed it had lied, Oliver had rehearsed a hundred things to say, imagined all the reactions Vanessa might have.

He raised his fist and knocked.

Vanessa looked surprised to see him, and that gave him hope. She didn't look angry, at least. But she didn't invite him in, either; she only stared at him, wide-eyed, clutching the door.

"I've made a terrible mistake."

Vanessa began to look, if not angry, then at least unhappy.

He stammered, words eluding him. After all the time he'd spent planning what he'd say to Vanessa, he found his mind blank. "I'm so sorry."

Vanessa folded her arms. "How did you finally figure it out?"

"Five—the Luyten—told me it had lied." He didn't know whether to refer to Five as *it*, or *he*, or *she*. None sounded right, so he found himself switching back and forth.

She gave a dry, humorless laugh. "Maybe it's lying now. Maybe you should find another starfish to corroborate Five's claim before jumping to any conclusions."

Oliver licked his extremely dry lips. "I know I should have believed you instead of it, but if you understood what it was like, how it gets inside your head." He stabbed a finger at his temple. "It knows exactly what buttons to push, it knows your fears and insecurities, all of your secrets." He took a deep breath, trying to control his rising emotions.

Vanessa's arms were still tightly crossed. She looked past him, into the street. "A limo?"

"I've been promoted. I'm the CIA Director of Science and Technology, and a special advisor to President Wood." Oliver wanted to tell Vanessa about his work, about the small part he'd played in the defenders project, but it was still technically classified. He'd been allowed to leave Easter Island now that eight heavily defended production facilities were up and running, and keeping their existence secret from the Luyten was all but impossible, but that didn't mean he could talk about the project with anyone he chose.

"Wow, congratulations," Vanessa said, sounding sincere, if not particularly enthusiastic.

"I'm going to adopt Kai—the orphan who discovered—"

"I know who Kai is," Vanessa said, cutting him off. She was back to looking surprised. "You told me you never wanted children. You said they made you uncomfortable."

"They do." He shrugged. "But someone has to take care of him." He'd hoped telling Vanessa about Kai would reform him in her eyes, make him seem worthy of forgiveness. That wasn't the reason he was doing it, but still, he'd hoped. He waited for some kind word he could build on.

"Why did you come here, Oliver?"

"I came to apologize. I should have trusted you. I'm sorry."

"Oliver—"

"The truth is, I believed Five because I couldn't believe you could really love me. It was so hard to see how you could. But, believe it or not, Five's psychological attacks have opened my eyes to—"

"Oliver."

He knew what she was about to say—he could read it in her eyes, and he didn't want to hear it. "Just spend some time with me, and you'll see. I'm not asking you to forgive me, just give me some of your time—"

"No," she said, simply, emphatically. "No. You're right, I can't forgive you for this. For leaving me in the middle of this." She started to lift her arms, then let them flop back to her sides. "Maybe the end of the world is supposed to make things like this seem insignificant, but for me, it hasn't. It's set me on a razor's edge. There's right, and there's wrong." Vanessa rubbed her upper lip, shaking her head. "And what you did was wrong. You were supposed to believe *me*. You were supposed to take *my* side."

Oliver had no response. Her answer was one he'd anticipated, but even imagining the words, he'd never come up with a reply.

He wanted to say goodbye but didn't trust himself to get the words out steadily. Instead, he nodded, then headed down the steps.

# 16

## Oliver Bowen

*May 21, 2030. Washington, D.C.*

With each swing of his arms, Oliver could feel his underarms gliding on slick sweat. He was short of breath, as if he were sprinting to the war room instead of walking.

A dozen or so people were talking in low tones, clumped here and there around the huge circular room, waiting for the meeting to start. The war room was built like an amphitheater, with the center the lowest point, and each subsequent ring of seats and electronics a few steps higher. Oliver spotted Ariel silently working her screen and took a seat beside her.

She looked up, nodded once, went back to work.

"Can you fill me in?"

Ariel stopped working. "I figured you knew more than I did. Five isn't keeping you updated?"

"Five does nothing but hurl insults at me, on the rare occasions when he deigns to speak to me at all."

Before Ariel could respond, President Wood entered, flanked by Secretary of Defense Oteri, Secretary of State Nielsen, and his senior advisor, his brother Carmine. He raised his voice to be heard, showing no interest in sitting.

"The starfish are massing around the cities housing defender production facilities. Every single facility. We don't have nearly as many defenders as we'd like, but unless someone in here says something to change my mind, I'm going to advise Premier Chandar to release what we have immediately. Their primary mission will be to defend those production facilities."

Raising his shoulders, the president waited, looking around the room at individual faces. He stopped on Oliver's. "Dr. Bowen. Oliver. What does our resident starfish have to say about all this?"

"He stopped communicating with me after Easter Island."

"Probably smart of it," President Wood said. He resumed his scan of the room. "So? Does anyone want to voice an objection? What do we risk by having them fight now, besides affording them less time to train?"

Evidently no one could think of objections. The Luyten were clearly aware of the defenders and understood they were a threat. The secret was out. Given that nine facilities were now in operation, it wasn't surprising.

"Can I make a suggestion?" Secretary of Defense Oteri asked. She was built like a bulldog—short, squat, with thinning black hair and a bulb nose. "Deploy one battalion first, so we can assess its effectiveness, maybe learn some things we can pass on to the other forces. It will take the Luyten time to mass numbers large enough to storm those facilities."

The president shrugged, looked around the room for reaction.

"We could send the Easter Island force into Santiago," said Wood's brother Carmine, who was tall and extremely thin, almost skeletal. "In fact, the Algarrobo nuclear plant is only twenty miles outside Santiago. If they could retake the largest power plant in South America while securing the defender production facility in Santiago, that would be huge. We need energy. Badly."

There were murmurs of agreement.

"We need to see what they're capable of on a mission before we set them all loose," Oteri added. "Once we set them loose, that's it. They become a fully independent fighting force—allies, more than anything."

"But if we set them loose in Santiago, aren't we giving the Luyten a chance to learn from that encounter as well?" Secretary Nielsen asked in his customary dulcet tone. Nielsen was soft-spoken, balding, with a full reddish beard.

Ariel waved her hand and waited for the president to recognize her like a child in class. "As the Luyten mass, their communication grid breaks down. They cut themselves off from one another as their web configuration folds. Do they have electronic communication?"

"Not much," Oteri said. "They have some they seized from us that they use to communicate across oceans and deserts and so on, but they don't have the capability to transmit visual recordings of a battle, or detailed schematics. They're used to passing information instantaneously, through their telepathic network."

Wood took a deep breath, let it out. "All right. I'll send a recommendation to Premier Chandar that we launch an attack on Santiago and the Algarrobo nuclear plant as soon as possible." Since the president was the World Alliance's minister of defense, it seemed certain the premier would go along with his recommendation.

# 17

## Dominique Wiewall

*May 25, 2030. Easter Island.*

When the colonel put his hand on her knee, Dominique wanted to hack it off with a knife, but instead had to settle for shifting to the left to dislodge it. How dare he use this, the culminating moment of all of their work, to pull this kind of stunt?

She'd been drunk the night she slept with him. Extremely drunk. Also wallowing in a modicum of self-pity, because it had been her birthday. She'd regretted it the moment it was over, before she'd even sobered up. When she did sober up, she more than regretted it—she'd been mortified. Not that Colonel Willis was unattractive, he was just...too military. A walking stereotype. It made him seem clownish in Dominique's eyes.

Shaking off the memory of his pale body rocking atop hers, Dominique focused on the feeds. They had three to start. Some might be knocked out once combat began, but hopefully not all. They needed to collect as much information as possible about the defenders' performance. It would be tricky, to pass on recommendations that might aid the defenders in subsequent engagements without passing on information that might help the Luyten, who would undoubtedly intercept everything they sent.

Her pulse was racing. These were her children. Many, many others had helped, but no one would argue that she was the primary architect. Besides everything at stake for humanity, Dominique felt in a very personal way that her life would be either vindicated or ruined in the next few hours. She was so glad she'd opted to stay on Easter Island. No one off the island would witness this, not even the premier.

Dominique was cautiously optimistic that the defenders would do well. The Luyten depended heavily on knowing their enemy's minds; they'd had no need to develop tactical expertise in battle. And while their weapons were sophisticated, most only had what was embedded in the biologically grown suit that fit them like a second skin. The defenders, by contrast, knew nothing but military tactics, and were armed to the teeth.

Dominique watched the feed from one of the little aerial butterfly cameras, which was temporarily perched on the helmet of the operation's commander, a defender named Douglas. He was traveling with the Airborne Battalion, briefing his officers in a clipped baritone, squatting in the hold of the huge stealth-enabled C-5, which was typically used to transport heavy artillery and buses. She enabled the sound.

"We establish two separate LZs. The first, five miles north-northeast of the objective." Douglas pointed to the spot on the relief map. The first LZ, which Dominique assumed meant landing zone, lit up in red. "The second, five miles south-southeast." He marked this one as well. "One squad from each drop zone will be designated as a security squad and will move as follows: From drop zone one, directly north. From drop zone two, directly south. The northern moving squad will secure Highway 60 and establish a perimeter defense. The southern moving squad will secure Highway 5. The full security squad will deny any Luyten movement from west to east—"

From what she knew of military tactics, the plan seemed solid. It soothed her drumming heart, how competent the commander sounded.

"—additional squad will be dropped in the southern LZ and will proceed to the area just north of San Antonio. Center of gravity, CP, and HQ will be established at that location, here, ten miles south-southeast of the objective."

A commander named Luigi was overseeing the defense of the production facility in Santiago, but taking the power plant was the more challenging of the two missions. Not only did the Luyten already hold it, but the defenders couldn't use large weapons to bombard the plant, because they needed it to be operational. To compensate, they were sending a large force—120 defenders.

"Here they go," Colonel Willis said, leaning forward. Dominique reflexively drew her leg away, afraid he'd use the shift in posture as an opportunity to reestablish an LZ on her thigh.

As the defenders jumped, two at a time, from the aircraft, they didn't appear to be almost three times as large as humans. The oversized aircraft and gear threw off Dominique's perception. But as they dropped to the ground in an open field adjacent to a forest, they were almost half as tall as the trees, and the illusion was shattered.

Douglas grunted orders to his men, as the butterfly camera

lifted off, giving Dominique a wider view of the terrain. A gentle slope led up to another wall of trees. The defenders fanned out, trotted across the field in what seemed like half a dozen steps, and disappeared into the forest.

It was strange, to think the Luyten didn't know they were coming.

Dominique glanced at the feed originating with the sea-based B Company. The company was in skiffs, heading toward the beach. They looked awkward, riding six to a skiff in boats meant to carry twenty humans. They would attack from the west, while the airborne company attacked from the east.

The butterfly camera panned down to provide a glimpse of defenders moving through the forest below, then up, to provide their first look at the power plant. It was shaped like a figure eight lying flat. Four enormous storage tanks on stilts stood behind it, and all of this sat on a platform surrounded by a placid artificial lake of steel-blue seawater, pumped in from the nearby Pacific. The lake was bisected by three breezeways. A Luyten-modified heavy construction vehicle was crossing one of the breezeways, its Luyten operator clearly visible. Half a dozen other Luyten were moving around outside the plant.

The crackle of small-arms fire erupted in the forest below. The camera swung toward the trees.

By the time Dominique could see what was happening, it was over. Two Luyten lay dead, their centers jellied with ordnance wounds. Defenders confiscated the fallen Luyten weapons, and the company pushed on.

"There goes the element of surprise," Willis said. "Though I doubt the defenders expected to make it right up to the gates without being spotted."

Willis's final words were partially drowned by an explosion coming over the feed, then two more on top of one another. The camera rose.

The Luyten had blown the three breezeways. Water surged to fill the gaps. The plant was now on an island.

"They'd better not set foot in that water. The Luyten will electrify it and fry them," Colonel Willis said, stating the obvious. Dominique was certain the defenders would realize that immediately. They weren't stupid grunts; their IQs were higher than the colonel's.

When C Company reached the edge of the forest they hung back, out of range of the Luyten weapons. B Company—the one coming by sea—had landed on the beaches and was spread out, waiting for orders. Now the question was how to reach the Luyten.

Fifteen minutes crawled by as the defenders continued to hang back. Dominique wished whoever was controlling the camera would set it back down on Commander Douglas so they could hear the defenders' planning, but it remained above the trees, providing a useless bird's-eye view. Another camera was embedded with B Company, the third at HQ.

Three A-7 Razorback Harriers buzzed over the horizon from the north, from HQ and the Engineering Company. Dominique couldn't easily see how three Harriers helped the situation, unless they used them to bomb the shit out of the Luyten position, which would mean destroying the power plant.

The first Harrier dropped low, close to the tree line. A defender sprinted out of the trees, leaped, and grabbed one of the Harrier's skids, as if it were trying to pull the thing out of the air. The Harrier was more powerful than Dominique would have guessed; it rose rapidly, the defender clinging to it with one hand. Each of the other two Harriers took on a hitcher and rose as well. They rose steeply, headed toward the air above the fusion plant with blinding speed.

The Luyten, brandishing Y-shaped lightning rods, opened fire as they drew close. The defenders returned fire, pumping hot rounds from the handheld mortar launchers in their free hands. Dominique's heart raced as she saw a Luyten go down. Then another, clipped on one limb and spun around.

From the beach side of the plant, defenders surged forward in twos, carrying the skiffs that had transported them to shore.

The first pair were hit by heaters, bursting into flame short of the artificial lake. Despite being thousands of miles away, Dominique felt singed by the heat that engulfed them, felt their loss like a sting as each managed a few steps before they fell, nothing but husks, black smoke rising from them.

Dominique took a deep breath, trying to calm herself. She hadn't expected to feel their deaths so strongly, to take them so personally.

The next pair made it, as the airborne defenders continued to lay down a blinding cloak of cover fire, the Harriers diving toward the plant, then rising just as rapidly. The pair hurled the skiff into the lake and retreated. The lake was shallow; the skiff landed with a splash and lay impotently on its side.

The third pair heaved their skiff beyond the first, and suddenly Dominique understood what they were doing: They were building a bridge out of the skiffs, which were undoubtedly composed of carbon fiber, and not electricity-conducting.

Another aircraft flew into view to the east, this one large, clearly not a fighter. Without slowing it dropped a pile of unidentifiable materials—slabs and poles.

One of the Harriers was hit. It spun in a tight circle,

dropping rapidly. The defender clinging to it let go, plum-meted a hundred feet, and landed in a tucked roll on the edge of the platform surrounding the plant. It came up firing, its shots uncannily accurate.

Seconds later lightning crackled, the pale blue zigzag land-ing just beyond the stranded defender. It trembled violently and dropped.

"Shit," Dominique said. Colonel Willis looked at her. She kept her eyes on the feed.

Ten or eleven defenders were down, maybe more. Each time one fell, Dominique felt it like a punch in the heart. Another skiff went into the water, this one hurled, flying end over end before landing. One more, and there was a ragged line in place, like stones across a brook.

Immediately, the defenders charged across it. The first few had no chance, but there was no hesitation in their steps as they leaped from skiff to skiff until they were hit, and fell.

C Company surged from the tree line. As they passed the materials dropped moments earlier, each scooped up rectan-gular sections and pilings.

As the battle raged to the west, the defenders to the east constructed a bridge, fitting pilings into slots in the large rectangles. They took Luyten lightning and heat fire, but it was tepid compared to what B Company had faced, because now the Luyten were under siege. Only one of the Harriers was still in the air, but it was wreaking havoc on the Luy-ten position. Maybe three dozen defenders had made it to the platform surrounding the plant.

Dominique watched as a defender, screaming with a rage that seemed all too personal, charged two Luyten block-ing the entrance to the plant. He put a dozen bullets in one while slashing the other open with an uppercut of his edged forearm. Before reinforcements could reach him, he stepped to one side of the door, swung his arm around, and pumped artillery bursts at the door from his forearm unit. Before the smoke had cleared, one of his comrades charged what was left of the big door, dropping his shoulder and battering it open.

Fighting at close range, the defenders made vicious use of their size and the built-in blades running down their limbs. To say they were fierce fighters didn't capture the jaw-dropping combination of rage and cold efficiency they displayed. Dominique found herself on her feet, roaring with her companions as the defenders tore the Luyten apart.

When the defenders dragged the last of the Luyten bodies from inside the plant, Dominique counted fifty-four. It would take a while, because the Andes to the east and the DeValparaiso range to the west would slow them, but more Luyten would come. They would come three at a time, from the nearest quadrants first, their numbers growing each day until they believed they had enough to retake the plant.

There had better be a lot of them.

# 18

## *Oliver Bowen*

*May 27, 2030. Washington, D.C.*

Oliver couldn't help thinking of Five. What was going through his mind, as he waited to follow the battles through the minds of his enemies? Was he nervous? Afraid?

"Mr. President?" Oteri gestured toward the wall of video feeds being transmitted from cities around the world. "The Luyten are attacking. Mumbai, London, Rio, Seoul."

The president, who had been huddled in a corner, discussing something with his brother, hurried over.

In London, they were all over the streets, already past the defense perimeter. Oliver watched as a half dozen barreled through Trafalgar Square. It was raining, so their lightning bolts were electrocuting fleeing civilians in wide arcs around the points of impact. Bodies lay everywhere, the ruined soles of their feet smoldering. Crisscrossing blue blades sizzled along the puddled ground.

"How did they get through the perimeter defenses so quickly?" Wood shouted.

Nielsen was scanning data on his portable system, his fingers flying across the keys, seeking some answer.

"*Look at Shanghai*," someone said.

They were in Shanghai as well, marauding through the darkness of the downtown area.

"They know the threat is real," Ariel said. "They were waiting to see what the defenders could do. If the defenders had stumbled in Santiago, I bet they would have gone back to their slow-and-steady strategy."

The population clock on the wall was racing backward. The human population was tens of millions fewer than it had been an hour before.

"They're coming from underground," Nielsen called out, still working his system.

"Underground?" Wood spun to face Nielsen. "How the fuck is that possible? All the subway lines were blasted precisely so they *couldn't* come from underground."

"They're coming through the sewers."

"The *sewers*? What do you mean, the sewers? They're as big as fucking elephants."

*Elephants without bones*. The voice in his head made Oliver flinch.

"Elephants without bones," Oliver repeated aloud.

"What did you say?" Wood asked.

"I didn't say it, Five did. Elephants without bones." On the feed from New York, Oliver watched one of the big, rectangular sewer grates glow red and drop away. He pointed at the feed. "New York. Watch." A Luyten squeezed out of the hole, its appendages folded tightly behind it until it popped free.

President Wood cursed a blue streak. He turned to Oteri. "Get the defenders out there."

"They've already been released," Oteri said. "Premier Chandar ordered it ten minutes ago."

For once, Wood didn't seem annoyed to be reminded he was not in charge. He seemed relieved.

It was difficult for Oliver to watch the carnage on the screens, but he couldn't turn away; it was his duty to stay apprised of what was happening.

What was happening was, people were dying. The streets of London, New York, Rio, Shanghai were littered with corpses as the starfish killed everyone in sight on their march toward the production facilities.

"Order civilian evacuation of the areas surrounding all production facilities. Those people don't know which way to run," President Wood said.

The Luyten were choosing routes that sidestepped combatants, instead wreaking havoc on civilians, who had nowhere to hide. Some of the Luyten were being picked off by stationary visual-recognition drones set up on rooftops, but each of the drones only worked once, then the Luyten knew where they were and took them out.

Their heaters were firing almost continuously, burning and melting people, vehicles, the sides of buildings, leaving behind a landscape that resembled a giant scar.

"Where are they?" Wood growled.

It was a rhetorical question. The defenders were now an independent army, allied with the human forces but formulating their own battle plans. From this moment on, the human forces would have no idea where the defenders would strike, what tactics and strategy they might use.

In Manhattan, the first Luyten reached the production facility's inner defenses and tucked behind buildings to wait for reinforcements. The ten blocks surrounding each production facility were heavily fortified. Silver heat shields the size of buses lined the perimeter; the turrets of heavy VRA guns poked from reinforced window slits in many of the old brick and concrete buildings. Oliver knew this sort of battle would not be as one-sided. In tight urban quarters their soldiers would be better able to hit Luyten, who didn't hold the element of surprise, and the automated weapons systems would take their toll. He was also aware that if they lost these battles, the war was lost as well.

# 19

## Lila Easterlin

May 27, 2030. *Atlanta, Georgia*

Cheena held the clunky box with its fat antenna up to her ear and said, "Talk to me, Hoochie. Anything new happening?"

The reply came after an absurdly long delay. "All quiet on the eastern front," a woman's voice squawked, causing Lila to flinch.

"Music to my ears," Cheena replied. "Death to fish."

Hoochie responded with a "Death to fish" of her own. Evidently it was their sign-off.

They were perched on a catwalk far above the floor of a defunct factory. Huge tanks lined the floor and walls, some hourglass-shaped, others spherical, a few tubular.

A voice burst from the walkie-talkie, paging Cheena. Cheena retrieved it. "Walk, tell me what you've got."

"I've got *defenders*," Walk said. "Two platoons were released from the Cheshire Bridge production facility an hour ago. Reliable source."

Cheena raised her fist in the air. She was eighteen. Her long legs and confident style made Lila feel twelve. "What do they look like? Tell me, tell me."

"Huge," Walk reported. "I mean, huge. And angry, like trembling with rage. It's not a good day to be a fish."

The three of them burst into cheers. Lila hugged Alfe fiercely, then Cheena. Finally, something to give them hope. More than hope, if the reports from Chile were true.

Cheena set the walkie-talkie down on its end. "I'd say this calls for a celebration." She stuck a finger in her jacket pocket, fished around until she came out with a little white ball of Lace. Setting it on the catwalk, she squeezed it until it popped, shooting a cloud of particles into the air. She and Alfe craned their necks, inhaled deeply. Lila followed suit.

Lace was a memory enhancer. You were supposed to think back to a time in your life and the drug would draw out those memories, making them super-vivid. It was also supposed to make you feel light enough to reach the clouds. Maybe Lila wasn't inhaling enough of it. She took another big breath, thought back to when she was ten. If she was going to relive a time in her life, she wanted to relive ten.

At first it only felt like she was reminiscing about the good times, which she often did.

*At Tybee Island Beach with her friend Margot and their dads. Eating oysters. Her dad singing oldies after he'd had a few beers. She and Margot making faces, singing modern hits to drown him out, only to have him sing louder.*

*Lila, stealing Dad's access code and reprogramming his phone to take on the voice of a porn actress from an interactive she found in his cloud. Then Dad, after toning down the language, leaving the voice intact for a week, so Lila had to endure lurid, "Ooh, you like that, don't you?" comments from his phone.*

The memories grew warmer, more vivid, washing over her in waves.

*Loblolly School. Seeing it again filled her with a glowing warmth, a profound comfort. She and Margot created Loblolly using a virtual-world-building kit, filled with characters their own age. It took them all summer, but it was worth it. Every day after school they'd meet in Loblolly and hang out with kids far more interesting than their actual classmates.*

"Lila?"

The voice was far away. Lila probably wouldn't have noticed if the voice hadn't called her name, if it hadn't been so familiar, and so frantic.

"*Lila.*"

She tried to open her eyes, but she just couldn't leave the place where she was. It was so perfectly where she wanted to be.

"Lila. Jesus Christ almighty, what the fuck are you *doing?*"

*She was eating a big, gooey block of frozen strawberry taffy at her tenth birthday party. Annabelle Toynbee was laughing and poking her in the ribs.*

She gasped, jolted back into the present by something. She wasn't sure what. The side of her face felt warm, almost hot. Her father was leaning over her, his shirt soaked with sweat in the V of the neck, and where his belly bulged against it. His eyes were wild.

He raised his palm, smacked her hard across the face.

Lila shrieked in surprise and rage, jerked herself up, her head still light, wanting to go back to the party.

"Wake *up*," Dad said. "Alfe, Cheena, you too. Jesus, what did you take?"

Dad smacked her again. Screeching, Lila swung, trying to hit him back, but missed. He grabbed her hand, yanked it.

"I'm *awake*. Stop hitting me." She took a huffing breath, trying to clear her head. He'd never hit her before, not on her worst day.

"Do you understand the situation we're in?" Dad asked. "I mean, do you fully grasp what's happening? Because you act like you don't."

Cheena sat up, looked groggily from Lila to her father. Alfe was blinking heavy eyelids, clearly still out of it.

"Yes, Dad, I fully grasp the situation," Lila said. "We're going to die. That's the situation. I'm not sure what good it does me, but I grasp the situation."

Dad stood, wiped his forehead with the back of his sleeve. "Come on, get up." Then in a louder voice, "They're *coming*, for God's sake."

She, Cheena, and Alfe struggled to their feet. Lila was fully in the present, her pulse racing, hallucinogenically vivid visions of Luyten crawling in the back of her mind.

"They're coming *now*?" Cheena asked. "We just checked in at all the outlying areas with the walkie-talkie."

"*They're coming now!*" her father shouted. "Through the sewers."

Her father must have gotten hold of some insane rumor. The *sewers*? How could they fit in sewers?

"Dad, are you sure?"

"I saw one," he said, his voice low, trembling. "Is that sure enough for you?" He grabbed her upper arm and pulled her toward the door. "*Move.*" He was almost crying.

They burst through the entrance, into sunlight. "Fast as you can run, Lila."

She ran, already breathless from fear, fed by adrenaline.

She felt her father, Alfe, and Cheena right behind her. The air was filled with the sounds of battle: booming explosions that vibrated underfoot, the rattle of gunfire, and, worst of all, the sizzle of lightning.

An image burst into Lila's memory unbidden, of a Luyten coming out of the trees, cooking people along I-16 with its heater gun.

The front door of Aunt Ina's house opened when Lila drew close, then closed as soon as everyone was inside. Aunt Ina, Uncle Walter, and a few others stood at windows pointing guns, waiting, watching.

Battle sounds were growing louder.

"The defenders are coming," Cheena said. "We heard it on the walkie."

Aunt Ina nodded from the window. "We heard the same on the TV. They'd better get here soon."

A dozen soldiers came around the corner of Cherry Street, covered in body armor, turning in one direction, then another. They were carrying serious weapons. Lila didn't know how to tell one sort of weapon from another, but she'd seen enough news footage to recognize the serious ones.

When they drew close, Lila's dad and aunt Ina ran out to speak to them. Lila couldn't hear what they said, but she heard the soldier who answered in a near shout.

"Get everyone to Brandon Elementary. We're setting up a defense there, and that's the *only* facility we're defending in the area. Most of our resources are devoted to defending the production facility."

"What about the defenders? Are they coming to help?" Lila shouted from the window.

The soldier, who must have been sixty at least, held up his free hand, gesturing that he had no clue. "We have zero communication with the defenders. Zero collaboration. We just have to hope they know what they're doing."

Just then, the emergency siren began to blow, startling the hell out of Lila. Just a little late to be of much help.

The soldiers continued on their patrol as Lila and the others headed toward the school.

They squeezed through a back door into one of the classrooms, where a hundred others were huddled, the smell of terror-sweat rife in the air. No one was speaking, save for the occasional murmur of assurance from parent to child, scattered whimpering from scared children. Lila and her people found a space near the windows, which looked out onto the playground behind the school.

Outside, soldiers squatted behind a mix of sleek new fighting vehicles and antique tanks that were spread in a semicircle to create a perimeter. Beyond them lay a ball field, then trees on all three sides.

Lila's father handed her a canister of water. She took it, grateful, dehydrated from running.

Dad studied her eyes one at a time. "Are you all right?"

"I'm fine," she said, not sure if he was asking if she was scared, or still stoned from the Lace.

An old man near the window shushed loudly. He was peering out, his mouth hanging open, jaw trembling. The voices outside had taken on shrill, urgent tones.

Lightning surged from between the trees—three, then four bolts. Two soldiers were thrown into the air by the force of the blast. Others, farther from the impact points, vibrated violently before collapsing to the grass.

Three Luyten surged out of the trees from the opposite

direction, barreling over swings and slides, their free arms pointed forward. There was a blinding flash, the screams of burning soldiers, who'd been facing the other way, toward the lightning blasts.

Lila squeezed her eyes shut as a half dozen more Luyten broke from the woods.

"Where are the defenders?" someone asked as they huddled on the floor.

Lila tried to think of something else. Anything else. Loblolly School, where she and Margot had gone to escape in that long-ago summer. Lila would keep her eyes closed and think only of Loblolly until it was over. Until she was dead. She whimpered, squeezed her eyes shut more tightly.

Someone in the room with Lila began praying. Her voice grew louder, more tremulous, as the sound of lightning bursts outside grew louder.

"Oh, no. No," someone moaned.

"We have to help them." It was her father's voice. "Anyone who can fight, we have to go now."

Lila's eyes flew open. Her father and half a dozen others were headed toward the back door, toward the smoke and the bodies and the starfish, so close now.

Then her father was outside, running, because the soldiers were dead and the Luyten were coming. He raced for the makeshift bunker where the dead soldiers' weapons lay amid their toasted bodies.

She saw a tall, balding man in a suit swing a fire ax at a charging Luyten. It cut him in two at the chest with a whip of its cilia.

*Over soon. Think of Loblolly School. All over soon.* Lila felt a warm wash of pee run down her thighs. She clapped her hands over her ears. One of them was speaking to her. She'd never felt something so awful, had never heard an accent so foreign, so evil and wrong.

Aunt Ina covered Lila's eyes, her trembling fingers not doing a thorough enough job, because Lila saw between the slats of her fingers, saw her father raise one of the big rifles as a Luyten galloped at him.

It gripped the arm holding the rifle and pulled it off.

Lila howled as her father spun out of the bunker. He landed at the foot of a toppled slide.

"*Daddy!*" Lila screamed.

She pressed her face to the window, suddenly unable to see her father because something was blocking her view. It was a pillar, bone white at the bottom, black above, that hadn't been there a second before. Just as quickly, it was gone.

The center of one of the Luyten blew out, leaving a trail of black meat behind as it toppled to the pavement.

Everyone was cheering. It was deafening. For a moment Lila was confused, because her father was dead and everyone was cheering. Then she saw them, impossibly tall on three knobby white legs. A defender leaped from the roof of the school above her, landed right behind one of the Luyten, and slashed it with the razor-sharp knife edges that ran down its arms and legs.

One of the defenders threw up its hands as a Luyten turned a heater on it. It took a heartbeat longer for it to die than it took a human soldier, but as it crumpled, black and smoking, to the ground, the Luyten wielding the heater was blasted by a weapon that was built right into a defender's forearm. The Luyten burst into half a dozen pieces.

Three surviving Luyten fled into the trees, a handful of defenders in pursuit.

The room went wild. Everyone was leaping in the air,

kissing, hugging, laughing, crying, shouting. This was something they'd never seen before: Luyten being beaten. Being slaughtered by these giant warriors, these fearless, powerful creatures who were on their side.

Lila understood the rush of joy and hope they felt, the relief after being so close to death, but she didn't feel it herself. She ran outside, ignoring Aunt Ina's calls that she come back.

She stopped a dozen feet from her dad, who was lying awkwardly, one leg bent under him, the other splayed up high, close to his face. The bloody hole, the bone jutting where his arm used to be, made her turn away, hand over her mouth. How could he be dead? How could he die now, just when there was hope? Lila wanted him to see what had happened to the Luyten.

It struck her that on the last day she'd ever see her father, she'd disappointed him. She'd gone off and gotten high, and he'd been forced to slap her out of her stupor. When she finally opened her eyes, he'd looked so disappointed in her.

Lila wanted to go to him now, stroke his hair, tell him goodbye, but she couldn't bring herself to do it, not with him like he was. Where was his arm, she wondered?

# 20

## *Oliver Bowen*

*May 27, 2030. Washington, D.C.*

"There, in Mumbai," Oteri said, pointing at the feed. Finally, a glimpse of a defender. He was pressed close against the buildings, his enormous body hunched. The streets were deserted; the emergency signal would have sounded by then, ordering everyone inside, away from windows. It was not simply a safety consideration—any human watching the battle became involuntary eyes and ears for the Luyten.

The defender paused, looked left, then right. The camera sending the feed rose above building level and panned the area, revealing another defender on the adjacent street.

"They're nowhere near the production facility," Ariel commented. She checked her system. "The facility is under Seshadripuram; they're out in Rajajinagar."

"Maybe they figure our forces are dug in around the perimeter, so they'll take the fight to the starfish." Oteri smiled. "The starfish won't be expecting that."

"For once those fuckers have no idea what's coming, or

from where," Wood said. "It's time they find out what that feels like."

"*Starfish!*" someone shouted, pointing at the Mumbai feed. There were three, their bright emerald, gold, and mustard skin fouled with sewage, galloping in a line perpendicular to the defenders' route.

One of the defenders spotted them. He said something into his comm and took off, parallel to the Luyten, one block to their right. Another defender took the street one block to their left. They were incredibly fast. Three legs allowed them to run upright, yet almost gallop.

"Go!" Wood shouted, like he was watching a running back heading toward the end zone. "Go, go, go!"

The defenders drew ahead of the Luyten, then cut inward on a crossing street. They stopped just out of sight of the approaching Luyten, pressed against buildings on either side, weapons raised.

"Get 'em!" Wood shouted. "*Yes!*"

Others in the command center joined in, shouting at the screen, as the Luyten passed the spot where the defenders had set up their ambush. The defenders stepped into the street and opened fire from behind.

The Luyten were hurled forward by the force of the shots, black blood splattering across the pavement. Deafening cheers filled the war room. The president leaped, swung his fist in the air, again, again.

Oliver couldn't tell if all the Luyten were dead at that point, but it didn't matter, because the defenders were on them in an instant, shooting each at close range before moving on.

Now the feeds from all of the cities showed either Luyten, defenders, or both.

"Look at that Manhattan feed," Ariel said. She expanded

it. Two defenders were standing in an alley. It almost looked like they were hiding.

"What are they doing?" someone asked.

A Luyten passed in the street. The defenders just watched it.

Oteri studied the scene, frowning, hands on her hips. "Either something went very wrong in their training, or everything went right. We'll know soon enough."

They spotted more defenders on the roof of Clayton Tower in Manhattan, watching Luyten movements and relaying them to troops on the ground. A few of the troops were involved in firefights, putting up some resistance, but most were actively avoiding the enemy.

Manhattan's production facility was beneath the tip of the island, much of it under the bay. The Luyten were converging on it. As each arrived it set up close to the outside layer of human defenses, creating a web encircling those defenses. If the soldiers holding it were overrun, they had nowhere to go but into the bay.

More Luyten arrived by the minute. Soon there were hundreds, maybe thousands. It was a terrifying sight, to see so many in one place. Oliver's heart was pounding; he turned his head, tugged at the collar of his shirt, which suddenly felt too tight.

The Luyten attacked. It came simultaneously, from all sides.

"Why are the defenders hanging back like that?" Oliver said. "Those soldiers need help, right now."

The Luyten wasted no time pressing in, trying to break through the perimeter. Mostly they stayed behind their cover, moving only when necessary. Oliver watched as a Luyten firing a human-made wall-buster from behind a truck suddenly bolted. Two seconds later, the truck blew to pieces.

Suddenly all of the Luyten scattered, just before a sphere the size of a coconut sailed from a high window inside the human defense perimeter.

"Tasmanian devil," Oteri said.

It exploded like a swarm of angry bees, the individual bits creating gaping wounds in wood, concrete, even the street itself, before burning out.

As soon as things settled, the Luyten began to reappear.

Just as suddenly, they disappeared again. Another Tasmanian devil flew from the same window.

"They're buying time," Oteri said, "hoping the defenders will show. We're in trouble if they don't."

Three Luyten flying in modified Harriers appeared high over the rooftops. They hovered there as the Tasmanian devil played out, then two swooped down, fired wall-busters point-blank at the window where the Tasmanian devils originated. The side of the building erupted, spewing concrete and steel into the street. Both airborne Luyten were hammered with small-arms fire. They were cut to pieces before their aircraft had time to fall out of the air and crash, one of them taking a chunk out of a building before dropping to the sidewalk, the other tumbling and spinning down the center of a street.

The Luyten kept coming, probing for a breach in the perimeter, firing captured human-shoulder-launched rockets that blew sections off the old buildings, their snipers waiting patiently for the soldiers to grow the least bit careless. The soldiers were using right-angle rifles with electronic sights to shoot without exposing themselves, because even before they poked a head out, the Luyten would know it was coming and blow it to chunks.

Oliver opened his mouth to ask what the hell the defenders were waiting for, when the first few stormed into view.

At that moment he realized what they were planning, and wondered if he was the last person in the room to catch on. They'd been waiting for the Luyten to pin themselves against the human defenses. They came with weapons blazing, screaming in maniacal rage. Luyten spun to engage them.

Immediately, a Luyten fell, two of its limbs blown off. It twitched and scrabbled on the pavement as if trying to right itself, then lay still.

"A pincer maneuver," Oteri said, seeming to relish her role as the room's military authority. "Perfect for this situation."

"The Luyten *had* to know it was coming," Ariel said. "Every human in the area is a set of eyes for them."

"But what choice did they have?" Oliver said. "They could have hung back, chased the defenders around the city, but their best chance to destroy the production facility was to get there before—"

Wood shushed him. Oliver shut up.

A defender's legs glowed red, then blackened. Writhing in agony it crashed to the ground, its head all but crushing a minivan as it landed. A second defender was firing blasts from its forearm-mounted weapon while pressing his other hand against a badly bleeding chest wound.

The humans continued to engage the Luyten, their fire tightly contained to avoid hitting defenders.

The Luyten were falling faster than Oliver could track; black blood was everywhere. Defenders pressed forward, spraying the Luyten with bullets, tearing them to shreds.

Moving as one, the Luyten surged forward, storming the defenders' position, trying to escape the trap they were in. The defenders fell back, letting them come. They waited until the Luyten were almost on top of them, then, shrieking, eyes wild, they attacked the Luyten close in, using their bladed limbs to slash Luyten open. The Luyten couldn't match the giants in hand-to-hand combat, and had trouble firing weapons with the defenders so close; their heat guns roasted as many Luyten as defenders as they tried to repel the onslaught.

Within a few minutes, all of the Luyten lay dead. At least half the defenders—Oliver estimated sixty or seventy—were dead or wounded as well.

The war room had gone silent during the final battle, but now President Wood raised his face toward the ceiling and let out an undulating whoop, part Native American war cry, part coyote howl.

People exchanged hugs and high-fives, but only briefly, because there were eleven battles still raging, and not all were as clean and beautiful as Manhattan. London, especially, was a mess. Teams of Luyten had each defender surrounded, while other Luyten had penetrated the human defense perimeter. There were no cameras inside the facility, but it appeared the Luyten were already inside.

"What's happening in London?" Oliver asked.

"They had only two platoons of defenders ready," Ariel said. "It looks as if there were too many Luyten."

"If the London facility is the only one we lose, this will be a very good day," Wood said.

# 21

## Oliver Bowen

*May 29, 2030. Washington, D.C.*

Although he hadn't slept in two days, Oliver had never felt so alive. They had a chance, a real chance, to win the war. The feeling of impending annihilation sitting on his chest like a gorilla for the past year had lifted, replaced by images of defenders swooping into cities, fighting like crazed superheroes. He couldn't get over how *fiercely* they fought. They seemed to hate Luyten more than humans did. When the last of the Luyten were dead, the defenders seemed downright frustrated that there were no more to kill.

Oliver passed Five's holding area. He paused. Five had been mostly forgotten; he was fed and watered, and otherwise left alone. Even Oliver hadn't spent much time thinking about Five recently.

Oliver activated a retinal scan that allowed him access to Five's room, and stepped inside.

Five was curled in a ball. Oliver had never seen a Luyten in that position. He had no idea what to say. He hadn't come to gloat. Honestly, he didn't know why he'd come. Five probably knew.

"You underestimated us," he said.

Five didn't move, didn't reply. Oliver wondered what he was feeling. Was he mourning their dead? Given their psychic bonds, they might all be emotionally closer than human brothers and sisters, parents and children. That is, if they loved at all.

The war was far from over; maybe Five was strategizing with his kind at this very moment, plotting their next move. The perimeter around D.C. had decayed enough that there were certainly Luyten close enough to Five for communication to be possible.

Oliver was tempted to get a rubber band and shoot some paper clips at Five through the barrier, to see if he could get him to at least move. It was a childish thought, but Oliver was feeling giddy. Odds were, Five wouldn't react to anything less than a blowtorch.

Studying the Luyten, Oliver wondered what it must be like, to be in constant contact with thousands of minds, some human, some Luyten, all at once. Could Five turn them off, or were they always chattering in his head? A human mind could never tolerate that.

"I guess you're not in the mood to talk." He paused a moment longer, then headed for the door.

# 22

## *Kai Zhou*

*June 11, 2030. Washington, D.C.*

A little boy in pants way too big for him ran past Oliver and Kai on the sidewalk, shouting, "A defender! A defender!" He disappeared through an open doorway, still shouting.

They paused, waited until the boy reappeared clutching a grocery bag of what looked to be carrots and potatoes to his chest. As he ran, hiking his pants with one hand, potatoes dropped out of the bag and rolled along the sidewalk.

"Oh, no," the boy said. He squatted to retrieve the fallen potatoes, causing even more to roll out. "Oh, no," he wailed.

Grinning, Kai went to help the boy secure the bag while Oliver retrieved the fallen potatoes. As soon as he was set, the boy took off again, down Third Avenue, still tugging to keep his pants up.

"Shouldn't we take the defender something?" Kai asked. He was eager to get back to their poker game, but he was also aware of their duty. The premier had made it clear, right after the defenders were released: *How can you help? Feed them.*

*They eat a lot, because they're big and they work hard.* When a defender needed food, all it had to do was go find humans. It made sense.

"You're right, we should," Oliver said.

They stopped in a bread shop, bought two large loaves of wheat, and headed in the direction the little boy had gone.

As they walked in silence, Kai occasionally looked at Oliver, still half expecting him to say something, to ask Kai questions the way his father used to. He wasn't at all like Kai's real father, who'd laughed and goofed around and played jokes on Kai. Most of the time Oliver didn't say much. It was strange to eat dinner mostly in silence, but it felt good to have dinner to eat, and a table, and someone taking care of him. Kai had had a nightmare the night before, where he woke up to find his bed had been moved outside, into the woods, while he slept. When he woke for real, in his own room, he'd felt such relief.

There were three defenders, actually. They were standing in the shadow of the Vietnam War Memorial, accepting food eagerly from kids and adults alike, their assault rifles leaned up against the memorial. They ate fiercely, the way they fought, showing no preference for any particular food, and no pleasure in eating it. The people feeding them were clearly enjoying themselves, though.

Kai held up his loaf until a defender plucked it away with two clawed fingers. He felt a thrill as the defender ate it like it was nothing. It felt good to do his part.

When the defenders had eaten their fill, they retrieved their weapons and left without a word. They weren't much for conversation, didn't say please or thank you, but as they trotted off to rejoin their company Kai and Oliver joined in when the humans applauded, shouting out lyrics from the defenders' song the band Hot Button had just released. Kai loved the song, played it all the time.

As they headed out of the park, Kai looked up at Oliver, who seemed lost in thought, as usual.

"Do you like football?" Kai asked.

"Sure."

"Maybe when the war is over and the NFL starts back up, we could go to a game?"

"Okay. I'd like that."

Oliver sounded a little hesitant, like he wasn't *sure* he'd like it but was willing to give it a try.

"What team do you like?" Kai asked. When Oliver hesitated, Kai added, "I like the Broncos."

"Me, too," Oliver said.

Kai suspected Oliver didn't know a touchdown from a ground-rule double, but he appreciated that Oliver was willing to lie to make Kai feel like they had something in common. It was a good sign. He was a good guy. Maybe one day it would feel natural to call him Dad.

# 23

## *Oliver Bowen*

*August 23, 2030. Washington, D.C.*

Oliver watched a cardinal perched in a tree outside his office window. He wondered what birds thought, when they were flying around in deep woods and came upon a Luyten. Were they at all surprised? Did they sense the Luyten were something different that didn't belong?

"Dr. Bowen?"

It was Carlotta Marcosi, carrying a screen. "You said you wanted to see the fMRI. Is now a good time?"

"Sure. Yes."

Marcosi set the screen on his desk. Oliver studied the fMRI video, trying to make sense of it. Brain activity was not his area, but he could read an fMRI well enough to know Five's brain activity was beyond bizarre.

"I don't understand what I'm seeing," Oliver finally said. "Do you?"

"Not really, no," Carlotta Marcosi said. Her hand was trembling as she pointed out regions of Five's brain. Apparently she was nervous about making this presentation to Oliver, who was, from her perspective, the big boss.

"We're struggling to link brain structures to functions. We do know there's a lot of repetition in the structures." Marcosi pointed to structures that looked like jagged mountain peaks, repeating again and again in Five's brain. "There's very little overlap in the pattern of chemical and electrical activity among these structures at any one time, though, so they're carrying out independent functions."

"Hmm." It boggled his mind, how complex their brains were. It would be so much easier if Five were willing to talk to him, although Oliver couldn't blame Five for not wanting to divulge information about how the Luyten brain functioned. They were, after all, studying Luyten physiology because of the potential to gain military advantage. Still, Oliver couldn't understand Five's recent boycott on any communication whatsoever. Oliver had grown so used to hearing that voice in his head that he missed it, in a masochistic way.

Not everything about the Luyten brain was foreign. They shared some neurotransmitter systems with humans, including serotonin, which had been the key to developing the defenders. But the Luyten brain also possessed dozens of mysterious neurotransmitter systems the human brain didn't.

When Marcosi finished briefing him, Oliver went to Operations for an update on the campaign. Now that it was often good news, Oliver was addicted to hearing the latest on the various campaigns being carried out by the defenders.

The news was always after the fact. The war was primarily taking place in Luyten-controlled territory, so surveillance of defender activity was strictly prohibited, because human knowledge of defender troop movement hindered defender effectiveness. Once a territory was under defender control, they alerted their human counterparts, often requesting that human forces hold captured territory. The defenders didn't have sufficient numbers to leave behind troops to hold territory after they captured it.

Oliver slipped into Operations and watched over shoulders as technicians updated three-dimensional maps. He worried that they might get tired of Oliver hanging around, although he wasn't the only one. There were usually two or three voyeurs from other departments hanging around Operations at any given time.

Suzanne Ramos, one of the technicians he'd gotten to know a bit, noticed Oliver and smiled. "Hey, the starfish whisperer."

Oliver had a thing for Suzanne, but she'd never know it. He was utterly incapable of flirting, and usually didn't know when a woman was flirting with him. He never would have known Vanessa was interested, if his late sister hadn't told him.

"Hi, Suzanne. What's the latest? In—" He stepped closer and examined the topography she was working on. "Southwest Africa?"

Suzanne leaned back in her chair. She was petite, her eyes bright. "There's no defender presence there yet. We're trying to assess what sort of Luyten presence there is. I still miss high-def satellite imagery; we're working with these little butterfly cameras that give you grainy images, plus the Luyten have a habit of routinely frying them to ash."

"What about in our backyard? Any progress since yesterday?"

"I-95 is clear from here to Baltimore. There's a lot of activity between Wilmington and Philly. We're guessing the defenders are trying to create a supply corridor from D.C. to New York."

Oliver couldn't help grinning. "That's just wonderful. It's hard to imagine, being able to walk from here to New York."

Suzanne leaned her head back until she was looking at Oliver upside down. "Even if there were no starfish, it's hard to imagine being able to walk from D.C. to New York."

"True," he said, wishing he had a witty comeback. One would come to him tonight, while he was watching a video or something.

"Here," Suzanne said, calling up a map of the area, divided into a green and red grid. Green squares indicated defender- or human-controlled territory; red squares, Luyten-controlled. There was still an awful lot of red—to the west, between D.C. and Richmond, covering the entire Delaware peninsula—but the green area was growing.

Large-scale battles between the Luyten and defenders were rare. Soon after the bloody battles to defend the production facilities, the Luyten went back to their net configuration— three Luyten defending territories of five to ten square miles. After retaking most of the strategically important facilities from the Luyten, such as power plants, factories, and mines, the defenders were now forced to locate and kill millions of Luyten, three at a time. Meanwhile, the Luyten had resumed their early strategy of sabotage and raids on vulnerable human populations.

"Thanks, Suzanne. Sorry to interrupt your work."

"Not a problem," she said, restoring the map of southwest Africa.

Back in the hallway, Oliver passed the room housing Five's holding cell. He hadn't been there in two months. There was little point, if Five wouldn't talk to him. He decided to pay Five a visit.

Five was facing the back of his cell. Oliver took a seat and watched Five do nothing for a while.

"When it looked like humans were on the verge of being

wiped out, I still spoke to you. I didn't blame you, personally, for it."

When the reply came, it startled Oliver, because he wasn't expecting it. *You spoke to me because you hoped I could provide you an advantage.*

"It wasn't quite that simple, was it? There was more than one reason."

*As usual you give yourself credit for being more complex and inscrutable than you are.*

Oliver let it go, not wanting to goad Five into once again hurling the ugliest contents of Oliver's own mind back at him to prove a point. "If my kind win, I won't take pleasure in your defeat." And every day it seemed more likely that they would win. The tide was turning.

*Yes, you will. You take great pleasure in dominating and debasing other species. It's what your kind does best.*

"*I* don't. I wish we could live in peace. I honestly do."

*No, you honestly don't.*

Oliver sighed, then closed his eyes. Five would never allow that what he *thought*—actively, consciously—should be given more weight than what the baser, more primitive, less controllable parts of his mind felt. Yes, he hated the Luyten, and hoped to see them rendered extinct as a species, but he didn't *want* to hope that.

*Yes, you do. You want to believe you're conflicted, because it makes you feel better. There's no conflict inside you. Your primitive side and your conscious side feel the same elation at the prospect of our extinction.*

"So I have nothing redeeming in my heart or mind. I'm just one big hate pie."

*You don't want me, personally, to die, if that makes you feel more virtuous.*

"No, I don't want you to die," Oliver agreed. "And no, it doesn't make me feel more virtuous."

*Yes, it does.*

Laughing at the hopeless absurdity of trying to interact with Five, Oliver stood. He was already tired of this game.

*Do you know why we arrived here so unprepared for war?*

"You arrived unprepared? You seemed awfully prepared to me."

*If we'd been prepared, you would have lost long ago. Our weapons are adaptations of civilian technologies we brought with us, for heat and power generation. We brought no weapons because we came as settlers, not conquerors.*

"You adapted to your new role quickly. And brutally."

*We're more deserving of existence than you. More will be lost if we're gone.*

"Don't you think that's a bit narcissistic?"

*No.* Evidently Luyten didn't possess ugly qualities like narcissism or bigotry. They were perfect, enlightened killing machines.

*We have many flaws. Understanding them is beyond you.*

"Of course it is." He should have left well enough alone. Now Five would probably yammer in his head all day, distracting him from his work, feeding him false information about Luyten brain function the way he'd fed him false information about Vanessa. "You can do so many things I can't, Five. But I can do something you can't. I can leave." Oliver spun and headed for the door.

*We want you to speak with President Wood on our behalf.*

Oliver paused, but didn't turn around. "About what?"

*Conditions for surrender.*

Oliver's heart began to thump, slow and hard. "Is this

more psychological warfare? Are you just setting me up to look like an ass."

*There's only one way to find out, isn't there?*

Never a direct answer. "Do you have the authority to negotiate this?"

*I won't be negotiating. I'm in contact with those who make the decisions.*

"You're in contact with them right now?"

*Shall I tell them you said hello?*

It could be nothing but a big *screw you* Five was orchestrating, but he had to take it seriously. "I'll contact the president."

"He's in a lunch meeting with Secretary of Defense Oteri in the West Wing," Five said.

"Silly me," Oliver said as he left Five's room. He continued as he hurried down the empty hall. "I was on my way to his chief of staff to request a meeting. With your helpful information, now I can barge straight in and interrupt the president of the United States. Unless the Secret Service agents stationed outside his dining room disapprove, of course."

Oliver hurried toward Chief of Staff Reinman's office.

# 24

## Oliver Bowen

*August 23, 2030. Washington, D.C.*

Oliver glanced around the Oval Office, took in the burgundy drapes, the ornate woodwork over the doors and on the crown molding, but it was difficult to appreciate where he was, because of what was about to happen. If it actually happened, this might be the most important event in human history, and Oliver was right in the middle of it.

"I'm not sure why I'm here," he said to Five. "Can't you speak directly to the president?"

*I can, but I don't want to. You're the only human who wants at least one Luyten to live. You're the closest thing we have to an advocate.*

Five was in his cage, which had been transported from CIA headquarters to the White House via a closed underground rail system Oliver hadn't known existed. The triptych of windows behind the president's desk had swung open to allow Five to be rolled right into the Oval Office. Oliver wondered if the windows had always opened like that, or if the president's people had installed it in case there was ever a need to meet with Luyten. Whatever the case, they'd gone through a great deal of trouble so Five could come to the president, rather than vice versa. Evidently it was crucial to keep up appearances, even if your opponent knew all of your effort was simply for appearance.

The president's private door swung open. Wood entered, followed by Secretary of State Nielsen and Secretary of Defense Oteri. Oliver stood, and to his surprise, so did Five.

As they shook hands, the president winked at Oliver, then clapped him on the shoulder. Oliver's throat tightened with pride at the private attaboy. He swallowed, trying to banish the emotion, which was extremely premature. It was yet to be seen if he'd accomplished anything.

The president turned to face Five. "I understand you wish to discuss terms for surrender?"

*Tell him he's correct.*

Relief washed over Oliver as he repeated Five's words.

"What terms are you requesting?" Wood asked.

*President Wood has been authorized by the premier to accept our surrender if we'll agree to incarceration in an internment camp. We see this as the best terms we will be able to negotiate given our circumstance, so we would, theoretically, accept them.*

Everyone in the room jolted visibly, as Five finished his thought aloud: "The problem is, once we enter the camps, we will be killed."

It took Wood a moment to regain his composure. He'd seen the recordings of Five speaking aloud on Easter Island, but no doubt hearing it live was another matter entirely. "No you wouldn't," he said, still facing Five. "If we sign an agreement in good faith, we'll honor it."

"Your intention is to honor it," Five said. "The premier is less certain. Others are certain you should exterminate us."

"Others such as who?" Wood asked.

"Such as your secretary of defense."

Scowling, Wood turned to Oteri. "Is this true?"

Oteri nodded tightly. "Yes, sir. That would be my counsel."

Wood moved a half step closer, pointed at Oteri's nose. "Another half billion people will die before this war is over. If we can save a half billion innocent lives by commuting a death sentence to life in prison, we'll take that deal every time. Erase any thoughts of going back on our word once we make an agreement. Wipe them out of your fucking mind right now."

He turned back to Five. "Is my secretary now on board with this agreement?"

"Yes. It may prove more of a challenge to convince other world leaders, including the premier."

"I'm supposed to convince *all* of them?"

"Ninety percent will do."

Wood grunted. "Only ninety percent."

Oliver couldn't help but feel disappointed. Somehow he'd imagined they would strike a deal then and there. It was a step in the right direction, though.

*Don't flatter yourself. There are dozens of these meetings being held.*

Right now? He thought it, rather than speaking it aloud.

*Now, or soon, or they were recently completed. The other meetings were conducted without the drama of face-to-face interactions. Leaders within range were contacted telepathically.*

How are the meetings going? Oliver thought.

*Mixed.* That was all Five would say on that, or any other topic. He fell back into silence as he was wheeled out of the Oval Office, onto the front lawn of the White House.

# 25

## Oliver Bowen

*October 10, 2030. Washington, D.C.*

Everyone would remember where they were when it happened. Oliver was tossing a football with Kai in their backyard. It was two hours before the news would go public. His comm alerted him to an incoming call from President Wood, indicating that full security was required to take the call.

"Holy crap." Oliver dropped the football. "I have to take this." He activated his phone's security protocol.

"Oliver." The president stretched his name into three syllables, as if relishing the sound of it. "I have news."

"Good news?"

"The best news."

Oliver let out a whoop. "It's over? Please tell me it's over." Kai had come over to stand close to him.

"The terms of surrender were signed ninety minutes ago. If you want to call what the starfish do with a pen 'signing.' More like doodling."

"Oh my God. I can't tell you." He fumbled for words, his

throat tight with emotion. "Thank you for calling me personally, Mr. President."

"Are you kidding? I should be driving over to give you a hug. You were an important part of this victory. I won't forget it. When everything settles down I want to talk about a position."

"Yes, sir." Oliver thought he might cry. He took a few deep breaths, tried to keep his emotions from overwhelming him. It was over, the war was over. Things would return to normal.

"Can you be here in an hour? I want to meet with my top advisors. There are things to be worked out."

"Yes, sir. Of course."

Kai stood looking at him, waiting expectantly.

"It's over. The war is over." And although he felt awkward doing it, Oliver gave Kai a hug.

He had to tell someone. An adult—someone he could absolutely trust. He was busting with the news. He had a few close friends, most of them back in St. Cloud, where he'd grown up. He could trust every one of them, but none seemed quite right.

Then he thought of Vanessa.

"I need to make a call; I'll be back in a minute." He went inside.

She answered, but didn't say hello, didn't say anything.

"Hi," he said.

"What can I do for you?"

"I wanted to share something I just heard."

"Oh? What's that?" She was clearly trying to control the tinge of anger in her voice.

"President Wood just called me." He took a deep breath, wanting to relish the moment, relish the words. "The war is over. The Luyten have surrendered."

He heard a choked sound escape her.

"It's over," Oliver said. "Can you believe it?"

"No. No, I can't."

He watched out the window as Kai threw the football straight into the air, ran a few steps, and caught it himself. Kai would have liked Vanessa; she was playful, always turning things into a game.

Oliver glanced at the clock. "Oh, crap."

"What is it?" Vanessa asked.

"It's still morning. No talking about the war in the morning."

It got a laugh out of her. Not a full, rich, Vanessa laugh, but a chuckle, tinged with sadness. Then she said, "I have to go," offering no excuse or explanation, just the simple declaration. "I appreciate you calling to tell me. It's wonderful news."

Staring at his silent phone, Oliver wondered if Vanessa still kept the voice-mail recording from the first time he'd ever called her. Whenever something went wrong, whenever things were bad, she could play that recording of him fumbling and stammering with nervousness, and they would both collapse into laughter. Surely she had erased it, after their divorce.

Maybe now that things were returning to normal, she would have a change of heart. All he wanted now was to have Vanessa in his life, and Kai, and to have a quiet, uneventful existence. Maybe he would decline the president's offer when it came, and go back to a university position. With his experience and a letter of reference from the president, he could take his pick of positions, could go in tenured. It sounded so good. Maybe that's what he'd do, as soon as everything settled down.

Oliver laughed aloud, suddenly realizing how absurd this train of thought was. There wasn't a university in the country that was operating at the moment. Maybe in a few years, though. Now that the war was over.

# 26

## *Lila Easterlin*

*October 20, 2030. Near Madison, Georgia.*

The gently sloping hill was covered with people, tents, and trash. There were people as far as Lila could see, from those high up among the copses of scrub pines dotting the top of the hill, to the throngs pressed right up to the outer fence, which had been set up to keep onlookers from getting too close to the real fence surrounding the detention camp.

It was like an enormous party. Everyone was drinking, singing, hugging, laughing. She could see the roadies for Hot Button setting up in a space between the laser fence and the real fence. Lila hoped they would sing the defenders' song more than once.

Alfe passed her a bottle of moonshine. It wouldn't be long before real booze, brand-name booze, would be back in stores, along with real soft drinks, real lipstick, real meat. She took a swig, then tapped Cheena on the elbow and held out the bottle. Cheena was dancing; Lila tapped her a second time, harder, just as another roar went up from the crowd, starting up high and spreading like a wave down the hill.

Lila scanned the valley, and finally spotted them. "There," she shrieked, pointing. Six Luyten moved across a long-neglected field of brown crops and tall weeds. They passed between a towering white silo and a row of combine harvesters. The cheers grew deafening as the Luyten continued on, between two rows of armed defenders, through the gates, into the enormous detention camp.

The crowd was still cheering as loudly as when the first two Luyten padded between those gates, two days earlier. Now the camp was getting crowded, even though it went on for miles, encompassing trees, hills, even a few buildings. It was a temporary solution, until a secure structure could be built. On the news there was talk of imprisoning all the Luyten in one place, maybe on an island. Lila didn't care where they put them, as long as they were miserable. Despite the premier's speech about saving half a billion lives, honoring our word, blah, blah, blah, she really wanted to see them all shot. She knew the defenders did as well—it was in their eyes as they watched the starfish shamble through the gates. They were an abomination; they didn't belong anywhere on Earth, except in the ground.

The crowd began to cheer again. It was a large group this time—thirty, forty starfish, clustered in their usual groups of three, forming triangles. One of them was crawling with baby starfish. The first time one of these momma and babies had appeared out of the trees, Lila had been mortified. Everyone had been mortified.

Lila threw up her fist and hooted, wondered if one of these was the one who'd killed her father. She felt the familiar stab of his loss, the aching sadness that was never far from the surface, no matter how drunk she got. He was really gone; she would never, ever see him again. It didn't seem possible.

And on the last day of his life, just before he ran out of the school to confront monsters, she'd argued with him. Along with the horrible moment of his death, she'd always carry the memory of him slapping her awake, asking her if she understood the situation, and her oh-so-clever answer. *We're going to die. That's the situation.* Would it have killed her to say, "I'm sorry"?

"Are these things going to be allowed to fuck?" Cheena asked, mercifully interrupting her thoughts. "I mean, are they going to be having kids in there, so there are more and more of them for us to feed until one day they bust out?"

Evidently Cheena wasn't much for listening to the news feeds. "Part of the treaty is the starfish agreed not to breed."

"They can control that?"

Lila shrugged. "I guess so, I don't know. I don't want to know any more about them than I have to. Let them rot."

More cheering, as more starfish appeared and took their perp walk.

Alfe leaned over to speak into her ear. "The defenders' parade's been announced. It's on Friday."

"Vascular. I can't wait."

Looking down at the defenders, at their stately, serene, strangely beautiful faces, their lean, powerful bodies, Lila had an epiphany. Now that her future was open, that's what she was going to do with her life: She would become a genetic engineer. She would study at the feet of the people who created the defenders.

Lila was confident she'd remember this moment for the rest of her life, because in this moment she'd found the blueprint for what was to come, and it felt so, so right.

"I wonder if they'll have any good music at the parade, or if it'll be all marching bands," Alfe said.

Lila rolled her eyes and sighed. "It's not about music. It's about honoring the defenders." She enunciated every word, like she would if she were speaking to a child. "If it wasn't for them, we'd all be dead."

"I know that," Alfe said, annoyed. "I'm not saying the music is the important thing. I was just *wondering*."

Lila didn't hear Alfe's last words. Another voice drowned him out—a voice in her head that felt like a razor blade dragged across her brain.

*I'm sorry I killed your father.*

Lila sunk to her knees.

*Very sorry.*

All around her, people shrieked, cried, clutched their ears. It wasn't just her—they were speaking to everyone.

*Sorry for your loss. Indeed.*

This was a different voice, although she didn't know how she knew that. Their voices felt horrible, like spiders had gone into her ears and were crawling around inside her head.

People were fleeing toward the road, where buses were parked, waiting to take the crowds home.

She looked at Alfe, who was plopped in the grass, his head between his knees. Cheena grabbed her by her tunic from behind, tugged her to her feet.

"Let's get *out of here*." She was shaking her hands, as if she'd gotten something disgusting on them and needed to wash. "Let's go."

Lila tugged Alfe up and they ran, letting the crowd carry them toward the buses.

*I'm truly sorry.* It was the first voice again, the voice of the monster who'd killed her father. It was speaking to her. Lila suspected the sound of that voice might drive her insane. She had to get out of there. She tried to run faster, but the crowd was setting the pace, and not everyone in it was young.

Her gaze was drawn down into the pens, toward one particular Luyten, a smallish, crimson one pressed close to the fence. There was no way to know for sure that it was the one who was speaking to her, but somehow she felt sure it was.

# 27

## Oliver Bowen

*October 21, 2030. Washington, D.C.*

They loaded Five into a semi. It was marked as a Killer Donuts truck, leading Oliver to wonder if the Killer Donuts Corporation was a government front. They made surprisingly good donuts, if that was the case.

As two men rolled down the back door of the semi, Oliver resisted the temptation to wave. Enough people thought his relationship with Five was sick and weird—no need to throw fuel on that fire. Oliver imagined Five would miss tormenting him.

*Having you as company is about as fulfilling to me as the company of a goldfish would be to you.*

Although Five had given no indication he was joking, Oliver couldn't help laughing. He turned away, headed into the shade of the oak trees on the side lawn of the compound, where he could speak aloud in peace.

"You'd really prefer to be in a camp? I could argue that you're more valuable as a liaison."

*I prefer to be with my kind.*

"All right." Oliver wondered what sort of reception Five would get. If he'd been telling Kai the truth back when they first met, Five had violated a basic rule set down by the Luyten leadership: no communication with the enemy.

*Luyten don't shun their own. Even those who've made terrible mistakes.*

"But in the end, it allowed you to be of some use to your kind."

*To facilitate our surrender. Yes, how useful.*

Oliver realized the direction of their conversation provided an opportunity to broach the subject many people were curious about. "Of course, there are lots of Luyten talking now." Oliver watched the truck pull away. "Can I ask why that is?"

*You already know the answer.*

"I *suspect* the answer. Given that Luyten motives are way beyond my comprehension, how could I possibly know I'm right, unless you tell me?"

*In this case, our motives should be utterly transparent, even to you. We're engaging in a campaign to "humanize" ourselves, because your kind are less likely to carry out genocide on a species that seems somewhat human.*

"You're scaring the shit out of people."

*That can't be helped. By communicating we become less alien. By sending a consistent message of kindness and contrition, we become less threatening.*

Oliver had to admit it made sense. In human wars, countries went to great lengths to dehumanize the enemy so their soldiers would feel less guilty killing them.

"Can I make a suggestion? Tell your kind to take on names, and introduce themselves when they contact someone. Names humanize."

Five didn't respond. Oliver frowned. "Five?"

The truck must have carried Five outside his telepathic range. He was gone.

His hands in his pockets, feeling somewhat melancholy, Oliver headed back inside. If not for what happened with Vanessa, Oliver could honestly have said he would miss Five.

# 28

## Oliver Bowen

*October 24, 2030. Washington, D.C.*

The defenders just kept coming. They were marching three abreast, and that was all that would fit across Pennsylvania Avenue. The crowd cheered, waved flags, tossed flowers and wreaths at the defenders, who crushed the offerings underfoot until the pavement was hidden beneath a layer of multi-colored mulch. Many carried weapons as they marched briskly, eyes front, their long faces proud, unsmiling.

They just kept coming. And these were just the defenders who'd been in the D.C. vicinity at the end of the war. There were hundreds of parades going on all over the world. Oliver wondered what all of these defenders would do now that the war was over. They could guard the Luyten, but that would require only a small fraction of them.

"How many defenders are there?" he asked Ariel. "Do you know?"

Ariel touched a finger to her lip. "You know, I don't. Millions. Several million. Maybe ten. We made as many as possible, as fast as we could. Every new defender meant fewer human lives lost."

"What are they going to do, now that the war is over?"

Ariel shrugged. "I don't think that's been discussed yet, not at the highest level. I guess they could be retired, given barracks and pensions. They could relax, watch jumbo TVs. Or they could be retrained to work in law enforcement, maybe construction?"

"Hmm." Oliver caught a glimpse of Kai, near the front of the crowd, waving at the passing defenders, who did not wave back.

"Why? Do you have an idea? I doubt anything's been decided."

"I was just curious."

Oliver leaned forward, tried to see if the end of the line was in sight, but the crowd was too thick.

The defenders just kept coming.

Oliver craned his neck to look in the other direction. "Where are they going, when they reach the end of the parade route?"

Then he remembered: His comm was working, the satellites were back in orbit. His comm located a camera farther down Pennsylvania Avenue and provided a link so he could see.

The defenders were turning onto Rock Creek and Potomac Parkway, and exiting along the long stretch of parklands. He linked to a camera in the park.

They were simply standing there. Not looking around, not talking to each other. Just standing. They had no idea what to do with themselves.

# 29

## *Oliver Bowen*

*November 11, 2030. Washington, D.C.*

Despite everyone being nothing but holographic images, the ethereal UN assembly hall nothing but keystrokes of computer code, the tension in the room was palpable.

Undoubtedly, the meeting the defenders were having at that very moment was taking place in a less impressive virtual environment, but the fact that they were having it at all was disturbing. Oliver didn't know what to feel about the defenders' closed meeting. By necessity, the defenders had been engineered to be fiercely independent, reliant on humans for nothing. It had worked—the plan had saved the human race, but no one had thought beyond defeating the Luyten.

Oliver admired the assembly hall, and fretted, while the assembly argued over whether they should have forbidden the defenders from meeting, cast about for scapegoats to blame for the awkward situation humanity found itself in, and occasionally digressed into debate about the wisdom of allowing the Luyten to live.

The hall had been restored to its full size and splendor, now that a network of satellites had been returned to the outer atmosphere. The structure was stunning, a masterpiece of classical Greek architecture with a dizzying, spiraling ceiling.

President Wood was recognized by Premier Chandar. Oliver lifted his head, paid closer attention.

"Our Japanese brethren have a profound saying that I think is relevant at this moment: Fix the problem, not the blame. The issue we should be discussing in the brief time we have available before the defenders join this meeting is how to tell them that while they certainly have the right to decide their own fate, they do not have the right to retain possession of our property." Oliver was always impressed by the president's ability to utterly erase his Brooklyn accent and his cocky, confrontational tone when speaking in public. "I'm of course referring to the substantial cache of state-of-the-art weapons we provided them. They're entitled to their rights as citizens, as set forth by the recently ratified UN decree, but they are not entitled to our arms."

Lorenzo Manzanillo, the prime minister of Nicaragua, jumped in without being recognized. An interpreter jumped in just as quickly. "Not only did we build the defenders' weapons, we built the *defenders*. I don't think their status as citizens—"

Premier Chandar interrupted. Her usual calm, dignified demeanor was completely absent; her long white hair was frizzy and unkempt. She looked as if she hadn't slept in days. "Excuse me, Minister Manzanillo. The defenders have finished their meeting and are asking to address this assembly."

It was the moment they'd been waiting for, the sole purpose for this meeting. The defenders had asked to address the assembly at noon, GMT, but had kept it waiting for...(Oliver checked the time) two hours and forty minutes.

The space between the bowl-shaped seating area and the dais where the premier and her deputies were seated expanded to accommodate the defenders' representatives. When the space was ready, Premier Chandar nodded to the chief of technology, and the defenders materialized.

There were seven defenders, chosen, Oliver had heard, because they'd distinguished themselves during the campaign. One was badly burned, his bone-white skin an angry, puckered swirl down one side of his face and neck, disappearing beneath his black dress uniform. Another was missing an arm at the shoulder.

It was the burned one who spoke, his arms dangling at his sides, fingers flexing and unflexing, as if they were hungry to clutch something. A weapon, maybe. He was breathing heavily, whether because he was nervous or just ramped up, Oliver didn't know.

"My name is Douglas. I'm not familiar with the protocols of this assembly, so I apologize in advance for breaching them."

He scowled as he spoke. All of them were scowling, actually. It seemed to be their default expression. "We have spent the past several days trying to determine our mission. During the war our mission was clear, and we were happy. Now we are not. We're left with nothing to want, no one to hate. You have suggested one solution, to provide us financial resources and vocational training. We've decided to decline your offer."

Douglas looked to the other defenders, who nodded, almost as if the decision were being made on the spot. They seemed awkward, now that they weren't in battle. Unsure of themselves.

"You are our mothers and fathers. We recognize and celebrate this. But we are not children."

Again, he looked to the others, who again nodded. One thumped his chest with his fist.

"We will create our own nation, forge our own identity, our own culture."

Douglas paused, as if to allow time for those assembled to digest what he'd said. Oliver couldn't digest it, because he didn't understand it. Their own nation? Did they mean that symbolically, or were they talking about a physical place, with borders, laws, an economy?

"Your population was culled substantially by the war. There were seven-point-two billion humans before the Luyten invaded; now there are two-point-nine billion." He spread his hands. "There is more than enough space, plenty of resources for all. We'll claim our prisoners, carry out executions, then leave you in peace."

*Their* prisoners? That didn't sound good. The uneasy feeling Oliver had been nursing became downright dread. Judging from the look on the premier's face, she felt the same.

"I'm not sure I understand. What are you proposing, exactly?" Premier Chandar asked.

Without hesitation, Douglas replied, "We want Australia."

# PART II
# AUSTRALIA

# 30

## *Lila Easterlin*

*May 18, 2045. Over the Coral Sea.*

"Can you see anything yet?" Lila's husband asked.

Lila leaned forward, looked out the window. There was nothing but thick, white clouds below. "Nope. My guess is, if I could see Australia, the cloak would have cut us off by now."

"True," he said.

"What's going on back in the world? Am I missing anything?"

"Most of the news coverage is about this plane full of diplomats heading for Australia. You're missing a lot of poop, though. As soon as you drove off, Errol started making that face that means he's pooping, and he hasn't stopped since."

A few of the emissaries sitting near Lila glanced her way as she burst out laughing.

"It's not funny. I hate poop. You're our go-to poop person. I'm in charge of vomit. I'd rather clean up a bathtub full of vomit than a diaper's worth—"

"Kai?" Lila said. Her phone had gone dead. She hadn't even gotten to say goodbye.

Oliver twisted in the seat in front of her, poked his head over the headrest. "You get cut off?"

"Yeah, Dad. Sorry—I know you wanted to say goodbye."

"Don't worry about it. We'll see him in a few weeks."

Lila slipped the phone into her jacket pocket as Oliver turned back around. It was a strange feeling, not knowing when she'd talk to Kai again. If only they knew what the defenders had in mind, whether this summit was meant to be a brief, ceremonial reestablishment of ties, or the initiation of detailed discussions and negotiations.

The silence was jolting, the sense of isolation unnerving, partly because it meant they had entered Australian airspace. She stared blankly at the stray tufts of Oliver's graying hair visible over the seat back. Oliver cleared his throat—a nervous habit. Lila was relieved to know the US Secretary of Science and Technology was nervous, too.

Then Lila thought to look out the window

Nothing to see yet; they were still above the smoky cloud cover. It was hard to believe Australia was down there. Over the past fifteen years it had taken on almost mythical dimensions in Lila's mind, and knowing she would see it any moment, see what it had *become*, set her heart pounding.

The Spanish ambassador, in the seat next to Lila, turned, as if noticing her for the first time. "Nervous?"

She nodded. The word didn't begin to describe the shades and layers of what Lila was feeling, but it would do as a rough approximation.

The Spaniard's white eyebrows pinched. "Were you even alive when the Luyten invaded?" Bolibar: His name came to her as he spoke. "Have you ever seen a defender?"

"I'd have to be sixteen years old to have never seen a defender." Lila wasn't sure if he was trying to flatter her, or what. "I've seen plenty. And Luyten." She closed her mouth. That was all she wanted to say on that topic. The last thing she wanted was to flip out on the flight in. Lila did not want to prove her skeptics right.

"Ah. I'm sorry," he said, reading her face. "You were a young girl? I'm sorry."

The second apology was for bringing up the painful topic, no doubt. It was impolite to bring up the Luyten invasion if you weren't sure the person you were speaking to was amenable to the topic.

Lila shrugged. "Who doesn't have nasty memories?" She forced a smile, turned back to the window, but it was too late. As they surged toward Australia, and humanity's first contact with their saviors in fifteen years, Lila's memories reeled out. She saw the Luyten, like enormous starfish dropping from the sky, twirling in one direction and then the other. She squeezed the armrest, trying to let the memory be, let it play out if it needed to. She'd learned that if she resisted it would only pull her in deeper, turn into a full-fledged flashback, and if she went into PTSD mode, they would yank her at the first opportunity. The pols in Washington would just love an excuse to pull her. Nobody wanted her there; it bugged the shit out of them that the defenders had specifically requested her. Lila suspected the only reason the president had signed off on the request was that he'd rebuffed the defenders when they first asked for Dominique, and he didn't want to start off on the wrong diplomatic foot by saying no twice.

Lila focused on her breathing, kept it smooth and even as she saw her fifteen-year-old self rushing into the shelter of the elementary school as the ground shook from explosions and the air crackled with the Luyten's electric fire, which stank like burning sweat. That first glimpse of a Luyten, galloping out of the trees on three arms. Her father, rushing outside.

Lila took a deep, sighing breath. It had been a few years since her last full-blown flashback, but it was inevitable, given the situation. Seeing defenders, actually standing before the massive things and talking to them, was bound to draw the memories back. It was worth it though, to be one of the first to see what sort of society they'd built. To have the opportunity to thank them personally. There weren't many humans she respected as much as she respected every single defender.

Bolibar was looking at her, probably wondering why she was sweating, and panting like a fucking Labrador.

"So what do you think's going to happen?" Lila asked him, mostly to deflect Bolibar's attention from what a wreck she was.

Bolibar grunted. "That's the big mystery, no?" He unsealed a pouch of dried fruit, offered it to Lila before helping himself. "I'm sure you sat through as many strategy meetings in your country as I did in mine, trying to anticipate why they suddenly want to reestablish ties." He stuck out his lower lip and shook his head. "My guess is their focus is technology. They want to exchange ideas. They've clearly made advances of their own since they segregated themselves." Bolibar waved in the air over his head, alluding to the cloak the defenders had developed that repelled both surveillance and missiles. What a shock it had caused when it went up, just two years after the defenders took possession of Australia. Everyone wanted to know how they had developed technology still beyond humans in such a short time. As far as Lila was concerned, that the entire population had IQs ranging upwards of 140 pretty much solved that mystery.

"If that's the case, why did they invite a plane full of politicians, and me? Why didn't they invite a bunch of techies?" Lila asked.

"I have no idea."

Everything made as much sense as anything else. The defenders' brains had been developed so hastily—few understood that as well as Lila—that it was difficult to guess what might be going on inside them. Dominique—Lila's mentor, one of the humans she respected as much as she respected defenders—admitted she had little idea what the hodgepodge of neurological tissue and circuitry she'd engineered really added up to, beyond its military capability. The defenders had retreated into self-imposed exile before they had a real chance to find out.

"Their motives aren't that simple, or that benevolent."

Lila turned in her seat to see who'd spoken. It was the Korean ambassador, Sook Nahn. She was a chubby woman, short, her features kind of scrunched.

"And what do you think their agenda will be, Secretary Nahn?" Lila asked.

"Sook," she corrected, giving Lila a warm smile that reduced Lila's knee-jerk dislike of her by about half. "They're militaristic beings. They eat, sleep, and breathe war and military tactics. When the war ended, they insisted on carting off millions of Luyten in cargo ships just so they could have the pleasure of executing them. My guess is they're seeking alliances. They've invited representatives from all over the world, but you watch: They'll peel off representatives from certain nations for private talks."

"Which nations are you referring to?" Bolibar asked.

Half smiling, Sook lifted her shoulders. "The like-minded ones. I'll leave it at that."

The most aggressive, militaristic countries, she meant. Lila could feel her hackles rising. What an uncharitable light to paint the saviors of the human race in. She was tempted to remind Sook that her scrunched little face wouldn't be on this plane if not for the defenders.

"It's an interesting perspective," Bolibar said.

"If you were describing humans instead of defenders, that characterization would seem the worst sort of stereotype," Lila said. "They're highly intelligent and adaptable. Who's to say their interests haven't branched out into science, the arts..."

Sook tilted her head, as if considering. "Who's to say." She didn't seem offended, or even ruffled, by Lila's heated defense of the defenders. In fact, she seemed amused, which made Lila even angrier.

"Maybe they've simply realized that our races need each other," Lila said, "that they exist because of us, and *we* still exist only because of them. We share a powerful bond."

Oliver had switched to the outside seat on his row to listen. "It's true—they may have no agenda at all. Maybe they just want to check in, because they feel ready now. More grounded."

"Trade," a man sitting half a dozen rows closer to the front called back.

"Maybe," Bolibar called, "but Australia is relatively self-sufficient when it comes to resources. Unless the defenders want Coca-Cola and a download of the new Peter Septimo album."

"Have you ever taken a close look at a defender's hands?" the man said. Lila moved her head left, then right, trying to see who it was. Finally, she caught a glimpse of Azumi Bello, the big, affable Nigerian ambassador. He held up his own hand, made a fist. "Their hands weren't engineered with fine-motor skills in mind. They were made to hold weapons. I can't imagine how they could mend boots with those hands, or manufacture dishes, or paint a picture."

"How did they create the cloak, then?" Sook asked. "That sort of technology would require extremely fine motor skills."

Azumi shook his head. "That, Ms. Sook, is a mystery."

Lila lifted her hand from the armrest, felt more weight than had been there a moment earlier. They were descending. She ran her hands over her thighs, wiping sweat. Fifteen years of wondering, and in a minute they'd have their answers.

People were leaving their seats, crowding around the windows, seeking a first glimpse of Sydney. The cabin was hushed as the jet broke through the clouds and a city took shape below.

"Oh," Bolibar said, clearly disappointed.

The city had barely changed. Visible below were skyscrapers, roads, vehicles, bridges. The jet descended, dropping below the tops of the skyscrapers.

"Oh," Oliver said, his tone laced with surprise and disbelief. As they dropped, the size of the city became more apparent. The skyscrapers were immense. Their jet was a toy that could nearly fit through an office window. The defenders had retained the look of the city, but had rebuilt it to their scale.

"Of course," Lila said softly. She meant it as a personal aside, but others looked at her, waiting for her to elaborate. "They're brand-new beings—their only point of reference is how humans do things." If everything was designed to defenders' scale, the city would be almost triple in size. The tallest buildings might be three thousand feet tall.

The landing gear ground into place beneath them. The FASTEN SEAT BELTS sign chimed. Reluctantly, the ambassadors returned to their seats. It was quiet as the jet descended. Everyone was peering out the windows, taking in Sydney.

They landed on a strip as long and wide as a small desert, then taxied to the airport for ten minutes.

As they lined up to get off, Bolibar grinned at her. "Here we go. Into the fray." There was a buzz of excitement, a plane mostly full of jaded politicos sounding like kids on Christmas morning.

Lila gave Oliver a playful nudge in the back. "Hurry," she said. He turned to look at her, his eyebrows raised. He was effectively here as her babysitter, someone the feds thought could control her, someone she would listen to if push came to shove. That made her smile. It was true, to a degree. But only to a degree.

Oliver had shown her the file the CIA worked up after the defenders requested her. She was impulsive, she drank too much, exhibited classic symptoms of PTSD. In short, she was damaged goods. Big surprise. Who the hell wasn't? *Them?* The clowns in charge were probably more damaged than most people; the difference was they were too arrogant to admit it.

As they approached the exit, Lila took a deep breath and swept her hair out of her face. Screw their file, she wasn't here for them. She was here for the defenders.

A defender was waiting on the tarmac. Lila had always found them strangely beautiful. So like the statues on Easter Island, if those statues were stretched, and stood on three legs, and had what looked like enormous shards of broken glass running down each side. Their faces were chiseled and angular, set on a long, almost neckless cylinder.

"Thank you for coming," the defender said as Lila stepped off the jet. He repeated this as each ambassador and special envoy stepped through the door, which meant he repeated the same phrase ninety-four times.

When they had all disembarked, the defender grimaced (or perhaps it was meant as a smile) and said, "My name is Vladimir. I will be your guide for the initial part of your stay. You must be hungry after your flight." The flight had been less than six hours from Geneva, and they'd been served a meal, but Lila nodded politely, a tight smile on her face as Vladimir gestured to their left.

Something large squeezed out of a hangar.

Even from a hundred yards, even after fifteen years, there was no mistaking the thing that rushed at them.

When Lila was next aware of her surroundings, she was sprinting across the runway, her terror given voice by a tight squeal on each outbreath. A Luyten. A Luyten was charging at them. One of the other ambassadors passed Lila, his arms pumping, his loose, old cheeks flapping, his eyes round with fear.

"There is no danger. No danger!" Vladimir called, and as before, with "Thank you for coming," he repeated the words over and over. Lila glanced over her shoulder and saw she wasn't mistaken: It was a Luyten. It wasn't chasing them, though. It stood beside Vladimir on five legs, something balanced on its sixth.

A silver tray. With food on it.

Lila slowed, stopped. The defender continued to shout, "No danger!"

"What the hell is going on?" It was Bolibar, suddenly beside her.

"Is it a...I don't know, a *reproduction* of some kind?"

"It doesn't look like a reproduction." Bolibar took a few tentative steps toward the thing. Lila followed. When the

Luyten didn't move they took a few more. Soon most of the ambassadors were standing in a loose circle, a hundred feet out from Vladimir and the Luyten.

"I am profoundly sorry," the defender said, bowing its head. "This was meant as a surprise, but not a cruel one. I will find out whose idea it was and surely he will be killed." He gestured toward the Luyten. "Please, eat. It won't harm you."

No one moved. In the stunned silence the same question had to be running through every ambassador's head: What was a Luyten doing here, alive? Hadn't they all been executed, their ship destroyed? The moment stretched as Vladimir held his gesture of invitation, his prominent brow leaving his sunken eyes hidden in a swatch of shadow.

Lila wanted to get as far from the Luyten as she could; the hair on her arms was prickling, her heart drumming.

Bolibar finally broke the circle. The Luyten extended the enormous tray toward him as he approached. There were a hundred delicacies on the tray, from caviar to a whole, steaming roast turkey. Lila tried to follow suit, because Bolibar was right: Establishing a positive tone from the outset was crucial; they shouldn't refuse a gesture of hospitality. But her feet wouldn't move. She kept seeing that Luyten breaking from the trees and charging at the school.

It must be reading her thoughts at that very moment. The idea horrified her, that this creature was in her head, knew that she was afraid, felt her revulsion.

She closed her eyes, took a deep breath, focused on turning her fear into searing hatred. Let the stinking starfish read that. Striding into the circle, Lila plucked a croissant from the edge of the tray, held her smile, and took a bite, resisting a desperate urge to flee from under the shadow of the massive beast.

Some of the other ambassadors followed. The defender's mouth stretched into a long, straight line of satisfaction.

Lila couldn't take her eyes off the Luyten. Few had seen one from this distance and lived. There were two bands of color around their pupils; their skin was heavily textured, thick and waxy. A half dozen randomly placed apertures contracted and expanded like giant anuses. They were interchangeable, Lila knew—each could be used for eating, breathing, excreting, mating.

"I don't understand," Oliver said to their host. "What is a Luyten doing here? Weren't they executed?"

"Some were killed. Some were kept." Vladimir lifted one of his arms and worked his three-fingered claw. "Our manual dexterity is quite limited. Our fathers built us to fight, not to live afterward. Luyten perform tasks we can't, or don't want to."

Lila looked to her left and right. The other ambassadors looked as stunned and incredulous as she felt.

"How many of them have you...kept?" Bolibar asked.

The defender wobbled its free leg. "Several million."

"Several *million?*" the ambassador from China said. He sounded very far away. She closed her eyes and took deep breaths, tried to clear her spinning head. Several million of them were here, all around her. Suddenly the lack of contact with the outside world seemed enormous. Through all of those strategy sessions, no one had ever brought up this possibility. Several *million?*

They choked down a few anxious bites of the feast, then Vladimir whisked them off in three limos the size of buses. Lifts took them to seats retrofitted to human size.

"Please relax and enjoy the sights," Vladimir said. "I'll show you our city, then I have a surprise for you that is very thoughtful of us."

"I'm sure it is," Oliver said, ever the diplomat. He was such a doofus. Lila loved her father-in-law, and he'd turned out to be a surprisingly effective administrator, adept at playing the Washington game, but he was such a doofus. As usual, he'd missed a big old spot shaving; there was a finger-sized line of dark stubble along the side of his otherwise freshly shaven face.

The city was bustling—it was downright packed with defenders. They were wearing clothes: massive three-legged jeans, business suits with ties like tarpaulins. Luyten were also plentiful, following deferentially behind defenders, repairing vehicles, cleaning the streets with steaming, high-pressured water.

There was no surprisingly advanced technology as far as she could see, but the vehicle they were riding in looked to have self-navigating capability, and the city was far from primitive. The more Lila saw, the more astonished she was that the defenders had constructed all of this in fifteen years. Of course they didn't sleep, and had millions of Luyten slaves to assist them.

"I keep expecting to see Five," Oliver whispered in her ear, "or hear his voice in my head. Assuming he wasn't executed fifteen years ago. I know chances are he's not in this vicinity, but if he is..." Oliver let the implications go unspoken. If he was, Oliver might be able to learn more than the defenders would be willing to share about what was going on with the Luyten.

"Does anyone know Sydney?" Azumi asked, his voice low. "Is the city *exactly* the same?"

186

It was a good question. Lila examined passing stores and high-rises.

"Does anyone see any churches?" a young, nattily dressed man Lila couldn't place said in a British accent. "The turrets of St. Mary's should be visible now and again."

Everyone looked toward the rooftops. No turrets. So it wasn't an exact replica. The defenders hadn't included churches, and she guessed they'd also left out some of the more frivolous things, like Luna Park, Sydney's famous amusement park. That was a pity—riding a gigantic roller coaster would have been vascular.

They passed several dozen defenders seated at tables outside a café, Luyten waiters scrambling around them. Lila wondered if the defenders had executed any Luyten at all. The defenders had been engineered to despise the Luyten, but you don't always kill what you despise, especially if you control them, and they are of benefit to you.

She inhaled sharply. Down a crossing street, a Luyten was strung up between two lampposts, partially torn in two, its blood puddled on the sidewalk below. "Look at that," Lila said, pointing. Her companions studied the scene until it disappeared from view.

Bolibar leaned toward the front of the vehicle. "Vladimir, what was that?"

"What was what?" Vladimir asked.

"It looked like a Luyten that had been lynched. It was dead, strung up by four of its limbs."

Vladimir shrugged. "It must have made someone angry."

Bolibar sank back into his seat, looking uneasy. Lila wasn't completely sure what to feel. On the one hand, she liked dead Luyten far more than she liked live ones. On the other, the means of its demise seemed a little excessive.

Their limo pulled to a stop in front of an especially imposing sandstone building, the doors set at the top of massive
steps. The sign on the façade indicated it was the MUSEUM OF
THE LUYTEN WAR.

"I think you'll be impressed by an exhibit developed especially for your visit," Vladimir said as the doors slid open.
Lila wasn't in the mood to relive the war after their encounter
with the Luyten on the tarmac, but she sucked it up, smiling
brightly as they marched up the human-sized wooden steps
that had obviously been installed just for them.

# 31

## *Oliver Bowen*

*May 19, 2045. Sydney, Australia.*

His hotel room was enormous. It made Oliver feel like a little boy, which was exactly what CIA interrogators attempted to do to their prisoners to gain advantage over them. It also reminded him of what Five had said, years ago, about his comic collection. It's so easy *a child could do it.*

At least the furniture was human-sized. Evidently their hosts had salvaged furnishings from human houses still standing outside Sydney. It was one thing—the only thing, really, besides his colleagues—that shattered the illusion that Oliver had shrunk to toddler size.

This trip was proving harder on him than he ever could have imagined. Mostly it was because of the Luyten, rising from the dead like boogeymen. How careless of the defenders, to allow them to roam free. Surely the Luyten were waiting for the right moment to strike. However, it had been fifteen years; if they were going to revolt, wouldn't they have done so by now? Then again, maybe they had, and failed.

Oliver eyed the TV on the wall. He'd noticed it last night but had been too tired to see what defenders TV was like.

"Television on."

CNN anchors Conchita Perez and Arthur Figgins materialized on the wall, reporting on the year's sea level rise figures.

"Entertainment. Comedy."

Oliver didn't recognize the television program, but he didn't watch much television, so that wasn't surprising. Maybe the link had been installed in their rooms so they'd feel at home, but Oliver didn't think so. The defenders watched human television.

There was a knock on the door.

"Come on in."

Smiling tightly, Lila said, "Ready?" It was obvious she wanted to talk, compare notes, but who knew if their rooms were being monitored? It would surprise Oliver to learn they weren't. They may not have an opportunity to speak privately all day; their hosts had scheduled a full slate, all of it chaperoned.

First up was a tour of the countryside, to Adelaide and back. Oliver was hardly in the mood for a quiet ride through the country, and for the life of him he couldn't imagine why the defenders had scheduled it. Had they genetically engineered giant trees to match their giant buildings? Would they encounter wallabies the size of dinosaurs?

Everyone seemed tense as they boarded the high-speed train. Their host was waiting for them.

"Hello, Vlad—" Oliver began, but Lila squeezed his elbow.

"I'm Lila Easterlin, US ambassador. This is Oliver Bowen, science and technology emissary attached to the US contingent."

It wasn't Vladimir. They all looked the same to Oliver.

Evidently Lila was able to distinguish one defender from another. Maybe that wasn't surprising; sometimes Oliver had trouble recognizing *people* after he'd met them a half dozen times. He wasn't good with faces.

"My name is Erik. I've been assigned as liaison for the North and Central American emissaries, because I have exceptionally good interpersonal skills."

Under other circumstances Oliver might have smiled at the oxymoronic nature of Erik's proclamation, but he only nodded while he studied Erik's face, trying to find a way to distinguish it from all the other long, angular faces.

"Please choose a comfortable seat and make yourselves..." Erik paused, frowned. "...comfortable."

Oliver and Lila sat across from the British contingent, Ambassador Galatea McManus and a military expert, Alan Nicely. Galatea was in her fifties, slim bordering on bony, with a lean, elegant face and red hair streaked with white. Alan was pudgy, impeccably dressed in a tight white tunic with tied lace cuffs and a matching bowler hat.

The train whisked them out of the city, into the exurbs of Sydney (much of the suburbs had evidently been consumed by the oversized version of the city the defenders had created). Massive new defender construction gave way to dilapidated human towns. Far fewer defenders lived in Australia than there had been humans, so it made sense the defenders' renovations left off in the outlying areas.

Erik joined them as they hurtled through the eerily deserted human towns.

"Erik, how many defender cities have been constructed?" Oliver asked as soon as he sat down.

"Several," Erik replied. An awkward silence followed, as Oliver digested the evasive answer.

Lila finally broke the silence. "Where were you stationed during the war, Erik?"

"I led the Eighth Airborne Battalion in England. My rank is colonel."

"Ah," Galatea said. "Did you spend any time in London? I might have passed you while running for my life."

They all chuckled except for Erik, whose flat expression didn't change. With serotonin absent from their biochemistry, the defenders would have a difficult time with humor. Lila had a better grasp on the defenders' limitations than Oliver. He made a mental note to avoid joking. Better to keep communication formal until they developed a better understanding of the defenders' psychological makeup. In many ways they were dealing with another alien species, although hopefully they would prove easier to comprehend than Luyten.

"I was in London late in the campaign," Erik answered. Abruptly, he turned to Lila. "I understand you studied under Dominique Wiewall."

"Yes, that's right." Oliver watched Lila adjust to the abrupt shift in topic. They'd been surprised, when the defenders requested Lila. She'd been fifteen when they left for Australia. For the past thirteen years humans had been incapable of monitoring the defenders, because of the cloak, but clearly the defenders had been watching them closely, and not just their television programs.

"What can you tell me about her?" Erik asked.

Lila tilted her head to one side. "What do you want to know?"

Erik leaned toward her. "*Anything*. Anything other defenders wouldn't know. What are her hobbies? Does she paint?"

"Um, no, she doesn't paint." Lila pressed a finger to her

lips for a moment. "She's not exactly the hobby type. She runs, a lot. And plays volleyball."

Erik folded his arms. "She's no-nonsense. Hardworking. Pragmatic. I suspected as much."

Lila grinned. "You've got her pegged. She holds herself to very high standards. If you want to find Dominique, day or night, look in her lab."

"Excellent. Excellent," Erik said.

There was something strange about Lila that had been nagging Oliver as he watched her, and Oliver finally put his finger on what it was: She was glowing; all of her irony and sarcasm had melted away when the defender singled her out for attention. Sometimes when the three of them were together, Oliver felt like Lila and Kai were speaking a different language, punctuated with odd tonality and wry non sequiturs. Suddenly Lila was back to speaking straight English.

As Erik went off to mingle with his other charges, the exurbs gave way to open country—alternating farmland and forest.

"So, Oliver," Galatea said, "I have to admit, I did quite a bit of research into you before the trip. I'm fascinated by your interactions with the Luyten, Five. I'm hoping you'll be willing to share some details I wouldn't be able to find in books."

"It was a long time ago, but I'd be happy to—" Oliver stopped speaking. The woodland the train had been traveling through had given way to open space again, only instead of farmland, all was blacktop, surrounding an immense factory. It must have been a mile long, fit with dozens of steel smokestacks, each hundreds of feet high. The paved lots surrounding the factory were filled with shiny, brand-new weapons: huge fighter jets that resembled manta rays; muscular tanks on four sets of treads on squat legs, sporting three independent turrets; building-sized winged monstrosities that might have been bombers. Chrome and silver sparkled in the sunlight, as if the weapons had recently been polished.

Alan stood, pressed his nose to the window. "Holy Christ."

"What sort of weapons are those?" Lila asked, her voice just above a whisper.

Alan didn't answer immediately. He studied the machinery passing by. "Those look like amphibian craft." He pointed at rows of chrome shovel-shaped vehicles. "But they have wheels. They may be dual-purpose. One thing's for certain: They're heavily armed. Heavily armed."

Oliver looked at Erik, who was leaning in their direction, eavesdropping. This was the reason for the ride in the country. The defenders didn't want to show them trees; they wanted to show off their military might.

Ten minutes later, they passed another factory.

Then another, twenty minutes after that.

Aircraft, artillery, guerrilla craft. Oliver's insides felt like liquid as he surveyed seas of shining metal. They must have a weapon for every defender alive. Unless they were making more defenders as well. Surely, surely, that was well beyond their technological abilities. Machines were one thing, genetic codes another.

A sound caught Oliver's attention. Overhead, defender fighter aircraft as big as houses flew drills. They were the same models human engineers had designed for them in their war against the Luyten.

"Look at those—it looks like Luyten technology."

Oliver followed Alan's gaze. Row upon row of assault sleeves, similar to the ones the Luyten used, filled a valley paved in concrete. Hushed whispers shot about the cabin.

Since they had Luyten slaves, it seemed they had access to Luyten technological knowledge.

If the Luyten were sharing technology with the defenders, who was to say they weren't passing information to the defenders, plucked out of the emissaries' minds?

"Shit," Oliver whispered. He closed his eyes, rubbed his temples. If the Luyten were passing information, what would the defenders learn? What would they want to learn? As far as Oliver knew, the UN had no ulterior motives, were not plotting against the defenders. There was also no overt indication the defenders intended them harm. They were emotionally unstable, yes. Maybe a bit paranoid. That didn't mean they were gearing up for war. Clearly they held humans in high esteem. Still, the weapons were alarming.

# 32

# Lila Easterlin

May 23, 2045. Sydney, Australia.

Among defenders, staring evidently wasn't considered rude. As Lila and her six companions explored Sydney on their own for the first time, defenders everywhere stopped what they were doing and stared. Some followed, until they had dozens trailing them, pressed close, carefully watching them.

Sook looked straight ahead, as if she was used to ignoring adoring stares. Galatea and Bolibar seemed bemused. Oliver seemed uncomfortable, although that wasn't unusual.

"How are you today?" Bolibar called up to a defender who was walking so close the blades along his leg were no more than three feet from Bolibar.

"Very well, thank you," the defender replied.

"Lila Easterlin?"

Lila turned to find a defender walking beside her. She examined him carefully, recognized the slight bump in his nose, the flaring nostrils. "Hello, Erik."

"You recognize me. I'm pleased."

"Well, you recognized me."

"Human features vary considerably, which makes it easier. You have blond hair, and you're shorter than most of the other emissaries. I noted those distinctions so I would recognize you."

Lila resisted making a self-deprecating crack about being short, afraid it would be lost on the defender. Her heart was racing.

"I came to ask if you would do me the honor of being my companion at the races this evening. It promises to be exciting."

Lila grinned. The way he phrased it, it almost sounded like he was asking her out. "I'd love to. Thank you for asking."

"Wonderful." He made a fist. "Everyone will be impressed with me, when they see you're my guest."

Lila laughed, not sure what to say to that.

After arranging to meet outside her hotel, Erik left to find the emissaries he was escorting to the Museum of Culture.

There were at least twenty defenders following them now. The defenders were treating them like rock stars, which amused the hell out of Lila, because she'd had posters of defenders on her bedroom walls until she was nineteen. She remembered trying to strike up a conversation with a defender once, while feeding it fried chicken. She'd so desperately wanted it to talk to her, but it just went on eating like it didn't hear her. She stifled a laugh, not wanting the others to ask what she was thinking. During the war she'd entertained such lush fantasies of having a defender friend, of going for walks with him, of the envious looks from the other kids. Of course back then the defenders had been too busy fighting Luyten. They hadn't gone for walks, hadn't made friends, even with each other. It was dumb, but she was excited as hell at the idea of having a defender friend.

# 33

## *Lila Easterlin*

*May 23, 2045. Sydney, Australia.*

Bolibar was chuckling as he stepped off the hotel elevator. Lila gave him a questioning look.

"Word must have spread about your date with a defender this evening, because I just received a call from a general named Hassan, who asked me to accompany him to a military banquet on Friday." Bolibar spread his arms. "Now I have a date as well."

When Oliver, Galatea, Azumi, and Alan joined them, they had similar stories that they shared as they all headed off to lunch.

Oliver had two engagements lined up. "When I informed the chief of housing and construction for the city that I couldn't join him for dinner on Thursday, because I had already agreed to join Brigadier General Thomas for an art opening, he seemed remarkably disappointed. Almost jealous."

"That's because you're being unfaithful to him," Galatea said, nudging Oliver's arm. It seemed a flirtatious gesture to

Lila. She wondered if something was brewing between Oliver and the British ambassador. God, she hoped so. It seemed as if Oliver was still waiting for his ex-wife to call, sixteen years after their divorce. It was about time he got laid and forgot about Vanessa.

"Given that they're asexual, you may not be far off," Oliver said, straight-faced. "To the extent they have affiliative needs, they have to funnel them into friendships. Since we created them, we represent high-status friends."

"If we created them, don't we represent momma and papa?" Bolibar said, grinning.

Oliver pointed at him. "Don't laugh. Not only do they have no romantic relationships; they have no parents—"

Galatea shushed him gently, gestured that a defender might overhear.

Oliver continued more quietly. "Their brains are derivative of human brains. There could be residue of human needs, like procreation and maternal attachment, built into their DNA, with no direct means of expression."

Oliver looked toward Lila for support, as Bolibar chuckled.

"Don't look at *me*," Lila said. "I only know how genetic codes express physically. The psychology is beyond me."

"It's beyond everyone," Oliver said.

# 34

## Lila Easterlin

*May 23, 2045. Sydney, Australia.*

She was winded by the time she spotted the sign—ROYAL RAND-WICK RACECOURSE—up ahead. The defenders had retained a lot of the original names of places after rebuilding them to larger scale, perhaps as a tribute. That seemed to be the case with the racecourse.

They had walked from Lila's hotel, because, as Erik put it, "that way, more defenders will see me with you." Erik was trying to walk slowly, but Lila still found herself striding briskly to keep up.

"I understand your husband is a professional poker player," Erik said.

He'd really done his homework. "That's right. His father, Oliver Bowen, introduced him to the game. Kai was beating Oliver soundly six months later, and he was barely thirteen."

Suddenly Lila missed Kai, and their son Errol, so badly it hurt. In the five years they'd been married, they'd never been apart for more than a few days at a time.

200

"I like poker. Most defenders like poker. It's war. Nothing but distilled military strategy."

"I've never thought of it like that," Lila said. "It is kind of like a war, isn't it? You fight until all but one player is dead." She didn't like looking at it in that light. Kai was a free spirit, an utterly nonviolent man. He didn't even like violent movies.

They were different in a lot of ways, she and Kai, yet they fit together so well. From the very start, she'd loved being around him. She smiled, thinking of their first day together. Kai had tagged along with his dad to a genetic policy conference, mostly as a way to get a free trip to Miami in January. He asked Lila to skip out on the conference banquet and go with him to a high-stakes poker game instead. An illegal game. Never one to miss out on something seedy, Lila had gone. It was exhilarating, something out of a movie. Kai had been so cool, so fearless, taking on the strange and colorful men and women huddled around the table. That time, it had been a war of sorts.

Kai lost money at the game, but on the ride home in a taxi he was in a great mood, almost manic as he deconstructed some of the more interesting hands for her. When Lila asked how he could be so happy after losing however much it had been—twenty or thirty thousand dollars—Kai explained that he never tallied wins and losses in terms of a single game. He said you played differently—defensively—if you were losing, and even good players lost 40 percent of the time. The trick was to take both a longer view and a shorter one. First, approach each hand as a new, discrete game in itself. And second, tally your wins and losses over the course of the past year. If you were a good player, in the long run you'd win more than you lost, and that was the only tally that mattered. When they got back to the hotel, Lila had led Kai down to the beach and banged his brains out.

She filed through the gate, surrounded by giants. As the only human in sight, she felt incredibly self-conscious. Everyone was staring at her. Everyone. They whispered to each other the way humans did when a movie star passed.

Their seats were close to the perfectly groomed dirt track, fringed with the greenest grass. "Wow, what terrific seats," Lila said. "You must have friends in high places."

Erik beamed. His smile was a stiff straight line, but wide.

Lila looked up and realized she couldn't reach her seat. Erik stood when he saw her trying to figure out how to climb up.

"May I help you?" he asked.

"Thank you. That would be wonderful." She held her hands out from her sides. Erik grasped her sides, lifted her ever so gently into her seat. Lifting her was clearly effortless for him.

Realizing she was blushing, Lila turned her attention to the track. A few defenders milled about by the starting gate, more down by the stable, along with several Luyten. The odds board, set out beyond the track, was active for the first race.

"Wait," Lila said. "Who rides the horses?" It hadn't occurred to her until then, because she had zero interest in horse racing. Kai wouldn't go near a track—he wouldn't gamble when the odds were against him.

"Horses?" Erik asked.

An electronic trumpet sounded. Confused, Lila looked out at the track. "Well, it's a race track, isn't it?"

A dozen Luyten scurried toward the starting gate.

"You race Luyten." Of course they did. They were too big to ride horses. Luyten didn't require riders. She should have noticed the starting gate and track were jumbo-sized like everything else, designed to race creatures bigger than horses.

"Which one should we bet on?" Erik asked. An electronic wagering system was built into the backs of the seats.

Lila eyed the Luyten, who were entering their respective stalls along the starting gate. They made her skin crawl.

What the hell, let them race. Why should she feel uneasy watching Luyten race, but comfortable watching horses race? Horses were noble animals. They deserved better treatment than Luyten.

She looked up at Erik. "My lucky number's always been four." Actually it had been three. She'd changed it when the Luyten invaded, clustered in groups of three.

"Four, then." He placed a bet. Lila didn't have any sense of the defenders' economic system, but she assumed it was capitalist, probably closely approximating the dominant human system.

The starting bell sounded; the barriers on the stalls swung open, and the Luyten surged out. Lila had to look away. Seeing them run at full gallop reminded her of her bad time. She tried not to be too obvious; she didn't want to disappoint Erik.

Around her defenders shouted encouragement or curses. The veins at Erik's temples were bulging as he shouted, his fist in the air, his eyes blazing with what might be excitement, but looked more like bloodlust or rage. As the shouting reached a crescendo Lila caught a glimpse of the Luyten crossing the finish line. Erik howled with pleasure. He thumped her on the back so hard it almost sent her tumbling out of her seat.

*"You did it. We won."*

Lila tried to smile as she struggled to breathe.

Defenders clamored past them down the aisle. Dozens of them pushed through a gate in the fence that surrounded the track as those still seated stomped their feet, creating a thundering that caused the concrete grandstand to tremble. One of the Luyten on the track took off, fleeing toward the stables. The defenders who'd come out of the stands chased it.

"What's happening?" Lila asked.

Erik pointed at the fleeing Luyten. "It finished last, and some of the bettors aren't happy with its effort. Watch what they do."

What they did was beat it. They could have used the razor-sharp shards along their sides, but instead they punched, kicked, and stomped it. Then defenders grasped each of its limbs and lifted it into the air.

"My God." Lila watched through her fingers. The spectators went wild as they pulled the Luyten apart.

# 35

## Oliver Bowen

*May 24, 2045. Sydney, Australia.*

"Why am I doing this?" Oliver said to his reflection in the bathroom mirror. He'd been waiting in the bathroom for two hours; for all he knew, he could be waiting another four. He had no idea when the rooms were cleaned; all he knew was they were, and he could not picture a defender making a bed with those stiff-clawed hands, so it had to be cleaned by a Luyten.

It could prove extremely advantageous if Oliver was able to contact Five. Beyond that, he wanted to speak to Five for personal reasons. He felt as if they had unfinished business, things that needed to be said.

The door opened in the other room. Oliver heard the muffled thud of something large walking on the carpeted floor. He took a couple of deep breaths, still looking at his reflection in the mirror, then turned toward the room.

The plum-colored Luyten gave no indication it noticed Oliver; it collected the damp towels he'd left folded on the dresser and headed toward the trash can.

"You know I've been waiting for you," Oliver said aloud, but softly. "Do you know where I can find him?"

The Luyten straightened, walked toward Oliver, then turned sideways to slip past him. It disappeared into the bathroom.

"Can you at least let him know I'd like to speak to him?" Oliver asked.

There was no response.

Oliver went to the bathroom door. The Luyten was cleaning the bathtub. "This is ridiculous. I know you understand me. I know you can answer if you want to." He turned his palms up. "Can you at least show me the courtesy of answering, even if your answer is 'no'?"

The Luyten went on scrubbing, as if Oliver weren't there. Maybe this was the Luyten's way of expressing their rage at the human race for signing a treaty and almost immediately breaking it. Oliver had to admit, it was well deserved. "I was against breaking that treaty, though," he said to the Luyten. "I'd like to speak to Five for personal reasons, beyond my role as an emissary."

The Luyten looked into the toilet, evidently judged it clean enough, and stepped toward the doorway.

Oliver stood his ground, blocking its path. "Say something. Lay out my deepest fears and insecurities. Tell me to fuck off and die. Say *something*."

It waited, perfectly still.

Oliver stepped aside.

The Luyten brushed past, collected its supplies, and closed the door behind it.

# 36

## *Lila Easterlin*

*May 26, 2045. Sydney, Australia.*

It was strange, to feel so small all of the time. Everyone on the pedestrian walk towered over her. The stone wall that ran along the river was waist-high to the defenders, but Lila couldn't see the river at all.

She watched defenders hurry to work clutching satchels, others stop into Perks Coffee, clutching giant Styrofoam cups on their way out, or sitting at tables outside. It could almost be a human street scene; the only thing missing was the occasional sound of laughter.

She spotted Erik a little way off leaning against the wall, looking out at the water. Lila called his name; he saw her, smiled, and headed toward her carrying something wide and flat, wrapped in brown paper. Under his arm it looked to be the size of a magazine, but it would come up to Lila's waist if he set it beside her.

"My special friend. Hello," Erik said, loud enough for passersby to hear. He looked around, as if seeking a reaction.

"Ready?" Lila said. She checked the time on her phone. "We don't have much time before I have to meet the others."

Erik blew air through his nose, a signature defender gesture that Lila had learned signaled anything from frustration to sadness to anger. "Are you sure you can't sit next to *me*?" His eyes were flat and emotionless, but his feelings were clearly still hurt from her unavoidable snub.

"I really wish I could, but Vladimir had a row of seats constructed just so the emissaries could sit together at the front." The performance had been planned for months, in their honor.

"Vladimir." His tone was surly. Then he seemed to remember the package he was holding. "I have something for you. Shall we sit?"

Pigeons flapped away from the bench they found facing the river. With Erik's help, Lila climbed into the seat. Erik propped the package on the seat between them. "I made this for you."

Lila canted her head at Erik, smiling. "For me? That's so thoughtful of you." She slid her finger under the spot where the paper was sealed, unsure what to expect. What would a defender *make* for someone? Pulling off the brown wrapping, Lila had to mask her reaction. It was an oil painting—a truly terrible painting, of a defender standing beside a human figure. There was little background to speak of, beyond smears of purple and green.

"It's you and me."

Lila inhaled dramatically. "It's *wonderful*. I love it."

"Do you really?" There was an undertone of desperation in Erik's voice. The gift obviously meant a lot to him.

And despite how awful the painting was, she did love it. She loved what it represented, found herself choking up. She sniffed and said, "I really do. It's the most beautiful gift any-one's ever given me."

Erik smiled, his mouth almost—not quite, but almost—curling at the corners. "That pleases me. I made it very small, so it would fit in your house."

"That must have been a challenge."

Erik raised his hand, looked at his three clawed fingers. His hands reminded Lila of *Tyrannosaurus rex* claws. "These aren't made for painting. I lash the brush to my hand with bonding tape."

"Do you do a lot of painting?"

Erik nodded. "It's my hobby. Everyone is encouraged to pursue a hobby." He grunted. "My work isn't good enough to merit display in the Defender Museum of Art. At least, that's the curator's opinion."

"Well, I think he's an idiot."

Erik beamed, his brow and mouth smoothing, giving him an almost serene countenance. "Our special friendship is…" He struggled for words, squeezed his hands together. "…it's the finest thing."

Lila wished she could go back in time to show her sixteen-year-old self this moment. She stood, brushed off her skirt. "Well, I should get going."

Erik stood. "Can I walk back with you?" He sounded desperate. "I can carry your painting for you."

"Absolutely. Thank you."

Lila felt safe walking beside Erik. On a conscious level, she knew the Luyten padding around were no threat, but she could never seem to convince the primitive part of her mind to relax. Each time one of them came into sight, she jolted, tensed to run. Just the sight of them felt wrong. Walking with Erik calmed that feeling.

"There's a defender named Ravi who's written a book that's becoming very popular," Erik said. He cleared his throat. "He writes that the fewer legs a creature has, the more value it has." He looked at Lila, as if trying to gauge her reaction. Lila nodded for him to go on. "Humans made defenders with three legs, because you see us as valuable, but not as valuable as humans. Mammals have four legs, insects six, and Luyten either six or seven. So killing a Luyten means nothing, but you should only kill a dog if you intend to eat it. Do you think this makes sense?"

"No, of course not," Lila said. "We engineered defenders with three legs so they'd be fast, because Luyten are fast. Believe me," she said with a laugh, though it was a little forced, "we weren't thinking about things like relative status when we designed you. We were thinking about survival." She thought about those dark days, before the defenders appeared. "It's hard to describe just how utterly the threat of extinction pushes aside everything else. Thoughts of who's better than who just stops mattering."

Erik frowned, clearly wrestling with what she'd said. The question had thrown Lila, left her flustered and uncomfortable, because she wasn't being completely honest. She had answered honestly, but there'd been more to his question than whether this wacky theory of leg count was correct. Erik was probing, trying to understand what humans thought of defenders *now*, and although no one ever said it aloud, Lila suspected that deep down, most humans viewed defenders as inferior.

# 37

## Oliver Bowen

*May 26, 2045. Sydney, Australia.*

On the elevator, Oliver watched his reflection in the polished brass door, trying to ignore the stares of the defenders sharing the elevator with him.

Lila was waiting in the lobby. She waved, as if he might not notice the only human in sight.

"How are you doing?" Oliver asked, squeezing Lila's shoulder.

She blinked slowly. "Well, let's see. Apparently I have a boyfriend."

"Erik?"

She nodded, smiling. "He gave me a gift, a painting of us. He painted it himself."

"Is it any good?"

"No," she said laughing. She made a face. "In fact it's *awful*. But in this case it really is the thought that counts."

Oliver had to agree. He touched her sleeve, drawing her away from the pedestrian traffic between the elevator and the exits. "How do they strike you? We all seem to be ending up with 'special friends,' but you're apparently getting to know Erik especially well."

"I don't know about *that*. I am spending a lot of time with him. He gets upset if he sees me with another defender. Humans don't seem to be an issue, but if I'm with another defender, it's as if I'm being unfaithful."

"So what's your impression of them?" Oliver wasn't getting many opportunities to talk with the others.

Lila sighed. "When I look at a defender, I see them storming over that school, fighting to keep us safe. I feel such overwhelming gratitude toward them. *Love*, even." She sighed. "But I have to admit, at times they scare me. Not Erik, but generally speaking." One of the elevators swished open; a half dozen emissaries stepped into the lobby. Lila waved to them. "The way they tore that Luyten apart at the racetrack. The huge stockpile of weapons…"

Oliver nodded, said, "The weapons were a shock. Thanks." They went to join the others, to wait outside for the limos that would take them to the theater.

Oliver found it interesting, how cliques always formed no matter the situation. He and Lila gravitated toward Bolibar, Galatea, Alan, Sook, Azumi—their little clique, bunched together on the edge of the larger crowd of humans.

"Who's in charge?" Sook was saying as Oliver and Lila joined them. "I mean, it's not Vladimir. He's some sort of midlevel official. Why haven't we met the leaders?"

"All these dinners and performances," Bolibar said. "Next they'll take us to an ice cream social. It's like they're trying to soften us up."

"Of course, the social events are mixed with these tours of their military might," Alan pointed out.

Azumi nodded. "It's an odd mix of activities, that's for sure."

Oliver had been wondering the same thing. They'd been in Australia for eight days and had yet to meet anyone in power. When he'd asked Erik if the defenders had a leader, Erik had proudly answered that they had three: Douglas, Luigi, and Ichiro. Why hadn't these leaders met with them?

A parade of limos pulled up in front of the hotel, and Vladimir stepped out of the one in the lead. Everyone stopped talking.

# 38

## *Lila Easterlin*

*May 26, 2045. Sydney, Australia.*

Their limo let them off in front of the State Theatre, which
had dozens of huge glass doors set under a bronze art-deco
façade. The marquee announced *Richard II*, in a limited
engagement. Below that, an announcement read, *Welcome,
Human Global Ambassadors*.

"I don't believe this," Bolibar whispered, sidling up to Lila
and Oliver as they were led down the aisle past hundreds of
defenders already seated for the performance. Lila only nodded, afraid to be overheard. The inside of the theater was
beyond ornate—the gold walls were festooned with lush
burgundy drapes and crusted with polished metalwork and
reliefs carved in marble. Lila guessed it was an exact large-
scale reproduction of the human theater it had replaced. It
comforted her, that defenders were interested in art, in Shake-
speare. What she'd witnessed at the racetrack was less alarming when offset by Erik's gift and this event. She wanted to

214

see the fine arts museum Erik had mentioned. Even if the art was terrible, it would raise her spirits to see it.

The defender playing King Richard wore a long white robe with gold inlay, and a crown the size of a bathtub, but if the defenders were attempting to act, it was not apparent to Lila. They recited their lines as if reading, moved about the stage perfunctorily, and as often as not looked at the audience rather than the character they were speaking to.

"You seem to have especially positive feelings for our hosts," Bolibar whispered to her as the performance dragged on. He made it sound casual but was probably more interested than he let on. They were all trying to understand the inscrutable beings they'd created.

Lila felt uncomfortable speaking during the performance, even in a whisper, but it felt rude to shush Bolibar, or ignore him. She kept her answer brief. "I'm so grateful to them that sometimes I feel like I'm going to bust." She could have elaborated, but their whispering was causing people nearby to glance their way.

Bolibar tilted his head in a very European gesture. "And your country, along with the Canadians, were grateful enough that they provided the displaced Australians with a new home?"

He left it a question instead of a statement. The flat, cold region running from North Dakota to Saskatoon that was now New Australia was not prime real estate.

"Spain didn't offer anything, as I recall," she whispered into his hairy ear. "There are degrees of stinginess."

He laughed, loud enough to make Lila flinch and nudge his arm. "How very true," he whispered. "We're a stingy people, the Spanish."

The defender playing Richard stopped mid-stanza. He

came to the edge of the stage. Lila sank into her seat, wishing she could hide. "Why are you laughing? Does this seem like a comedy to you? Maybe you think you can do better?"

Embarrassed, Bolibar shook his head. "I'm—"

"We've worked hard to get this right for you. And you're laughing at us?" The defender reached out almost casually with its front leg and slashed Bolibar across the stomach.

Lila sat frozen as Bolibar's insides slid out. His mouth hung open, his eyes wide with surprise as he slowly tipped forward.

"Uncalled for!" a defender shouted. It was Erik. He stormed up the center aisle, leaped onto the stage, stiff-armed the defender playing Richard. "Deeply uncalled for." A dozen defenders followed him onto the stage, roaring. Some attacked Richard; others leaped to defend him.

As they fought, one of Richard's legs was torn, or bitten, or cut off, and it fell into the seats, slashing open the Chilean ambassador's back from shoulder to waist. As she screamed in agony, a few ambassadors crowded around Bolibar, crying out for medical attention as he bled out onto the seat and the polished floor. In the seats behind them, defenders roared and jostled. Lila could do nothing but stare at Bolibar, her jaw working, but no sound coming.

One of the defenders onstage fell into the seats, his nose nearly severed, blood pouring from the gash in his face. He landed on the Tunisian ambassador. Lila could hear the ambassador's back snap before he disappeared under the defender.

"Come on," Oliver said, grabbing Lila's arm. She yanked her arm free. "We can't leave him." Bolibar was clearly dead, but somehow it felt wrong to bolt. She was in shock, she realized. It had all happened so quickly, so unexpectedly. She'd barely had time to be afraid.

By some silent assent, the combatants suddenly broke off.

Erik, who was mostly unharmed, motioned to Luyten at the back of the theater. The Luyten scrambled to clean up the carnage, dragging away defenders and pieces of defenders. One reached across half a dozen rows and plucked the limp mess that was Bolibar. Lila stumbled to her knees and crawled out of the way.

She and Oliver joined the rest of the emissaries at the back of the theater as Luyten mopped the blood. A dozen conversations were carried out in harsh, shocked whispers. Lila turned to Oliver, but she couldn't speak. They only passed a look. It said all they needed to say to each other. *This is much worse than we thought.*

As the last of the dead were carried away, Vladimir went to the front, waved his arms at the murmuring crowd, and said, "Please. Quiet, please. Please, sit. Let us continue."

Lila was sure she'd misunderstood. Continue? As in, continue the play?

The lights dimmed. Actors returned to the stage, including a Richard understudy. They waited, looking expectantly at the emissaries.

"This is insane," Azumi Bello hissed. "We're just supposed to sit back down? People are *dead.* The defenders must allow us to notify their kin, their embassies."

"Too much is riding on this," Priyanka Vadra, the Indian ambassador, hissed. "Let's just do as they say for now."

Dazed ambassadors shuffled down the aisles. Lila looked around, seeking—she didn't know what she was seeking. The real defenders, maybe—the ones who'd saved her life.

Lila was sure she wouldn't make it through the rest of the performance. Surely she would faint, or be unable to stifle her overwhelming urge to run. The seats around Bolibar's blood-stained one were empty; ambassadors were glancing around, eyes wide, afraid to move or speak. Lila risked a glance back at the section where defenders were seated. They were watching the performance as if nothing had happened.

Vladimir was not happy when their small contingent insisted on walking home, rather than riding in the limo. They told him they needed air, and time to mourn their friend.

"They're insane," Azumi said as they waited for the light—an enormous red moon hovering far above them—to change. "Did you see their reaction?" He shook his head, his arms folded tightly. "They're insane."

"They have less regard for life than we do, I don't disagree," Oliver said, "but 'insane' implies their thinking and behavior is incoherent. I have to disagree."

"They're insane," Azumi repeated.

"Poor Bolibar," Galatea whispered.

"Let's set their mental state aside for now," Sook said. "We have to decide what to do."

The red light blinked, turned green.

"We should demand they lift the cloak so we can contact our governments," Galatea said.

"We should *leave*," Azumi said. "This is a *madhouse*."

Lila shushed him. Half a dozen defenders were trailing behind them.

Azumi lowered his voice. "They kill like it was nothing." He gestured toward a Luyten operating a bulldozer on a construction site they were passing. "Starfish everywhere. And this 'special friend' nonsense. I have a wife; I don't need a brigadier general defender at my side every minute of the day."

"We can't leave yet," Lila said. "Even if it's dangerous, we

218

have to know what we're dealing with, why the defenders invited us here."

"I agree," Oliver said.

Azumi sighed theatrically. "Fine. Then let's demand we get down to business. We're here on a diplomatic mission, so let us proceed with the diplomacy. No more plays. No more special friends. I'm telling General Baxter I'm not available for any more films, or lunches, or cocktail parties."

"You're breaking up with General Baxter?" Galatea asked, in mock shock. Everyone burst out laughing.

"*Yes*," Azumi said, "I'm breaking up with him."

Lila didn't have the heart to do the same with Erik. In any case, she wasn't sure she wanted to. His violent nature disturbed her, but hadn't they made him that way? The human race was alive because Erik and the other defenders killed so efficiently, without fear. All humans bore some of the responsibility for that. In some real sense, the defenders were the blameless ones; they were simply expressing what they'd been engineered to be.

The question was, since there was now no need for killing, could the defenders extinguish their violent instincts, or channel them into socially appropriate behavior? There was no alternative, really, unless the defenders decided to stay isolated. Lila thought they could do it, given time and guidance.

"Let's not forget, they have positive qualities," Lila said.

Sook laughed harshly. "Were you just in there?"

Lila ignored her. "This special-friend thing is a good sign. They crave close relationships, especially with humans." She glanced at Sook. "Yes, I was in there, but what about *them*?" She gestured toward the defenders following. "Most of the defenders adore us."

"I don't think it's a good idea to encourage these close relationships." Azumi made a chopping gesture. "We should keep our relationship with the defenders strictly professional."

Up ahead, a Luyten was loading a delivery truck with pallets of oversized milk cartons. It was crimson, on the small side. Lila slowed, studied it as they passed.

She couldn't be sure.

"Are you all right, Lila?" Azumi asked.

Her heart was pounding. She wanted to ask the Luyten if she was right, if it was the one, but there was no point. It knew she was asking, and it chose to stay silent.

She continued past it. Had it shown itself to her on purpose? If it was the Luyten who'd killed her father, wouldn't it go out of its way to avoid her? Maybe it wasn't the same one. There were millions of Luyten, and even if the crimson ones were rare, there still must be thousands of them.

# 39

## *Lila Easterlin*

*May 27, 2045. Sydney, Australia.*

Lila couldn't reach the doorbell. She considered taking it as a sign to leave while she still could, but hope and fear drove her to keep this dinner date. The hope was that Azumi and Sook were wrong, that the defenders were, at their core, human. The fear was that Erik might get angry if she didn't show. Lila was afraid of them. All of them, even Erik. She couldn't deny that. But unlike Azumi and Sook, she saw good in them as well. It was incumbent on her—on all of them—to get to know these creatures, to understand what they were capable of, not only when they were at their worst, but when they were at their best, too.

Having convinced herself to go through with it, Lila knocked. The heavy door hurt her knuckles and made almost no sound. She pounded the door with the side of her fist. That produced a tiny thump.

Footsteps approached the door from the inside; it swung open.

"Please come in and admire my home." Erik held the door open for her.

It was a modern-looking house, sparsely furnished save for the walls, which were covered with enormous paintings that Lila had no doubt were Erik's work.

Erik led her into the dining room, which was dominated by a simple but solid rectangular table and four chairs. Erik helped her into her seat as a Luyten approached holding a bottle of wine.

"I'm sorry I don't have a smaller glass. I should have asked you to bring one from your hotel room."

"Don't worry about it, it's fine." It was a fishbowl. The Luyten filled it a quarter of the way.

She considered the painting closest to her. It was a portrait of a defender's face floating on an otherwise empty canvas. "Are you part of an art community? Do you talk technique with other artists, share ideas and such?"

Erik seemed perplexed. "If I share what I know with other painters, they'll improve, weakening the quality of my work by comparison."

Lila wasn't sure how to respond. It wasn't surprising, really, that they saw the creation of art as a competition. And really, how far off was that from how humans thought of art? Erik was saying it aloud, but how many human artists thought the same way?

The steak the Luyten set in front of Lila was absurdly large. It was far smaller than the piece it served Erik, but still, it must have weighed six pounds. It was cut into pieces, probably to match Erik's, since he would have trouble handling a knife. Handling a knife for the purpose of carving his dinner, anyway.

"I'm so sorry about your associate, Bolibar," Erik said. "It was uncalled for, what happened."

"Thank you. It's such a shock." Lila had been avoiding the topic, waiting for Erik to broach it. She put down her utensils for a moment. "You know what was especially tragic? It was all a misunderstanding. Bolibar wasn't laughing at that actor; he was laughing about something completely unrelated to the performance."

"That *is* a shame." Erik was making quick work of his beef. He chewed each enormous bite once, maybe twice before swallowing it and taking another. "So *many* killings seem to arise out of misunderstandings."

Lila smiled, nodded politely.

"Did you see me fight, though?" Erik asked, his eyes lighting up. "Maybe you couldn't see because there were so many defenders on the stage." He pointed his fork at his chest. "But *I'm* the one who killed him."

She had decided to leave the wine rather than risk spilling it all over her blouse, but now she lifted the glass with both hands and took a swig. It was quite good—peppery, sharp, with a hint of licorice.

"Who makes the wine?" Lila asked.

Erik shrugged. "Charles. He took over an existing vine-yard north of the city."

"It's really good."

"Is it?" Erik took a drink. "Charles's is the only wine I've ever tasted, so I have nothing to compare it to."

"If the defenders negotiate trade deals, I'm sure a lot of human wineries would be eager for a chance at the defender market."

"Yes."

Lila waited for him to elaborate, but evidently "Yes" was

the extent of it. "What sort of goods or services do you think defenders would be likely to offer, when trade relations open?"

"I don't know," Erik said. "I'm not involved in business and commerce."

Lila thought of their weapons factories, and wondered if they were planning to go into the human weapons business. That was an unpleasant thought.

After dinner, they carried their wine to the living room. With the equivalent of three or four human-sized glasses in her, Lila felt more relaxed. Erik seemed more at ease as well. When he saw Lila take a seat on the rug rather than try to climb onto a chair, he sat on the floor across from her, his back against the sofa. He looked at his glass, smiled, took a drink. "We rarely drink more than a small amount."

"Why is that?" Lila asked.

Erik closed his eyes, spoke as if reading from a page written on the backs of his eyelids. "A warrior is always in control of himself. Alcohol compromises that control."

Lila nodded. True enough. They were developing their own standards of behavior, their own culture. In time it would mature. She crossed her legs and leaned back against the chair.

Erik crossed two of his legs, his expression playful.

"Is this an inappropriate posture among defenders? In Vietnam, it's considered rude to sit with your legs pointing at someone."

"A warrior maintains balance, both feet on the floor if he is standing or sitting in a chair, both legs on the ground if he is sitting on the ground." Erik swung his third leg over his other two and laughed. His laugh was loud, and had a mechanical, slightly panicked quality to it.

She studied his enormous face, his deep-set eyes. They

seemed almost human in that moment. Maybe it was the wine. "Sometimes it's okay to allow ourselves to be a little off balance, when we're among friends."

"True." He lifted his glass, held it up to the light before taking another drink. "My comrades are jealous of me, because our friendship is especially special. I'm becoming famous."

Lila wasn't sure how to respond. Defenders just didn't get modesty. "That's nice. I'm happy for you."

"Part of it is my excellent social skills, but part of it is you." He considered her. "What is it about you, do you think, that sets you apart from your companions?"

She told Erik the story of the first time she saw a defender, leaping off the roof of the school to save her. How in the last days of the war she'd hung posters of defenders in her room, read everything she could about them, daydreamed about having a defender as a special friend.

By the time she'd finished, Erik was beaming. "And now you have one."

"That's right." She yawned, covered her mouth belatedly. "I'm getting tired." She stood, opened her arms. "Can I give you a hug goodbye?"

"A hug?" Erik seemed taken aback.

Lila dropped her arms. "It's okay, a handshake will do just as well."

Erik looked off at the wall for a moment, then shook his head emphatically. "Handshakes are formal. You're right, special friends should hug."

Erik leaned forward to stand, but Lila motioned to him to stay put. "If you stand I'll be hugging your legs."

She went over and wrapped her arms around his torso, amazed by how solid, how muscular he was. It was like hugging an oak tree. Slowly, tentatively, he set his hands on Lila's back. His hands were shaking. Lila pressed her cheek against his shoulder. It felt good—safe—to be in his arms.

Erik's chest hitched. He seemed to be struggling to control his breathing. She looked up. He looked uneasy, his eyebrows pinched.

"Let me guess, warriors don't hug," she said jokingly.

Erik didn't smile. He was trembling.

Lila hugged him tighter. This was what she'd really dreamed of when she was a teenager, she realized. Not going to the mall with a defender, but being held by one, being rocked to sleep in his protective arms, told that no one could ever hurt her again…

Before she knew it was happening, she was crying. Deep, howling sobs racked her as she clutched Erik, her face buried in his shirt. This day had ground her down to a nub. Seeing Bolibar killed, the bloody fight. Erik squeezed her tighter, his body shaking. Lila looked up. Erik was crying, too.

Tentatively, she rocked him, left and right, left and right. He seemed soothed by the motion. As she rocked him, she realized something: She'd looked up to the defenders as father figures, but Erik didn't see her as a daughter. He saw her as a mother.

# 40

## *Lila Easterlin*

*May 28, 2045. Sydney, Australia.*

Lila woke at dawn and couldn't go back to sleep. Her shoes lay on the end of the bed where they'd fallen when she kicked them off, exhausted and a little drunk, the night before. Even in the faint gray light she could still make out speckled stains on the toes. Bolibar's blood. She'd packed only one pair of heeled shoes, and even if defenders' shoe stores had sold black pumps, they wouldn't have had them in Lila's size.

Erik's painting was propped on the dresser. Besides the human figure's hair being yellow, it bore absolutely no resemblance to Lila. It wasn't even clear it was a woman. The face was twisted, its expression a grimace, to the extent its expression could be made out. Erik's face was rounder in the painting than in real life, his complexion pinker. He looked more human in the painting. Peering closely, Lila realized she looked a bit like a defender.

There was a sharp knock on her door. *"Lila?"* The tone

of Oliver's voice set her heart thumping. She sprang from the bed and flung open the door.

Oliver was staring at his feet. "Azumi is dead. Drowned. Defenders found him in the river."

"*Drowned?* How did he drown?"

Oliver looked up. "I don't know. I guess he could have climbed over that stone wall if he tried, but why on Earth would he do that?"

Lila dragged her hand through her tangled hair. She knew Oliver was thinking the same thing as she. Azumi hadn't climbed over the retaining wall—he'd been thrown. He'd angered some defender, probably through the same type of misunderstanding that cost Bolibar his life. Or maybe it was that general, the one he'd broken up with. That made a sick kind of sense.

There were no police. As they'd witnessed on the night of Bolibar's murder, defenders meted out justice spontaneously, and haphazardly.

"Where is his body?" Lila asked.

"They buried it. They collect up all the dead each day— defender and Luyten, and now the occasional human—and bury them in pits." He shrugged. "That's how they did it during the war; I guess they saw no reason to change."

"So we can't see if there are visible injuries on his body."

"I'm not sure it matters," Oliver said. "It's not like they're going to check him for DNA and search for his killer."

Poor Azumi. He'd so wanted to leave. It was almost as if he'd had a premonition. With a sudden jolt, Lila realized she was the first to argue that they should stay despite the danger. Everyone else had agreed, though; it wasn't as if they all would have packed up if she hadn't opened her mouth.

"There's other news as well," Oliver said. "We're finally meeting with the Triumvirate, on Friday."

# 41

## *Oliver Bowen*

*June 1, 2045. Sydney, Australia.*

Oliver had imagined the Triumvirate as larger than the average defender, their faces a bit more animated, but of course that was silly. They'd all been created from the same genetic blueprint, and epigenetic variation wouldn't create such extreme differences. The defenders on the dais, sitting in enormous plush seats that looked suspiciously like thrones, looked to Oliver like any other defenders.

Well, that wasn't exactly true. One was badly burned. Oliver recognized him as Douglas, the defender who'd addressed the United Nations when the defenders asked for Australia.

"Was Francesca the only Venezuelan representative, or is someone taking her place?" Galatea asked, whispering in his ear.

"I don't know. I think she was their only representative."

Francesca Villanueva, the fifth emissary to die, was in the wrong place at the wrong time. Two defenders got into an argument over the placement of a chair alongside a parade

229

route, and one of them—her "special friend"—accidentally slashed her before she could get out of the way. She'd been a stout woman in her sixties. Like Bolibar, she'd been the sort of person who laughed easily, although that trait hadn't played a role in her death.

"Here we go," Galatea said. She squeezed Oliver's forearm, let her hand linger before taking it off. Lila thought Galatea was flirting with him. Galatea touched a lot of people, but he wondered if maybe Lila was right. He liked Galatea, and if the circumstances were different he probably would have asked her out. But here, with everything that was going on? If anything was going to develop, it would have to wait.

Oliver glanced at Lila, who was sitting two seats over, beside Alan. She smiled at him.

The defenders' minister of defense, whose name was Walter, took the floor in front of the dais. As Walter began talking of their admiration for humans, their recognition that without humans, they would not exist, Oliver relaxed.

"We wanted this time of solitude to decide who we are, what sort of life suits us," Walter said, reading stiltedly from a teleprompter. "What we've come to realize is, we crave the challenges that come with being part of the larger world. We want to learn from our mothers and fathers, to engage them in athletics, to study at their universities."

Engage them in athletics? Oliver tried to picture a defender playing tight end for the Denver Broncos.

"We want to integrate. And to do that, we'll require accommodations." Walter stepped closer to the ambassadors. He squatted over the one vacant human-sized chair in the front row, pretending to sit. A few ambassadors laughed politely at the attempt at humor. Oliver couldn't bring himself to smile, even insincerely. The empty chair was Bolibar's.

"As you can see," Walter went on, "we're not designed for human structures. We cannot be dignified if we must squat and crawl through spaces not built to accommodate us."

Walter returned to the center of the floor. "To successfully integrate as equals, we'll need fair representation and voting power in the world body, and other political bodies where appropriate." A map of the world materialized behind Walter. Some areas were highlighted in orange. "We will also require places to live in addition to Australia. Certain blocks, towns, states, and provinces. We've mapped out those places."

Oliver leaned forward, squinting at the map. New Orleans. The San Francisco Bay area. *France*. A large swatch of central China. What looked to be much of Nigeria and Cameroon. There were dozens of separate spots, maybe a hundred. Was that Jerusalem?

"You want us to give you these places?" Priyanka Vadra asked, her tone measured.

"We welcome humans to live in the areas we will control, but they will be refashioned to accommodate us."

*The areas we will control*, not *the areas we* would *control*. It suggested they didn't see this map as open to negotiation.

"Are these locations negotiable?" Oliver called out.

He half expected Walter to look to the triumvirate for guidance, but Walter simply closed his eyes, as if searching for words, or patience. "Our cartographers worked very hard on this map." He sounded almost hurt. "The percentage of territory we'll control is in direct proportion to our estimated population as compared to yours, adjusted for our larger size. We can make the calculations available if you'd like to examine them."

How thoughtful of them. What they were asking was surely out of the question. The decision would ultimately be made by the United Nations, but Oliver couldn't imagine the world agreeing to these demands.

Oliver pictured the mile upon mile of state-of-the-art weapons the defenders had manufactured. Now their purpose was clear. The human race was militarily weak. It was still recovering from the Luyten War and the global economic depression that followed. They'd needed bridges far more than tanks, and after the Luyten, no one had the stomach for human-on-human conflict, so there'd been little will to divert resources toward weapons manufacture.

"There's one other thing we'll require," Walter said. He held out his open hands, as if in supplication. "We were left with no means to procreate. To repair this oversight, you can provide us with the expertise to create more of our kind. We plan to establish a production facility here in Sydney, staffed by visiting genetic engineers, and headed by your own Lila Easterlin."

Oliver's blood went cold. Galatea reached up and squeezed his shoulder.

Smiling a flat defender smile, Walter gestured toward Lila. "She was recommended for this prestigious position by Colonel Erik, who distinguished himself in Great Britain during the Luyten War."

"Jesus." Oliver's lips were numb. He looked at Lila, who was staring at Walter, wide-eyed. Were they insinuating they expected her to stay in Australia permanently? Suddenly their insistence that she be the US ambassador made chilling sense.

The huge door swung open; a Luyten padded in carrying refreshments. That was another issue: If the defenders got what they wanted, would they expect to bring Luyten with them? Oliver was confident they would.

"After you've had something to eat, please take time to

contact your respective governments and tell them the good news," Walter said. "We have lifted the communications cloak for this evening."

Heading toward the Luyten, Oliver resisted the urge to sprint from the room and contact Washington immediately. The other emissaries seemed to be struggling with the same urge. People were taking as little food as seemed polite. They ate hurriedly, eyeing each other as if silently asking how long propriety dictated they remain in the hall. Who knew what the defenders thought was proper? Perhaps the defenders wouldn't have thought it unseemly if they all stampeded out of the room, shoving each other out of the way. For all Oliver knew, grabbing others by the hair and slamming their faces into the wall might not raise defenders' eyebrows.

He moved through the crowd, following Galatea as their small contingent sought a space where they could talk.

Lila was clearly struggling to keep her composure. "We'll fix this. Don't worry," Oliver said into her ear.

"You can't be sure of that. What if the negotiations boil down to me staying, in exchange for San Francisco, or *France*?" She shook her head. "I can't fucking believe this."

"Washington won't tolerate an emissary being taken hostage. Not a chance."

Lila took Oliver's plate from his hand and set it on a table. "I want to hear them say that."

# 42

## Lila Easterlin

*June 1, 2045. Sydney, Australia.*

Erik was waiting for Lila right outside, on the steps of the Parliament Building. He galloped over as soon as she appeared.

"I just heard the news. Isn't it *wonderful*? It's an honor for you to be chosen to head up our reproductive efforts."

Lila searched Erik's face for some clue, something to signal whether he was truly so clueless he believed he'd done her a favor, or if he was so calculating he would maneuver to force her to stay just so he wouldn't lose his special friend.

"Erik, I have a family at home. I have friends, a house. I can't turn my back on all of that and stay here."

Erik considered. "You'll have me. You can buy a new house—you'll be paid *very* well." When Lila didn't answer, he added, "Now we won't have to say goodbye."

This couldn't be happening. Lila put her hand on her forehead and struggled to think clearly. Could they really do this to her? Things were so bizarre in the world right now that anything seemed possible. She looked up at Erik. "I just want to go home. I want to see my husband, my son, for God's sake. Please say you'll help me undo this. Tell them you made a mistake. *Tell them anything.*" She closed her mouth, realized she was shouting.

Erik looked stunned. Trembling, his voice barely controlled, he said, "Do you have any idea how hard I worked to arrange this? I risked my *life* for you."

To this point, Oliver had been standing slightly behind Lila. Now, almost casually, he stepped between Erik and Lila. "I'm sorry, but we have to contact our government as soon as possible. Come on, Lila." He took her elbow and guided her away.

Erik turned to watch her leave.

# 43

## *Lila Easterlin*

*June 3, 2045. Sydney, Australia.*

It was a meeting unlike any Lila had ever attended, starting with the location. Surely they could have come up with another place in this oversized city where fifteen humans could meet without fear of being overheard. She glanced at the opening of the pipe, a circle of light and color fifty yards away. Actually, she couldn't think of any. Even meeting in a sewer pipe in a smallish group, the defenders might notice and send in a spy bug.

"I understand why the UN won't tell us anything. I just don't like it," Sook was saying. "We're the ones who are here; we're the ones who are actually negotiating with these psychopaths."

Galatea snorted. "Negotiating. I'm surprised you can keep from lacing that word with sarcasm."

Sook smiled grimly. "It took effort."

Wanting to hear what those outside her little group thought, Lila headed for another cluster of people chattering in low tones. She took care not to slip on the moss growing inside the enormous sewer pipe.

"—problem is, they're so adversarial, so zero-sum in their thinking, they see any compromise in their position as weakness," Nguyen Dung, the structural engineer from Vietnam, was saying as Lila joined the circle. A few of them nodded to Lila, acknowledging her.

"If only there were some way to negotiate where we didn't *seem* to be negotiating, where on the surface we appeared to be capitulating. Like, 'Okay, you win, we'll—' Whatever." Ahmad bin Nayef, the ambassador from Saudi Arabia, tugged on his elaborately braided mustache.

"The problem is, they won't budge off the *precise* demands they made at the outset," Nguyen said. "What would they do if we offered them *more* than they're asking for? Say we offered them all of Asia, Europe, and North America. I wonder if they'd reject it, because it wasn't *exactly* what they demanded?" He sighed. "Not that we're going to offer them all of that."

"What *are* we going to do?" Lila asked. "If the defenders doggedly insist we meet their demands, what will the UN do?"

No one answered. No one wanted to bring up the prospect of war. It was unthinkable, to fight another war, against such a savage and well-armed foe. *Foe*. The defenders *weren't* their foes—that was the irony.

"I *can't* see the UN giving in," Ahmad said.

"Lila? Can I speak to you?" It was Oliver. He'd missed the start of the meeting, saying there was something important he had to do.

"What's up?" she asked as they walked toward the circle of daylight, their heads down.

"Let's wait till we're outside." Lila glanced at Oliver, realized that whatever it was he wanted to tell her, he was badly shaken by it. They hopped out of the pipe and walked along the massive, bowl-shaped concrete aqueduct the sewer pipe drained into.

"Washington wants me to locate Five. Badly."

Lila laughed humorlessly. "Sure. We can go door-to-door. 'Pardon me, have you seen a starfish missing a limb and blind in one eye?'"

"I know." Oliver threw his hands in the air in frustration. "I don't even know if he's alive. They're telling me to do everything I can. Everything."

"Why do they want you to speak to him so badly?" It seemed as if the Luyten were an afterthought at this point.

Oliver swallowed. "They want to know what the Luyten would do if they invaded Australia."

Lila stopped walking. "*Holy shit.*"

Oliver held up a hand. "They're not going to invade. You know Washington bureaucrats—they're gathering information, doing their due diligence so they fully understand their options."

A preemptive strike. It made sense, but it sent a chill through Lila. "How would they even do that, with the cloak in place?"

Oliver shrugged. "I guess they'd fly in low under the cloak. We don't have near the number of planes and heavy weapons the defenders do, but if the world combines resources again, re-forms the Alliance, we still have a hell of a lot of weaponry. And we wouldn't be fighting a guerrilla war—we could bomb the hell out of this continent."

They came to a tunnel beneath an overpass, turned, and instead headed up the lip of the bowl toward street level.

"I guess I see where I rate as an ambassador in Washington's eyes," Lila said. "They're doing an end run around me."

"Don't take it personally. They don't trust anyone who hasn't worked for the government for at least twenty years."

"Especially someone who's unstable and unpredictable. I might go all PTSD on them." The truth was she was relieved not to be caught in the middle of all their shit. In fact, she felt sorry for Oliver. "How do *you* feel about them considering this?"

"Oh, I think it's a terrible idea. A war?" He shook his head. "It shouldn't even be on the table. We're too weak, militarily. Last year the US military budget was seventeen percent of what it had been before the invasion." His shoulder sagged slightly. "But I still have to locate Five, if I can."

They were getting close to street level; Lila paused, not wanting to go there and be forced to speak in a whisper. "You know, if the Alliance had already decided to invade, they wouldn't tell you."

Oliver thought about it. "No, they wouldn't."

They still had no evidence, direct or indirect, that the Luyten were passing on the emissaries' thoughts to the defenders. The Luyten didn't seem to speak to the defenders at all, ever. They clearly understood, and took direction, but they never spoke. Because they couldn't read the defenders' minds, they'd have to speak aloud, and, as Five had demonstrated, they were capable of speaking aloud if they chose.

"If the Luyten *are* reporting to the defenders, just by asking you to get this information, they're tipping their hand. And putting you in an incredibly dangerous position at the same time." She made a sweeping gesture, encompassing everything around. "Right now, every Luyten in this city knows the UN is at least considering an invasion."

"Evidently they're willing to take that risk." Oliver folded his arms across his chest. "I'm guessing this is how their logic goes: If the Luyten tip off the defenders that we're considering an invasion, and that I'm seeking information to facilitate that invasion, the defenders will kill me. *No*—they'll kill all of us. And if we're all killed, that signals to the UN that the Luyten may be allied with or controlled by the defenders. If there's a good chance the Luyten will fight alongside the defenders, the Alliance is not going to invade under any circumstances, because they know they can't win."

They continued walking. As they came over the rise and reached the street, a brisk wind hit them.

"That would be a pretty fucking ruthless plan."

Oliver tried to smile. "I sure don't love it. But the stakes are high enough that I think that might be the plan."

Of course, now the Luyten knew this hypothetical plan, and if they were tipping off the defenders, the defenders knew it as well. In which case they *wouldn't* kill the emissaries. Yet. Lila pinched her temples. She couldn't believe they were back to dealing with these telepathic monsters.

# 44

## *Lila Easterlin*

*June 6, 2045. Sydney, Australia.*

Lila blew on her hands, wishing she'd packed gloves. There were so many things she wished she'd packed. Her family. Extra shoes. Valium. She was so tired of this pipe.

"How can they even consider such a thing?" she asked. "The defenders haven't once threatened military action." Lila couldn't believe they were even arguing about this.

"Those little tours of their military stockpiles weren't intended as a threat?" Sook countered. "A quick strike while the defenders are still contained is our best chance to end this before it gets out of hand."

Somehow, word had leaked to the others. Lila hadn't leaked it. She knew Oliver hadn't. So at least one of the other emissaries had been briefed by their government. For all Lila knew, all of the countries had told their emissaries.

"We've been told an invasion is one option 'being considered.' What do they mean by 'being considered'?" Oliver asked. "Certainly, every option available should be *considered*, but are they *seriously* thinking about launching an invasion?"

"They can't be," Galatea said. "Not unless the defenders demonstrate a real willingness to use their weapons against us. Not even a willingness—an *eagerness*." Galatea was standing so close to Oliver their shoulders were brushing. She was wickedly hot in her proper British uptight way; Oliver should be banging her nightly, relieving the crushing stress they were both under. But was he? Of course not.

"*Who else would they use them against?*" Alan asked. "The trees? Cats? They've spent the last fifteen years building weapons to use against us. There's no other logical conclusion to draw."

"You sound almost eager for it to happen," Lila said. Her disdain for Alan was growing by the day. She was barely able to look at Alan when she talked to him. He clearly fancied himself a strong-willed, swinging-dick alpha male, but the more they disagreed, the more he came across as a petulant child.

"I wouldn't say *eager*," Alan said. "But if we learned anything from the Luyten War, it's that when we're threatened, we have to take decisive action to defend ourselves. Immediately."

"So the reason we had so much trouble with the Luyten was that we were too easy on them?" Lila asked, incredulous. "Go tell that to the four *billion* people who died fighting them."

"I didn't—"

Oliver cut Lila off. "Why don't we stick to the things we can control? If there is an invasion, whether we agree with it or not, we would be at ground zero surrounded by defenders. If we aren't killed in the initial bombing, the defenders will surely fix that."

It was a sobering thought. If only they could contact Five. Five might be able to warn them away, either by providing some insight into the defenders' intentions, or by telling them the Luyten would fight on the defenders' side, either by choice or out of fear of reprisal.

The Luyten's silence was frustrating. After the war, they'd certainly been chatty enough. *We're terribly sorry!* they'd shouted at the human race. Had they meant it even slightly?

Humans had double-crossed them, though. They'd handed the Luyten over to the defenders, believing the defenders were going to slaughter every last one of them. But not every human had agreed with that action. Lila had been against allowing the defenders to take custody of the Luyten. So had Oliver. Five knew that. So did the crimson fucker who'd killed her father.

*Sorry I killed your dad*, the crimson one had said to Lila. Were they even capable of regret? Were they haunted by the lives they'd taken? Maybe Lila should get in its face and ask it, point-blank.

She waited for a lull in the argument, then clutched Oliver's sleeve. "Come on."

Oliver followed her out of the sewer pipe without comment, evidently relieved to have an excuse to escape the tension.

"I think Alan may be a psychopath," Oliver said when they were outside. "I disagree with Sook, but I respect her. Alan just seems eager to see people die."

"I may know how to locate Five," Lila said. "Though it's a long shot."

"My best idea was going door-to-door. I'll take a long shot."

As they climbed the steep grade of the drainage bed, Lila picked up her pace. "Do you remember which street we were on when I spotted the crimson Luyten? I want to have a little talk with him."

Oliver, immediately grasping her plan, looked skeptical. "Five told me those apologies were nothing but a strategy to improve their chances of survival. A goodwill campaign to rebrand themselves."

"From everything you've told me, Five is kind of an asshole. I'm not sure I'd put much stock in anything he said."

"Which is why we're trying to get information from him that might affect the likelihood of a global war."

Lila pointed at him. "Good point. In any case, I'm not planning to play on its sense of regret; I'm going to play on its sense of self-preservation."

With Oliver striding to keep pace, Lila stormed up the concrete bed, onto Elizabeth Street. Defenders paused to stare. One waved. Oliver waved back. Lila kept walking.

"Where are you?" she said under her breath. She was angry at Sook and Alan, and potentially the entire human Alliance, but for now she turned that anger toward the crimson Luyten. If the Luyten didn't regret killing her father enough to help them, she was planning to find a two-by-four and beat the hell out of it. She could, too. The telepathic pinwheel wouldn't be able to lift a tentacle to defend itself with defenders around. Odds were, if she attacked it, half a dozen defenders would join in, and they could have a good old-fashioned starfish pull. It seemed as if defenders were always in the mood for a good starfish pull.

"Where are you?" she called. "You can hide, but I'll keep asking until I find you. Slaves can't hide for long."

She turned the corner onto Campbell Street, and stopped short. There it was, unloading crates from the back of its delivery truck.

*I owe you nothing.*

Lila stumbled as the words clawed her mind.

*I lost Luyten who were closer to me than you're even capable of imagining.*

"I didn't kill any of them. I was *fifteen*." Lila heard Oliver's sharp intake of breath as he realized she was speaking to the Luyten.

The Luyten went on stacking crates, slowly, deliberately.

*We signed a peace treaty with you, and you handed us over to these monsters.*

Lila had no comeback for that one. She'd been only fifteen when that happened as well, but the information she was trying to obtain wasn't for her benefit, it was on behalf of her entire species, and her species had betrayed the Luyten in spectacular fashion. There was no denying that. She took a deep breath, willed herself to calm down. "I'm sorry. I'm sorry for those you lost, and for threatening to attack you. I wouldn't have actually done it."

*Yes, you would.*

Lila opened her mouth to tell the Luyten that she knew what she was and was not capable of, that it could take its telepathic righteousness and stuff it into one of its seven mouth-asses. Then she remembered she didn't have to speak for it to hear her.

"Did you get all that?" she asked.

*Yes.* It turned away, headed toward the sidewalk with a dolly full of crates. For a moment Lila thought the Luyten was ending the conversation. Then she remembered it could drive its truck eight miles and they could still hold the conversation.

"So is that the only reason you deigned to speak to me, to tell me you owe me nothing?"

*I want you to understand that I'm not acting out of a sense of obligation, or fear.*

A defender walking by stopped to look at Lila and Oliver. Lila turned to Oliver, so it would look as if she were speaking to him. "Then you'll tell us how to find Five?"

*Five sends Oliver his regards.*

Her heart thumping, Lila repeated this to Oliver. Then she added, "Will he tell us what we want to know?"

Without the slightest pause, the Luyten replied. *We would do nothing. We would seek safety underground, even if the defenders tried to compel us to fight. And they surely would.*

She repeated this to Oliver, word for word.

He nodded. "Now we know. Assuming they're telling the truth."

*You should also be aware that the defenders know you're contemplating an invasion.*

"What? How do they know?"

Oliver started to ask what it had said, but Lila waved him off.

*A Luyten told them. It's difficult to break us when we're psychically linked, but the defenders know to isolate us before they interrogate. They learned that from Oliver.*

That did it, then. There was no way the Alliance would attack if the defenders knew it was coming.

*They don't. They know you're* contemplating *an attack. None of you here in Australia knows for sure. The defenders are confident there will be no invasion.*

As they headed back to the meeting in the sewer pipe, Lila wondered why the Luyten had decided to answer, if it truly wasn't out of a sense of obligation or fear for its life.

Then it came to her. It was so obvious, now that she thought about it. They'd like nothing better than to have the

Alliance wipe out the defenders, and weaken itself in the process. Then the Luyten could wipe out humanity. Surely the Alliance had thought of that. Of course they had. They had no intention of invading; this was all a feint, meant to get back to the defenders, so humanity would be in a stronger negotiating position.

# 45

## *Lila Easterlin*

*June 9, 2045. Sydney, Australia.*

Faruk Demir sidled up to Lila as they were leaving Ayami Ogego's funeral service.

"Any word?"

Lila shook her head. "There won't be. Either it'll happen or it won't." They speculated in coded whispers; everyone had an opinion, but no one knew anything for sure. Meanwhile, the defenders were busy making plans for their diaspora. At this point the official response to the defenders' "request" was "We're considering it." If they were really considering it, the ambassadors had not successfully conveyed to their respective countries just how unstable the defenders were.

"Has anything been communicated to you about...your own status?" Faruk asked.

"Nothing."

She was tired of people asking, and she found herself getting irritable when the issue was raised. It seemed inconceivable

248

that she could be compelled to stay in this lunatic asylum, yet even if the defenders' other demands were resolved through peaceful means, it was conceivable the defenders would simply refuse to allow Lila to leave. What could Washington do, send in Navy SEALs in the middle of the night to steal her back? Actually, that might be their plan. The thought of being trapped here, with the other emissaries gone, was intolerable. She wouldn't let Kai join her, no matter what. She wasn't going to risk his and Errol's lives.

Lila waved goodbye to Faruk as he headed toward whatever event was awaiting him next. His special defender friend was especially needy, and must hold a privileged position, because he rarely seemed to work. Lila had a free hour and decided to walk in Victory Park.

She admired the elaborate flower beds. Defenders seemed to favor sunflowers, likely because of their size. Lila wondered if they drew pleasure from flowers, or if they planted them simply because parks were supposed to have flowers.

Maybe she could negotiate some sort of guest-worker status with the defenders. That was a thought. She could agree to fly to Australia three or four times a year for a few weeks. She could tolerate that. The defenders were, after all, her life's work. If they wanted more of their kind, she and Dominique could work on creating new defenders who were less volatile. These new defenders might even take on leadership positions, become examples for the existing defenders on how to be more reasoned, and less violent.

Her mood lightened as she walked, and planned. She was also feeling better because there were no Luyten around, she realized. Usually there were a few in the park, planting flowers or picking up the defenders' trash. They never gave any indication they noticed her, but she knew they knew exactly who she was, and how she felt about them, and that bothered her.

Lila spotted a glint of green plastic buried in fallen leaves. She kicked it loose: a flattened Lido Lemonade bottle. She chuckled. "Bits of us are still here, even fifteen years later."

A deafening honk made Lila jump. It was followed by another, and another. To her left, where she could see the road nearest her, defenders poured into the street.

"Oh, no." Had they really done it? No. Surely it was a drill.

A deep roar, like the sound of a raging fire, rose from the east. Lila looked toward the sky.

The sound grew louder.

She jumped at the first *thump*. It was followed by a dozen more. Missiles rose overhead, angled toward the coast.

The roar from the east grew steadily louder, punctuated by ever more *thump*s.

Hundreds of Alliance bombers came into view on the horizon.

Many were being blown out of the sky by surface-to-air missiles, but they just kept coming, filling the sky. Cluster bombs shot from the bombers and curled toward the buildings below. She felt the impacts deep in her chest. Clouds of dust and debris rose as if in slow motion.

A terrible sadness enveloped Lila as she watched. The bombs kept dropping, leaping out of the fighters, surging toward the ground like they were eager to meet their targets. She watched, hand over mouth, as Victory Tower—the tallest building in the defenders' so recently constructed city—seemed to slide sideways before tipping, crushing several other buildings as it crashed to Earth.

From horizon to horizon, the sky was filled with Alliance bombers. There were so many explosions they blended together to create one endless, deafening boom.

She had to find shelter, or she was going to die. Lila kicked off her shoes—heels for the funeral—and ran, her palms covering her ears. They'd planned to rendezvous in the sewer pipe if the invasion came, but it was too far. She had to find something nearby. She raced toward the streets.

Above, defender fighter jets roared into view, flying higher than the invaders. They fired cannon bursts, creating a series of blinding flashes, like a sudden burst of fireworks. Alliance aircraft seemed to disintegrate, raining onto the smoldering city.

As Lila reached the street she realized how stupid she'd been to kick off her shoes. There was broken glass everywhere.

Hearing gruff shouts, she ducked behind a parked vehicle. A platoon of defenders thundered past. On the other side of the street, a convoy of vehicles roared by, defenders squatting elbow to elbow in their beds, no doubt on their way to retrieve the heavy weapons stored out in the country. They must be loving this—more war at last. She thought of Erik, wondered where he was. They were special friends no more.

A new sound lit the air: dozens of huge booms, far away. Artillery fire, maybe naval gunfire? Alan had said the Alliance would pound the city from ships. Lila stumbled, caught herself, and pushed on as the tops of buildings disintegrated.

Pain lanced the underside of her foot. Lila stopped, balanced on one leg to examine it. A nasty shard of glass was sticking out. Eyes watering from the pain, she pulled it out and tossed it aside.

Something slammed into the side of her head, knocking her down. Blackness swept over her as she lay on the sidewalk, her cheek pressed to the concrete. She fought it, struggled to get to her knees. At first her body wouldn't respond; her hands opened and closed spasmodically, clawing the pavement. Through sheer force of will she made it to her knees, touched the side of her head. There was a deep, straight gash an inch above her ear. It felt as if her scalp, her hair, was hanging lower than it should. Her hand came away bloody.

Struggling to her feet, Lila staggered on.

She wondered if Oliver was still alive, if the others had reached shelter in time. Then she thought of Kai, their little man, Errol, and she nearly sobbed.

Up ahead, one of the enormous exhaust grates built into the sidewalks was leaned against a storefront, exposing a huge open hole. Lila ran bent at the waist, listing to the right, correcting, drifting right again until she reached the hole.

There was an enormous ladder, the rungs too far apart. She hugged one of the ladder's vertical bars, paused, and took one last look at the city, the bombers overhead like a chain-link steel roof, the air stinking of soot and gasoline. Then she slid into near darkness.

She reached a huge horizontal sewer pipe as the earth above continued to rattle, the *boom*s only slightly muffled. She sensed she wasn't nearly far enough underground to be safe if a bomb landed nearby, but looking around, she couldn't see a way to go lower.

Then she spotted an opening, and limped a hundred feet deeper into the tunnel. Shrouded in darkness, there was a ragged hole in the side of the enormous pipe. She stepped through and found herself in a wider tunnel, freshly dug, angling downward. It was pitch-black.

Every fiber in her was repulsed by the thought of climbing into that hole.

A bomb struck fairly close; dirt rained down onto her head. The open wound burned. She had to go farther down. Alan had said the Alliance would pound the city for hours, maybe days.

Lila sat, then eased herself down the steep grade. The thought of being alone in a dark tunnel for hours or days terrified her to the core.

She kept sliding, freshly dug earth tumbling down with her. Once she was down, would she be able to climb back up? The thought sent bright stabs of panic through her as she dropped. It was too late to go back.

The tunnel leveled out; Lila spotted a faint blue glow ahead. Cautiously, she got to her feet, walked the final sixty feet, the light growing brighter. She reached a curve in the wall and, heart drumming, followed the curve a dozen more feet.

The tunnel opened onto a dimly lit room packed with Luyten. Some were curled into balls; others stood along the walls. One was wounded; it lay near the center while two others tried to stanch the bleeding from a half dozen ragged gashes.

Lila turned and fled back through the tunnel, running blindly, hands in front of her, expecting to feel a Luyten's cilia wrap around her ankle at any second and drag her back into the room where they would tear her apart. She reached the slope, stumbled in the soft earth, landed face-first, sprang up immediately, and clawed at the dirt, panting in fear. Overhead, bombs thumped like the whole city was being reduced to dust. Lila felt blood dripping off her hair onto her shoulder and chest as she scrabbled in the soft dirt with her hands and feet, trying to find purchase.

She'd managed to climb twenty feet or so, the angle growing steadily steeper, when she lost her grip and slid down again.

Lila pressed her forehead into the dirt and shook her head. There was no way. She was trapped.

It occurred to her that if the Luyten were chasing her, they would have caught her before now. She turned and sat, listening to the sounds of Luyten moving around in the bunker. Five had told Oliver they were going to remain neutral. Maybe they meant it.

She leaned against the tunnel wall, drew up her knees. This was insane. The World Alliance was bombing defenders while Lila took refuge in a shelter filled with Luyten.

Lila shrieked and scurried backward as a thick Luyten appendage pressed against her. She backed into the shelter, where the Luyten squeezed past her and continued into the shelter.

The Luyten in the shelter simply ignored her. Rather than risk being in the way of other arriving Luyten, she sat against the wall, in a wedge near the exit where the wall angled.

Looking around the makeshift shelter, she spotted crates of food tucked into the far corner, plastic barrels of water. Blue iridescent lights jutted from the walls at rough intervals. Lila wondered if the Luyten preferred the blue tinge because it approximated the light of their home world, because it made it more difficult for defenders to detect them, or simply because it had been easiest to pilfer from their masters. One thing was certain: They'd prepared for this. Thanks to Oliver, they'd had warning.

Every Luyten in the shelter could hear her thoughts. In the dim light, her mind conjured unbidden images of Luyten cooking cars full of screaming people, crawling up from the sewers in Atlanta, bearing down on her father...

Yet in the end, when they'd lost, they set down their weapons and marched into those camps, leaving themselves at the mercy of humans. And Lila's people had betrayed them.

Why were they tolerating her presence now, she wondered?

# 46

## Oliver Bowen

*June 9, 2045. Sydney, Australia.*

Head down, shirt pressed to his mouth, eyes half closed against the dust and blinding flashes, Oliver ducked under a huge pipe that was probably a standard household-sized plumbing pipe in this Brobdingnagian city.

The explosions went on and on.

Oliver paused, then turned to Alan, who was behind him. "How long is this likely to go on?"

"Until any more bombing would be pointless. Then they'll send in troops and drones."

That wasn't an answer. "Well, how long is that likely to *take*?"

"There it is," Galatea called out, pointing. Sure enough, there was the pipe where they'd held their covert meetings. The still-smoking wreckage of a bomber was strewn to one side of it. They picked up their pace, eager to have cover, although a drainage pipe wouldn't lead far enough underground to shield them from a direct hit.

Galatea, who was a few paces ahead of Oliver, stopped suddenly.

"What is it?" Oliver caught up to her and peered inside.

The pipe was full of bodies. Twenty or thirty of their colleagues lay in a burnt, bloody tangle thirty feet inside the pipe. Oliver turned away, gasping, trying to catch his breath. The sight in the tunnel had knocked the wind out of him.

"They must have been spying on us," Sook said. "They knew we were meeting here, and when the invasion started, they guessed we'd seek refuge here."

"We have to get out of here," Alan said. "They might come back."

"I have to see if Lila is in there," Oliver said, struggling to keep his voice steady. "Go on, I'll catch up."

"No," Galatea said, putting a hand on his shoulder. "I'll help you." She turned to Sook and Alan. "Shout if they come."

# 47

## *Oliver Bowen*

*June 9, 2045. Sydney, Australia.*

At the start of the Luyten War, Luyten had dropped from the sky like falling stars. This time it was humans who dropped from the sky.

"It looks like most of them are dropping over there." Sook pointed to the west.

During the long, cold night in a restaurant sub-basement, they'd finally agreed that their best course of action was to leave the safety of the basement when the bombing stopped and find Alliance soldiers to take them to one of the ships off the coast. Oliver couldn't leave without finding Lila, but Galatea had convinced him it would be both suicidal and pointless to wander the city looking for her. Wiser to get a platoon of soldiers to search for her.

"We're better off heading east," Alan said. "Most of the force will be coming off the boats." They headed east along the top of the drainage bed, less than forty feet from Trafalgar Street. Because Alan had a degree in military history to go along with his extensive knowledge of modern weapons, they were grudgingly following his lead for the most part.

Another wave of Alliance paratrooper planes buzzed overhead. Then, moments later, another.

"Here comes the full invasion," Alan said. "They'll drop a few kilometers west of the city, then sweep this way."

Cautiously, Oliver lifted his head above street level. The city was unrecognizable—a postapocalyptic nightmare. The enormous scale of the infrastructure meant that much more wreckage. In places, Trafalgar Street looked impassable.

"If all goes well, how long will it take before the Alliance is in control?" Galatea asked Alan.

"Based on how quickly they've put boots on the ground, I'd say they're planning a quick, violent assault. Either they control the continent in a matter of weeks, or they won't control it at all."

Oliver clapped his hands to his ears as dozens of defender fliers roared by overhead. Oliver recognized them as the ones lined row upon row at one of the first factories they'd passed on the initial tour. They were enormous, angry-looking things, almost rectangular save for a pointed nose, loaded with turrets and cylinders that were clearly weapon systems.

"I was hoping the Alliance had gotten all of those during the bombing."

"I'm sure they got some," Alan said. "Hopefully, most."

The thumping of many pairs of boots in the street sent a thrill of fear through Oliver. Risking a glance, he saw defenders carrying automatic rifles, running in step. Their eyes were wide and wild, their teeth clenched.

Gunfire erupted. Two of the lead defenders dropped heavily; the rest scattered left and right. Two more were hit by what must have been large-caliber ordnance, because it tore right through the defenders' body armor, spraying flesh, blood, and bone.

Oliver and his companions watched from their cover as the defenders disappeared down side streets, behind vehicles. From the west, a baritone moan and a metallic clicking rose. More of the defenders' gigantic weapons.

"We should get out of here," Oliver said, but no one moved. They were mesmerized by the sight of defenders fighting humans.

"Look," Galatea said.

Oliver looked where she was pointing, and saw a defender climbing out a third-story window clutching an assault rifle. He perched on the ledge right above the spot where the Alliance shots had originated, and jumped.

The defender hit the debris boots-first with staggering force, yet stayed on his feet. Howling, he unleashed a barrage of rapid, booming fire, point-blank. Oliver couldn't see the human troops hiding in the debris, but he knew they were dying.

Four Alliance soldiers broke from their cover. Screaming, his face twisted with rage, the defender turned his fire on the fleeing soldiers.

When he finally stopped, they were in pieces.

"Let's go," Oliver repeated. This time, everyone moved.

# 48

## *Lila Easterlin*

*June 9, 2045. Sydney, Australia.*

Seemingly all at once, the bombing stopped. Lila had been half dozing, in a twilight state where Luyten and defenders lurked in the corners of her vision, constantly jolting her from any chance of real sleep. Now she woke fully, listened for the muffled thump of bombs exploding overhead. All was silent.

Lila jumped as something dropped into her lap. It was a defender-sized package of cereal. Weetabix. She turned to see a Luyten returning to its place beside the food stores.

"No milk?" Lila called. The package hissed as she ran her finger along the airtight seal.

# 49

## Oliver Bowen

*June 9, 2045. Sydney, Australia.*

The bridge across Sydney Harbor was gone. From behind an overturned piece of a bombed fountain in Dawes Point Park, they watched a flotilla of defender submarines head out toward the sea, silent, dipping under the water then resurfacing like porpoises crossed with tanks.

"It's going to take us forever to get to the beach with the bridge gone," Sook said.

"Hopefully we'll encounter some Alliance troops before then. We just have to keep moving toward them," Alan said, pointing in the direction he thought they should go.

"*Down*," Galatea hissed. Everyone ducked. Oliver had a tight view of the street running along the river through a cracked place in the fountain. He counted four defenders as they passed, walking single file, the first three carrying assault rifles, the fourth something larger and heavier, with two enormous barrels and a shoulder brace.

When the defenders were out of sight, the emissaries waited

five minutes, then headed toward the beach. They stuck to the backstreets, which were tight alleys to the defenders but felt wide and exposed to Oliver. They had to backtrack often to navigate around fallen buildings, and did their best to stifle coughs that might give them away as the smoke-filled air tortured their lungs.

Oliver was sick about being separated from Lila. It had been a tremendous relief when it turned out she wasn't among the bodies in the pipe, but if she hadn't made it to the rendezvous point, where was she? He didn't want to believe she was dead in this rubble. Surely she'd sought shelter, was holed up somewhere.

They'd wound a third of a mile from the downed Sydney Bay Bridge when they hit a wall of rubble a hundred feet high, stretching out of sight in both directions.

"Which way?" Sook asked.

A small jet appeared over the rooftops and paused directly overhead. They pressed into the doorway of a department store, but the jet darted down, hovered thirty feet above the street, facing them. It was like a toy, no bigger than a bicycle. From its muscular appearance—like a jagged bullet with wings—it was clearly defender made.

It whisked off.

"A spy drone. They know where we are," Oliver said. "They'll be coming. Run."

They ran north along the edge of the mound, looking for a breach they could squeeze through.

"Can we climb over it?" Galatea asked.

The soft hiss of aircraft engines broke through the din. Three defender Harriers swooped into view, hovered, then landed in a semicircle, pinning them against the mound of debris.

Doors whisked open and defenders jumped out of the craft, charging at them, snorting, their eyes glowing with rage.

"*Hold fire!*" a defender in officer's gold and black fatigues shouted. "Hold. I think those are the ones."

The officer stepped between two defenders and peered at the emissaries. "You." He pointed at Oliver. "You're Lila's father."

"Yes," Oliver said.

"Erik? It's Galatea." She took a step forward. "It's good to see you."

"We're not combatants," Alan chimed in. "We had no idea this would happen."

"Do you know where Lila is?" Erik asked, ignoring them. He sounded ready to tear Oliver's head off and crush it in his fist.

"We haven't seen her since before—" Oliver stammered, not wanting to use the word *invasion*, or *attack*. "Since things went bad."

Erik motioned to his troops. His meaning was evident: Kill them.

Oliver held up his hands. "I can help you find her. I know places she might be. Don't hurt Galatea, Alan, and Sook. Take them into custody, and I'll help you." He named each of his companions intentionally. It was harder to kill people if you knew their names. He didn't know if that applied to defenders.

"Lila is strategically valuable. We need her," Erik said, as if someone had questioned his motives.

"Yes, I understand that," Oliver said. "Let me help you find her."

Erik eyed them from under his heavy brow. "Why?" Erik asked. "Why did you do this?"

How could Oliver answer a question like that? A truthful answer could get them all killed. Silence wouldn't improve their odds, either.

Alan started to answer, but Oliver spoke over him. "You asked for too much."

Erik glared at him. "We asked to be treated as equals. We asked for respect. You gave us parades, but you don't want to live with us as equals. You think we're a joke."

Behind Erik, a series of huge aircraft roared by. Erik turned and watched them for a moment. They were heading north, away from the Alliance forces.

"We don't think you're a joke," Oliver said. "We take you very seriously."

"You will." Erik studied the emissaries a moment longer, then turned toward one of his men. "Take them into custody." He pointed at Oliver. "You, come with me."

265

# 50

# Dominique Wiewall

*June 9, 2045. US Pacific Command Station, Guam.*

General Willis rose from his seat. Dominique guessed that, in the general's mind, he was *springing* from his seat, but the truth was that his aging legs didn't have much spring left in them.

Squinting, Willis approached the satellite feed, where a number of enemy aircraft were traveling north. Dominique guessed they were planning to attack the enormous Alliance fleet from the rear.

Dominique sat ramrod straight, watching the feed, still unable to accept that this was really happening. They'd attacked the defenders. The *defenders*.

The aircraft just kept going. Up the coast, out over the Coral Sea.

"*They're running,*" Willis said, sounding almost jubilant. He'd been slumped in his chair since the defenders' coastline antiaircraft system had picked off all fifty-six of the bombers carrying nuclear warheads. He shouldn't have been surprised—the US had almost perfected a spectroscopic technique for remote detection of nuclear weapons before the Luyten invasion had derailed the program. The defenders had been granted full access to US military databases during the desperate days of the war.

Dominique watched the feed. "Where are they running *to*?"

No one answered. The defenders had no safe harbor outside Australia.

More aircraft appeared, following the same route.

In Melbourne to the south, a fleet of defender warships hugged the coast, *avoiding* Alliance forces. Pacific Command hadn't known about those warships. Thanks to the cloak, all they had was what the emissaries on the ground had told them. They had no idea how large the defender army actually was.

Dominique watched the aircraft. What were they up to? If they pulled a substantial part of their forces out of Australia, the Alliance would take it in a matter of days. Dominique pinched the bridge of her nose, trying to think like a defender. They were fighters. They were ruthlessly aggressive. They—

"They're going on the offensive," Dominique said aloud.

Everyone in the war room looked at her. Mouths fell open. Admiral Adler cursed under her breath.

"They're just going to cede Australia to us?" Willis asked, pointing at the blips that represented the Alliance ships and aircraft, a force ten times larger than any ever before assembled in one place.

"Humans always protect their homeland, because they have no choice," Dominique said. "They can't leave their children behind, their parents. Defenders have no children to protect, no old people."

On the virtual map, some of the defender aircraft headed west, between Australia and Papua New Guinea. Others split off and headed east, toward the Pacific. Closer to Sydney, several Alliance aircraft carriers were flashing red on the map.

"What's going on there?" Willis asked, pointing at the carriers.

Laura Dramis, their tech, zoomed in, giving them a tight aerial view of one of the aircraft carriers. It was canted at a thirty-degree angle, sinking.

"Holy shit. Did they get hit by aircraft, or rockets? Why didn't our perimeter defenses take them out?" Willis asked.

Peter Hernandez spoke directly to someone in the fleet in a quick, clipped exchange. He spun in his chair. "The attack came from underwater, but sonar did not detect any foreign bodies below. There are reports of defenders surfacing in big *sacks*, like the ones the Luyten used."

That they had weapons based on Luyten technology shouldn't have surprised anyone. The report from their weapons expert on the ground had said as much. But that wasn't the problem right now; the problem was the conventional defender aircraft and warships leaving Australia. Yet more were taking flight out of New South Wales, heading due north.

"Get every ship to send some butterfly cameras under that water, see if they can locate the enemy visually." Willis reached out, squeezing the air like he was clutching a shoulder. "No. First, tell them to detonate depth charges, tight in, close to their ships. Detonate them as shallowly as possible."

"General, you need to redeploy your forces," Dominique said, interrupting. "Most of the world's major population centers are defenseless right now." She couldn't believe the Alliance had put him in charge of the invasion. How did these old, incompetent relics always manage to retain power?

General Willis glared at her, then swept a backhand at the

map. "I can see it as well as you can, Miss Wiewall. I'm not blind."

No, he was just an idiot.

"You're here to provide insight into the defenders, not advise on military strategy. Now let me do my job."

He went on arranging for the defense of their naval forces as precious minutes ticked by. He went about it methodically, deliberately, as if to show Dominique who was in charge.

"*Now*," he said, finally, dipping his head toward Dominique in mock deference, "divert forces to pursue the unfriendlies leaving the vicinity. Send warnings to strategically significant targets and major population centers to be on full alert."

Dominique realized that by threatening the general's ego, she'd delayed the deployment by ten or twelve minutes. They were on their way now, though. She relaxed, but not much. She'd pictured this war taking place in Australia. How foolish of her. She of all people should have known better.

She of all people. When the president refused to let her be part of the diplomatic mission to Australia, she should have tried harder to change his mind. Maybe she could have defused the situation before it even started.

# 51

## Oliver Bowen

*June 9, 2045. Sydney, Australia.*

There were no human-sized seats in the aircraft, so Oliver stood clutching the pant leg of a fire suit hanging from a hook above him, trying to stay on his feet as the Harrier weaved and dove and banked. He watched what was left of Sydney through the bottom of a window. Human soldiers ran from the cover of one bombed-out building to another. A platoon of defenders vaulted over rubble, looking eager to kill.

"Where are our heavy weapons?" Oliver heard Erik shout into his comm.

"Most have been redeployed," a gravelly-voiced defender replied.

"Redeployed to where?"

"Moscow, Mumbai, Washington, Shanghai..."

Oliver had a moment of thinking he must be dreaming this. Surely this wasn't happening. Kai was in Washington.

"What about Sydney?" Erik asked. "What about me?"

"If the Alliance doesn't turn its force to engage us in their cities, you're going to die."

Erik turned toward Oliver, shock and fear evident on his face. It was reassuring to see Erik was afraid to die. "I need Lila. We have to find her."

"I agree." His mind was racing. Besides being major population centers, there was something about the cities the defender on the comm had mentioned that struck a chord.

Then it came to him: They were all cities that held mothballed defender production facilities. They were going right after those facilities. Surely the Alliance had thought to destroy those facilities before they launched the invasion. Surely.

Below, blackened rubble and fires were replaced by the green calm of grass and trees. Belmore Park. Since Lila hadn't returned to the hotel after the funeral, and she clearly hadn't gone somewhere with Erik, Oliver's best guess was the park. She spent a lot of her free time there; the normal-sized trees and plants made her feel less like a child, she'd said.

The Harrier dropped close to the ground, its enormous rotors causing the trees to bend and sway like reeds as leaves were torn from branches and blew in all directions.

They cruised along the main walkway, everyone aboard seeking some sign of Lila. Now that they were here, Oliver realized how futile this was. If she'd been here when the bombs began to fall, she would have sought shelter. Not in buildings adjacent to the park, though; she was too smart for that. She would have sought low, protected ground, or better yet, climbed down into a sewer.

"Watch for open sewer holes, or other places she might have taken cover." Of course, all of this assumed Lila had been in the park when the invasion hit.

# 52

## *Kai Zhou*

*June 9, 2045. Washington, D.C.*

Kai was fairly certain Tony Vellikovsky had a third seven in the hole. He so hoped he was right, because if he was, there was no way Vellikovsky could cut loose, and Kai had just drawn the ten he needed for a straight.

Kai saw Vellikovsky's bet. "Raise." He pushed another eighty thousand into the pot.

Vellikovsky looked pained, yet pleased. He saw the bet, raised another eighty.

Just in case he'd read it wrong and Vellikovsky had a full house instead of a set of sevens, Kai saw the raise, flipped his hole cards. "Straight."

Vellikovsky leaned toward the cards, as if he doubted Kai's assessment, then he looked up at Kai. "You called my raise with a jack-nine?" He pushed away from the table and stormed over to the gallery. "Honey, did you see this?" He gestured toward Kai. "He called my raise with a jack-nine." He turned back toward the table. "Can you even *spell* 'poker'?"

272

Kai smiled. "Sorry, Tony. Insults don't sting much when you're raking the insulting party's money toward you."

"You play like a twelve-year-old." Evidently, Vellikovsky wasn't finished. "Seeing my raise when you *know* the odds are against you, just in case you get lucky?" He pointed at Kai. "You won the hand, but you're an idiot. I don't know how you've lasted this long. *Ben*." Finally, he sat down.

With great effort, Kai kept the smile on his face, but he could feel himself flushing, with embarrassment and anger. No one called him that. No one called him Benedict Arnold.

The next hands were dealt; he tried to concentrate.

He'd never even met Mandy Caron, the author of the book that insisted on defining his life, yet he hated her more than everyone else he hated on Earth combined. The book itself painted Kai as being far more instrumental in winning the Luyten War than he'd actually been, but it was the title that people remembered, even though it was meant to be ironic.

*The Boy Who Betrayed the World.*

"Ante is thirty thousand," the dealer announced.

"And thanks for the rotten cards," Vellikovsky said to the dealer. "All night, you've been handing me shit. You deal me a set, then finish off his straight."

"Come on, this is getting embarrassing," Kai said, his patience gone. "Stop with the tantrum and play your goddamned cards."

Someone in the gallery spoke over him, shouting, "Jesus, they're invading Australia!"

Kai jumped from his chair. "What? Who?" The last time he'd spoken to Lila, everything had been okay.

"The Alliance."

"What Alliance?" Vellikovsky said. "There is no Alliance."

The guy projected the feed onto the wall so everyone could see. There were four POV screens, most of them aerial shots

273

above a city in smoking ruins. Planes filled the sky, some of them enormous, like nothing Kai had ever seen. They were like flying aircraft carriers.

"We're invading the defenders?" Kai asked. Lila had hinted at problems, but *war*? He pulled out his comm and tried to reach Lila at the number she'd given him, although he knew it would be blocked. It was.

There was an emergency exit to the left of the gallery. Kai headed for it, ignoring the alarm that sounded when he shoved the door open. Unless they'd airlifted the emissaries out before the assault, Lila was in that ruined city. So was Oliver.

First, he had to get Errol. It would change nothing about what was happening in Australia, but suddenly Kai had an overwhelming need to have Errol with him. It was ironic— most mornings he was relieved when the nanny showed up to care for the boundless, chaotic force that was Errol. Now all he wanted was to be with him.

He'd clambered down two flights, taking the steps three at a time, when he finally stopped to catch his breath and think about what to do. He needed to understand exactly what was happening. Breathing hard, his fingers shaking, he activated the news on his phone.

The newscaster said the defenders had delivered an ultimatum, demanding huge territorial concessions, and threatened military action if their demands weren't met. That must have been the problem Lila had alluded to but couldn't talk about. In response, the World Alliance had re-formed, and attacked Australia.

The newscaster, who had been rattling off details in a breathless voice, suddenly went silent.

"We've just received new information. The conflict may be expanding beyond Australia. The Federal Emergency

Management Agency is directing civilians to evacuate the following cities."

The names of the cities appeared below the feed. Atlanta, Chicago, Los Angeles, New Orleans, New York, San Francisco. Last on the list was Washington, D.C. The list was alphabetical. It was most definitely not in the order of cities most likely to be hit by a counterstrike.

Kai sprinted down the stairs, heading for the garage under the hotel.

# 53

## *Oliver Bowen*

*June 9, 2045. Sydney, Australia.*

Something small and black was skipping across the grass, blown by the Harrier's rotors. Oliver squinted. It was probably a piece of trash, but it looked heavier, almost like a shoe. He watched it roll and bounce along.

"Hang on. What is that." He pointed at it. Erik switched to Oliver's side and peered out the window.

"What is what?"

"There." Oliver pointed. "Is that a shoe?"

Erik lifted a pair of binoculars, trained them on the object as it skipped across a walkway and came to rest, pressed against a curb.

"It *is* a shoe." He dropped the binoculars and turned to the pilot. "Set it down."

Before they'd even touched ground, Erik was out of the Harrier, running toward the shoe. He was as desperate to find Lila alive as Oliver was. They could have won the defenders over, in time, if they'd been more patient, but the Luyten War had left humanity too skittish, too scarred. So instead the defenders were heading for Moscow, Mumbai, Washington. Oliver had no illusions about what they would do when they arrived. They were angry.

Erik was halfway back when Oliver caught up to him. Oliver took the shoe Erik handed him, barely had to glance at it. "It's Lila's." She'd brought only two pairs of shoes, and bemoaned the limitations of her footwear almost daily.

Erik cupped his hands around his mouth. *"Lila? Lila."*

Oliver scanned the horizons. The sewer grates were huge iron things, too heavy for a human to lift.

*Cold.*

That voice in his head, so familiar even after fifteen years.

"Five," he said under his breath. Cold? It wasn't cold. It was hot, even hotter than usual with so many buildings on fire.

Oliver turned, looking for some sign of Five. Was he nearby?

*Warmer.*

"What?" Oliver said aloud.

Erik frowned. "What?"

"Nothing." Warmer. Like the children's game? Oliver took a step in the direction he was facing.

*Warmer.*

"This way," Oliver said, with no idea where he was going.

A half dozen defenders padded behind and beside him as he trotted down the street. He was hot. Not red hot yet, not burning, but hot.

"Lila?" he called.

The pop of gunfire erupted to their left and behind them. Oliver dropped to the ground. He heard a shout—a human shout—then more gunfire as one of the defenders went down and the others ran for cover.

Oliver lifted his head enough to see human soldiers racing from the corners of buildings, peeking from behind buses, more of them pouring in from around an enormous block of concrete that had once been part of a building. He crawled on his belly, away from the soldiers, in the direction that was "hot."

*Hot.*

Behind him, he could hear defenders returning fire, someone on a comm, maybe Erik, calling for air support, or a tank, anything big.

*Hot.*

It was all Five would say to him. For all Oliver knew, Five had been hot-and-colding him not toward Lila, but toward this ambush.

*Very hot. Red hot.*

Oliver glanced around. He almost laughed out loud when he saw the rectangular gap in the sidewalk to his left, the thick steel grate leaning up against the side of the building.

*Boiling.*

He clawed his way to the opening, swung his legs around, and grasped a steel pipe that was one side of an oversized ladder.

He slid twenty feet to the floor of a sewer pipe, looked left, then right...

*Scalding.*

He went right, wary that Five might be leading him toward a divorce-sized pit. He didn't understand why Five was helping him.

There was a breach in the pipe. "*Lila?*" he called.

"*Oliver?*"

Oliver ducked through the breach, then took a few anxious breaths before plunging ahead, down a freshly dug tunnel.

Toward the bottom he saw a blue glow. He called again, "Lila?" Rushing around a bend in the tunnel, he saw Lila, the side of her head a bloody mess. She was in a room packed with Luyten, who were doing exactly what Five had said they would do if humans launched an invasion.

Lila launched herself at Oliver and hugged him fiercely. "You're alive. I can't believe it," she said.

Above them there was a mechanical shriek, like metal being twisted. One of the defenders' big weapons had arrived. He'd sorely hoped they would surface to find live human soldiers and dead defenders.

Lila let go, and Oliver examined the wound on her head. It was difficult to see much in the dim light, but from what he could see, it was bad, even if not life-threatening. It looked like she'd been partially scalped.

"How the *hell* did you find me?" Lila asked.

"Five."

Lila looked surprised. "Why would he help me?"

Oliver shrugged. "Maybe he's trying to make amends for breaking up my marriage. Maybe they want to deliver you into the hands of the defenders. I have no idea." He motioned for her to go first.

She took a few steps, then paused. "I think he did it for Kai."

"For Kai?"

"That's right. I have no idea why I think that. I just do."

"*Lila?*" He could just barely hear the voice. Erik, shouting from street level.

"That's your special friend," Oliver said, gesturing toward the surface.

"Oh, no," Lila said, her voice low, and soaked in dread.

# 54

## *Kai Zhou*

*June 9, 2045. Washington, D.C.*

His car inched along. Kai was sure he could walk faster than
they were moving, especially with the amount of adrenaline
rushing through him, but not for twenty miles, carrying Errol
and a trunk full of food and water. FEMA's emergency navi-
gation system had been activated, so Kai's vehicle was under
auto-control meant to maximize traffic flow out of the city.

He watched the news, keeping the feed small so Errol
wouldn't see it. Kai glanced at Errol, strapped in the back.
He was sleeping, his cheek pressed against the side of the
child seat. Errol's peaceful face was a stark contrast from the
images on the feed. When the defender force reached Mumbai, a piece of it had peeled off and attacked. They went right
for the most densely populated spots, killing as many people
as possible. Along with conventional weapons, their forces
were equipped with chemical weapons. Huge fish-shaped fliers swooped low over neighborhoods, releasing gas. It was

killing everyone, inside buildings and out, burning lips, eyes, lungs. Forty minutes after the assault began, everyone, everywhere in the city, seemed to be dead.

The retired general commenting on the feed said that was why the defenders had ceded Australia so quickly: In Australia their soldiers would be mixed with Alliance soldiers throughout the city; the battle would have to be fought street by street. The defenders had far fewer soldiers, so they were at a strategic disadvantage. By going on the offensive, they could capitalize on their strength: huge weapons of mass destruction; chemical weapons humans shrank from using against one another and had consequently ceased manufacturing decades earlier.

They were on their way to D.C., and they were targeting civilians. Kai dug deeper into the news feeds, seeking information about the fate of people trying to evacuate. Would the defenders target people obviously leaving the city, or just let them leave?

He found a panicked personal text feed from a woman named Sangita who was trapped in Mumbai. The people in Mumbai hadn't had enough warning for any organized evacuation to begin, so the arteries out of the city hadn't been clogged with evacuees. So Kai had no idea if the defenders would attack fleeing refugees.

He took a deep breath and dragged his hair out of his eyes. After the conversation he'd had with Lila, he probably knew more about the defenders than any other person on this highway. The defenders were killing as many people as possible, not just seizing strategic territory, and they wouldn't hesitate to target evacuees.

The feed went dead. Kai didn't bother checking his

phone—he knew what had happened. The defenders were taking out the satellites, just like the Luyten had knocked out the satellites.

Kai glanced at Errol again, then ahead at the sea of taillights inching steadily along. They weren't going to make it out in time. Kai suddenly knew this with such certainty that it felt as if he were remembering, not anticipating.

He looked out the side window. They were on a long overpass; beneath them was block after block of industrial sprawl, blanketed in darkness save for the occasional glow of yellow streetlights. It was all but deserted, not the sort of place the defenders would target.

Kai climbed into the backseat and unstrapped Errol. Errol's eyes fluttered open, then closed again as Kai drew him out of the seat and held him. Kai had to override the safety lock to open the door in a moving vehicle. Clutching Errol to his chest, he looked down at the pavement rolling by. It wasn't an illusion: They were moving at the pace of a swift walk.

Switching Errol to his left hand, Kai moved to the edge of the car, grasped the hood with his right hand, and stepped out, immediately breaking into a trot. He stumbled, then regained his footing. Slowing his pace, he let the car pass him, then fell into step behind it. He popped open the trunk, grabbed the backpack he'd filled with the things they would need as soon as they arrived at the refugee center, and headed off to look for a way down.

He found a stairwell a quarter of a mile on. Errol was crying in his ear, disturbed by the jostling. Kai's thighs burned as he descended to street level. Errol was heavy.

When they reached the bottom, Kai jogged with Errol's head pressed to his chest until he was too tired to go on.

He was gasping for breath. Too much poker, not enough

exercise. He looked around. Across the street was a yard filled with construction vehicles, enclosed by a cyclone fence topped with barbed wire. To his left was an electrical power station, nothing but wires and big generators. To the right, a big old warehouse. Kai headed for that.

"I want to go to my bed," Errol said. It was after ten; the poor guy was exhausted.

"Try to sleep on my shoulder," Kai said, knowing that was nearly impossible.

The warehouse was locked, its big bay doors chained and padlocked. Kai didn't think he could carry Errol and the pack much farther without rest. He circled the building and found fire escape stairs in the back. The only thing he could think to do was climb to the roof and wait up there.

Errol protested when Kai set him down on the gravel that covered the roof. Kai shushed him, ran a hand over his hair, coaxing his head into Kai's lap.

From the roof Kai could see the line of vehicles fleeing the city, a million lights that turned to pinpoints in the distance. The tall buildings rising from the downtown area were mostly dark.

The last thing, the very last thing in the world Kai wanted his son to go through was a war. He hated the Alliance for starting this. Surely they could have found some way to resolve the dispute. Anything would have been better than this.

It looked as if a storm was coming. On the horizon the stars winked out and the sky grew darker. Kai saw something moving inside the darkness, and that was when he heard the engines. On the causeway, people were fleeing their vehicles, running toward the exit ramps.

The aircraft were deceptively fast. In what seemed no more than a minute, they reached the city. Antiaircraft fire erupted from a dozen locations; tracer rounds rose, along with surface-to-air missiles. Aircraft were hit, but not enough of them. Bombs began to fall. Kai pressed his hands over Errol's ears, knowing it would not be enough to block the sound.

When the first ones hit their targets, it was like thunderclaps. Errol jolted fully awake, squealing in surprise and fear. Kai hugged him, still covering his little ears.

"It's okay. We're okay," Kai said, but Errol wouldn't be able to hear him over the bombs, so he was only consoling himself.

There were a few American fighter jets in the sky, but not many. Most were in Australia. By now some must be on their way back.

Kai watched the Washington Monument fall, disappearing into billowing smoke. The rest of the important buildings were too low for him to see from his vantage point, but he had no doubt they were gone, too. There was only one area that was being spared, just north of downtown. Maybe Logan Circle. The old defender production facility was under Logan Circle.

Kai ducked, held his breath as the planes passed overhead. As he'd hoped, they saved their bombs for riper targets.

What he hadn't anticipated were the parachutes. Defenders hung below black nighttime chutes, dropping in the outskirts of the city. One came down only a few blocks away. He heard shrieking as the defender's automatic rifle roared to life before it even landed among the people fleeing on I-395.

Hardly able to grasp what he was seeing, Kai watched the defender deliver sharp bursts into the backs of fleeing figures, tearing holes in them.

The defender's crazed shout, its maniacal, wide-eyed expression reminded Kai of a thousand clips he'd watched of the Luyten War. If anything, this defender seemed more battle-crazed than those in the clips.

When everyone in range was dead or dying, the defender jogged up the street, toward the city center. He was going to pass right by the building where Kai was hiding.

Errol was screaming. His nose was running, his eyes wide and terrified. Kai tried to shush him, but that only made it worse, so Kai swept Errol up and, keeping as low as possible, carried him to the far end of the roof, praying that the added distance, combined with the explosions in the city center, would prevent the defender from hearing Errol.

After a few moments Kai lifted his head; he could see the defender two blocks away. They were safe, for now.

The downtown area was in flames. Defender bombers continued to pound it. They were doing the exact opposite of what the Luyten did, Kai realized. Where the Luyten took the wilderness, driving people into the cities, the defenders were attacking the cities, driving everyone into the wilderness.

Kai had to get out of the city.

# 55

## *Oliver Bowen*

*June 9, 2045. Sydney, Australia.*

The Harrier set down on the roof of a building that looked mean and unforgiving. Oliver guessed it was the defender equivalent of the Pentagon. The door swung open. Wordlessly, Erik gestured for them to step out, where two armed defenders were waiting.

"She needs immediate medical attention," Oliver said.

Erik grunted, gestured more emphatically for Oliver to step out. He did as he was told, then reached up to help Lila down. She looked hideous, the hair on one side of her head caked with dried blood, her scalp red meat. Her knees nearly buckled as she stepped off the Harrier.

One of the defenders waiting for them took Oliver by the shoulder; the other took Lila by the arm.

"No, we stay together," Oliver said, dragging his feet as the defender pulled him toward a doorway.

Lila's eyes were wide, suddenly alert. She turned toward Erik as the defender pulled her toward an open elevator.

"*Don't you do it*. If you kill him, you might as well kill me, because I won't help you. You know I won't."

Oliver stiffened, and redoubled his effort to get away from the defender holding him.

"*Wait*," Erik called to the defender holding Oliver. "I'll take him."

The defender released Oliver's shoulder.

"Come on," Erik said.

Oliver hurried to catch up with him. "I want to see my companions. Galatea, Sook, Alan. You gave me your word they wouldn't be hurt."

Erik stopped walking. "You want to see your companions? I'll take you to them." He turned, then stormed through the doorway, which led to an immense escalator. Oliver climbed onto it, then had to jump from step to step as Erik, not satisfied to let the escalator carry them along, strode down the stairs.

When they reached the lobby, Erik curled around beneath the steps, crashed through a door, and breezed past a security checkpoint with Oliver running to keep up. They headed to the end of a long hall. Erik pushed open another door that led into a walled courtyard. He held it open for Oliver.

"There you go."

Oliver stepped through the door. Erik slammed it shut behind him. His friends were piled beside a fence, their bodies riddled with bullets.

# 56

# Dominique Wiewall

*July 10, 2045. Colorado Springs, Colorado.*

Everyone stood as President Carmine Wood breezed into the war room, flanked by his brother, the former president Wood, and his wife and chief advisor, the former actress Nora Messina.

Dominique still couldn't believe she'd been flown to Colorado Springs to join strategic command. As far as she knew, no one else on General Willis's invasion team even held federal positions any longer. Maybe as the chief engineer of the defenders she was considered irreplaceable.

She felt a certain sick satisfaction that Willis would end his days as the modern face of incompetence and failure, but she wasn't proud for feeling it. There was nothing good about any of this.

"Good afternoon, gentlemen, ladies," the president said in his nasally voice. He was getting old; there was a noticeable bend at the top of his spine. He'd seemed so much younger seven years ago, when he'd been elected not through his own accomplishments but because of his wildly popular brother, who was credited with helping to turn the Luyten War around when all seemed lost.

"We're losing," the president said with no preamble. He allowed a moment of silence to stretch, to emphasize his words. "But you already knew that."

Yes, Dominique knew that. The defenders held most of the world's major port cities. They held the Panama and Suez Canals. They held Gibraltar and Morocco, so they controlled the Mediterranean Sea. They had superior weapons, maintained air and sea superiority, and held all of the defender production facilities. They didn't sleep; they just kept coming, day and night, wearing down humanity's superior numbers.

Something else had become clear, at least to Dominique: They carried boundless rage toward their creators for designing them so carelessly. Deep down they knew they were fucked-up, that there was something missing at their core. In a very real sense, Dominique was responsible for that rage.

When she'd been charged with creating them, her focus had been 100 percent results oriented. It had never occurred to her to give any thought to the quality of the defenders' lives. She'd designed their hands to shoot and climb, not paint; she'd designed them to be tough and angry, not content.

She'd designed killers.

"During the Luyten War, when things looked their worst, we took decisive action," the president was saying. "I believe it's time for decisive action again." Dominique had missed some of what he'd said. She needed to stay on task.

An aide activated a map of the world. There were yellow circles set over about a dozen major world cities, all of them currently under defender occupation.

"Based on our current intelligence, it will be a matter of

months, if not weeks, before the defenders are able to erect cloaks over the territory they hold and install their spectroscopic nuclear detection technology. Once that happens, our military options become extremely limited."

Dominique leaned forward in her chair, examining the cities with the yellow circles over them. New York, Los Angeles, London, Beijing, Tokyo, Seoul, Moscow, Mumbai, São Paulo, Mexico City. The Alliance couldn't possibly be planning what she thought they were planning.

"All told, the Alliance has seventeen cruise missile submarines on the open waters, doing their best to evade defender naval patrols." President Wood II rested his hand on a table and took a deep, sighing breath, as if he didn't want to say what he needed to say. Surely everyone in the room knew what he was going to say. "We're going to target the defenders' centers of gravity with nuclear strikes while we still can."

No one stated the obvious. There were still millions of people living in those cities under defender occupation. Bombing them meant bombing human civilians.

"The defenders will not be expecting this," the president said.

No, they wouldn't. Neither would the people living there. Dominique listened carefully as Peter Smythe, Wood's secretary of defense, filled in the details. The strikes would kill an estimated 20 percent of the defenders' forces and a quarter of their weapons capability. It would cripple their communications for a short time, during which Alliance ground forces would launch an all-or-nothing assault on their remaining assets.

A woman Dominique didn't know raised her hand. "I'm assuming Premier Santos made this call?"

"The premier is against this action," Wood said. "We're

acting in concert with China, Russia, India, and half a dozen other countries."

There was stunned silence. The Alliance had split? This was worse than Dominique thought.

"Ms. Wiewall," the president said. Dominique raised her head. "How will the surviving defenders react to this action?" he asked.

"I can't answer that question," Dominique said.

"I'm sorry?"

Dominique shrugged. "I'm not a military strategist. Their reaction will be whatever gives them the best chance of defeating us. Your military people will have to advise you on what that would be."

# 57

# *Kai Zhou*

*July 11, 2045. Mapleton, Utah.*

"There they are." Luis pointed at the horizon, where tufts of white smoke rose toward the sky. Kai had been expecting mushroom clouds, like the ones he'd seen in pictures of Hiroshima, but these were thinner, maybe because they were tactical nukes rather than big bombs.

No one said anything as they cruised along Route 89, elbow to elbow in the back of the open troop transport. Even if Kai felt like cheering the deaths of tens of thousands of defenders despite all the human lives that were being snuffed out at the same time, someone within earshot might have loved ones living in Los Angeles.

Kai wondered what he would have done if, when they were informed yesterday about the nuclear strikes, Atlanta had been one of the targets. Would he still be here, willing to fight? No. Not a chance. There would have been nothing he could do to save Errol, but he wouldn't be carrying a rifle now.

He understood that it was necessary. It was still a terrible thing to do.

Kai fingered the plastic sack holding the radiation shield he'd been issued. *They'll help*, Sergeant Schiller had said as they lined up to get one, *but there's no guarantee you won't get sick. I'm not going to lie to you: You probably will get sick. But with the shields, you'll live.* How comforting. In an ideal situation, they would have twenty thousand big, expensive radiation hazmat suits to hand out, but this was not an ideal situation.

The convoy pulled off the highway at the next exit. They passed a shopping center with a Target, an Applebee's, CVS, Golden Dragon Chinese. A little farther along they passed a strip mall. Just beyond it, they turned into a neighborhood, past a big sign that read WINDMILL PLANTATION.

It was one of those endless suburban neighborhoods. The expansive lawns, now nothing but neck-high weeds, must have needed constant watering during the hot summers. Most of the residents had probably worked in Salt Lake City, commuting an hour to work every day. It was long deserted. Everyone had fled during the Luyten War (either that, or the Luyten had killed them), and afterward none of the survivors of the war had reason to return and claim a free house in neighborhoods like this one. There was nothing here, no point in living here. There were plenty of free, fully furnished houses closer to the cities.

"Four to a house," Sergeant Schiller called as the transport ground to a stop.

Kai followed Luis, Shoelace, and Tina toward a big beige house sitting on what must have been two acres. Tina reached the door first, pushed it open, and jumped back with a shriek.

"It's a *nest*."

Kai joined Luis and Shoelace at the door to take a look.

Sure enough, some Luyten had made itself at home. Fabric stretched all over, cutting the room into weird semi-enclosed chambers. He'd seen videos of Luyten nests, but he'd never seen one for real. He stepped past the others and went inside.

"You're sick," Shoelace said. "Seriously ill."

"What?" Kai glanced back at Shoelace. "You afraid a few starfish stayed behind? Maybe one's still hiding out in here?" He ran his fingers over the fabric. It was tight as a drum, and softer than it looked.

"Let's just find a place to sleep," Shoelace said.

Sleep. That was the magic word. Kai followed Shoelace and the others down the driveway, toward the next house. He was so tired. When was the last time he'd gotten even five hours' sleep at once? During basic training? Had they gotten five hours a night during basic? He couldn't remember. And in the morning they were going into a city that had just been nuked. Yes, he needed some sleep.

The next house was fine. Without a word they split up, located bedrooms, and dragged mattresses—still in dusty sixteen-year-old bedding—into the living room.

As Kai lay down, his thoughts immediately turned to Errol and Lila, as they always did, and he felt the now-familiar stab of pain and panic. Were they all right? Kai knew Lila's aunt Ina would protect Errol with her life, but the defenders had overrun Atlanta. Bombs and bullets had flown. Kai had no way to know if they'd survived, and what was happening to them if they had. He was tortured over his decision to report for military service.

Lots of his comrades had young kids, though; that's why they were here, to fight for those kids, for their future.

"Do you ever wonder what would happen if the defenders won?" Tina asked from the mattress to Kai's left.

294

"Come on, shut up. That's the last thing we need to think about," Luis said. He was sitting on the couch, thumbing through a tattered book of comic strips he'd found in one of the rooms.

"I'm just asking. I'm not saying they're gonna. But if they did, what would they do? Would they just be in charge? Like, they get to be the presidents of all the countries, and we don't get to vote?" Tina sounded almost relaxed. All of these people, his friends, seemed to be taking it in stride. Kai could barely stand it; each moment of being here, in this strange house in a strange town, missing his family, filthy, tired beyond anything he'd ever imagined, was torture. The defenders didn't sleep, but people needed sleep or they'd just break down.

Kai was breaking down. He wiped a tear as it rolled to the bridge of his nose. He'd always thought of himself as tough, like steel, forged in the streets of D.C. during the Luyten War. He didn't feel tough now. He felt like that twelve-year-old kid hiding in a bathroom, lost, cold, scared, ready to accept help from anyone, even a starfish.

"I just want to understand what we're fighting for," Tina went on. "They can't put us all in prison camps like we did with the Luyten. There are too many of us. How would they feed us if we were all in prison camps?"

"Would you shut up?" Luis said. "You don't know what you're talking about. Yeah, they're going to build a prison camp the size of Texas and put us all in it."

"*Then what are they gonna do?* That's what I'm asking?"

"*I don't know.* Nobody knows." Luis spit on the carpet, studied the glob of spit for a moment before rubbing his boot over it. He stabbed at his temple with one finger. "They're crazy. They're psycho. There's no telling what they'd do."

The front door swung open. Sergeant Noonan stuck his head inside. "Everybody outside. One minute. Let's go." Then he was gone.

"Oh shit." Tina fumbled with the zipper on her pack, stuffing the things she'd just set out by the mattress back inside.

As Kai lifted his pack and slung it on his back, he wondered, what now? What fresh new hell was coming their way?

They joined their squad outside. Kai watched some of the latecomers, crashing out through front doors and sprinting down driveways so they wouldn't be late.

When everyone was assembled in a loose line on the sidewalk, Sergeant Schiller raised his voice and said, "The stilts are coming. They're making an all-out siege, from both coasts."

Kai exchanged a *Holy shit* look with Shoelace.

"Their bombers are on the way, supported by a fighter squadron. After that, in all likelihood one airborne division, possibly two, will parachute into the area. They're trying to take Salt Lake City and the surrounding area as a jumping-off point for an overland siege of our center of gravity in the Cheyenne Mountain bunker."

"How many will be coming by land after the paratroopers?" someone down the line asked.

"All of them," the sergeant answered.

That got the whole division buzzing. The sergeant waited, hands clasped behind his back, letting the chatter die down naturally.

"So this is it. We must stop them here. Two additional reinforced divisions will be setting up to the north and south of our position. The rest of our western forces are scrambling to intercept the ground forces before they get here. We have a lot to do before they get here, and not much time."

* * *

Kai looked out over the neighborhood. It was teeming with activity. Bulldozers were pushing vehicles into piles to form barriers; the few engineer soldiers they had were setting land mines in the road. Tanks and artillery were spreading out, finding protected spots. Soldiers were dispersing, seeking cover in houses, strip malls, wooded areas. Many wore tan camo, but most were dressed in jeans, stained sweatshirts, work boots, sneakers—whatever clothes they didn't mind getting dirty, or bloody. Many had nothing but a pistol. They hadn't been through even the cursory basic training Kai and his comrades had received. *Shoot at their faces* was probably the full extent of their training.

"We shouldn't have dropped those nukes. It just pissed them off worse." Tina was watching the horizon, where smoke rose from a copse of scrub pines that had been torched to improve sight distance, but her eyes were glassy, unfocused.

She had a star-shaped scar on her temple. Kai wondered how she'd gotten it; he was aware that the thought was bizarre, given the situation, and probably a sign that he was losing his grip.

"It just sped up their timetable," Shoelace said. "They were coming one way or another."

"At least we would have lived a few more weeks," Tina replied. She sounded listless, more depressed than afraid.

Kai waited for someone to contradict her, but Shoelace went on cleaning his rifle, leaning up against the side of the house. Luis was listening to music with earbuds, his head bobbing, eyes closed.

A group of eight or nine terrified people was standing in the weeds nearby. They might have been an extended family—men and women, ranging in age from early teens to their sixties. More volunteers kept arriving all the time, answering a desperate last-minute call.

"When the sergeant said, 'This is it,' he didn't mean the war's over after this, did he?" Tina asked, stubbing out a cigarette on the house's foundation.

"If the defenders overrun our center of gravity and kill the president, drive a wedge through the middle of the country, and meet in the middle..." Kai shrugged. "It's over for the United States, that's for sure."

Tina considered this.

Kai had been watching the recently arrived group out of the corner of his eye. Now two of them broke off and approached: a stocky guy in his forties, and an Asian woman Kai guessed was his wife.

"Excuse me," the stocky guy said. "We're sorry to bother you, but we're not clear about our role here. The officer who briefed us didn't tell us what we're supposed to do."

"Shoot at their faces," Tina said without looking at them, as smoke trailed out of her nostrils.

Kai rose. "Come on." He put a hand on each of the newcomers' shoulders and led them back in the direction of their group. "First, find an empty house, a drainage ditch, some cover to fight from. We're facing a superior force, so we spread out, make them come to us one group at a time." He let them absorb this for a moment before continuing. It was a lot to take in. "The first thing that's going to happen is, you're going to see *our* fighter planes overhead. That means their bombers are close." The two newcomers nodded, looking grateful, and so utterly lost and out of their element. Kai knew the feeling; four months ago he hadn't known a howitzer from a supply truck. "The defenders will have fighters to protect their bombers, and their fighters are more advanced than ours, so that might not go well, depending on how many planes they have and how many we have." Kai pointed at each of the newcomers in turn. "*Don't shoot at the planes.* You're just wasting ammunition. Stay down."

The woman looked up, blinking rapidly, trying not to cry. He knew that feeling, too. There was that moment when you realized this was real, that the defenders really were coming, and they were coming to kill you. Kai gave the woman a moment to get hold of herself, then he went on.

"Soon after that, more planes will come, and defenders will parachute out of them. When you see the defenders coming, that's when you start shooting."

"Go for their faces," the stocky guy said.

"That's right." Defenders were hard to bring down with bullets designed to kill humans, especially given the extensive body armor they wore. Your best bet was a face shot; that way you knew they wouldn't get back up. They were fast. So fucking fast. "Don't move around; movement draws attention to you. Stay put."

Kai raised his eyebrows, waiting for any questions.

"Thank you." The guy held out his hand. "I'm Jaden, by the way." Kai shook Jaden's hand, then shook the woman's hand. Her name was Julie. Jaden and Julie. He wished them luck.

As he walked back toward his friends, Kai heard the fighter jets' engines coming from the east. A moment later they shot past overhead, going to intercept the defenders' aircraft west of their position.

"I'm not as limber as I once was," Shoelace said to Kai as he rejoined his friends. Kai raised an eyebrow, not sure what Shoelace was getting at.

"I'd like to kiss my ass goodbye, but I don't think I can reach it anymore."

Kai burst out laughing, and Shoelace joined in. Kai gave him a hug, and they clapped each other on the back.

They could hear the aerial battle, but couldn't see it. Kai had seen enough of them to know what was happening. The defender fighters were big, almost twice the size of the human model. The defender model looked a lot like the Alliance's YF-23, and what it lacked in maneuverability, it made up for in speed and firepower.

A half hour later, they heard the rumble of bombers. Kai and his friends headed inside the house they'd chosen, to ride out the initial bombing. It was a nondescript house near the center of the development; there was no reason it should be targeted over thousands of others spread over dozens of square miles, but some of them were going to get hit. It was all about odds, an oversized game of Russian roulette.

Slinking over, looking almost apologetic, Jaden and Julie's clan came up behind them.

Tina waved them on. "Come on in, if you're coming."

Anyone who wasn't terrified by the sight of defender bombers on the horizon was afraid of nothing. They were so big, and flew in such tight formation, that it was like a steel storm cloud blanketing the sky. As the air vibrated with the sound of their engines, Kai did what he'd always done in these situations: He closed his eyes and played poker in his mind. He found he could enter a trancelike state if he concentrated hard enough. It didn't eliminate his terror, but it gave him distance from it.

The bombs began to fall. Mobile antiaircraft guns boomed. The newcomers huddled on the floor behind the couch. Lisa was thumbing through a coffee-table book of dog breeds. Luis listened to his music.

Somewhere down the street, a house took a direct hit.

Kai heard pieces of wood and concrete *thunk*ing on their roof. He drew the five of clubs and the eight of hearts, and waited to see the bet. Maybe he would bluff. He did more bluffing in imaginary games, because imagining others playing out a hand wasn't as absorbing as playing the hand himself.

Unbidden thoughts of Lila broke into his game. Kai saw her as she'd been the first time they met, at a genetic engineering conference Oliver had taken him to. Kai had asked to go only because it was in Miami, in February. When Kai saw Lila, trailing behind his dad's friend, Dominique Wiewall, he'd ditched his plans to go to the beach and, to Oliver's confusion and surprise, sat through an utterly incomprehensible presentation just so he could be near Lila. She'd been so wonderfully not what he associated with academic types. Dyed blond hair in dreadlocks, too much eye makeup, her expression daring you, just daring you, to piss her off and see what happened. That night, he'd convinced her to go with him to a poker game.

The silence startled him out of his semi-dream state. He lifted his head, went to look out the windows with the others, at the ruined houses, the leaning mailboxes, the scorched and battered ground. Smoke acted like a thick fog, making it difficult to see more than a few hundred yards, but he could see enough damage to get a sense of where they stood.

"Ninety minutes," Luis said. "I figured they'd be at it until nightfall, at least."

"I think they're in a hurry," Kai said. "It shook them, when we bombed our own people to get them. They thought they knew what to expect from us."

"Yeah, well, they forgot they ain't starfish." Luis pointed at his temple.

Something was unsettling Kai. For a moment he didn't

know what it was, then the sound registered. The low rumble of aircraft.

"Oh, come on," Luis said, crying up at the ceiling. "Can't you give us a few hours first?"

"You talking to God, or the stilts?" Shoelace asked.

"Anyone who'll listen."

Shoelace tilted his head to one side and smiled grimly. "Then you're talking to no one."

They filed onto the back porch and watched the distant transport planes spit defenders. The paratroopers dropped feetfirst, their sky-blue parachutes not deploying until they were close to the ground. Heavy artillery pieces dropped out of one of the planes, their larger parachutes deploying almost immediately.

Kai eyed the tank at the top of the hill, nestled behind the blockade of vehicles the dozers had constructed. Its presence was somewhat comforting.

Shoelace turned to Jaden. "I don't want to be rude, but a dozen shooters in one location is a waste. How about you take your people and set up a few houses down the road?"

When they were gone, Luis and Tina took up positions in upstairs windows. Kai took the back door. Shoelace chose a window facing the front and knocked out the glass with the butt of his rifle. Kai pulled the sliding glass door open; he left the screen closed, figuring it provided a bit of extra camouflage.

"I'd like to say today is a good day to die, but I'm not feeling it," Shoelace said. "Today would be a shitty day to die."

"I'm with you there."

Soon they heard gunfire. It was distant at first, coming from the north. It grew closer.

Then it was everywhere. A thousand battles, going on

simultaneously. That was the way you wanted it if you were facing a superior force—harass the enemy, slow them down.

Before he'd stepped into line the day he'd volunteered to fight the defenders, Kai had zero interest in military strategy. Now it was the only thing that did interest him, besides poker and his family. He figured he had better odds of staying alive if he knew what was going on, and why.

Kai scanned the backyard, watching for movement. There was an in-ground pool back there, the water murky and greenish brown, and a shed too small for a defender to use as effective cover. Beyond that was a line of pine trees, then the backyards of houses facing the other way.

At any minute, the first defenders would appear. They'd likely come along the road in front, but they might come through the back.

"You know what I'm craving right now?" Shoelace asked.

Gunfire erupted from the street in front of the house.

"Do you see anything?" Kai called.

"No."

Kai ran to join Shoelace at the front windows.

The face of a defender appeared over a rooftop across the street. It had climbed onto the roof. One of its eyes closed, the other sighted down a rocket launcher. Kai ducked away from the window as an explosion shook the house. It must have hit the house next door.

Kai went back to the window. Another defender had joined the first, peering from the roof. Everyone in Kai's house held their fire. Shooting at them from this distance would only serve to get the rocket launcher pointed in their direction.

Three defenders broke from between two houses up the street.

The tank at the top of the hill *boomed*; the roof of the

house across the street exploded, shooting wood and black tile into the air.

Kai sprang up, took aim, but the three defenders who'd been on the move were already gone. He ran to the back door and spotted human soldiers in the backyard, running. They passed out of sight. A moment later two defenders appeared in pursuit. Kai raised his rifle, squeezed off a few tight bursts that missed. Then they were gone. They were so fast.

Upstairs, Tina and Luis were firing at something in the street.

Shoelace opened fire, then paused. Cursing, he dove away from the window. Defender bullets ripped through the window, shredding the wall beyond in a wide arc.

Two or three more defenders opened fire on them, their bullets thumping into the front of the house, shattering windows. Kai heard shouted orders outside, then a roar. Outside, the air suddenly grew bright orange.

Smoke poured in through the windows.

"They torched us," Shoelace said as Luis and Tina barreled down the stairs.

"Down," Kai said.

They huddled near the floor by the back door as the room filled with smoke. Kai coughed. His eyes burned. The defenders would pick them off as soon as they stepped outside, but they couldn't stay inside. Kai glanced over his shoulder: The curtains and window frames were burning, the flames climbing the wall.

Luis held up a set of keys on a yin-and-yang key chain. "I found these upstairs. Maybe there's a car in the garage."

It was a chance, at least. They followed Luis, who pulled open a door leading to the garage. Thick, black smoke poured out. Kai yanked up his shirt, covered his mouth and nose, and followed the others, stumbling down wooden steps, blinded by the smoke, coughing uncontrollably, hoping the car was in the garage.

Then it occurred to him: The car had been sitting in the garage, untouched, for fifteen years. There was no way it was going to start. They'd panicked; they hadn't thought it through. He tried to shout to the others, but nothing came except racking coughs.

Crawling on hands and knees, he turned and headed back up the stairs into the kitchen. Dragging himself onto the porch, he curled up in a ball, coughing uncontrollably in the cool air. There was a defender out back, watching the house. The smoke must have covered Kai's exit. He tried to stay perfectly still, hoping the roar of the flames and the crackle of burning wood would muffle his cough, because he couldn't hold it in.

In the kitchen, Kai heard someone else coughing. Keeping low, he ducked inside. Shoelace was sprawled on the blackened linoleum. Kai grabbed his hand and dragged him partially outside.

Through the porch's slatted wood floor, Kai saw that the inner supports beneath the porch were on fire. The porch would go up in a minute or so.

He heard a shout. The defender watching the back of the house hefted his rifle and trotted off. They were moving on.

"We have to go," Kai said, barely recognizing the voice coming from his singed throat. "You ready?"

Coughing furiously, Shoelace nodded once. Kai staggered down the porch steps with Shoelace right behind. They got clear of the fire and dropped to their knees in the grass, still coughing.

"Hold still," Shoelace croaked. "You're on fire." Shoelace smacked at the cuff of Kai's pant leg, extinguishing the flame.

Lifting his head, he looked past Kai. "*Oh, shit.*"

Kai followed Shoelace's gaze. Half a dozen defenders were heading their way. He looked around for somewhere to hide. If they ran, they'd be spotted for sure. The shed was too far, the storage bin for pool supplies too small.

The pool. "Come on."

They crawled through the gate, stashed their weapons along the fence, and slipped into the warm, swampy water.

When the defenders drew close, Kai whispered, "Under," took a deep breath, and ducked underwater.

He couldn't see anything but green silt floating in brackish water. Because good soldiers don't do much talking in the midst of battle, he couldn't count on hearing the defenders pass. His best bet was to hold his breath as long as possible, though not so long that he surfaced gasping for air.

Tina and Luis were dead. It was the first moment he'd had to register that. They were still in the garage. How had all four of them been so stupid? When Kai saw that key in Luis's hand, he'd instantly formed an image of the four of them bursting through the garage door, careening down the street and out of harm's way. In a car that hadn't been started in fifteen years.

Stupid, stupid.

Kai's damaged lungs began to ache. He guessed they'd been under no more than thirty or forty seconds, probably not long enough for the defenders to pass. Worse, he needed to cough. His lungs were twitching, his throat tingling madly.

If he was going to cough, better to do it underwater, where the sound wouldn't carry. He let it go, expelling most of the air from his lungs, then held on a few more seconds before gently lifting his face above the water.

A defender was standing directly over him. Kai took a deep, slow breath through his nose as Shoelace's face surfaced beside him. The defender looked left and right, then moved on.

Two more came into view. Like the first, these two were focused on threats from nearby houses and other areas that provided potential cover; none thought to look in an old swimming pool.

When they were out of sight, Kai and Shoelace pulled themselves out of the pool and retrieved their rifles.

"We should touch base with HQ, find out where we're supposed to rendezvous," Shoelace said as water dripped off him and pattered to the concrete.

Kai took a deep, sighing breath, then looked off at the smoking wreckage. The thought of heading back into that insanity made him want to cry. If they went, they would die. He was certain of that. Kai didn't want to die. He wanted to see his son again, his wife.

It was time to fold, he realized. Time to collect what chips he had left and leave the table. He looked at Shoelace and said, "I think we should find a house that's still standing and crash there until this thing is over."

Shoelace chuckled, but Kai gave him a level look. "No, I'm serious." This war was so big, so complicated, no one would miss two soldiers. "We can get some sleep, read a book."

Shoelace gave Kai a pained look. "Kai, I can't do that. Like the sergeant said, if we don't stop them now, we're not going to."

"We're not going to," Kai said. "We both know that."

"We at least have to *try*." When Kai didn't respond,

Shoelace shook his head, then took a few steps toward the house, which was now nothing but a big bonfire on a concrete foundation. "You know what these stilts are like. You know that better than I do."

"I don't want my son to grow up an orphan the way I did."

"I have *four* kids!" Shoelace shouted. "I'm afraid they won't get to grow up at all." Suddenly his face just fell. He looked at Kai, shook his head slowly, ponderously, then held out his hand.

Kai shook it. "See you again sometime."

"Sure. You know, if the defenders take the area, you'll be caught behind enemy lines."

Kai shrugged. "They won't bother me if I keep my head down."

Shoelace headed in the direction the defenders had gone. Kai watched him walk for a moment, then he went in the opposite direction. He had about two days before the full defender ground force would arrive. By then he needed to be stocked up with food and supplies, and to be in a basement somewhere.

His stomach was a knot of guilt, more for letting Shoelace down than anything else. The rest of them would fare about as well with or without him. As far as he was concerned, he didn't owe them anything.

A half mile away Kai found Jaden, Julie, and their family. There was a stream running under a little bridge on the access road that led into the housing development. They'd taken a position under the bridge. Not a bad move, all in all.

They were all dead.

# 58

# Dominique Wiewall

*July 11, 2045. Colorado Springs, Colorado.*

Orders were shouted. All around the war room, rapid conversations took place. Dominique left her swivel seat as unobtrusively as possible, and went to stand by the exit. Not that she was planning to go anywhere; she just felt like she should get out of the way, because she was of no use in this situation. Worse, she felt as if people were silently asking the back of her head why she'd made the defenders complete psychopaths.

"They're securing oil fields and refineries as they advance on Baghdad," some colonel shouted. He was near the front, looking at a live feed of a tactical map. "Long-range rockets launched from the Persian Gulf have hit the center of gravity in Baghdad. No word on the status of the premier and other leaders working there."

A civilian in a black suit was suddenly at Dominique's side. He offered her a bottle of water. "You all right?"

She accepted the water with a nod of thanks. "I'm just trying to stay out of the way. I'm not of any use in this situation."

Someone shouted to the president. She watched him climb the steps, two at a time, then huddle with two strategists. "To be honest," she said laughing, "I'm not even sure why I'm here. I was on the Australia team."

"Oh, I can answer that, Dr. Wiewall. The operation in Australia was recorded—everything is recorded; we're being recorded right now. The president went over that recording, so he knows who fucked up and who didn't. You didn't."

Dominique laughed harshly. "No, I only *designed* the bloody things. I didn't fuck up at all." If felt good to say it, to get it out in the open.

"You had to be quick. Not to mention, you saved the human race."

She stepped closer, grateful for the words, for a sympathetic ear. "I'm still responsible for what they are. I should have considered what they'd be *like*, not simply how effective they'd be in battle."

The man gave her a kind smile. "I'm not sure you're being fair to yourself."

She offered the civilian her hand. "I'm sorry, I don't know you."

"Forrest Rosenberg. Secret Service."

"Thank you for telling me about the recordings. I feel better, knowing everyone in the room doesn't think I'm an idiot."

"No problem."

# 59

## *Kai Zhou*

*July 11, 2045. Mapleton, Utah.*

A wounded defender lay beside the road. His side was flayed open, his arm gone above the elbow. Shrapnel wounds, from a tank round or a howitzer. Probably a tank. The defender had torn a strip from his pants to use as a tourniquet. The arm that was missing was the one that had held the defender's built-in weapons system. His rifle was nowhere in sight.

"They left you behind?" Kai called from a distance. They just left their mortally wounded behind to die, like they could care less about each other.

"Yes," the defender said. He was in obvious pain. Maybe they were short on morphine and didn't want to waste it on a hopeless case.

"Do you want me to, you know." Kai touched the rifle strapped across his back.

"If you want to kill me, I can't stop you." The defiance, the hostility in his voice, was unmistakable.

Kai held up his hands. "Hey, I didn't mean it as a threat.

I meant, if you wanted me to do it as a favor." Why was he talking to this stilt? Maybe it was just morbid fascination. He'd never spoken to one before. Even lying there, mortally wounded, the thing scared the shit out of him.

He took a few steps closer. "Why are we fighting? I mean, we're supposed to be allies."

"I'm a soldier," the defender said, as if that were all the justification he needed.

Kai nodded. "Fair enough."

The defender licked his thin lips.

"Do you have water?"

"No." He sounded almost embarrassed to admit it.

Kai pulled his canteen from his belt, unscrewed the cap, took a few more steps toward the defender, and underhanded the canteen to him.

He went on his way.

As he walked, it occurred to him that this wasn't the first time he'd provided comfort to the enemy. He laughed out loud. What was it about cold-blooded killers that brought out the maternal instinct in him? Maybe Oliver could explain it.

There must be something about him, though. How many times had he wondered why Five picked him that night? There had been thousands of people within Five's psychic range. Tens of thousands. Yet he'd chosen Kai. What had he sensed in Kai's mind? Was it weakness? Kindness? That Kai was an outsider?

His entire life, everything he was, hinged on Five's decision to choose him. Kai would have died in that bathroom if Five hadn't goaded him into making a fire. If not for Five, he never would have met his father, or Lila. There would have been no Errol. He carried the burden of being the Boy, but what was that, compared to life, a father, a wife?

Yet he still hated the son of a bitch.

It had been such a shock, to learn Five might still be alive, hiding in a bunker with the rest of his kind.

Stepping over a guardrail and cutting down a ravine, Kai headed across the parking lot, toward the shopping center they'd passed on the way in. He kept his rifle at hand, but there was no one in sight, friend or enemy. The two stores on the end of the shopping center had been shelled, probably by the defenders' bombers.

Kai felt more alert, better rested than he had since the day the invasion began. He'd slept fourteen hours straight the night before. With his judgment sound and clear, he felt more certain than ever that he'd made the right call. His allegiance was to his family, and himself, not to the nitwits who'd thought attacking the defenders was a good idea.

As he approached the Target, he reviewed his mental shopping list. Food, if by some miracle there was any left inside. New reading material—fiction, preferably set long ago in some other place. Socks. The house he'd chosen to hole up in had plenty of abandoned clothes, but no warm socks.

He ducked through shattered doors, praying it hadn't been completely looted, and immediately spotted bodies.

They were soldiers, recently killed. One was draped across a checkout lane with big defender bullet wounds in his neck and face. Another, a young woman, was lying facedown in the big center aisle. There were five or six others.

Kai couldn't understand how a defender could fit through the doors to get inside and shoot them. It was a big space with a high ceiling, so once inside a defender could move around, but the entrance was too tight, unless they got down on their bellies and shimmied through the double doors.

He walked the periphery of the store. It grew darker as

he moved away from the front windows, but that was fine with Kai—he'd grown to associate darkness with safety. It reminded him of the early days with Lila. Every weekend he'd take the bus to New York to visit her. For months he stayed in a depressing, smoky hotel room on those visits because Lila wouldn't let him stay over. She lived alone, and she was happy to have sex with him—she just wouldn't let him sleep over. It baffled him for the longest time; all he could think was, she didn't want things to get too serious.

Kai smiled wanly, remembering the night she finally let him stay over. It turned out she slept with all the lights on, the TV blaring old romantic comedies. She'd been embarrassed for Kai to find out.

After a few sleepless weekends in Lila's brightly lit and loud bedroom, Kai tried to convince her to sleep with the TV and lights off. He was there, he'd said. That would replace the lights and TV. She would be safe.

Lila got angry. Everyone was fucked-up in some way, she'd said. Everyone coped in their own fashion. She wasn't going to give up the things that comforted her, so if they were going to have a future together, they'd have to find a solution that didn't involve turning the lights out.

When she'd finished, Kai was speechless. It was the first time Lila had suggested there was a "they," and a potential future for them, and Kai had been dumbfounded with happiness. Lila took his silence for anger and said, "Are you saying you weren't damaged by the war, that you don't have any scars?"

Kai couldn't keep from laughing. "Lila, I'm the Boy Who Betrayed the World, remember? What do *you* think?"

He bought earplugs and a sleep mask, and moved in.

There were big doors in the back, to cart pallets out of the delivery area using a forklift. Kai checked the delivery area to make sure there were no unfriendlies skulking around. He was about to start shopping when he heard a voice.

Catching the door before it shut, he went back inside and spotted a soldier looking up at him from the floor. She was lying at one end of a thirty-foot-long bloody streak. She'd dragged herself along the floor that far.

Kai squatted beside her. She'd taken three or four shots to her thighs and lower abdomen, the oversized bullets taking pieces out of her.

"Can I have a drink of water?"

Kai had left his canteen with the defender. He sprang up. "I'll get some."

He pulled a canteen off one of the bodies, found a medic's bag on one of the others, and grabbed that as well. On the way back, he called HQ to request a medic. They didn't mention him being AWOL; in all likelihood they'd lost track of him, thought he was dead. They told him they couldn't afford to send one, so he would have to bring the wounded soldier back to them.

What was he supposed to do, pull her in a little red wagon? She was middle-aged, Indian or Middle Eastern. Kai helped her roll onto her back. When she'd managed a few gulps from the canteen, he set it aside.

"I told them I was a stockbroker," she said, gasping. "They said that meant I was smart, so I should be in demolition."

"I told them I was a gambler. They gave me a rifle."

She didn't laugh.

"What's your name?" Kai asked.

"Sudha. Are they all dead?"

Kai nodded.

"I couldn't reach it," she said, her voice a hoarse whisper.

"Reach what?"

315

"It was all set." She looked at the ceiling. "Shit. It was all set."

Kai looked up, tried to see what she was looking at, but it was too dark. The only light in the room came from an open bay door.

"Then they got Aiken, and I couldn't reach it."

He looked at the blood streaked across the floor. She'd been trying to reach something. He followed the line in the direction she'd been going, and saw another soldier, dead, lying beside a forklift.

Demolition. *It was all set.* "You wired the store with C-4?" he guessed.

Sudha swallowed, nodded.

Kai pointed at the body. "Aiken had the detonator, but he was killed, and you couldn't reach it in time."

She nodded again.

They were going to lure defenders into the store, go out the front, and blow the roof down on top of them. But the defenders caught them before they were ready.

"How are we doing out there? Are we holding them off?" Sudha asked.

Kai nodded vaguely. He had forgotten about the medic's bag. He rummaged through it, found some pre-dosed morphine shots, and gave one to Sudha.

"Where's the detonator?" Kai asked.

"His comm. Push SEND and..." Sudha mimicked the sound of an explosion.

Kai unpacked the medic's kit and did what he could, which was to cut Sudha's uniform away from the bullet wounds, pack the wounds, and cover them with bandages. Despite how many he'd seen in the past five months, he still hated the sight of wounds.

"I called for a medic, but they said they couldn't get one out here just yet. We're on our own for now."

Sudha didn't seem surprised. "A lot of wounded."

It was getting dark. Kai went inside the store and gathered some bedding. He made Sudha as comfortable as he could, gave her a second shot of morphine, then spread out a pile of blankets for himself.

"You going to try to get some of them?" Sudha asked as they lay in the near darkness.

"I'm thinking about it." He hadn't been. Not consciously, anyway. Now a sick dread blossomed in him as he realized he was. He could devise some way of luring them inside while he hid outside.

"If I'm...not here when they come, turn on the generator. It's hooked to lights and a portable stereo at the front of the store. If I'm around, I can draw them in."

"Sudha, I'm not going to use you as live bait. I'll get us both out of here."

"I want to die." Her tone was almost scolding. "My children are dead. I signed up so I could get killed."

Kai didn't know what to say. He still wasn't going to prop her up with a rifle and leave her here while he hid outside with a detonator. He wasn't even sure he was going to try this.

When Kai woke, it was still dark outside, and Sudha was dead. It took him a moment to realize what woke him: engine noises, growing louder. Kai pulled a blanket over Sudha's face, then took his flashlight and went over to her friend Aiken. He found the comm. The SEND key was painted red.

If he was really going to do this, he needed to get to work.

An alternative plan would be to hide in a pile of clothes

until they were gone. Then he could find a little red wagon and use it to haul the generator back to the house where he was staying. He could watch movies until the war was over.

Glancing one last time at Sudha, Kai killed his flashlight and trotted toward the front of the store, as the defender vehicles approached, sounding like a hundred Harley-Davidsons revving. He ducked as powerful spotlights painted sections of the store white.

Squatting behind a checkout counter, Kai peered out at the front parking lot. He counted seven defenders—likely a reconnaissance team coming in advance of the main ground force.

If he turned on the generator, they'd have to go around to the back and make their way to the front of the store. That's when he'd slip out the front and blow the roof. The problem with that plan was, not all of them would go inside. Soldiers would be stationed at the front and back entrances. The demolition team's plan was to turn on the generator before the defenders arrived, then hide somewhere outside, out of sight. It was too late for Kai to do that.

No—better to go with the alternate plan. Hide, then haul away the generator. Kai headed toward Men's Clothing.

He spied a side door—a fire exit. The defenders might miss that one. He could turn on the generator, wait for them to get into position, then slip out the side door.

He shifted from one foot to another, unsure. Five or six fewer defenders wasn't going to turn the tide of the war.

If that was the case, why had he volunteered in the first place? He could have stayed with Errol. Had it all been to avoid the shame, the disdainful looks of people who wondered why a healthy twenty-eight-year-old wasn't fighting? Not entirely. He was a pragmatist, but not a complete cynic.

He believed in the social fabric that bound him to others. He just wasn't sure he believed in it strongly enough to die for it.

The comm sat in his sweaty palm. To hide felt like a betrayal of Sudha and the others who'd died after rigging the C-4. Of course, he was the Boy Who Betrayed the World. Betrayal was his specialty. Wasn't that why he'd gone AWOL?

He headed for the generator, moving as quickly as he could in the near darkness.

Running his hands over it, he located the power switch. Before doubts and second thoughts could creep back in, he flipped it.

A bank of overhead lights flipped on, blinding him. Music blasted from a stereo near the front windows. He recognized it—a Frank Sinatra song, "Baubles, Bangles, and Beads."

Bent at the waist, Kai sprinted for the side door, marveling at the synchronicity of hearing Sinatra at this moment. Lila loved Sinatra. For some reason she loved old hokey 1940s music. At first he'd made fun at her antique taste, but in time it had grown on him.

Easing the side door open, Kai looked outside, just in time to see five defenders whizz by in a transport vehicle. On the main road beyond, dozens more defender vehicles were winding along the main road, almost bumper to bumper. He wondered how he was going to get out of there.

First, he had to get out of the store. Kai heard muffled footsteps, then the creak of the big swinging doors that separated the main store from the back. Defenders were in the store with him. From the open side door, he looked left and right. He didn't see any defenders, so he slipped out, eased the door shut, then raced across the parking lot and ducked behind a van.

Keeping his head low, Kai moved from vehicle to vehicle,

heading toward the front of the store. Soon he could see two defenders guarding the front entrance, rifles ready, peering inside. Sinatra was singing "Between the Devil and the Deep Blue Sea."

Heart pounding, Kai looked at the comm. If he was going to do it, it had to be now. Ducking as low as he could behind a big black pickup truck, he pressed the detonator.

Nothing happened.

"*Shit.*" They were demolition people, for Christ's sake— how could they have screwed up something as crucial as a detonator? Kai pressed the key again, and again. It was no use. He tried to think of reasons why it might not be working. Usually the solution to a mechanical problem was something simple and obvious.

The comm's light lit when he pressed the SEND key, so it had power. Was he too far away? That could be it; he was a good two hundred yards away.

With every muscle clenched in anticipation of discovery, Kai lifted his head, saw the two defenders peering into the store, probably puzzling over the dead bodies and sudden music.

He bolted from behind the truck and ducked behind a Toyota thirty feet closer. He tried the detonator. Nothing.

He ran for another car, fifty feet closer to the store. One of the defenders turned to speak to his companion just as Kai ducked. Heart hammering, Kai steeled himself, expecting a shout of discovery, the roar of rifle fire, but it remained quiet.

He pointed Aiken's comm at the Target, tried the detonator again.

The explosion startled him. Pillars of fire erupted from under the eaves of the store's roof, then the roof dropped out of sight, as if it had been pounded down by a giant fist.

The defenders outside the store were thrown backward by the blast. One slammed into their transport; the other landed on the ground on his back as steel, wood, and plaster rained down.

Maybe Kai should have felt elated, but in that moment all he felt was scared. He'd made his presence known, and now they'd be looking for him. He needed to hide. The car he was hiding behind was locked. Looking around, he spotted a row of vehicles that had been melted by a Luyten heater gun years earlier and no one had ever bothered to haul away. He raced over as the defenders' second transport vehicle came roaring around from behind the stores. The driver was the lone passenger.

Kai chose a white Honda minivan. The back half of the van was badly melted, the back tires nothing but puddles around the rims, but the front was intact and open. As he shut the door, he heard a shout that curdled his insides.

The transport vehicle roared toward him.

They'd spotted him, or maybe spotted the movement of the closing door. He should have crawled under a vehicle, he realized, not inside.

Could he surrender? He'd never heard of defenders taking prisoners. Kai watched as the defender trained his rifle on the van, waiting to get close enough for a clear shot.

Kai dove across the front seat, threw open the passenger door, and rolled out as gunfire tore through the van, rocking it. The windows blew out, raining glass down on Kai.

He crawled along the row of vehicles, seeking cover, an angle from which to return fire with the pathetic rifle dangling from a strap on his back. When he reached the end of the row he looked for the other two defenders. He spotted one, moving along the row, bent, looking for Kai. Kai turned to make a run for cover. The other defender was blocking his way, rifle raised.

Kai put his hands up and opened his mouth to tell this giant towering over him that he'd had enough, that he was ready to fold.

The rifle roared. Bullets hit him, like teeth tearing into his shoulder, his hip, his thigh. The impact spun him around, then the ground seemed to come up and catch him. He thought he would pass out, but he didn't; he just lay there panting.

"How many were in there?" he heard one of the defenders ask. The defender sounded far away.

"Four."

"What about the one who was outside with you?"

"He's not hurt too bad."

"Get him and let's go."

They drove away. In wide-eyed shock, Kai took in his own body. His right side was nothing but raw, open meat. It hurt. He knew it was going to get much, much worse, unless he died first.

Most of his right hand was gone. He pulled out his phone with his left, called Shoelace. It rang long enough for Kai to suspect Shoelace was dead, then, miraculously, Shoelace answered.

"Kai. What's up?"

"I'm in bad shape, Shoelace." The pain—the real pain—suddenly kicked in, all at once. It was worse than he'd expected. It was blinding, intolerable. "I'm shot, like, three or four times."

"Oh, shit. Are you near help?"

"I'm way behind the lines. I just wanted to tell you, I got some of them. Four of them. Blew a roof down on them."

"That's killer, Kai. Good for you." Shoelace sounded like

he was crying. "Where are you, buddy? I'm gonna come and get you."

"That's really nice of you." Kai grunted as another truly hellish wave of pain lanced through his side. His hand, or what was left of it, was still mostly numb. "I'd appreciate that."

Kai got most of the way through telling Shoelace where to find him before he blacked out.

# 60

## Lila Easterlin

*July 13, 2045. Sydney, Australia.*

Lila took a break from her work and went to the single window in her office/jail cell. From forty defender-sized stories high, she could see much of Sydney, stretching to the river and beyond. It looked just as it had when the last of the Alliance forces had fled or been killed. As far as she could see, not one shard of glass had been swept. The streets were mostly deserted, the bulk of the defender population off fighting elsewhere.

Elsewhere. Lila had only a vague idea where that might be. The Internet she had access to was a static Internet—a snapshot in time the defenders uploaded just before they began knocking out the power sources that allowed the Internet to function. It told her nothing about what was happening in the outside world. Everything she knew came from the bits of news Erik chose to share.

Time to get back to work. She was monitored at all times and didn't want some defender poking his head in to tell her to get back to work. They never threatened; they just told her what was expected of her. The threat was implicit.

Sitting at her human-sized desk in front of her human-sized computer, Lila considered the files she'd compiled—the first steps toward creating a defender production facility in Sydney. Erik assured her the personnel she'd need to actually construct and run a functional production facility would eventually join her.

That certainly set her mind at ease.

She kept thinking of Kai dropping food into that church basement. *The Boy Who Betrayed the World.* Now here she was, drawing up plans to create more of the creatures her species was at war with. They were quite the couple.

Ironically, she was able to draw most of the information she needed from the Internet. Project Defender had been top secret during the war, but because it had been a truly global effort, detailed specifications for the project had been made available to the world scientific community after the war. It was all there, right down to the genetic codes.

She knew her cooperation was all that kept her and her colleagues alive, so as far as she was concerned, she didn't have a choice. Maybe the heroic thing to do was to let the defenders torture her as she steadfastly refused to cooperate, but she didn't have it in her to be that kind of hero. Her hope was that the information she was gathering would never be put to use.

If they'd only let her make changes. She kept coming back to that. She would do this work gladly, enthusiastically, *tirelessly* if they'd let her improve on the design. But no; other humans would check her work, and if it was discovered that she had tampered with their genetic code in any way... The threat was implicit.

There was a knock at her door, which meant Erik was paying her a visit, because no one else knocked.

"Come in."

"How are you today?" Erik asked as he let himself in.

"I'm lonely, and I'm worried about my people, and yours." She always gave the same answer, yet Erik kept asking.

"I'll have to find time in my schedule to visit more often. I don't want you to be lonely."

Lila had decided Erik was simply incapable of grasping that loneliness involved yearning not just for company, but for the company of specific people.

"How nice," she said.

Erik made himself comfortable in the plush defender-sized seat near the window. He planted all three of his feet firmly on the floor, as a warrior does. There was no more banter between them, no playful moments.

"Our most renowned philosopher has come out with a new treatise."

"Oh? Is this Ravi?"

Erik seemed pleased. "You remember him. His new treatise argues that when you created us, you left out the things you value most in yourselves."

"What would those be?"

"Your capacity for joy, humor, and affection. Ravi refers to them as the three pillars of madness. He argues that we're superior for lacking them."

Lila folded her arms, stared at the slate-gray carpet. They knew there was something missing in them, and they were angry about it. Maybe they had a right to be. She had no energy for this; she was tired of carrying the weight of how carelessly the defenders had been designed. She'd been fifteen and running for her life at the time.

"Maybe you are superior for lacking them. I don't know. What I do know is you lack them because your brains lack serotonin, and they lack serotonin because it renders Luyten incapable of reading your minds. Like your third leg, there was a reason for the design decision."

Erik grunted, folded his arms, mirroring her posture.

"How are my colleagues?" Lila asked.

"They're well." Erik wouldn't tell her where they were, what they were doing. All she knew was one of them had admitted that the emissaries knew the invasion was being considered. Lila couldn't imagine any of them divulging that information, except through torture.

"Can I see my father-in-law? Just for a few minutes?" After every meeting with Erik, she promised herself that next time she wouldn't beg. But she was so lonely; so scared and depressed.

"I've told you, if any of you were to go out in public, you'd be torn apart."

"Yet *you* don't tear me apart."

"Because I know you. I know you're not the same as the rest of them."

Maybe it was inevitable. No matter how much you admired a people, when you went to war with them you so quickly learned to hate everything about them.

# 61

# Dominique Wiewall

*July 15, 2045. Colorado Springs, Colorado.*

When President Wood announced that the covert operation to take out the defenders' center of gravity at Easter Island had failed, the room went silent.

Dominique hadn't realized just how much hope she'd staked on a few dozen elite Alliance forces. She wondered what went wrong, how they'd been discovered before making it into the underground complex to detonate the nuclear device.

That was to be their game changer: take out the defenders' high command, throw them off balance. It had been a brilliant and psychologically fascinating move on the defenders' part, to take Easter Island, reinforce it, and make it their center of gravity.

Dominique rubbed her eyes, which were burning from lack of sleep. The war just went on and on; there was never an opportune time to sleep, and hadn't been for the past five months. Mostly, Dominique slept in her chair in the war room.

"We have to find a way to get populations in occupied territories to rise up," Peter Smythe said. He punched his palm. Smythe had been a baseball star, once upon a time. Despite that, he wasn't an arrogant dickhead. Dominique appreciated that. "That's the defenders' weakness: The forces they leave behind to hold captured territory are wafer-thin. If they had to keep backtracking to put down insurrections, we could wear them down."

Trying not to show the exasperation she felt, Dominique went to the back for more coffee. They'd been broadcasting pleas for resistance to the captured populations almost from the start, but the defenders were ruthlessly effective at making gruesome examples of anyone caught listening to those pleas, let alone plotting resistance.

With the coffee warming her hand through the Styrofoam cup, Dominique studied the big map at the front of the room. The defenders were positioning themselves to storm their facility, as well as Alliance headquarters in Baghdad. Those were their two primary targets. So far, Alliance forces were repelling the defenders in both locations, but the defenders were choking off supply routes, and once those were under defender control...well, you can't fight without food and fuel.

"How are you holding up?" It was her Secret Service guardian angel, Forrest.

"Tired. Depressed." She looked up at him. "They're my children. At the end of the day the defenders are my children, and they've done unspeakable things. You know?"

Forrest put a hand on her shoulder and squeezed. His touch felt good, nourishing. "I don't think you can think about it like that. The mistake was provoking them, not making them."

Dominique nodded, wiped a tear from the end of her nose. "I think we're all well past our breaking point. Hang on. We'll get through this."

"Somehow," Dominique whispered.

"Somehow."

# 62

# Kai Zhou

*July 15, 2045. Provo, Utah.*

"Kai? Come on, Kai, you have to get up."

Kai didn't want to wake up. Waking meant returning to the pain—the relentless, maddening pain. But someone was tugging on his cheek, pulling him awake, away from his only means of escape. Whoever it was had better have a very good reason.

"Let's go. You have to get up."

Kai opened his eyes. The pain was there, waiting for him.

"Come on." It was Evelyn, the nurse who was playing the part of MD and chief surgeon in the tent that was playing the part of hospital in this nightmare farce. Evelyn put a hand behind his head and lifted, as if she were trying to get him out of bed, which was absurd.

"What are you doing?" he groaned.

"You have to get up. Right now. You have to walk out of here."

Although there was no morphine running through Kai's

veins, because there was no morphine at this mobile hospital, Evelyn's face was hazy and swimming as it hung over him. "What are you talking about?"

Evelyn lowered her voice. "There are three defenders outside. They're going to burn the hospital. If you can walk out under your own power, that means you're strong enough to work, which means you can live. Do you understand what I'm saying?"

Suddenly Kai was wide awake. His wounds were throbbing exquisitely, simply at the thought of standing and walking.

He lifted his head and looked at his wounds more carefully than he'd been willing to before. Most of his right hand was gone. The bandage over his thigh sagged in the middle where there was a hole that resembled a crater. His shoulder was only partly there. There was just no way.

Only, he could see in Evelyn's eyes that he had no choice.

"I have to keep moving, we don't have much time. *Get up*." She hurried away.

Gritting his teeth against the grinding pain, Kai slid over to the left side of the cot—on his uninjured side. It wasn't too bad as he let his left foot slide out from beneath the sheets and drop until it reached the dead grass on the floor.

When he tried to swing his right leg around, blistering pain shot up his thigh, across his side. Gasping, every fiber in him not wanting to do this, he let his right leg drop until it touched the ground, and grimaced as fresh pain shot up the leg.

He took a moment, allowed the worst of the pain to recede, then used his good hand to push himself upright.

He screamed, then realized the defenders might hear him. He bit his lip, staggered to his feet, putting most of his weight on his left leg as tears rolled down his cheeks.

The world grew fuzzy—he was passing out. "No. No." If he passed out he'd never wake up. He took a few deep, whooshing breaths, trying to clear his head.

"Okay," he hissed. He took a step on his bad leg, and immediately shifted the weight back to his good leg. He felt blood dribble down his pant leg, off his shoe and into the yellow grass in a series of streams. He didn't know which wound it was coming from. Maybe all of them. He took another step, stifled a scream that instead turned into a high mewling, then grabbed the end of the next cot to steady himself.

There was a man lying in the cot, his eyes open, watching Kai. A tube trailed from the man's chest, draining blood. Avoiding eye contact, Kai took two more steps, leaving the man behind.

If anything, it got harder as he went. His limited energy quickly became depleted, and his injured leg dragged. Two defenders were waiting, one on either side of the door as he staggered out of the tent, covered with sweat, trailing blood, gasping from the pain.

The defender on the left said, "You—go back inside." Kai stared straight ahead and kept walking, not sure if the defender was speaking to him, and not wanting to find out.

"*You*," the defender barked. Reluctantly, Kai looked up, saw the defender staring down at him. "Go back inside."

"I'm fine," Kai stammered. "I can work."

"With one hand?"

"I can—" Kai tried to think. What could he do with one hand? What would the defenders value?

His pulse slowed as it came to him. He looked the defender square in the eye and said, "I'm a nuclear physicist. I worked at the North Anna Power Station, in Virginia."

The defender studied him for a long moment, then motioned him to step to one side. "Wait there."

Kai waited, remaining on his feet through sheer force of will. He'd never even been inside a nuclear power plant. Hopefully the people he was assigned to work with would cover his ass until he figured it out.

# 63

## Dominique Wiewall

*July 15, 2045. Colorado Springs, Colorado.*

It had taken Dominique less than twenty minutes to stuff her belongings into a rucksack, but when she reached the hangar, the transport plane was already on the tarmac, its engines revving. Trying to tamp down rising panic (and the irrational, childlike voice in her head saying they were leaving her behind on purpose, as punishment), she swung the bag over her back, put her head down, and ran. Surely they wouldn't leave people behind. Of course, they were leaving everyone behind; all of the soldiers defending the facility, all of the noncrucial facility personnel they couldn't fit in the transport plane. They were leaving them here to die. The defenders had their underground command complex surrounded. Anyone still inside was going to die.

"Come on, let's go." Forrest was standing at the bottom of the stairs, waving her up. She hustled inside, took a seat along the wall. The president, his wife, his brother Anthony the ex-president, and a dozen others were already strapped in, but there were still plenty of empty seats. She wasn't late; it was a relief to know she hadn't been holding up the flight.

Soon others were rushing across the tarmac: Smythe, the secretary of defense; President Wood's adult daughter, Solyn. Meryem Cevik, chief of the Secret Service, was the last. They were in the air by the time she was in her seat.

They climbed at a steep angle; there were no windows nearby, so Dominique couldn't see what was going on. That was probably a good thing; if they were going to be shot down, Dominique didn't want to know in advance.

As the plane leveled off, so did Dominique's pulse. The president and his inner circle left their seats almost immediately, retreating toward the cockpit.

They weren't ever going back to the United States. No one had said that out loud, but Dominique knew that if the president was fleeing to the Arctic, things weren't going to turn around. How could they, at this point? The defenders had dispatched troops from Turkey to the south, Iran to the west, and Syria to the east, and were closing in on the UN command complex in Baghdad. They controlled the seas, the air. They controlled 90 percent of the world's power sources.

She'd engineered the defenders to be vicious warriors, brilliant tacticians, so they could defeat the Luyten and save the world. She'd designed them too well. And too poorly.

"Dr. Wiewall?" Forrest set a hand on her shoulder. "The president would like to see you." With the buzz of the engine vibrating underfoot, Dominique made her way to the front of the plane.

The president and his advisors were standing around a technician operating a shortwave radio that was now their sole means of communicating with Central Command in Baghdad. He looked up as Dominique entered the war room.

"Dr. Wiewall, the premier has asked for your assistance in drafting a peace proposal to present to the defenders."

Dominique nodded. She was not surprised by this news. She'd learned a few things standing around war rooms for the past few months, and one of those things was that once you can't resupply your center of gravity and your troops, it is time to surrender.

# PART III
# OCCUPATION

# 64

## *Kai Zhou*

*October 8, 2047. Washington, D.C.*

The defender watched the dealer turn the card. Kai watched the defender, who sat up straighter in his chair and licked his lips. Now Kai knew both of the defender's hole cards. They were so absurdly easy to read, so clownishly bad at masking their reactions.

"Bet twenty-five thousand." The defender, whose name was Sidney, slid oversized chips into the pot with his clawed fingers. The motion aired out Sidney's armpit, causing his stress-stink to waft in Kai's direction. When defenders were nervous they sweated profusely, and the stink was incredible.

Kai called the bet. This was a good hand to lose. It wouldn't be obvious, given that Kai had a smaller two pair. He saw the bet and raised forty thousand, not worried about scaring Sidney into folding, because defenders didn't know what the word meant. If they had a bad hand, most of the time they tried to bluff. They hated losing. Everyone hated losing, but defenders had turned sore losing into an art form. Kai had seen it once firsthand, when a defender named Francois had crushed Pete Sheehy's head after Sheehy wiped him out with a bluff. What a horrible thing that had been—as bad as anything Kai had seen in the war.

Kai flipped his cards, feigned disappointment as Sidney revealed his paired king-ten, and watched as the defender gleefully raked in the pot.

"You're a Poker World Series champion," Sidney said.

"Yes, I am."

"I'm an outstanding player, if I can beat you."

"That would follow, yes." The other human players at the table might have picked up the slightest hint of sarcasm in Kai's tone, but they wouldn't dare smirk. Kai's own face generated nothing but earnestness as he looked up at Sidney.

If Kai had known from the outset how much defenders revered poker, he could have saved himself the stress of spending two months working at a nuclear power plant with no idea what he was doing. He really owed the people at that plant; they'd risked their lives covering for him.

Kai shifted to the left, then the right, trying to find a position that made his hip and side ache less. Sometimes it was hard for him to believe he was not yet thirty years old. He felt eighty.

Sidney raised old Paul Heller's bet fifty thousand, proclaiming the raise with such ham-handed bravado that even a hamster would know he was bluffing. Kai folded.

He had probably been safer as a fraud in a nuclear power plant than he was playing poker with defenders. Once in a while you had to beat them, or they'd suspect you were patronizing them and they'd kill you. But you'd better be sure they were in a good mood when you beat them, or else they'd kill you then, too.

"Poker is war, disguised as a game," Sidney proclaimed, apropos of nothing, as he raked in the pot after Paul folded.

Head down, Kai restacked his dwindling pile of chips. He still found it difficult, stacking chips and handling cards with only his left hand. Maybe he always would.

Poker wasn't war; war was war. And if you lost a war, you'd better let the victors beat you at poker.

Kai's phone vibrated. He checked it, saw it was a message from Lila.

> Erik and I are going to dinner tonight. Can you pick
> up Errol?

It was so stupid, so pointless to be jealous, to feel angry at Lila for a situation she could not possibly control. Yet that's what Kai felt as he read the message. Erik had turned their marriage into an incredibly dysfunctional sort of polyamory.

Yes, he punched, taking his frustration out on the keys. He wanted to say more, but there was always the risk that Erik, or some defender at ultra-paranoid Central Command screening messages for subversive content, might read his message. Another night of babysitting while his wife and her platonic lover went out on the town. Kai wasn't sure how much more of this he could stand, but in the new order of things, he had no choice but to stand it.

# 65

## *Lila Easterlin*

*October 8, 2047. Washington, D.C.*

It was stupid, but Lila found herself getting choked up watching the demolition of Disney World on her computer. Maybe it was because Disney World so perfectly represented the modern human world, with its combination of commercial crassness and creative audacity. She watched bulldozers flatten snack bars, wrecking balls topple Cinderella's Castle and the monorail. Did the defenders really need to supersize Orlando in that direction, or were they trying to make a statement about how childish humans were? She took a big swig of coffee; she was hoping the caffeine would kill the pounding headache she had. She'd stayed up too late, drinking too much and popping too many pills.

It was stupid that the destruction of Disney World was bothering her. The real tragedy was the destruction of all those works of art at the Met, MoMA, the Louvre, on and on, to make room for defender artwork. They could have removed the human works of art instead of destroying them, but who was going to question defenders' instructions?

Even with all of that space devoted to defender artwork, nothing of Erik's was on public display. It gave Lila childish pleasure, yet she also felt sorry for him. That was the difference between how she and Kai felt about the defenders: They both hated them, but Lila also pitied them. Maybe if she'd been shot by a defender, and dealt with the pain Kai dealt with on a daily basis, she'd find it hard to pity them.

"Lila? You ready?" Minka stood in Lila's defender-sized doorway.

"Sure." She closed the feed on the demolition, grabbed her phone, and joined Minka in the hall. "Who's doing the review?"

"Pierre."

Lila groaned inwardly. Pierre was a walking neurosis. Lila wasn't sure if defenders were capable of developing PTSD, but something had to account for how far from the defender norm Pierre was when it came to being tightly wound.

Pierre was waiting outside the delivery room (as they referred to it when no defenders were present). "How many?" he asked as they approached.

"Eight hundred," Lila replied.

"Eight hundred exactly?"

"Eight hundred exactly." Eight hundred more defenders, with their dead souls and sociopathic narcissism. With the advances in genetic engineering made between the end of the Luyten War and the beginning of the Defender Ascension (as the defenders had named it), Lila could have engineered them to be so much more stable, if they'd let her. But no. The new defenders couldn't be in any way superior to the existing ones.

Lila and Minka followed Pierre down concrete stairs to the parade floor, where the new defenders were lined up, ready for review.

She should kill herself. Blow her brains out, or jump from a bridge. More of these monsters only added suffering to the world. If she wasn't such a coward, if she didn't love Kai and Errol so much, she would remove herself from the equation. They would get someone else to oversee production at this facility, but that rationalization was wearing thin for her. Lately she felt so disgusting most of the time. Most humans who learned what she did for a living shared her contempt for herself.

Other officers tended to strut around during a review, making it more a ceremonial show than a true inspection, but Pierre looked the new defenders up and down as if expecting some to be missing fingers, or major organs.

Lila waited by the door for more than an hour before Pierre finally nodded his approval. "Brothers," he called, "welcome to the world."

Lila and Minka stood aside as the new defenders paraded past, five at a time, up the stairs to join the hellish world they'd all created together.

Lila dropped her purse on the kitchen counter and headed for her room. She had twenty minutes to get ready to go with Erik to this thing, whatever it was.

"Lila?" Erik called from his room. "Is that you? Come here, please."

"Coming." She always felt uneasy, being alone in the house with Erik. It made her feel too much like his wife.

He was lying on the bed, wearing what looked like a giant pair of boxer shorts, his artificial legs on the bed beside him.

He looked less than imposing lying there, his stumped flesh-and-bone legs ending just below the knee, the last few inches of his legs deeply notched to accept the bionic appendages, his friction sores salved.

"Can you help me with these?"

"Sure."

She clamped and locked his limbs into place as gently as she could, trying not to aggravate the open sores. The fit was never perfect, and friction was inevitable. The arms weren't as bad.

# 66

## Dominique Wiewall

*October 8, 2047. Ellesmere Island, Nunavut, Canada.*

She hated the cold. Absolutely despised it. She'd turned down a postdoc at UMass in favor of LSU solely because it was warm in Louisiana and cold in Massachusetts. That she might live out the rest of her life in the northernmost outpost on Earth was a biting irony.

As she did at the start of every information-gathering session on the Internet, she checked her sister's Facebook page. There was nothing new. Richelle was still working on a construction project for the defenders in Sarasota, Florida, building a government office facility, working right alongside Luyten. As always, Dominique had to resist the urge to leave an anonymous message that only Richelle would understand, to let her know Dominique was still alive. She'd never actually do it, of course. If by some wild chance the defender intelligentsia checked her account that day and realized what the message was, they could trace the computer's IP address, and ultimately discover that the computer in question was issued to CFS Alert, the northernmost continually inhabited outpost in the world, one of those out-of-the-way locales they hadn't bothered to formally conquer. Dominique wondered why they couldn't have fled to some out-of-the-way Polynesian island. There were plenty of those the defenders hadn't bothered to conquer, either.

With her daily check on Richelle out of the way, Dominique got to work, starting with a check of the *New York Times*. Most of it was fluff now, stories of pets finding their way home from a thousand miles away, coverage of construction projects, details of the planned changeover in the NFL from human players to defenders. Very little helpful information. No one put anything helpful in writing; the president and his people assumed significant communication was happening the old-fashioned way: face-to-face. That left the good people hiding out at CFS Alert frustratingly uninformed.

Dominique wasn't sure what good it would do them to be informed. There were fewer than fifty people at CFS Alert. They had no weapons to speak of, no army to command. The war was over. They'd lost. Still, they were one of the last vestiges of free human leadership, of legitimate human authority, and they had zero information.

Dominique lifted her hot cocoa, blew on it, took a sip. It was powdered and not very good, but how much was she going to miss it when it was gone? They would deplete their food stores by spring, by which time they'd have to know how to live off the land. Dominique shuddered at the thought of dried seal blubber for breakfast. They should fly south and surrender. Only they couldn't, because they'd be executed for fleeing, and for being important and powerful people. No, what they needed was a way to communicate with people in the larger world that didn't give away their existence, let alone their location.

There was a rap on her door.

"Come in!" she shouted, to be heard over the howling wind outside.

Forrest squeezed inside and closed the door, gasping from the morning cold. "That'll wake you up in a hurry."

"That's why I'm still in here," Dominique said, suddenly feeling energized. Forrest did that to her, and it was time and then some that one of them crossed that invisible line and overtly acknowledged the obvious attraction between them. Dominique wondered if they were both taking it slow because it was fun to be in this early, flirtatious stage. It was a breath of warm spring air in an otherwise barren, stifling existence. Maybe they should just go on like this. Only Dominique was tired of sleeping alone; Forrest's warm body would be so much better than her army-issue electric blanket.

"Does that mean you're not going to breakfast?" Forrest asked.

Dominique made a show of struggling to her feet. "No, I'm coming. I just want there to be a tunnel between the barracks and the cafeteria. I don't want to see any more *snow*."

"I can fix that. Come on."

Dominique pulled on her coat, hat, and gloves. Grinning, Forrest took a scarf off her coat hook and blindfolded her with it. Laughing, Dominique let Forrest take her hand and lead her outside.

The wind bit her skin, immediately unpleasant.

"Did you see they're demolishing Disney World?" Dominique asked as they walked.

"I did."

"I mean, Disney World. The Taj Mahal was one thing, but *Disney World*? Mickey's home?"

"The bastards."

"The problem is, they're not playful. It made sense at the time—if you're designing killing machines, you don't want them to be playful, but now that they run everything, it's a problem..." She stopped short, pulled off the scarf as a flash of insight struck her. It just dropped into her mind, the way some of the best ideas arrived. "Holy shit. I think I've got it."

"What's that?"

"It. *It.*" The defenders didn't have a playful bone in their bodies. That meant they would turn their prodigious noses up at video games, theme parks, anything that hinted of frivolity. Never in a million years would they visit a virtual playscape. And just to make doubly sure, she could use one of the obsolete ones. Earth2 would be perfect. Dominique recalled reading an article about how Earth2 had been saved from deletion by a virtual historical preservation group, because it was the first, the oldest virtual playscape to be widely used. If they could get the word out, humans could meet inside Earth2 and speak freely, without fear of being overheard.

"Let's get inside and I'll explain."

With a dozen people watching over her shoulder, Dominique navigated to Earth2. She chose a default avatar and consulted the map. If any people were there at the moment, a central, urban destination seemed the most likely place to find them. She chose a city called Haven and teleported in.

Her avatar—a slim, pleasant-looking woman of indistinct ethnicity—appeared on a street corner in what looked like a typical early-twenty-first-century city. It was deserted.

Dominique directed her avatar to walk.

"You can fly, you know," President Wood said—Anthony Wood, not Carmine. From the moment they'd arrived at

CFS Alert, President Wood had been back in charge, though nothing was ever said. Carmine seemed fine with the change, almost relieved; Dominique wondered if it had been his idea.

Dominique craned her neck to look at the president. "How on Earth would you know that?"

President Wood shrugged. "Do the math. I was twenty-five when Earth2 was all the rage." He gestured at the old-fashioned keyboard, which must have been at least fifteen years old. "Press and hold the function key, then hit PAGE UP."

She did. Her avatar spread her arms and rose into the air, soaring higher the more Dominique pressed PAGE UP. When she got above the buildings she went exploring for signs of life.

There was no one on the streets, no one at the beach resorts, no one in Medieval Village or on Vampire Island.

"*Someone* must visit occasionally. I can check every few hours," Dominique said.

"Over there," Carmine's wife, Nora, said, pointing as the avatar passed over an amusement park.

A lone car whipped around an impossibly steep curve on a roller coaster. Dominique dropped her avatar lower, until they could see a single head inside the car. She found the exit to the coaster, and landed there to wait.

The avatar was tall and slim, a black woman with her head shaved except for a ponytail. She paused at the coaster's turnstile exit, taking in Dominique's avatar.

Hi, Dominique typed. Earth2 had an audio function, but Dominique thought it prudent not to use it to start, given their desire to remain anonymous.

Hi. You know, everything's free in here. You can grab a better avatar, dress her in anything you want.

Thanks, I'll work on that when I've got time. But listen, I'm here with someone important who needs your help.

Someone important? Is it Jesus?

"Just what we need, a smartass," President Wood said. "It must be a kid. Who else would be trolling around in there?"

Ha. Ha. Not quite that important. How old are you? Dominique typed.

82.

Seriously. This is incredibly important, more than you can guess.

I'm 13.

"Told you," Wood said.

Her name was Eclipse, at least inside the game. Dominique was happy to keep it at pseudonyms. She told Eclipse her name was Island Rain, but Eclipse could call her Rain.

What can I do for you, Rain?

"Now we're getting somewhere," Nora said.

Bring some adults with you and come back.
Tomorrow, noon Eastern Time. Will you do that?

I will if you ride the Avalanche with me.

Chuckling, Dominique typed, You got it. She followed Eclipse to the coaster's entrance.

# 67

## *Kai Zhou*

*October 8, 2047. Washington, D.C.*

When the key rattled in the gargantuan front door, Kai tensed.

"Mommy!" Errol howled and scrabbled off the couch to greet Lila.

Kai smiled a greeting as Lila came into the living room carrying Errol. Erik followed behind her.

"Was Errol good?" Lila asked, sitting on the couch.

"I was good," Errol answered, before Kai could.

"He was fine."

Lila excused herself and headed to the bathroom. Kai turned back toward the TV with Errol in his lap as Erik eased into his giant stuffed chair.

"What is this?" Erik asked, frowning.

"*Forever After.* An old situation comedy."

Erik picked up the remote and changed the channel to one of the new shows. It was a cop show, with a defender playing the lead. The defender was so bad he was painful to watch, standing out among his professional human costars like a Little Leaguer trying to play shortstop for the Atlanta Braves.

There was no romance in the new shows, and little humor save for the hammy plays-on-words the defenders could understand.

Kai watched obediently until the defender-cop got into a shootout with a dozen bad humans, then he took Errol to bed.

Lila joined him a few minutes later. "Sorry. Erik wanted me to stay until the commercial. I have to get back in a minute." Glancing toward the closed door, Lila kissed him quickly. "Meet me in the laundry closet later?"

"It's a date," Kai said.

As Lila pulled off his shirt, Kai grimaced, repulsed by his own wounds. "I'm just disgusting," he whispered. The skin was thick and puckered in the spots where he'd been shot, the damage radiating out in starburst patterns.

"Are you kidding me? War wounds are sexy." She kissed his ravaged shoulder, his caved-in side. "If you had scars from a hernia surgery, *that* would be disgusting."

He pulled Lila's shirt over her head, dropped it on the dryer. Her skin was soft and perfect. He caressed her breast with his good hand, took her nipple between his lips. She closed her eyes, arched back onto the washing machine, her breath quick but silent. They were running both the washer and dryer to create noise so they wouldn't be overheard. Kai slid Lila's skirt and panties to the narrow strip of floor between the appliances. Lila kicked them off, eased back onto the washer with Kai's help.

They knew this closet well, could maneuver without making a sound into the three positions that were possible in the cramped space. You could be incredibly careful, incredibly quiet, when you knew you'd be killed if you were discovered.

Kai slid his half hand behind Lila, gripped her ass as well as he could, expecting her to recoil from the feel of what looked like a pincer—nothing but a thumb and index finger on the end of his wrist. She only pressed closer, worked him inside her, wriggled her hips to get just the right angle.

His thrusts were careful and deliberate, both because he didn't want the washing machine to rock, and because his body was far more fragile than it had been before he'd been shot. Sex hurt now. He could feel things grinding in his injured hip and rib cage, but tried to ignore the discomfort as Lila dug her fingernails into his neck and pulled his face close to hers, her body tensing and relaxing in waves as she whispered incredibly filthy things in his ear. Since the defenders had outlawed sex, it had become a truly forbidden pleasure, something only crazy-reckless people did. It had done wonders for their sex life.

Afterward, they took separate routes back to the living room and told Erik they were going to walk to the Timesaver to get some sodas. Erik glanced their way and nodded before returning to his TV show, giving them permission like he was their father.

It was cold outside, but Kai didn't mind. When he was outside, away from Erik, away from the TVs that doubled as monitoring devices, he felt infinitely more relaxed, more alive. He inhaled deeply as they walked, looked up at the sky.

It seemed as if the stars should be different, now that the rest of the world was unrecognizable, but they were bright and white on a black background, just as they'd always been.

"I had a game with the usual gang before the tournament,"

Kai said as they cut through the fenced backyard of Erik's house, out through the gate and into an alley.

"How'd you do?"

"Up eleven thousand."

Lila popped a Tick, offered one to Kai. He shook his head.

"Marcus said this resistance movement is serious. They had to expand Earth2 to hold all the people visiting. It's packed in there. He said there are rumors the inner circle is planning something big."

"Something big." Lila sighed.

"I'm sure it's not any sort of direct confrontation. Unless they've lost their minds, they'll stick to their plan, borrowing from the Luyten playbook. Conquer the world from the edges, in. Disrupt the enemy; harass them."

Lila nodded. Not in approval, Kai knew—just acknowledgment. "I'm pretty sure that's a human playbook. The Luyten borrowed it from us."

They emerged from the alley, their chins tucked against the cold wind. Lila swept her hair back. "They're so stupid. They're just confirming the defenders' paranoid worldview. It'll only make things worse."

"I'm not sure things could be worse."

Lila glanced at him, must have seen something in his eyes. "Kai, please don't get involved in this. When the defenders stomp this out, they're going to use a very big boot."

"I haven't decided what I'm going to do. For now I'm just watching." Sometimes Kai had no choice but to push back when Lila made a pronouncement like that.

"The defenders don't want to admit it, but they still look up to us," Lila said. "If we play it right, we could get them to back off willingly."

"They look up to *you*. They hate the rest of us." They'd had the same argument before, and it was pointless, because they had no control over the rebels' actions. But Kai couldn't let it drop. "You can't let go of that last shred of hope that these monsters will turn into the defenders of your childhood, the heroes who rode in to save the day." Kai tried to check the sarcasm in his tone. "You know better than anyone: They're engineered to understand nothing but force."

"They're engineered to *use* nothing but force, and to respond to it effectively. They don't know what to make of kindness. It knocks them off balance. If you hug them, they regress into a childhood they never got to have."

"Maybe we should launch a hug attack." Kai threw his hands in the air. "A guerrilla love offensive. Leave bouquets of flowers on their doorsteps."

Lila didn't smile. "Keep your voice down."

"I'm so sick of keeping my voice down. I'm sick of having sex in closets. I'm sick of *Erik*." They turned onto Monticello Street, which was mostly deserted on the cold night. A few defender vehicles, like tanks with wheels, cruised by. "It's like Erik is your husband now, and I'm the nanny."

"I don't like it any better than you do."

"You like Erik better than I do."

Lila stopped walking. "What's that supposed to mean?"

"You stick up for him. When I say something mean about him, you don't agree with me, you make excuses for him." Wisps of white condensation escaped Kai's mouth with each angry breath. "'He's not as bad as the others are.' 'He can't help it, it's the way he was designed.'"

"It *is* the way he was designed, and he *isn't* as bad as most of the others."

Kai looked at Lila and realized that at this moment, he

didn't like her. It was the first time he'd ever felt that way, and it scared him. "I'm not sure I can go on living this way."

Lila let her head loll back until she was staring at the black sky. "If there was any way for us to get out of that house, I would pack up in a heartbeat."

"He won't let *you* leave, but he'd be happy to see me and Errol gone. We'd probably be able to see you as much that way as we do now." It wasn't the first time Kai had thought about moving out, but it was the first time he'd said it out loud, because he wasn't sure how Lila would react. Now he knew. She looked devastated.

"You would want that?" she asked.

He licked his chapped lips. "I just wonder if it would be better for all of us."

"You think it would be better for me if I lived alone with a defender? You think I'd be happier with you and Errol gone?"

Kai put his head down. "No. It's just that, the way things are, Erik is tearing our family apart. I'm trying to think of a way to fix that."

Lila reached out and took his hand. "The way we fix it is, we don't let him. From now on, when you say something negative about Erik, I won't make excuses for him. I'll pile on. I promise."

They continued walking. The red and yellow lights of the Timesaver reflected in puddles on the sidewalk ahead.

"Fucking Erik," Lila said. "Clueless arrogant asshole."

"Selfish prickless bastard." In the shadows alongside the Timesaver, Kai noticed the Dumpster was so full the lid was jammed open.

"Grandiose pinhead," Lila said.

Kai squeezed her hand. The green Dumpster tucked alongside the Timesaver was filled with bodies. Others were stacked in front of it, leaned up against both sides. In the tepid light of streetlamps and store signs, blood-soaked skin appeared black instead of red; deeply shadowed eyes were nothing but black sockets. A single Luyten corpse lay wedged between the Dumpster and the wall.

They kept walking, around to the front of the store and inside. They picked out their sodas and headed to the check-out counter.

"So what happened out there?" Kai asked the clerk, a teen-age girl in tight jeans. He tried to sound casual.

"There was a traffic accident," she said, shrugging, like she was just making conversation.

"A bad one?"

The clerk shook her head. "Not too bad. A woman backed into the front of a defender's SUV. Evidently. He got angry."

Kai nodded, glanced at the TV mounted over the wom-an's shoulder. She was being careful with her words, in case someone was listening. What she probably meant was, the defender rear-ended the woman's car, then went berserk, even though it was his fault.

They thanked her and headed home, both of them looking away as they passed the Dumpster. It was possible there had been more casualties. Sometimes people still risked retrieving murdered loved ones and burying them, even though bodies were supposed to be left out for the sanitation trucks to cart away. Kai felt sorry for people who worked as trash collec-tors. That would be one grim job.

"We have to do something. We can't live like this," Kai said.

"I agree. The only thing we disagree on is tactics."

Kai limped along, his bad leg starting to give him trouble. There was no point in arguing; both of them were too stub-born to be shifted from their opinions.

# 68

## *Oliver Bowen*

*October 11, 2047. Washington, D.C.*

There was a letter in Oliver's mailbox. It was handwritten, with no return address. Oliver tore it open, withdrew an index card with a single thing written on it: Earth2.

Even if he hadn't recognized Kai's handwriting, he would have known the message was from Kai. No one but Kai and Lila knew he lived there. He headed back inside his little basement apartment, decorated primarily with Marvel comic book memorabilia, and sat at his computer.

He'd never been much of a gamer, even back in high school when dorky kids like him were supposed to hide there until they could escape into adulthood. Now he called up Earth2 and set up an account.

He was surprised to find the place roiling with activity. Avatars hurried here and there on foot, in cars, via flight. It seemed bizarre that so many people would be playing an old-fashioned online game. And actually, most people weren't playing, exactly—they were meeting. Performing a three-sixty, he saw three separate groups of avatars congregated together, deep in conversation.

He directed his avatar toward the nearest group, about two dozen people sitting in a circle on a beach. As he approached, they stopped talking.

"Private meeting," someone called in a metallic voice, or maybe his audio settings made it sound metallic.

Oliver turned his avatar around, headed for the second group. It probably would have been more efficient to check the instructions and find out how to fly, but he was in no hurry.

He was still surprised by how easy it had been to slip off the defenders' radar. He'd been a major political player, heavily involved in the Luyten War, the defenders program, yet the defenders had simply lost track of him, and didn't seem to be actively trying to locate him. If they had a weakness, it was this lack of attention to detail.

As he swung open the door of the old-fashioned diner where the second group was meeting, a few avatars looked his way, but no one said anything. Oliver took a seat toward the back.

"If you try that, they'll catch you, and they'll kill you," a blond, square-jawed avatar said to what appeared to be a golden retriever standing on its hind legs.

"They won't catch me. And they won't catch you, either, if you follow my instructions. They can't trace you if you're using my baffle software."

"Can we get back on subject?" a Valkyrie-looking woman dressed in purple furs said.

"We *are* on the subject," the retriever said. "Our charge is to develop techniques to disrupt their electronic communications. How are we off subject?"

His heart pounding, Oliver directed his avatar back outside. If this was what it appeared to be...

He joined another meeting. They were discussing how to locate US Army weapons caches hidden during the previous century.

Oliver raised his fist in the air and whooped. A resistance movement. This was what he'd been waiting for. He navigated his avatar out of the second meeting, wandered around until he found a pedestrian—an Asian woman wearing a blue sweater and a pair of khakis.

"Excuse me, is there someone in charge of operations here?"

"You mean, here in Fiddler's Green?" she asked.

"No, for the whole thing. All of this." He gestured to encompass all they could see.

The woman put her hands on her hips. "You're looking for Island Rain."

Oliver's heart hit another gear. Island Rain? Why did that moniker sound familiar?

Then he remembered. Dominique Wiewall. She'd been from the Caribbean. There'd been only one thing on her office wall—a poster of her home, with *Island Rain* printed across the bottom. Could it possibly be Dominique? But how could she have survived? He'd assumed she'd been with the US leadership in Colorado Springs when the country fell.

"Where can I find her?"

The woman laughed. "You can't just wander in and see Island Rain. You have to earn your place, work your way up. Are you new? You look new." She looked Oliver's avatar up and down.

"Let's assume I'm new, but I'm someone with expertise

Island Rain would want to know about. How would I go about getting a message to her?"

"Hmm." The woman folded her arms. She was quite good at realistic mannerisms. Oliver's avatar was just standing there, arms dangling at his sides. Of course, that pretty well captured his mannerisms in real life. "I could message JJ, the captain of Fiddler's Green."

"Would you? I'd appreciate it." If it was Dominique, how could he signal her? It would be a bad idea to speak her name, probably not smart even to mention Easter Island. Something subtle. "Ask him to tell her a fellow admirer of Moai needs to speak to her." Oliver was elated to have something constructive to do. Something he was good at.

# 69

## *Lila Easterlin*

*October 15, 2047. Washington, D.C.*

The morning rush hour pedestrians moved into the street, or pressed against the buildings, to let a defender pass on the sidewalk. It reminded Lila of vehicles clearing out to let an ambulance pass, only people moved more quickly to get out of the way of a defender.

Lila stood in the gutter an extra moment to allow the throngs to unclog, then stepped back into the flow of people on their way to work. She waited for the light and crossed Victory Avenue, which was a hundred feet wide at least, one of the new defender streets. The city was transforming into an enormous visual illusion. On one block everything looked normal; on the next everything was triple in size.

There was a new indoor rifle range on Ichiro Street, bearing the familiar NO HUMANS sign. She'd never seen a NO LUYTEN sign; evidently even while target shooting the defenders needed someone to fetch their iced tea.

She was so tired. Typically her insomnia would get a little

worse each night, building to a crescendo where she was too exhausted to think, and that would break the cycle and she would sleep fifteen hours straight. This time it just kept getting worse. She was beyond exhausted, but her thoughts kept spinning, as if they'd discovered their own power source independent of her sleep-deprived brain.

She was so afraid of what might happen if this resistance turned out to be more than a bunch of posturing blowhards. What was it about humanity that always led it right back to killing as the solution to its problems? If someone would just listen, she was sure she could get them out of this mess without firing a shot. The defenders had weaknesses; their ability to respond to a physical attack wasn't one of them. Why couldn't other people see that?

If only there was some way to jump-start the process, to get the defenders to see that they'd be better off if humans were in charge, or at least sharing power. That would mean getting them to be less paranoid. Saner. Happier.

Lila laughed out loud. Couldn't they all use that? She certainly could. The problem with the defenders was that they were engineered to be paranoid and unhappy. The only way to change it was to alter their genetic code.

She slowed her pace. What if she did it now, subtly? There was no one checking the new defenders' genetic coding at this point. Would the existing defenders notice if the new ones were less disordered? If she could somehow reintroduce serotonin into the design, the new ones would still be violent and have negligible social skills, but they'd be less empty inside.

It would be incredibly risky. Her defender superiors had expressly instructed her to make the new defenders exactly the same as the existing ones. If they caught her messing with the formula, they'd pull her legs off, then stomp her to jelly.

But if she made the alterations at the source codes, and no one checked her work, she'd be the only person on Earth who'd know.

Up ahead, the back of a parked semi rolled open, and a Luyten climbed out. Lila stopped walking and waited for it to cross the sidewalk and head down an alley between two shops. She would never get used to them; they would always make her skin crawl...

With a jolt, she realized that if she were to introduce serotonin into the brain chemistry of defenders, the Luyten would be able to read their thoughts. How could she have overlooked that fact, even for a minute? The thought gave her chills. Jesus, what if she'd gone ahead with it, not realizing what she was doing?

"Lila?"

Lila turned to find a beefy guy and a skinny blond woman keeping pace beside her. She didn't answer, because she wasn't sure she wanted to confirm her identity to these people. They were clean and relatively well dressed, not the sort of people she associated with the threats and hate messages she occasionally received.

"We need you to come with us, please," the guy said. He had a heavy New York accent—Brooklyn, or the Bronx. In fact, he was wearing a New York Yankees Windbreaker.

"And why would I want to do that?" Lila shot back. Now Lila wasn't sure; these people might be a threat after all. She looked around, saw two defenders within earshot. If she screamed for help, would they respond? They might if she made clear who she was.

"We've been authorized to speak to you in private, by the president of the United States."

That got her attention. Usually when people lied, they tried to keep it plausible. "Oh, really? How did you contact him, through a Ouija board?"

"He's alive. They're both alive, actually. Anthony Wood is back in charge." The man stepped in front of her; when she tried to walk around him he stuck out an arm to stop her, but stopped short of grabbing her. "Please, Dr. Easterlin. We need your help. We're all on the same side here, aren't we? You're only helping them because they're not giving you a choice. Right?"

She knew he was playing on her insecurities, but the words still stung. "What is this about?"

"It's about exactly what you think it's about."

Lila looked at the woman, who had yet to utter a word. She looked to be about Lila's age, late twenties. "Did you agree ahead of time that he would do all the talking?"

"My work comes later," she replied. There was something about her, a nervousness, or maybe just too much caffeine.

Lila eyed them both for a moment longer, then shrugged. They'd sparked her curiosity. "Okay. Let's go."

The big guy stuck out his hand, introduced himself as Clete. The woman was Danika. As the three of them headed down Monticello Avenue, Lila tried to guess what they wanted. They must need her expertise for some sort of attack they were planning. Wouldn't it be bizarre if they'd come upon the same idea as she, about altering the newly produced defenders in some way? But what sort of alteration would possibly help them? Whatever it was they wanted, she wasn't sure she would help. If they were simply planning to blow shit up, kill a few defenders, then no way was she sticking her neck out even an inch.

They led her to the Renaissance Hotel. Lila had had lunch there once, back when it was a four-star gem; now it was in serious decline. The carpet in the lobby was stained and

# DEFENDERS

threadbare, the walls in need of a paint job. Few humans traveled for business, none for pleasure, and the place was too small for defenders.

There were no suitcases in Clete and Danika's room, no indication that anyone was staying there save a briefcase lying closed on the bed. A slimy, unidentifiable lump sat on top of it. Danika went over to the lump, bowed her head as if in prayer. Clete hung back near Lila.

Danika picked up the lump with a quivering hand. She held it high, looked up at it, and stifled a sob. "I used to be a high school teacher. I taught algebra and trig." Still holding the lump, she looked at Lila. "I don't know why it's important to me that you understand, but it is. Maybe it's because I'm going to be you for a little while."

"What do you mean, you're going to be me? I haven't agreed to go along with anything yet, and given how weird this is beginning to look, I doubt I'm going to."

Clete took a step back, placing himself between Lila and the door. Suddenly Danika was the chatty one, and he was the introvert.

"I had a child, just like you. She and her father were killed when the defenders invaded Los Angeles. When I found out, I promised myself I'd join them in heaven as soon as I could. But I wanted my death to count for something first."

Danika lowered the lump toward her face. She opened her mouth, pushed the lump between her lips.

"*Wait. What is that?*" Lila asked. Lila thought Danika must be eating poison, but how would that make her death count? The lump was slick on the outside, like it was sheathed in stretched plastic—a deflated balloon, or a condom.

Danika slid it farther, into her throat. She gagged, pulled it out. Whatever it was, she was trying to swallow it.

369

"If someone doesn't tell me what's going on right now, I'm leaving." She turned toward Clete. "And if you try to stop me, I'm going to scream like you wouldn't believe."

"Take your time," Clete said to Danika. "Relax. Relax your throat. Let gravity do the work."

Lila spun toward Danika in time to see the lump disappear. Danika made a terrible choking sound; her eyes grew huge as she pressed her hand to her bulging throat.

"There you go. That's it," Clete said softly.

When it was down, Danika cried out in a mix of horror and relief. "It was bigger than the ones I practiced on. *Much* bigger."

"Maybe they didn't want to risk you choking in practice. Or maybe your throat is tighter because you're tense."

"*You're damned right I'm tense.*" Danika was on the verge of hysteria.

"For God's sake, what did you just swallow?" Lila asked.

"A bomb," Clete said. "Now she's going to walk into the heart of the production facility and detonate it."

For a moment Lila was speechless. When she finally regained her voice, she shouted, "Are you out of your fucking minds? There are people in there. Some of them are my friends. Besides that, there are eight other facilities. They'll just divert production to the others."

"No they won't," Clete said, "because we're hitting all of them at once."

"How are you bombing the Easter Island facility?"

"All but that one," Clete allowed. "It will still cripple their production capability."

Lila's head was spinning. She wasn't sure she was on the same side as these people. She should be, but they were talking about bombing *her* facility. She'd designed it, she ran it, and some of her friends were in it. And this woman, this math teacher, was about to kill herself.

"Wait a minute—you don't look like *me*. They're not going to let you waltz into the lab just because you have my ID."

"She's the same height and weight as you, the same hair color," Clete said. "That's all defenders use. They can't tell one face from another. We're counting on the human workers to instinctively keep their mouths shut."

"So you can blow them up. How nice." He was right about the defenders not being able to distinguish human faces, though. Erik had told Lila as much. Still, this was insane.

Danika stood. "I need your ID."

"You also need the pass code," Lila said, not sure she was going to give it to her.

"We have the pass code." Danika reached to check Lila's pockets.

Lila slapped her hand away. Danika reached again, drew Lila's ID out of her breast pocket.

"I'm sorry if you don't agree with this," Danika said, "but the president does. His people do."

Lila didn't see how this would bring down the defenders. Unless... "There's more to the plan. More to come." Lila said it aloud, but mainly for her own benefit. Clete and Danika already knew it.

At the door, Clete and Danika clasped hands. Maybe hugging risked detonating the explosive, or maybe they didn't know each other well enough to hug. Danika was clutching a thin satchel, which Lila guessed held the igniting agent—something Danika would inject to induce a chemical reaction.

Then Danika was gone, and it was just Lila and Clete. Lila wasn't sure if she wanted to stop them or not. She hovered in the middle of the room, deciding whether to scream, try to get past Clete, or do nothing. In the end, she took a seat in a stuffed chair by the window.

"How will you know if she's successful?"

"We're close enough that we should hear the blast." Clete pulled the briefcase off the bed, took it to the little hotel desk, and pulled out a laptop.

Curious, Lila leaned in to see what he was doing. Clete opened Earth2 and got an avatar up and running.

"Is that your means of relaxing during stressful situations?" Lila asked, knowing full well what he was doing.

Clete looked up from the screen, said nothing. Lila moved closer to the computer so she could read what Clete was typing.

It was nothing surprising or enlightening. He was communicating with an avatar named Sandovar, saying all had gone well so far. He was keeping the message intentionally vague.

After a few minutes he signed off and closed the computer. He stood, sniffed, wiped his nose with the back of his hand. "Now comes the hard part."

"The *hard* part? We haven't gotten to the hard part yet?"

He gave Lila a hard, direct look. "We have to make it look like this happened against your will."

That had crossed her mind. After the explosion the defenders would assume she was the one who bombed the facility. When they found her alive, she'd be a prime suspect, and they weren't ones to wait for a trial, or even facts, before they started meting out punishment.

"And how do we do that?"

Clete looked at the floor, like he was suddenly feeling terribly sad, or ashamed. "It has to be immediately obvious to them."

Then she understood, and felt a sinking in the pit of her

stomach. It had to be immediately obvious, as in, she had to sport the bleeding, swollen face of someone who'd put up a fight. She wasn't convinced their plot would do any good in the long run, yet they had dragged her into it, risked her life, and now they needed to kick the shit out of her so the defenders wouldn't kill her. She was supposed to stand there while this asshole beat her.

She looked up, returned Clete's level stare for a moment, then punched him in the face.

Teary-eyed with pain, Clete clutched his nose. His fingers came away bloody. "*Why did you do that?*"

Lila punched him again, in the eye this time. The blow landed with a satisfying *smack*.

Clete started to fight back. His first punch felt like a hammer blow to Lila's cheek.

373

# 70

## *Lila Easterlin*

*October 15, 2047. Washington, D.C.*

The man at the front desk called, "Jesus, are you all right?" as Lila stumbled past. She kept walking.

She couldn't see out of her left eye. Although she knew it was because it was swollen shut, a small, scared voice in her was sure she'd been blinded. Her nose wouldn't stop bleeding. Before he left, Clete had said that was good, let the blood pour all over her shirt. She had the worst headache of her life, and felt like she had thick clumps of mud plastered to her cheek, her lower lip, her forehead. Lila wondered if the kicks to her face had been planned ahead of time, or improvised.

Outside, she texted Kai to meet her at home while she waited for a cab to happen by.

The cabby, a woman in her seventies, said nothing about Lila's injuries. She nodded when Lila gave her the address, and took off. Lila had to get back to her house—to Erik's house. When he saw her face, Erik would believe her story and protect her.

She still hadn't heard an explosion. As the taxi hurdled over the cracked, pothole-laden streets, Lila guessed the explosion must have happened by now. She must be out of hearing range.

When she got home, she went straight to the freezer. She found a defender-sized bag of frozen brussels sprouts, collapsed on the couch, and gently pressed the bag over her eye.

She jerked the bag from her eye. What was she doing? She didn't want the swelling to go down. Easing herself to her feet, she tried to jostle her pounding head as little as possible. She had to find Erik, tell him what happened. Maybe she could act like she was trying to warn him, trying to prevent the blast.

The door flew open. Erik stormed in, flanked by two defenders in combat gear.

"Erik." Lila stumbled, fell to her knees, and caught herself on Erik's ottoman. She was acting, and she was not. It was easy to act like you'd been beaten senseless when you had. "They're going to bomb the facility."

In an instant Erik was at her side. He helped her lean up against the ottoman, then studied her face, her bloody shirt. "We caught her. She was trying to pass herself off as you, but I know what you look like." He reached out, then brushed her hair with the gentlest of touches before turning to the soldiers. "Find a doctor."

Both soldiers froze. "We were told to kill her."

"Did you hear what she just said? How do you think she sustained these injuries?" Erik shouted. "By helping them?"

They left to fetch a doctor.

"It was a coordinated attack. Five of our production facilities were hit." He studied her face.

"What is it?" She touched her nose. "Am I bleeding again?"

"I'm trying to read your expression. Part of you must be glad about these attacks, even if you tried to stop them."

The front door clicked open. "Lila? *Lila*." Kai rushed to her, pushing between her and Erik. "Oh my God. *What happened?*"

"I was attacked by rebels," she said.

Kai slid his hand behind her back. "We have to get you to a hospital."

"I've already sent for a doctor," Erik said. "I have everything under control. I'd suggest you make sure your son is safe. Things could get bad out there."

"Where is he?" Lila tried to sit up further.

"He's at Charlie's, down the street." His voice tight, he added, "I'll get him."

Erik relaxed visibly after Kai left. If anything ever happened to her, she wondered if Erik would kill Kai. She was confident he'd make sure Errol was taken care of, but she worried about Kai.

"What did you mean, 'things could get bad out there'?"

Erik turned on the TV, tuned it to the channel that was not a channel—the Eye in the Sky, the live feed only defenders could access. He tuned it to a surveillance camera on a street corner in a city Lila didn't recognize, where defenders were going berserk. The air was hazy; in the background smoke poured from the broken windows of a wide, flat building Lila recognized as the Moscow production facility. They were pulling people out of a grocery store and lining them up against the wall. A defender was going down the line and shooting each person in the head. Three men broke away from the wall and ran: They were torched by a defender with a flamethrower. In the street, four defenders in a jeep were strafing the upper floors of office buildings with automatic weapons.

"I'm so relieved you weren't involved in this. I knew you wouldn't be."

Lila looked at her hands, to avoid having to watch the screen. Most of the people being butchered hadn't been involved in it, either.

"They're going to execute the woman who impersonated you tomorrow. Why don't you join me for the execution? I have excellent seats."

After nearly choking with surprise, Lila managed to say, "I'd like that." Erik had presented it as an invitation, but Lila knew he wasn't asking her, he was telling her. Her presence would prove her loyalty and give the other defenders in power a chance to see what had been done to her face.

# 71

## Dominique Wiewall

*October 18, 2047. Ellesmere Island, Nunavut, Canada.*

She wasn't sure whether to feel ecstatic or dejected. They'd disabled five production facilities, but not seven. When those two were added to the Easter Island facility, the defenders could still roll out about 80 percent of the new troops they'd planned, if they ran the facilities full tilt, cracked the whip on the technicians. Security would be super-tight at those remaining facilities, so hitting them again wasn't an option.

Someone knocked. "Come in!" she called, hoping it was Forrest.

It was. Gasping from the cold, he pulled off his gloves, a big, goofy smile on his face.

"What?" Dominique said.

"Nothing." He went on smiling.

*"What?"*

"Have dinner with me?"

Dominique gave him a puzzled look. They had dinner

together every night, though usually he didn't phrase it quite like that. Usually it was "You going to dinner?" or "You ready?"

She checked the time on her screen. "Dinner's not for another hour and a half. Unless you're taking me to a swanky new restaurant I don't know about."

He clapped his hands together, spun in a half circle. "Damn. You guessed my surprise."

Lila raised her eyebrows.

"Okay, maybe not a *new* restaurant. Blake agreed to cook us dinner early, so we could have the cafeteria to ourselves for a change."

"*Blake* did? Wow, what did you have to trade for that, your last pair of warm socks?"

"Don't even ask." Forrest looked pained.

"Wait a minute," Dominique said. She put her hands on her hips. "Are you asking me out?"

Forrest nodded. "Bad idea?"

Dominique shook her head. "Excellent idea. I could use some cheering up. Or should we be celebrating? I have no idea."

The meal was creamed spinach and corned beef hash on toast, not exactly swanky restaurant fare, but they each claimed one of the remaining bottles of beer in their ration, and Dominique found herself excited by the idea of a shift in their relationship. Any change was welcome, but even if they weren't trapped in this arctic hell, Dominique would have liked this guy.

"Did you hear Barry shot a walrus?" Forrest asked. On the way over they'd agreed not to talk about the resistance. All anyone ever talked about was what was going on through

Earth2. There'd be plenty of time for that when the others arrived for dinner.

"I didn't. How nice. I mean, nice that we'll have fresh meat." She tilted her head. "Do walruses have meat, or just blubber?"

"Mostly blubber, I think."

"I can't say I've ever had blubber."

"It's considered a delicacy in some cultures," Forrest said.

Dominique grinned. "What cultures are those?"

Forrest cleared his throat, shrugged. "I can't list any specific cultures, but rest assured, it's a delicacy in some cultures."

Laughing, Dominique put her hand over Forrest's, which was resting on the table. He looked down at their hands, turned his over, spread his fingers.

"So what was it like, studying at COGE?"

Dominique turned her gaze toward the low foam-tiled ceiling. "Weird. Exciting, but weird."

"You really weren't allowed to leave the island?"

"Not for the first three years. I was in a college run by the equivalent of the CIA. They were teaching us things the US government denied it knew how to do."

Forrest shook his head. "How times have changed. It's hard to imagine there were such hard, fast lines between countries back then. State secrets. Cold wars. It all seems stupid now."

The door flew open; Dominique and Forrest quickly unclasped their hands, as if they'd been caught doing something wrong.

It was the president. "We think the defenders have infiltrated Earth2."

Both Dominique and Forrest leaped from their chairs and followed Wood through the supply room, into the operations room. Nora was at the computer. Dominique watched over her shoulder as she controlled Island Rain. Rain was in a bar, speaking to two male avatars. One was dressed in a black ninja outfit, the other in jeans and a T-shirt. Both were clearly newbies, given their generic appearance and the stiffness of their movements.

Nora glanced up at Dominique. "I have a very bad feeling about these two, but you'd know better than I."

*We both have military training. I'm conversant in all manner of explosives, and Daniel was a Navy SEAL. We're ready and eager to strike at the enemy.*

Dominique pressed her hands to her face. "Oh, shit," she whispered.

"What should I reply?" Nora asked.

Dominique just stood there, her mind not working.

"Dominique? What should I reply? Something that'll tell us for sure."

"We can't know for sure, but—" She cursed under her breath. "Give them an opportunity to brag, or try to piss them off."

Nora typed. *You don't sound intelligent enough to be Special Forces and Navy SEAL. Are you sure I'm not talking to two kids playing G.I. Joe?*

There was an inordinately long pause, during which no one in the room said a word, or even breathed heavily. Finally, a reply came.

*My IQ is 147. Daniel's is 139. If you suspect there's a child in this conversation, check the mirror.*

"Shit," Dominique nearly shouted. "Oh, holy Christ."

"You're *sure*?" the president asked.

"They're defenders. The awkward phrasing, the arrogance." She gestured at the avatars. "The IQs he mentioned are right in the defender range." She stared at President Wood, the implications sinking in. The defenders could locate them.

"Everyone be ready to leave in one hour," Wood said. "Fuel the plane. Concentrate on packing survival gear—we'll have to land and ditch the plane before we reach defender territory."

Zipping her coat as she ran, Dominique headed for her quarters to get packed.

# 72

## Lila Easterlin

*October 18, 2047. Washington, D.C.*

It took forty minutes to reach the Capitol Shopping Center's parking lot, and another half hour to find a parking space. Most of that time Lila relived Danika's execution, over and over. Only it hadn't been an execution: It had been an exhibition on torture, a primer on all the things defenders would do to you if you defied them. Why was it that the mind insisted on lingering on exactly the things you most wanted to forget?

Lila tried to drag her thoughts back to the present, to the vehicles parked everywhere—in fire lanes, on the grass medians, along the road leading to the shopping center. No one was sure if the defenders had a reliable way to keep track of who was complying with their designated shopping day and who wasn't, but no one wanted to risk finding out.

"Not Target," Kai said.

Lila paused. She'd automatically headed toward Target, forgetting that it held bad associations for Kai. She scanned the big shopping center. There was a Hobby Town, but neither of them had a hobby. The grocery store didn't count (food was a staple, so buying it didn't stimulate the economy). She pointed their cart toward Office Depot.

"I wonder if the defenders understand that a lot of these people can't afford to buy random shit. A rash of bankruptcies isn't going to stimulate the economy."

"Yeah, I wouldn't say that too loud."

As soon as they got inside, they split up and began filling their cart with things they could actually use—preferably bulky items that made the cart appear full.

Lila grabbed a printer and tossed it in the cart. She was heading toward the printer ink aisle, but it was slow going. The store was packed.

Everyone she passed looked at her intently for a moment, then quickly looked away. Fortunately her stitched lip, bandaged cheek, swollen left eye, and bruised forehead would heal. It was probably 50 percent better already.

When they weren't gaping at her, Lila watched other people's faces. She was morbidly fascinated by the shift in the default human expression since the defender occupation began. People rarely smiled, and rarely looked angry or even annoyed. They tried to keep their faces flat, emotionless, but undertones of fear and something like sadness, or self-pity, bled through. Back in the days of the Luyten War everyone looked openly afraid, but something about this situation caused people to try to tamp their emotions.

Kai found her in the printer ink aisle, limped over, and dropped four reams of paper in the cart. "You can never have too much paper."

A defender came around the corner, his arms full of boxes. "Shit," Lila whispered.

"Here. People aren't buying enough of these." The defender

dropped three identical boxes into their cart. According to the box, they were roll sorters. Lila had no idea what they were, but she now owned three.

"That should be enough," Kai said. "Let's get to the checkout line before he comes back with more."

Another defender was patrolling the checkout line. Lila watched as he grabbed some big-ticket electronics at random from a pile and added them to an old woman's cart. Evidently her cart wasn't full enough. Lila was about to share a coded snide comment with Kai when a voice trumpeted in her head.

*I have information for you.*

Lila's purse slipped from her fingers. She gripped the shopping cart with both hands to stay on her feet.

"You okay? What's the matter?" Kai asked.

Why would a Luyten speak to her? As far as she knew, no Luyten had communicated with a human being since the invasion of Australia.

*There are bathrooms in the back of the store. Beyond them is a fire exit. I've disabled the fire alarm.*

"I have to go to the bathroom. I'll be right back." She forced a smile, left the line, and headed toward the back of the store.

The exit was at the end of an L-shaped hallway. When she got outside Lila eased the door closed, maintaining her composure despite the presence of the scarlet-colored Luyten, waiting between two Dumpsters. It was in the prone position, three appendages on the floor, three folded.

As she stepped toward it, Lila glanced around to make sure no one was around.

*There are no humans nearby, or planning to come back here anytime soon. That much I can tell you.*

"I'm not particularly worried about humans. What do you want? I need to get back inside before I'm missed."

*I'll try to be brief, but it's important I be clear. The defenders were more rattled by the attacks on their birthing facilities than you know. They've decided that, as things stand now, they're far too outnumbered by humans to maintain control.*

"I know. I got their marching orders. They've got me spitting out defenders as fast as the facility can create them." The strangeness of the situation hit Lila anew. A *Luyten* was talking to her, probably the one that killed her father.

*Their plan is to reduce the human population as well.*

The Luyten's words silenced all of her internal chatter. "They're going to cull us to a manageable number?"

*Yes.*

"What's a manageable number?"

*Between a quarter and a half billion.*

What was the current world population? Lila had no idea.

*Two-point-three billion.*

"You're telling me they're planning to kill off more than three-quarters of the human race?"

*Yes.* The Luyten sounded almost sad. She wondered if it was telling the truth.

The Luyten stood; it towered over her. Suddenly she wished she'd brought Kai with her. It could kill her in an instant.

*I have no reason to hurt you. We're not like the Defenders. Violence is not our default response.*

But lying was, if Five was typical of their species. The Luyten would have much to gain if they could convince humans to go after the defenders in earnest. Much to gain.

*Defenders have started clearing out of some heavily populated areas. They're preparing to use chemical weapons in those areas. You can confirm that.*

"All right. I appreciate the warning. I'll pass it on." She found herself monitoring her own thoughts as she reeled them out, then monitoring the thoughts of the monitor. It was a maddening loop.

*If all we had to offer you was a warning, it wouldn't do much good. You can't beat them on your own.* It took a step toward her; she tensed, resisting the urge to step back. *We have a common enemy. You've come up with a brilliant plan to defeat them, but you need our help.*

*Don't be shocked.* The Luyten interrupted itself as Lila reacted to what the Luyten was suggesting.

"*Holy shit.*" The words just came out. Lila glanced around, relieved that there was still no one around, because she'd just shouted. *You're proposing we ally with you against the defenders?* She thought it instead of speaking it. The words were enough to get her killed on the spot, if the wrong ears overheard. "Hold on. What 'way to defeat them' are you talking about?" That detail had slipped past while she absorbed the rest.

*Restoring serotonin to the defender's brain physiology. The new defenders will act as unwitting spies; we'll pass on the defenders' plans and strategies to your commanders.*

Lila had forgotten about her wild idea.

*Once the new defenders are in place, humans and Luyten attack simultaneously. We can serve as ground forces. As soon as your commanders know what they want from us, we'll know, and we'll follow their orders—*

It was insanity. Yet what did the Luyten have to lose by proposing it? *And if we did? What would keep you from turning on us once the defenders were gone?*

*There won't be many of us left after such a war. And as I said, violence isn't in our nature; we prefer compromise.*

*Unlike the defenders.* Its tone shifted; it whispered into her mind. *They're insane. You made them too quickly.*

Lila barked a bitter laugh. "Yes, well, we were in a hurry."

*I know. I'm sorry. We're sorry.*

Lila couldn't believe she was having this conversation. "Why are you talking to me? Why don't you talk to the rebels? They're the ones making the decisions."

*Because we trust you.*

She laughed at the absurdity of the statement. "You trust *me*? I fucking hate you. I hate you more than I hate the defenders."

*We're aware of that. More important, so are you.*

Lila shook her head. Oliver was right—they were baffling. Their words were clear, but following their logic made your head ache. "I'll pass this on, but that's as far as I'm getting involved. I'm a scientist. I have a family. I'm not playing Joan of Arc for you."

*Fair enough. You can go now. That's all I wanted to tell you.*

"I can go now. Thanks—thanks for your permission." She turned to go, then hesitated. She couldn't resist asking.

"Are you the one who killed my father?"

*Loblolly School*, it said. *All over soon.*

The words chilled her. Barely a day went by when she didn't hear those words, the twisted attempt to console her with words spit from the hole of a monster coming to tear her to pieces. She looked at the massive thing standing over her.

"You ruined my life."

The Luyten made a draining sound, like water being flushed down a toilet. Maybe to them it was a sound of regret, or apology. Everything bad, all of the suffering in her life, could be reduced to this Luyten.

"I don't need your apology, if that's what you're offering."

*No. But believe me, you need what I'm offering.* The Luyten raised two of its appendages, as if waving goodbye. *The defenders will go on killing until there's no life left.*

"No one's going to trust you."

*Maybe not. But you're right: We have nothing to lose by trying.*

Lila turned to go back inside, saw there was no knob on the outside of the door. "Great." She headed around the back of the strip of stores at a brisk jog. Kai would be worried.

She spotted him in the parking lot, heading back toward Office Depot after stashing their purchases in the car. When he saw Lila jogging toward him, he stopped.

"Where'd you go? I was worried."

Lila slid her hand under Kai's bicep, then turned him toward the car. "I just spoke to my father's killer."

They inched along toward the exit.

"Do you think it's telling the truth?" Kai asked.

"I don't know. It can't be." She looked at Kai. "It can't be, can it?"

"I don't know. I could see the defenders doing that. Let's assume for a minute it is true. What do we do?"

Lila curled into the corner of her seat, pressed her temple against the cold window. "If it has to be done—and I'm not saying I'm convinced it does—I'm not the only one who could do it. The Hong Kong facility is still operating. We could pass along the Luyten's message to someone involved in the rebellion. One of your poker friends, maybe. Let them decide if it's a good idea, and if they do, they can contact Kim Han, the head genetic engineer at the Hong Kong facility."

Kai shook his head. "Honestly, I'm not sure that's a good

idea. If we decided this had to be done, I don't think we can risk telling anyone—no one at all—until the altered defenders are in place. There are bound to be people dead set against allying with the Luyten—people who'll give us up to the defenders in a heartbeat to stop us from exposing our throats to the Luyten."

The weight of Kai's words felt like a rope around her neck. "Kai, we can't possibly make this decision by ourselves. If we went ahead with this, we'd be putting *everyone's* life at risk—"

"If the Luyten is telling the truth, everyone's life is *already* at risk. Four out of five, Lila. I don't like those odds, not for us, not for Errol, not for anyone."

Lila was about to scream at Kai to let her finish, but she caught herself. She wondered if it had been a mistake to tell him at all. She hated herself for wondering that. "This is all moot, because I'm one of those people who are dead set against allying with the Luyten. I don't trust them. No way. If I discovered someone was doing what we're talking about doing, I'd squeal to the defenders, too."

Kai pulled out of their lane, cut in front of a car doing its best not to let them out. The driver leaned on his horn. Lila gave him the finger and glared until he looked away.

*Tell me what we can do to prove we can be trusted*, the Luyten said in Lila's head.

"It just said, 'Tell me what—'"

"I heard it," Kai said. He shuddered. "I forgot just how bad that feels."

"There's nothing they could do that would make me trust them."

"They have no pinkies, so I guess a pinkie-swear is out."

Lila burst out laughing. Maybe it was knowing the Luyten

had heard Kai's ridiculous remark that made it funny. Maybe she just needed an excuse to laugh, to release some of the tension building up inside her as it sank in that the Luyten might back her into a corner so she has no choice but to do this. *If* she could do it. She wasn't even sure she could. It would be an incredible feat. "We don't have the right to make this decision, either way."

Kai chuckled humorlessly.

"What?" Lila asked.

"I'm the Boy Who Betrayed the World." He waved a hand in the air. "This is what I do."

Sometimes Lila forgot how heavily that weighed on Kai.

"What if we talk to my dad? We could get *his* opinion, at least," Kai suggested.

"That sounds like a plan." Anything to take the weight of this decision off Lila's shoulders sounded good to her.

# 73

## *Dominique Wiewall*

*October 18, 2047. Over Alaska.*

"Here they come," Smythe said. The TV screen in front of Dominique's seat sprang to life, giving her an aerial view of the compound that had been her home for the past eighteen months. The deep rumble of defender bombers dominated the audio feed.

Bright flashes lit the compound as the defenders' bombs hit their targets. It reminded her of a Fourth of July finale—there was a cascade of intense explosions, followed by silence. She'd had no doubts the defenders would find their hiding place, but it was shocking to see it destroyed, unnerving that they'd located it so quickly.

"As soon as they discover there are no bodies in that rubble, they'll be after us," Forrest said.

"They're already after us," Dominique said. Forrest gave her a questioning look. "They're thorough bastards. They'll have launched two forces—one to bomb us, the other to hunt us down in case we run."

Forrest only nodded.

Dominique appreciated that in all these months, no one had ever likened her to Dr. Frankenstein. It would be such an obvious connection to make. In fact, in all the time she'd been at CFS—and before that Colorado Springs—no one had ever made a snide comment about her role in creating the defenders.

"Do people ever say things behind my back, about my role in all this?" she asked Forrest in a whisper.

He leaned in close, whispered in her ear. "The president said if anyone ever criticized you, he'd have their head on a stick. They wouldn't dare."

That explained it.

Moments later, the little town of Gakona, Alaska, came into view a thousand feet below. After eighteen months at CFS Alert, Gakona seemed like a thriving metropolis. It consisted of maybe fifty buildings surrounded by nothing but wilderness. Not that they were going to be spending any time in Gakona. Their C-295 banked right, heading toward an airstrip at an air force atmospheric research compound six miles outside the town.

They descended quickly to minimize the risk of being spotted by a patrol, although they'd chosen the location because there seemed little reason for defenders to be in the area. The landing strip was set amid thousands of what looked to be windmills with rotors pointing skyward. Someone on board probably knew what they were, but at the moment Dominique wasn't the least bit interested in them. They were in defender-controlled territory, and would only be going deeper in. They were the enemy, and if they were caught, they'd be killed.

When the plane came to rest, Dominique hustled outside with the rest and helped unload their supplies as Blake,

Sheena, and a few others ran off to locate the BvS10 arctic transport vehicles they'd found in the base's online inventory.

Before long, the vehicles rolled out from behind a lime-green aluminum building. They looked like oversized SUVs on tracks. As they pulled up, Dominique hefted a box of MREs to load into the flip-up storage compartment.

Two hours later, Blake's portable radar picked up a squadron of defender fighters heading in their direction. They took the vehicles off-road, bouncing and jarring, weaving through the forest until, they hoped, they were hidden from view. They killed their lights and sat in the dark for twenty minutes before continuing.

With the sun sinking into the trees, they stopped for the night at a long-abandoned logging camp a hundred miles from the nearest paved road. A row of rectangular red clapboard cabins reminded Dominique too much of the barracks at CFS Alert. Rusting appliances—a meat locker, water cooler, washers, dryers—were piled by the weed-choked ruts that passed for a road in front of the cabins.

Dominique grabbed her gear and headed for one of the less decrepit bungalows. She glanced back, looking for Forrest. He was talking to Carmine Wood in front of the lead vehicle. Dominique didn't want to invite him to share a cabin in front of an audience. She'd have to wait.

Between the cabins, she could see a rickety metal pier on a shallow river, with a contraption that reminded her of a giant sewing machine built into the pier. She pulled open the door, and stopped dead.

There was a Luyten nest in the cabin. Still clutching the

doorknob, she watched as President Wood swung open the door of the next cabin. He paused as well, looked at Dominique.

"There's one in there, too?"

Dominique nodded. She checked the next cabin down. Same thing. The Luyten must have used it as a safe base, back during the war. Normally you wouldn't find this many nests together, so far from human targets.

"Chief? Look at this." Forrest was squatting beside an abandoned truck. Dominique followed Wood over.

There was a Luyten tunnel entrance, camouflaged within a trash dump behind the truck. Forrest was kneeling amid the rotting paper, bottles, and cans, peering into the hole.

"They had quite a compound here," Wood said.

"I wonder if there's any chance they left weapons behind," Forrest said. He pressed his face close to the ground, trying to get a better line of sight into the tunnel.

"You're not thinking of climbing down in there, are you?" Dominique asked.

"I doubt you'd find much," Wood added.

Forrest shifted left, then right, still trying to get a line of sight. "I don't have anything else productive to do. I think I'll grab a flashlight and take a look."

Dominique resisted the urge to kick his leg, which was splayed beside her foot. She could think of something productive they could do.

"*Jesus!*" Forrest shouted, jerking back.

"What is it?" Wood asked.

He flattened onto his stomach and slid partway into the hole. "I thought I saw something. I swear, it looked like a baby Luyten. Then it was gone."

A sharp cry of surprise startled Dominique. She whirled.

A Luyten was standing behind them. Dominique gaped at it, then noticed another standing between two of the cabins, fiddling with the exoskeletal battle suit it was wearing.

"They're *armed*!" Dominique shouted.

She wasn't the first to notice. Sheena stood unmoving, her rifle leveled at the Luyten closest to her.

"How the *fuck* did they get hold of weapons?" Wood hissed.

Dominique wasn't concerned about where the weapons came from. If the Luyten chose to use them, they were all dead. But if the Luyten wanted to kill them, they would have done it by now.

"Sheena, put the rifle down," Dominique said. "You know that's not going to help us."

Sheena lowered the muzzle, but held on to the rifle.

"They're not killing us," Wood said, half to himself. "Why aren't they killing us?"

"You *did* sign a treaty with them," Dominique pointed out.

*Leave now.* The words blasted through Dominique's mind. From Forrest and the president's reactions, they'd received the same message.

"That's the best offer I've gotten in a long time," Wood said. He raised his voice. "Let's go, into the transports."

No one had to be told twice.

As they crawled along the logging road in the dark, intent on putting a substantial amount of distance between themselves and the Luyten before setting up a camp, Dominique had an epiphany.

"They never gave up those weapons," she said aloud.

Everyone looked at her.

"How could we possibly verify that all of the Luyten turned themselves in after the war? They knew we couldn't. Some of them retreated deep into the wilderness instead. They know we're on the run ourselves and not a threat, so when Forrest started poking around in their tunnels, they decided to simply come up and tell us to get the hell out of Dodge."

"If you're right, there must be more than one of those compounds. They could have them all over the world," Forrest said.

"I'll bet you anything they do," Dominique said. They were like fleas on a dog; every time you thought you were rid of them, there they were again.

# 74

# Oliver Bowen

*October 20, 2047. Washington, D.C.*

From his parked car, Oliver watched kids shooting baskets, a couple playing tennis, joggers circling the track. He marveled at the mundane scene. There wasn't a defender in sight, nothing to indicate that everything had changed.

He spotted Kai and Lila, pulling into a space at the other end of the parking lot. Oliver stayed in his car as they got out and headed across the soccer field, slipped through the gate, and headed down the hiking trail. He allowed three minutes to tick off on the car's clock before he stepped out of his old Toyota and followed them into the woods.

They were waiting about a quarter mile in, Kai sitting on a fallen tree, Lila pacing.

Lila gave Oliver a fierce hug; Kai smiled and nodded, clearly in pain from the short hike. Every time Oliver saw Kai, he hoped to see some noticeable improvement, but they were more than two years removed from Kai being shot. This might be the best he was going to get. It was a depressing thought.

"So what's going on?" Oliver asked. He'd been surprised to find the note in his mailbox.

"We were contacted by a Luyten yesterday," Lila said.

"A Luyten?" Oliver clutched Lila's arm. "A Luyten spoke to you?" He'd never expected to hear those words again.

As Lila laid out a horrific story of plans to exterminate most of the human race, of the offer of a Luyten alliance, Oliver's insides roiled. He would need to find a bathroom as soon as their meeting was over. It was a familiar sensation, one he hadn't missed in the least since he went into hiding.

"You can't trust Luyten," he said when Lila was finished. "If we did manage to wipe out the defenders, they'd turn around and wipe *us* out. I have no doubt of that."

"So what you're saying is, with or without the Luyten's help, we can never revolt, because if we win, the Luyten will turn on us," Kai said.

Oliver hadn't really thought about it like that before. He wondered if Island Rain's people had. "If we overthrew the defenders, we'd have to get them to surrender before their numbers were too badly compromised, so they would still be an effective deterrent on the Luyten."

"That's quite a balancing act."

Oliver's feet were getting tired. He sat on the log, stared off into the bare winter branches. As far as he was concerned, it was too dangerous to do anything the Luyten wanted them to do. They were too powerful, too clever; they'd find an utterly unexpected way to turn things to their advantage. "As soon as we create defenders the Luyten can read, we've ceded all control to the Luyten."

"I agree," Lila said. "It's too dangerous."

Movement among the trees caught Oliver's eye. Gold patterns, shifting among the bramble and tree boughs in the woods. Oliver stood, straining to see.

Kai stood as well. "What?"

Oliver knew what it was. As it moved closer he could make out the limbs, the eyes. The real jolt of terror hit him when he saw that one of the eyes was nothing but a ruined mass of scar tissue.

"Did either of you bring a gun?" Oliver asked. Although a gun wasn't much use against a Luyten.

"Holy shit," Lila said. Five was clearly visible now, passing between trees, branches cracking as it pushed through the underbrush.

*I'm not going to hurt you*, Five said. He stepped onto the path.

"Where did you come from?" Oliver said. "Of all the places in the world the defenders could have sent you, you ended up here?"

*I ended up in San Antonio. I've been traveling for two days to get here.*

"Traveling? How the hell can you travel?" Lila asked. "What, you told the defenders you had something you needed to do, and hopped on a bus?" So Five was speaking to all of them, not just to him. That was new.

*The defenders stopped keeping track of us individually a long time ago. They're impatient with mundane details. We keep things running without being told. They're happy with that arrangement.*

That confirmed Oliver's experience, and was useful information to be filed away. The defenders were not without their weaknesses.

"I take it you've been sent to convince us to agree to this alliance?"

*That's right.*

Oliver couldn't help but laugh. "You send the Luyten who killed Lila's father to pitch the idea to her, and the one who broke up my marriage to close the deal with me. You guys must be short on talent."

*We need to convince Lila because of her unique position. By extension, we need to convince you as well. Who better to reform your feelings about us than the ones most responsible for forming those impressions in the first place?*

"I probably wouldn't have taken the divorce as hard if you weren't simultaneously trying to wipe out my entire species."

*That was never our intention. Once you surrendered, we would have stopped.*

"Yeah. Things didn't work out that way, though, so we'll never know." Oliver waved toward himself, like a guy in a fistfight offering his opponent a free shot. "Go ahead, then. Convince me."

Five eased into the Luyten prone position. *Neither of our species needs this entire planet. With your losses, and ours, there are enough resources for everyone. We would accept any reasonable arrangement, whether it be complete segregation or intense intermingling of our two species.*

*We feel the deaths of our own more acutely than you can imagine. If we're allowed to live in peace, we'll go to almost any length to avoid violent conflict with you.*

Oliver waited until he was sure Five was finished. "You once warned me that you could be lying at any time. I learned that lesson the hard way." He thought of Vanessa, let all the bottled-up anger in him come to the surface. "You took pleasure in fucking up my life. Personal pleasure. It had nothing to do with the war. You just wanted to see me suffer." Oliver stepped closer to Five, stabbed a finger at him. "I treated you with respect. You were my prisoner, but I never treated you like one."

*No, you didn't. That's one of the reasons we're coming to you, and Lila, and Kai.* Five stepped around Oliver, went over to Kai. *I'm sorry for your injuries, my friend.*

Kai nodded tightly.

*Yes, I used you when you were only a boy. I was desperate. I'm sorry. And I'm still grateful for the help you gave me.*

Oliver thought Five was pouring it on a little thick. He could barely reconcile this warm, grateful beast with the slick son of a bitch he'd known back in the day. He suspected he was still a slick son of a bitch, manipulating them the way he'd manipulated both Oliver and Kai years before.

Five turned back to Oliver. *You're right. I was intentionally cruel to you. I hated you all the more because you treated me well, and made it harder for me to see you as a bug whose life wasn't worth much. Killing something while simultaneously feeling her pain is truly indescribable. I think it drove us a little mad.*

"You're just bursting with sincerity, aren't you?" Lila said. "I'm getting all misty-eyed."

Five made a gurgling noise. *We're not all in agreement, either. Many of my kind are against this. You're not sure you can trust us? Imagine if you knew with absolute certainty that nearly all of your potential allies hated and feared you, that they wished you dead. Imagine proposing an alliance with people who, after signing a peace treaty with you, immediately handed you over to monsters to be exterminated.*

Oliver swallowed hard. How easy it was to remember

all the atrocities the Luyten had committed, but forget the betrayal they'd perpetrated on the Luyten.

He had the urge to clap his hands over his ears and hum. Five's arguments were compelling, but Oliver didn't want to be convinced—he wanted to hold on to his certainty that the Luyten couldn't be trusted.

*We can be petty, just like humans. Can't you allow that we might also share more noble human qualities, like remorse, kindness, integrity? I don't want to be your enemy. I don't want to stand by while two billion of your people are killed. I'm ready to fight at your side.*

Oliver's throat tightened. He turned away, took a few steps down the path. "Get out of here. I need to talk to my family."

Without another word, Five left. None of them spoke until Five was out of sight, although they knew Five could hear them regardless of where he was.

"I think our first step is to confirm defenders are in fact evacuating some densely populated areas," Oliver said.

*Karachi, Shanghai, São Paulo, Jakarta, Calcutta, Tehran, Chicago—*

"*All right*," Oliver said, clenching his eyes shut. He pinched his temples, already sick of hearing that voice in his head. He looked at Lila and Kai. "I'll find out if it's true. It's less risky for me to do it. Let's meet back here in two days."

Lila and Kai nodded. Oliver looked off through the woods, toward the spot where Five had disappeared. Was he lingering just out of sight? Was he going to stay within telepathic range of Oliver for the duration? Surely he was; that's why he'd come. The thought made Oliver queasy.

"So, how are you, Dad?" Kai asked.

Oliver looked at him, thrown by the question. "I'm sorry

I don't get to see you and Lila as often as I'd like. I know it's not ideal to have to meet like this—"

"No, Dad, it's not about that. If I was in your position, I'd do the same thing. I'm just asking. How are you?" Kai started to say more, then stopped, folded his arms across his chest. "Isn't that why we're fighting them, so we can stay human? Talk to each other about nothing? We're so boxed in. So blocked off. We don't talk to each other anymore." He shook his head sadly. "We've gotten so screwed up from all of this."

Oliver wasn't sure how to respond. Kai was right, but Oliver didn't know if he remembered how to talk about nothing, how to relax and just be a family. All he could think to do was give Kai a hug, so that's what he did. Kai hugged him back, nodded as they separated.

Oliver turned to find Lila waiting, arms open. He held her, blinked back tears, Kai's words echoing in his mind. He was right, they needed to stay human. As human as they could, anyway.

"I'm okay," Oliver said as he let go of Lila. "I'm still collecting my comics. DC now. I'm working on a complete run of *Superman*."

She smiled. "That's a tough run to complete."

"How about you?" Oliver asked. "You finding any games to play in? Besides the fiascos with the defenders, I mean."

As Kai ran through the players in his regular games, Oliver felt relieved to discover he could still have a conversation.

# 75

## *Oliver Bowen*

*October 23, 2047. Washington, D.C.*

He was standing in the shower, drying himself off, when he heard the sound of a coin dropping into a vending machine. It was the sound his phone made when he had an incoming text message. He dropped the towel and rushed into the living room, dripping wet and cold.

Peter—

Here are the statistics for the products you're interested in. Good luck with your business venture!

Diane

He opened the attachment, scanned the numbers. His heart sank as he read down the columns. Shipments of filet mignon, jumbo shrimp, and leg of lamb coming into Karachi, Shanghai, São Paulo, and the other cities Five had listed had dropped precipitously. They were the foods only defenders could afford, the ones defenders favored. Shipments of those foods to major cities not on Five's list had actually increased somewhat.

A human inquiring about defender troop movement was a dead human, but there were many ways to determine if a specific population was on the move.

"Oh, Christ," he said under his breath.

Oliver began typing a quick note of thanks to Alissa Valeri, who'd been a top-notch data hound at the CIA.

The doorbell rang. Almost no one knew he lived there; the door hadn't rung in a month. He went to the window.

For a moment he didn't recognize the woman standing at his door, then it registered.

It was Vanessa.

Fingers trembling, Oliver flipped the lock and opened the door. "*Hi.* How did you find me?" She looked older than when he'd last seen her. That had been almost ten years earlier, when he bumped into her at a Nationals game. She was still beautiful. Oliver pulled the door open wider so Vanessa could come in, but she stayed where she was.

"*Will you please get that* thing *out of my head?*" she said.

"What? What thing?"

Vanessa's eyes narrowed. "You don't know about it? Honestly?"

"Vanessa, I have no idea what you're talking about."

Vanessa closed her eyes, spoke very slowly. "The alien is trying to convince me to reconcile with you."

"*What?* Oh, no. You've got to be kidding." It made sense. Five was trying to fix what it had done, to prove his sincerity.

Vanessa was studying him carefully. "You had nothing to do with it? You didn't ask it to do this?"

406

"God, no. I wouldn't inflict that monster on my worst enemy." He reached out as if to touch Vanessa, but hesitated. "I'm so sorry about this, Vanessa. Believe me, I know what it's like to have that monster in your head."

She gave Oliver a sarcastic smile. "You'll be happy to know it takes full responsibility for the misunderstanding between us."

Even her indirect reference to his tragic blunder made him cringe. What an idiot he'd been back then. "Well, that's big of him."

"Can you get it to leave me alone? I'm going to jump off a bridge if it doesn't stop."

Oliver heaved a big sigh. "I'll try. He has to be within telepathic range to hear me, and he has to be willing to speak to me. Although lately, the latter's been less of a challenge than it used to be."

"So you've been in touch with it recently?"

Oliver kicked himself for letting that information slip. He'd been a CIA bureau chief, for God's sake. "Five contacted me, yes."

"What did it want? To reminisce about the good old days?" A touch of bitterness leaked into her tone. She swept her long black hair, now infused with strands of white, out of her face in a gesture that was painfully familiar.

The smart thing would be to latch on to Vanessa's suggestion, laugh it off, but Oliver couldn't bring himself to tell her an outright lie. "If you really want to know, ask me again in six months and I'll tell you." One way or another, it would be safe to tell her in six months. By then the secret would be out. Because, Oliver realized, if he had a say in this, they were going to go through with it. Not because Five's little gesture of remorse had moved him in the slightest; it was the cold, hard data in that email message that convinced him. If they did nothing, 80 percent of the world's population would die. If they acted, they put the final 20 percent at risk, but at least everyone had a fighting chance. If the Luyten double-crossed them, so be it. They'd beaten the Luyten once; they could do it again.

Vanessa had said something. Oliver had been so lost in thought he'd missed it. "I'm sorry, what did you say?"

"I said, I'm sorry to bother you." She glanced over her shoulder. For a moment Oliver wondered if someone was waiting in the car for her—a husband or boyfriend—but he couldn't see the street from his door. "I would have called, but the Luyten refused to give me your number. Although this was probably too sensitive to talk about on the phone anyway."

"You're probably right." He wanted to ask if she *was* married, or seeing someone. He knew that she and her second husband (whose name Oliver had forgotten—all he remembered was, it wasn't Paul) had divorced six or seven years earlier. Fifteen years ago, he would have been stupid enough to ask that sort of question. Not now, though.

He held out his hand, and Vanessa took it. "It was good seeing you, Vanessa. I'll get Five to leave you alone. I promise"

"Thank you. It was good to see you, too."

She turned. Oliver closed the door and went to the window to watch her climb the steps. For a moment the terrible sadness returned, the hollowing loneliness that had tormented him after their divorce. He turned his thoughts to the work ahead, and the pain receded.

# 76

## *Lila Easterlin*

*October 24, 2047. Washington, D.C.*

Kai pointed into the woods. "Look at that."

Lila spun, scanned the terrain. She didn't see anything through the lattice of bare branches, nothing moving on the floor of fallen brown and orange leaves.

"Higher."

She followed his pointing finger up into the trees, and spotted it: a huge woodpecker perched on a dead tree, poking at it with her long beak.

"A pileated woodpecker," Kai said. "They're rare."

She was about to ask where Kai the city boy had learned about woodpeckers when she spotted Oliver heading toward them, head down, hands in his pockets. Lila tried to read his face for a hint of what he might have found out, but Oliver always looked worried.

"Not good news," he said as he reached them. "Defenders are definitely clearing out of the cities Five gave us, and not out of others. I think the Luyten are telling the truth."

409

He looked at Lila. She knew what he was going to say, and she didn't want to hear it.

"I think we have to accept their offer."

Lila cursed, turned away.

"I wish I was more confident we can trust them. I'm not at all confident about that, but, honestly? I think it's our only chance."

She didn't want to agree to this. *She* would be the one who would actually hand the Luyten the power to wipe them out; it would all be on her shoulders.

"What other choice do we have, Lila?" Oliver asked. "Do nothing, while the defenders gas two billion people, quite possibly including your family?" Lila looked up at him. "They wouldn't kill *you*, because you're too valuable, but I could picture them whisking you off to Easter Island just before they gas the entire D.C. area."

"It would take at least three months to get enough altered defenders trained and in place. What if the defenders carry out their plan before then?"

*That's why they've pressured you to ramp up production. They want to reinforce their numbers before they act. They want overwhelming force before they reveal their intentions, in case you fight back.*

"Hello, Five," Oliver said. "Are you in the immediate vicinity."

*I'll be there in a minute.*

"Why do you risk coming here if you can communicate with us from eight miles away?" Lila asked.

*I think it's important that we meet face-to-face.*

"You don't *have* a face," Lila said.

"If we do this, we'll need able military commanders and strategists ready to go, all over the world," Oliver said, ignoring her crack. "How are we going to recruit them, now that Earth2 is no longer an option?"

It hurt Lila to hear him say it aloud. Almost as soon as she'd learned Dominique was still alive, Lila was back to not knowing if she was or not.

*We'll contact them directly, as soon as the altered defenders are in place.*

They could do that, couldn't they? Every time Lila thought she grasped the magnitude of the Luyten's advantage, another facet of it surfaced. If they were allied with the Luyten, humans would suddenly have an effective means of communication with no chance of defender interception.

"What about weapons?" Kai asked. "The defenders have total control of weapons."

Five pushed out of the brambles behind them.

*Getting access to weapons will be the focus of our initial attacks. We'll use improvised explosive devices and suicide attacks. In the United States and Russia, there are large caches of outdated weapons buried in various unguarded locations. We'll liberate those as well.*

"You have all the answers, don't you?" Lila said. Then she thought about what Five had just said. "Hang on, your initial attacks? Are you picturing a guerrilla war, like you fought against us?"

*Of course. When you're facing a larger, better-armed force, it's the most effective—*

Five stopped there, Lila assumed, because it was reading her thoughts. She laughed out loud, relishing a rare moment when a Luyten looked foolish. "You see it now, don't you? That's not going to fly against defenders."

"What? Why?" Oliver asked.

*This is why we need to work together.*

"*What is?*" Oliver asked.

Lila turned to face Oliver. "Guerrilla wars work because the larger force can't catch the enemy. They attack, then duck back into the woods, or melt back into the population."

"So?"

Lila folded her arms. She was going to have to spell it out for him, wasn't she? "The defenders don't care *who* they kill. As soon as you start attacking, they'll turn and lay waste to the population, just like they're planning to do anyway." Oliver was nodding now, and so was Kai. "They're not going to go chasing after each individual attacker; they're going to point their tanks at crowds and open fire."

Oliver looked toward Five, but he'd gone silent. Lila kicked at a fallen branch, feeling a little smug, waiting for someone to pick up the pieces, if they could.

It was Five who broke the silence. *The initial attacks will be Luyten only. They'll be small. The defenders will think we're attempting the coup on our own, and they'll turn their guns on us. Soon after—very soon after would be our preference—humans will rise up, and we fight a war on a million fronts, all at once.*

"How exactly are we going to get a billion people to rise up, more or less all at once?"

*When the time comes we'll push everyone able to fight. We can be very persuasive.*

"You're going to persuade a billion people?" Oliver looked dubious. "I'm not sure anyone's going to respond to Luyten shouting orders at everyone at once."

*Oh, they won't be generic orders. We'll speak to each person individually, by name. If we have to we'll shame them into fighting, or scare them.*

"A *billion* people? Have you done the math on that? It'll

take forever," Kai said. "We'll have to target certain block leaders, rely on them to spread the word."

*Oliver, do you remember the MRIs and CT scans you subjected me to while I was your prisoner? Remember the curious repetitive nature of my brain structures?*

"Sure."

*If a species evolved with the ability to exchange thoughts with many others at once, wouldn't it make sense that this species also develop separate, parallel processing centers of conscious thought?*

Oliver looked stunned. "You can think—and communicate telepathically—on multiple tracks simultaneously?"

The implications of that boggled Lila's mind. Dozens, maybe hundreds, of separate lines of thought all going on at the same time in one head? The entire species thinking like that, and communicating telepathically. All of those lines of thought connected in a vast web. They were even more alien than she'd imagined.

*Do we have a deal?* Five was looking at her.

Lila grunted. "I imagine you knew we had a deal before I was aware I'd made up my mind. That's not to say I don't have deep reservations about this."

*Humans draw a hard line between thinking something and saying it aloud. I'm asking you to say it aloud.*

Lila considered Five. How had they arrived here, at this insane moment? She wanted to tell this creature to go to hell. But that wasn't an option; even she understood that now.

"Yes. We have a deal."

# 77

# Dominique Wiewall

## October 24, 2047. Southeastern Alaska.

A Harrier swooped by, just above the tree line. Forrest, who was driving their BvS10, jerked the wheel, taking them off the road and pulling to a stop.

They listened to the thump of the Harrier's propellers. Dominique watched out the window, praying it didn't turn back.

"Do you think it saw us?" Forrest asked.

"I don't know. It was close. It could have."

"If it did, they wouldn't necessarily engage us," Peter Smythe said from the back, crowded in with a dozen others. "They might call in reinforcements first."

What was there to do, though? Ditch the vehicles and head off into the woods with whatever they could carry? In the side-view mirror Dominique saw the door open in the next vehicle back. The president stepped out, his eyes turned toward the sky. Dominique and Forrest got out as well.

"Do we just hope they didn't see us?" Wood asked.

No one answered.

"What are the odds? Sheena?" He turned. "Did they see us? Your professional opinion."

Sheena looked into the treetops. "It's a close thing, but I'm going to say no. The foliage is too thick, and we're on something that's barely a road; they wouldn't expect to find us here."

Wood nodded, satisfied. "Let's take a break since we've already stopped." He raised his voice. "Twenty minutes, everyone."

It was fascinating to Dominique to watch Anthony Wood lead. Not once had she heard anyone question why Wood should be in charge, given that the United States no longer existed, and his brother, not him, had been the sitting president when it fell. No one questioned him because everyone *wanted* him to be in charge. He was that good at it.

"I'm going to take a walk, stretch my legs a little. Want to come?" Forrest asked.

"Sounds good." Dominique barely remembered what it felt like to take a walk, let alone a run. She'd run almost every day of her life until she found herself at CFS Alert, where there was nowhere to run but outside, where the snow was always three feet deep.

They headed off down the logging trail. Forrest checked his watch. "We'll go nine minutes, then turn around."

There was nothing to see except trees and brush, the same view they'd had for days, but it was nice to pass it slowly, to hear the wind and the occasional bird. "How far do you think we are from the nearest town?" Dominique asked.

"Probably less than fifty miles. We're getting into more densely populated territory." Forrest took her hand, and, glancing back, Dominique realized he'd waited until they were out of sight of the caravan before doing so. The few people who had coupled up over the past eighteen months were all discreet about it, probably because they were aware of how many of the others were lonely, and recently widowed. Some didn't know whether they were widowed, whether their children were dead or alive. She was so grateful she didn't have children.

"I'm so tired." It came out before she could stop it.

"Me, too."

"I'm not sure I understand the plan. We're just going to slip into some town and hope the defenders don't notice us?"

Forrest glanced at his watch. "I'm not sure there is a plan. Maybe a few of us slip into one town, a few into another."

"I doubt the president would split us up like that. It would mean we were giving up the resistance."

"No, you're right."

Forrest paused, frowning. Dominique was going to ask him what was the matter, then she heard it, too: an aircraft engine, getting louder. They bolted into the woods. Dominique ran, arms up to keep branches from whipping her face, following Forrest's back. The engine grew louder. She heard another, farther away.

Forrest stopped abruptly, ducked behind a tree. Dominique squatted behind him, panting, a plume of vapor jetting from her open mouth.

A Harrier roared past, flying low, following the logging trail. Just before it flew out of sight, a defender in full battle gear appeared in the rear doorway and leaped out. A small chute deployed as it dropped.

"Oh, no." Dominique leaped up.

Forrest caught the back of her jacket and tugged her back down. "We're unarmed. We're no help to anyone."

Gunfire erupted in the distance. Panicked shouts. Dominique squeezed her eyes shut as screams reached her, the sounds of people dying, of her friends dying.

"We have to get out of here," Forrest said.

"There might be survivors. Wounded. We have to see."

"Right now we have to run." Forrest took her hand, led her deeper into the woods. They ran down a slope, and when they came to a stream Forrest surged right through; Dominique followed, her feet numb as soon as they hit the water.

Far behind them, she heard the *whump* of an explosion, followed closely by two more. They were taking out the vehicles, so anyone they missed would be left to freeze, with no shelter, no supplies.

They had nothing, Dominique realized. No blankets, no food, no weapons. She slowed, called out, "*Wait.*" Forrest stopped. As he turned she could see from his expression that there was no need to point out the seriousness of their situation.

The sharp crack of a branch sent a fresh jolt of fear through her. She and Forrest dropped to the ground and crawled on their bellies until they were hidden by a copse of trees. Slowly, carefully, Dominique raised her head to look in the direction of the sounds.

Two defenders topped the rise a hundred yards away, both clutching rifles. She looked at Forrest, passed a silent question: Should they run, or stay down and hope the defenders missed them? Neither seemed a good idea.

A voice boomed in her head. Dominique nearly cried out in surprise. *Run. Two hundred yards, directly away from them.*

She exchanged another look with Forrest, who nodded. What did they have to lose? They sprang up as one, sprinted away. A clump of trees was between them and the defenders, masking their flight. They'd covered a hundred yards before

Dominique heard a shout of discovery from the defenders. Ahead through the trees, she could see bright shifting colors—four Luyten, heading toward them.

*We'll carry you: Dominique, run to me, orange; Forrest, run to violet.*

She didn't want to put her life in the hands of a Luyten, but she saw no choice. As she approached the orange Luyten, it swept her up with its powerful cilia, like ropes roughly lashed around her legs and waist, pressed her to its stony body, and ran like hell.

Dominique's head bounced and jostled; the forest passed in a sideways blur as the defenders' shouts grew louder. A blast rocked the ground a dozen yards short of them, just as they reached a steep hill—a cliff, really. The Luyten kept going; Dominique wanted to shout for it to stop but couldn't muster the breath. The Luyten half climbed, half fell down the steep ravine, using the cilia on all of its free limbs to clutch and scrape at the rocks and dirt as they plunged hundreds of feet.

It hit the ground upright and galloped across a shallow river, then broke into trees on the opposite bank. Forrest was nowhere in sight; Dominique wondered if they'd fled straight into an even worse fate. If the Luyten had wanted her dead, all they would have had to do was wait. But if they didn't want her dead, what *did* they want with her?

*What we want right now is to keep you safe*, the Luyten said. *Then we want to get you and Forrest to Washington, D.C.*

Dominique was stunned. "Why would you want to do that?"

*Because we've agreed to an alliance with your people, and you have expertise that can help us.*

Dominique was positive she'd misunderstood, or more

likely the Luyten had misspoken. An alliance? The idea was simultaneously chilling and absurd.

Yet as the Luyten slowed, and uncovered the camouflaged entrance to a tunnel in the ground, Dominique had to admit the idea also made an odd sort of sense.

# 78

## Lila Easterlin

*October 25, 2047. Washington, D.C.*

Lila's hands were shaking as she called up the defenders' specifications—the genetic recipe Dominique Wiewall had developed to create the defenders. To introduce an entire neurotransmitter system into the existing framework, which had been meticulously designed to create an intelligent organism that functioned *without* that neurotransmitter, was a staggering proposition. Even with a trained staff assisting her, it would have been a challenge. But alone? It was going to take a long time. How long, she couldn't guess, because she wasn't sure how she was going to do it. It would be far easier if she could redesign the defenders from scratch, if she weren't also trying to hide the fact that she was doing this. Then she could simply back up and start over with the specifications for a human brain, and design something close to a defender. But these defenders had to look *exactly* like the existing ones, and to act like them.

As she typed a few tentative variations, she watched the

genetic code transform before her eyes. Without the Mizrahi protocol, which translated genetically expressible characteristics into genetic code, it would take years to design these changes. It was amazing, really, that she hadn't had to think in terms of adenine, cytosine, guanine, and thymine since graduate school. All of that was automated.

Lila jumped as a voice blared in her head.

*Minka is coming to see you about an employee. She'll be at your door in less than two minutes.*

Lila masked the program she was working on, called up a productivity report. She had no idea the Luyten was eavesdropping, but it made sense—they had as much riding on this as she.

After Minka left, Lila waited, in case she thought of something else and returned.

*All clear*, the Luyten said before she could resume work on her own.

When darkness came Lila texted both Kai and Erik to tell them she wouldn't be home until late. She went on working, knocking back coffee, driven by anxiety, blocked not only by a dawning understanding of how difficult, if not impossible, this was, but by doubts about whether she should be doing it at all.

At 3 a.m. she packed up and went home. If she stayed all night it might raise suspicion. On top of that, she wasn't making progress. Not real progress, anyway. So far she was only learning what *wouldn't* work. As she turned off the lights, it occurred to her that if the Luyten were telling the truth about the defenders' plans, then in a very real sense every day she failed to create the blueprint for the altered defenders, millions of lives could be lost. Not that she needed to feel any more pressure.

Halfway home, the Luyten's voice blared in Lila's head again.

*Please turn around and go back to your office. Make a portable copy of the defenders' blueprint. Take it to Oliver's apartment.*

"Are you fucking kidding me? If I'm caught carrying a copy of—" She shut her mouth, thought the rest. *Of the blueprint, I'll be killed on the spot, and if I'm followed to Oliver's apartment, he'll be killed.*

*I'm passing on this request from Oliver. You'll understand when you get to his apartment.*

"Why can't you just tell me now?"

*I could, but it would ruin the surprise.*

Lila slowed, pulled into an empty Wendy's parking lot, and turned around. *The surprise?* Lila couldn't help but laugh. How long had it been since she'd had a surprise that wasn't a shitty one?

*Surprise.* Your own people are dropping bombs on your head. *Surprise.* While you were a POW, your husband was shot a half dozen times.

*This is a good surprise.*

"Stop eavesdropping."

*I literally can't.*

"Then have the courtesy to pretend you're not eavesdropping."

That seemed to shut the thing up.

As she knocked on Oliver's door, Lila tried to imagine what could possibly be on the other side that would surprise her. What she really wanted was to hear that she didn't have to do this, that they'd come up with another plan to avert the coming genocide, but that seemed too much to hope for.

The door swung open; instead of Oliver, Lila found herself face-to-face with a ghost.

"Oh my God," Lila whispered. "I can't believe it."

Dominique grinned. "I can't believe it, either."

Lila launched herself, wrapping both her arms and legs around Dominique, who dropped to the floor under her weight, laughing.

"You're going to help me?" Lila asked, speaking into Dominique's shoulder. She noticed Oliver, standing in the doorway to the kitchen, watching the two of them and grinning. Another man Lila didn't recognize stood behind him, watching over Oliver's shoulder.

"Let's get to it," Dominique said.

"I'll make some coffee," Oliver said.

Lila leaned back so she could look into Dominique's eyes. "Tell me we're doing the right thing."

Dominique shook her head. "I used to think I knew when I was doing the right thing, but no more. At least we're doing something. I'm not much in love with the status quo."

Lila wished she could be so laissez-faire about it. The tightness in Dominique's brow suggested she might be putting on a brave front, to take some of the pressure off Lila. That would be just like her.

# 79

## *Oliver Bowen*

*December 28, 2047 (two months later). Washington, D.C.*

Oliver stared down at the phone, his heart pounding. If he was going to call her, he needed to just do it; there was never going to be a moment when he felt calm and collected making this call.

He punched Vanessa's number, raised the phone to his ear.

Vanessa answered on the third ring. When she heard his voice, she said, "How did you get my number?" She didn't sound angry, only surprised.

"The same way you got my address."

"Ah. Of course."

"I just wanted to check in, make sure my friend stopped bothering you." Since the defenders had taken over, talking on the phone had become an art. You had to avoid using key words that would trigger their automated filter and bring your call to their attention.

"Yes, he has. Thanks for intervening."

"I'm just glad I was able to get in touch with him."

Vanessa started to speak, stopped, breathed a sigh into the phone. "I have to say, it's given me a new appreciation for what you went through. Your friend knows just what buttons to push."

Oliver felt a weight lifting from his shoulders. "Thank you for saying that." He looked up, found himself staring up at his Marvel superhero FOOM (*Friends of Ol' Marvel*) poster. It reminded him of Five's take on why he'd gone back to collecting comics, all those years ago.

"It's impossible to understand what it's like, until you experience it yourself," Vanessa said.

Oliver wondered if that had been Five's strategy all along—not to try to convince Vanessa to reconcile with Oliver through his words, but to give her a taste of what Oliver had gone through. Although Five never would have been able to capitalize on Oliver's doubts about Vanessa's fidelity if the doubts hadn't been there to begin with.

"It still doesn't excuse what I did," Oliver said.

"Let's not go there," Vanessa said. "That was a lifetime ago."

"It certainly feels like a lifetime."

"'May you live in interesting times.' That's what the Chinese used to say, if they wanted to curse someone."

Oliver laughed. "We've certainly lived in interesting times."

"We certainly have."

There was a pause. Oliver listened to the sound of Vanessa's breathing.

"Well," Vanessa said, "thank you for calling. I'm glad we talked."

"I am, too. You have no idea."

Oliver set his phone on the coffee table. That one call, those four or five minutes, had brought him more peace than all the hundreds of hours of psychotherapy he'd undergone after the war. He went over Vanessa's words in his mind, wanting to commit them to memory so they could go on salving that wounded place.

What would his life have been like, if he and Vanessa had stayed together? Certainly he would have laughed more. She'd been such a light and playful presence, had been able to bring out a playful side of him he hadn't even known about. That side of him had shriveled and died during the divorce, and the war. Maybe he would have rediscovered it with Galatea, who had reminded him of Vanessa in a lot of ways, but really, how well had he known Galatea?

He wished he could talk to Vanessa again, but next time he wouldn't have a handy excuse. Maybe that was okay, now that Vanessa had apparently forgiven him.

Did he still have feelings for her after all these years, or were they only memories of feelings? Over the years he'd spent so much time thrashing himself for losing the love of his life that he'd rarely stopped to think about whether the present-day, flesh-and-blood Vanessa was still the love of his life. How would he know that, unless he got to know her again?

He picked up the phone. What was the worst that could happen?

She answered on the first ring, sounding surprised. "Hi, again."

"Hi. I was just wondering: Would you like to have coffee sometime?" He closed his eyes, held his breath.

"Sure. That would be nice."

"Great. Great." Oliver stammered, feeling like the awkward doofus he'd been that first time he called Vanessa and left a message. He'd asked her to go to the Smithsonian. He winced at the thought of it. The Smithsonian. How romantic.

*Is this a good time to ask for your forgiveness?* Five asked, as soon as Oliver was off the phone.

Oliver considered. "I appreciate the gesture you made," he allowed.

*We're going to be allies. It's important we trust each other.*

Oliver chuckled at that one. "It's a lot easier to trust someone when you can read his mind. You don't have to take it on faith; you *know* that if I have any say in it, we'll keep our word to you."

*I wish I could open my mind to you, so you could know I feel the same.*

"Yeah, well." Oliver went over to look at the FOOM poster. All of the major Marvel superheroes were represented, racing, jumping, and flying like they were coming right out of the poster at you. Silver Surfer led the way. Usually it was Spider-Man, or the Hulk. Wasn't Silver Surfer the only alien among the Marvel superheroes? Oliver was pretty sure he was.

*So far we've contacted two hundred fifty-seven people with strong military leadership experience, all over the world.*

"*What?* I thought we agreed to tell no one until all of the defenders were in place."

*We're not telling them about the defenders. Each thinks we're negotiating only with him or her, about humans and Luyten mounting joint attacks. We have to get your commanders used to the idea of this alliance.*

Oliver was not at all comfortable with the idea of the Luyten choosing the human leadership, but he didn't see another option. They knew who might be open to this alliance, and they would know immediately if someone could not be trusted.

*Exactly.*

"Now if only I were sure I could trust you."

*We've also salvaged more than two thousand tons of weapons the US and Russian governments stashed during the cold war,* Five went on, ignoring the comment. *As the first altered defenders are put in place, we'll begin the Luyten-only attacks on the defenders' least-defended weapons storage facilities. The first wave of altered defenders have been produced, by the way. They're a week into language training.*

Oliver felt a surge of adrenaline. There was no turning back now; this was really going to happen. "Do they seem all right?" He hadn't spoken to Lila and Kai in more than three weeks, he realized.

*I think so. Since I can't read the others, I have no basis for comparison. They're not like you.*

"How so?"

*Their minds are howling storms. Even before they learn language, their minds are always churning. If these are the minds of defenders with a crucial neurotransmitter added, I can't imagine what the others' minds are like.*

# 80

## *Kai Zhou*

*January 8, 2048. Washington, D.C.*

Erik leaned forward in his chair, looked past Lila, over at Kai for the third or fourth time. Kai suspected Erik was looking for signs that Kai was pleased about the Luyten attacks. Short of giggling and pumping his fist in the air, Kai couldn't imagine what it would take for Erik to pick up on Kai's feelings. Kai was taking no chances, though; he was wearing his best damned poker face.

"I hope you appreciate my allowing you to watch this," Erik said to them. "I'm not supposed to."

"Oh, we do appreciate it," Lila said. Kai piped in with an enthusiastic grunt. If only Erik knew who he was sharing the defenders-only news with. Not that this was all new information—the Luyten kept them updated.

On TV they were showing a satellite image of six or seven Luyten dragging two stunned defenders out of a high-speed locomotive that was lying on its side. The Luyten had blown the track moments earlier, sending the train spilling across the desert sand in sub-Saharan Africa. Looking down from above, Kai couldn't make out how the Luyten were killing the defenders, but it was clear they were. The stolidly toned news commentator explained that the train had been carrying portable rocket launchers, Tasmanian devils, and other small arms, which were now in the hands of rogue Luyten.

"We were wrong, to let the Luyten live," Erik said. "We should have executed them all. Plans are being set in place to do just that. Humans can just as easily perform the tasks Luyten do."

Why bother with two species of slaves, when one will suffice? Erik's logic was impeccable. Kai couldn't wait to see Erik's expression when the real uprising began, when humans and Luyten fought together.

The defenders would go berserk. He hoped the human population wouldn't lose its nerve.

Erik glanced over at him again, and Kai had a moment of clear, almost prophetic insight: When the uprising began, the first thing Erik would do was hunt Kai down and kill him. The only way Kai could prevent it was if he killed Erik first. The realization knocked the wind out of him.

It wouldn't be easy; Kai wasn't going to beat Erik in a shootout. He would have to come up with something Erik would never expect.

# 81

## *Lila Easterlin*

*January 10, 2048. Washington, D.C.*

"These in-person meetings are getting too dangerous," Oliver said. Like everyone there, he was wearing black and silver, the defenders' colors. The Luyten were taking the brunt of the defenders' rage, but the defenders were tense, and they were quicker to kill humans as well. Not that there was much evidence that wearing their colors improved your chances of surviving, if you crossed paths with a particularly cranky defender.

"Maybe from now on we should only communicate remotely, through Five," Dominique said.

As if on cue, Five galloped out of the woods. Lila felt a surge of something like affection. She tried to tamp it down, but couldn't. It was hard to remain suspicious of someone (or some thing) when your life was in its hands (or appendages), and vice versa. Maybe that was part of their plan, to lull the human race with the warmth of camaraderie.

Or maybe she should get over it, and stop being so suspicious.

It was astonishing to think this was really happening. People and Luyten were going to be fighting, and dying, side by side.

*We're recruiting more humans for leadership positions every day,* Five said. *As we launch new attacks, we're able to gauge people's reactions, and identify those who not only approve of the attacks, but wish they could take part in them.*

"Not everyone approves of the attacks?" Oliver asked.

*Oh, no. Some are afraid the defenders' retaliation will spread to humans. Others are working for the defenders— they're only interested in ingratiating themselves by feeding the defenders information.*

"If you know who those people are, shouldn't we be doing something about them?" Kai asked.

"Like what?" Lila asked. She didn't like the implications of the question.

*I'm glad you brought that up,* Five said. *Do you want us to supply names?*

"Hang on," Lila said. "Why would we want their names?"

"Because they have to be killed," Kai said.

After all this time, she realized, Kai still felt some sort of connection with Five. Both of them did—father and son. The Luyten had been right, to move heaven and Earth to get Five here in person.

Lila looked from Kai to Five, and back again. As Kai followed her gaze, his stolid expression turned dark, almost accusatory. Lila had a moment of wondering if Kai knew her so well he knew what she was thinking, or if Five had plucked it out of her mind and passed it on to Kai. That was the thing about having a Luyten present—you couldn't help but feel paranoid.

"Let me get this straight," Lila said. "We're going to kill people—*humans*—because aliens tell us they're spies?"

"We're all in, Lila," Kai said. "If we can't trust the Luyten, well, we're fucked. We've already crossed that bridge."

"So we're just going to *off* people? What are we going to do, slip into their houses when they're asleep and cut their throats, trying our best not to wake their kids? Lure them into alleys and beat their skulls in with steel pipes?" She looked at Oliver, Kai, and Dominique. "Who's going to do this? Us?"

*We can identify former Special Forces, CIA operatives, army snipers, and provide assignments directly to them. Most will want contact with some sort of human leadership first, to make sure our authority is legitimate.*

"And we're the human leadership?" Lila said. She brushed her hair out of her face. "Is no one else getting uncomfortable with this?"

"We're *all* uncomfortable with it," Dominique said. "None of us wants to decide who lives and who dies."

"But when push comes to shove, you will."

Dominique didn't answer.

"While we're on the topic of leadership," Oliver said, "I think I should point out that Dominique is the highest-ranking government official involved in this action. I'd like to suggest we officially acknowledge that, ultimately, she's in charge."

Dominique raised both of her hands. "Whoa, hold on. Don't put that on me. Four voices, four votes."

"What happens in the event of a tie?" Oliver asked.

"We talk it out."

Lila nodded agreement. "Can we vote on this assassination idea?"

"Yes," Dominique said, her voice clipped. "All in favor of authorizing the assassination of known human traitors?"

Everyone but Lila raised a hand.

*For the record, most of us are in favor as well,* Five said, *although we won't personally kill humans under any circumstances, for obvious reasons.*

Somehow Lila didn't find that reassuring.

*We're planning to escalate the attacks tomorrow. We're going to hit armories where at least one altered defender is stationed.*

"They're not going to like that," Kai said.

*No, they're not. More of us are going to die, but we can't let up. A few more days, and then the real war begins. Is three days from now an acceptable time frame?*

They looked at each other, then Oliver said, "Yes."

*Good. In the meantime, we're going to try to evacuate the cities where gas attacks are planned. Those are obvious first-strike targets, with the defenders already cleared out.*

# 82

## *Oliver Bowen*

*January 12, 2048. Washington, D.C.*

In the end, Oliver suggested he and Vanessa go for a walk. Oliver was a nonperson, so meeting at a coffee shop or restaurant carried risk, and he felt uncomfortable suggesting they meet in his apartment. So they met near his apartment and circled the block, their chins tucked against a chilly wind.

They caught each other up on their lives. Oliver told her what it had been like to be in Australia when the war broke out. How he'd be dead if not for Lila.

Vanessa described watching from her bedroom window as the first bombs dropped on D.C., then hiding in her basement, terrified, as the bombers flew overhead, evidently saving their bombs for more densely populated areas.

"I've never felt as alone as I felt in that basement," Vanessa said. "Most of the time, I'm happy on my own. I enjoy my own company; I thrive in the silence. But when you're terrified, when you're watching bombs drop on the roofs of your city, suddenly it's awful to be alone."

435

Oliver was surprised by Vanessa's honesty. It reminded him of the early months of their marriage, when he'd felt closer to her than he'd ever felt to anyone.

"I tried calling my mom, but the phones were out by then. The power was out; I was in the dark. I would have given anything to hear another human voice." Vanessa's mother, who'd lived in Albuquerque, died in the war. So did her brother, and an uncle.

A defender came around the corner. Oliver tensed, ever afraid one of them would demand ID and somehow see that his was fake. He and Vanessa pressed close to the wall to give the defender plenty of room to pass. As the thump of the defender's boots faded, Oliver's pulse returned to normal.

Vanessa noticed how tense he'd become. "I don't know how you do it. I could never disappear like you did, and worry all the time about being discovered."

Oliver shrugged, put on a brave face. "The trick is to hide in plain sight. If you seem to be avoiding them, they get suspicious. I really had no choice; even with Lila's protection, sooner or later they would have killed me because of who I was."

"You hated it when they drafted you into the CIA. Do you remember? You absolutely didn't want to do it."

Oliver nodded, watched a concrete mixer roll by, driven by a man who must have been ninety.

"But you adapted. You thrived." After a pause she added, "I didn't think you would."

The comment took Oliver by surprise. He nearly stopped walking before regaining his composure. "No?"

She touched his shoulder. "You were such a gentle man; too gentle to fight a war, I thought." She must have seen something in his expression, because she quickly added, "Don't get me wrong, I *liked* that you were gentle—it was one of the reasons I married you. But I confused gentle with weak. You're not weak."

"Thank you" was all he could think to say. When he first joined the CIA, he'd been afraid he was too weak. He wouldn't necessarily have used that word, but that was the crux of it. Over the years those fears had vanished. Still, it did his heart good to hear Vanessa say she didn't think he was weak.

"We probably should have done this a long time ago," Vanessa said. "Get things right with each other. Lots of divorced people reconnect and become friends after some time passes." She glanced at him, smiled. "We shouldn't have waited twenty years."

Oliver nodded. His throat had tightened; he didn't trust himself to speak, but he was afraid Vanessa hadn't seen him nod, and he didn't want her to think he didn't agree with what she'd just said. So he added, "I missed you," almost choking on the last word.

Vanessa studied his profile. Oliver kept his head down, face forward, not wanting her to see how choked up he was.

"I missed you, too."

How long had he imagined taking this walk, having this conversation? He felt…he couldn't put it into words. His senses felt sharpened; he felt lighter than he had in ages. The wars hadn't made Vanessa sour and brittle, or depressed and anxious, as it had so many people. At her core she was still the same woman. There were wrinkles around her eyes, the softness of middle age showing under her chin, but it was still Vanessa. She'd made it intact through two wars; Oliver wondered how she'd fare in a third.

"I want to tell you something I'm not supposed to tell anyone. But for now, you can't ask me for details."

Vanessa swallowed. "This is the thing you talked about on the phone. 'Ask me again in six months,' you said."

Oliver scanned the street, looking for any sign of defenders, or security cameras. It would be too dangerous to go into specifics, but he felt he had to say something, or he would be lying to Vanessa in a very real sense. "There's another storm coming, Vanessa. Very soon."

She slowed. She understood exactly what he was saying—Oliver could see it in her reaction. "You're sure?"

"I'm positive."

"As bad as the other storms?"

Oliver squeezed his eyes shut for a second. "Just as bad."

Vanessa took this in, then nodded. "Good to know."

A few blocks ahead, the row of colorful three-story connected houses ended, replaced by the towering frames of new defender construction, cranes and bulldozers, and piles of rubble—the remains of the human buildings that had been demolished to make room for more defender dwellings. Hopefully, they would never be completed.

"We'd better turn around," Oliver said.

They headed back the way they'd come.

Vanessa took out her phone, tapped the keys for a moment, then held it up. "I haven't listened to this in twenty years, but today, I need a laugh."

Sounding like he was speaking from inside a can, Oliver heard his own quavering voice. "Yes, Vanessa, this is Oliver Bowen? My sister, Leslie Bowen, gave me your number, and I hope you don't mind my calling you, but—"

As they laughed, Oliver watched for defenders. If a defender happened by and saw two humans laughing as hard as they were, it would raise suspicion.

# 83

## Kai Zhou

*January 12, 2048. Washington, D.C.*

The crawlspace under Erik's house was large enough for Kai to walk upright. When Kai and Lila had owned their own house, it had been a struggle to move around in the crawlspace with his back bent, squatting. And that had been before the war, when his body was strong and fully intact.

Kai located the plumbing that went up to the kitchen, listened to each of the pipes in turn with the stethoscope he'd brought. He marked the one connected to the sink, which he'd purposely left running, with a red X, then went to find the main circuit panel.

He felt like he was deceiving Lila by planning this without telling her. But there was no doubt in his mind that Erik was going to try to kill him; he was too good a poker player to misread what he'd seen on Erik's face.

He flipped the breaker switch leading to the heater for Erik's pool. Erik would never notice it was off; as far as Kai knew, Erik had never been in the pool—it was just a prop, a display of his wealth and power.

Rerouting the wiring was the hard part, especially with only one good hand. During basic training he'd received cursory instruction in booby-trapping, including about two minutes on how to electrocute someone using a house's typical 110-volt setup.

An hour later, shaking from the exertion, his hip throbbing, he had the wires from the pool's heater wrapped around the pipe leading to the kitchen faucet. In theory, when the time came all he had to do was flip the breaker, then get Erik to touch the faucet. He hoped he'd done it right.

# 84

# Dominique Wiewall

*January 18, 2048. Washington, D.C.*

It was a pathetic war room. In place of interactive high-definition electronic maps, they had paper maps and push-pins on the walls. And Spider-Man. Dominique didn't even feel qualified to participate in planning an insurrection. She was a geneticist, for God's sake.

*We're in direct contact with hundreds of high-ranking officers with combat experience,* Five said in her head, probably from miles away. *They'll be making the military decisions.*

"I know, I know," Dominique said. "They're just my *thoughts*, Five. That's where we express our private doubts and insecurities. If we're all going to live together in peace and harmony, your kind is going to have to learn to politely ignore what you hear us thinking."

*Sorry. You'll have to excuse my manners, but thousands of my people are being slaughtered at the moment, and each time it happens, it feels a little like dying myself. I'd appreciate it if you'd cut me one fucking inch of slack.*

Dominique swallowed. "I'm sorry. I forgot for a moment."

Oliver took a sip from his third or fourth cup of coffee, politely ignoring the altercation. He had three days' growth of dark stubble on his face, and smelled like a defender. Dominique wasn't sure how to tell him that if he didn't have time to shower, he should at least change his shirt.

They were all on edge. Forrest had his face buried in his computer, trying to find a way to hack into the defenders' video feeds to give them a better idea of what was going on out there. He cursed under his breath as he pounded away on the keyboard.

"Five, how are the evacuations in those cities going?" Oliver asked.

*Chaotically. Some people are trying to get out, others are staying put. The defenders are saying no one who stays will be harmed, and anyone who tries to leave without a pass will be killed. Meanwhile, we're doing our best to panic people into fleeing. If we can create stampedes out of the cities, the defenders won't be able to kill as many refugees. The defenders are frantically trying to understand what's happening.*

"How do they think people learned about their plan to gas those cities?"

*They're guessing it happened through an intercepted communication.*

Oliver nodded. "So they're not suspicious that some of their own have been altered?"

*That would be an impressive leap of logic, don't you think?*

"Don't underestimate their capacity for paranoia," Dominique said.

Someone knocked on the door.

Oliver jumped like he'd been goosed. He looked at the Invincible Iron Man alarm clock sitting on a nearly empty bookshelf. "Oh, shit. I invited Vanessa over. I didn't realize what time it was."

Dominique surveyed the room. "How were you planning to explain the battle maps?"

"I told her to come for coffee, but the real reason I invited her was to warn her of what's about to happen, and hopefully convince her to stay here with us."

Another knock. Oliver went to answer it.

It wasn't Oliver's ex, it was Lila, who stormed in, dropped her bag on the couch, and went to the map. "What's happening?" Her eyes were red, and her nose sounded plugged.

"Didn't we agree you should go to work, as usual?" Oliver asked.

"I infected myself with rhinovirus yesterday, then played up the symptoms like I had the flu."

That seemed risky to Dominique, but she kept her mouth shut. Lila liked to be in the middle of things. Dominique could relate.

"*Here we go!*" Forrest shouted. "I got it, I got it."

Everyone hustled to see the laptop screen. "We can choose country, then city or town, over here." Forrest pointed at a menu to the right of the screen. "Then scroll through the various feeds." He toggled through a dozen views of D.C. until he found one that showed a handful of defenders with rifles shooting dozens of Luyten, who'd evidently been hiding in a warehouse. The Luyten were fighting back (in fact, one defender was down and unmoving), but they were cornered and outgunned, and they were dying. There were twitching, bullet-riddled Luyten everywhere.

"It's time," Oliver said, staring at the carnage. "Let's send the call out to the human side of the resistance. They're being slaughtered."

*Not yet—we have to allow the images of Luyten resis-*
*tance to spread. It will make it much easier to convince your*
*people to fight at our side.*

"Are the images spreading?"

*Yes. Quickly. We've recruited human allies who are mak-*
*ing sure.*

"What about the Luyten in the wild, the ones who are
armed?" Dominique asked. "Couldn't they help?"

Lila turned. "What Luyten in the wild?"

"We stumbled on a camp of armed Luyten in Alaska. They
looked like they'd been there since the war. If there's one
camp, there must be others." She was surprised this was news
to them; she'd assumed if she knew about them, the others
would by now.

"Five?" Lila sounded supremely uneasy. "Are there others?"

There was an uncharacteristically long pause. *Yes. Some of*
*your military strategists are aware of them, and have plans*
*for them.*

"*How many?*" Lila asked.

*Several million worldwide, Lila. And yes, to what you're*
*thinking. That was the original plan.*

Dominique looked at Lila. "What was the original plan?"

Lila folded her arms. "They were planning their own
rebellion. Why else would they have secret camps all over
the world? And I'll bet they were breeding as fast as they
could, weren't they, Five? You were biding your time, waiting to grow an army big enough to wipe out the defenders,
and then us."

*Look out your fucking window, Lila. We're dying by the*
*thousands. If you still can't see past your own hatred of us,*
*then I give up. We're monsters, bent on killing. You're angels,*

*with nothing but noble intentions. Are you satisfied? Now, get the hell out of our way. The rest of us have work to do.*

There was no missing Five's rage. It burned inside Dominique's head like a blowtorch.

"He's right, Lila," Oliver said, speaking gently. "Since we formed this alliance, they've done everything they promised, and more."

"Except tell us about the existence of *millions* of other Luyten."

"They told others. I'm guessing they withheld the information from us because they knew how you'd react. Can you blame them?"

Lila looked at Oliver, her eyes like razors. Dominique had seen her angry like this a few times before; it had never ended well. She needed to defuse the situation before things got out of hand.

"Well, *you* can't blame them, that much is clear," Lila said, her tone acid. "What is it about Five that makes you crave his approval so desperately? Even after he broke up your marriage, you still want his approval more than you want your wife back."

Oliver's face trembled, with rage, hurt, or both. "You don't know anything about what I want."

Lila opened her mouth to reply just as the doorbell rang.

"That's Vanessa," Oliver said. He went to the door.

"Five, tell us the Luyten's original plan, so we can understand," Dominique said.

Oliver led Vanessa into the room; Dominique nodded a brief greeting, as Five replied.

*Stay out of sight. Multiply. In about thirty years, if we weren't discovered, we'd have had enough strength to rise up against the defenders. Humanity would be forced to choose a side.*

"But you changed your plan when you learned about the defenders' plan to cull the human population. You couldn't stand idly by while it happened," Dominique suggested.

Vanessa looked utterly confused. She was hearing only half the conversation. Oliver whispered something to her.

"Or they saw it as an opportunity," Lila said. She headed for the door. "I'm going to go. Five is right; I'm only getting in the way."

No one tried to stop her. Dominique was tempted, but it was probably best for her to be elsewhere; the stress was getting to her. The stress was getting to everyone, even Five. Hell, Dominique wished she could leave, too.

Oliver was still whispering to Vanessa. Her mouth dropped open. "Oh my God."

*Your military strategists are offering a range of opinions, from launching the human side of the uprising immediately, to waiting several days. The consensus seems to be to wait another hour or two. So that's what we plan to do.*

"Explain to me again how you're going to convince people to pour into the streets, poorly armed, against defenders armed to the teeth?" Dominique asked.

*Wake up, John Smith, your people are rising up, and they need your help. Get the ax from your garage and report to your commander on Main Street. I'm hiding under your house. Don't make me come in there and get you.*

The room erupted with laughter, except Vanessa, who looked confused, and scared. Oliver whispered something else, clearly trying to console her.

"That would get *my* ass into the street," Forrest said.

*It won't take much prodding. Most humans are ready to fight.*

Forrest nodded. He looked dead on his feet, his eyes half shut, his hands shaky. It occurred to Dominique that this might be a good time for them to go back to the little apartment they'd commandeered and get a couple of hours' sleep. Oliver would probably appreciate some time alone with Vanessa, and in this little studio apartment that wasn't going to happen unless Dominique and Forrest left for a while. When she suggested getting some sleep to Forrest, he didn't argue.

# 85

## *Kai Zhou*

*January 18, 2048. Washington, D.C.*

Kai went to the kitchen, plugged the sink, and turned the water on full-blast. He was so nervous his stomach ached. The water overflowed, spilling across the counter and onto Erik's tile floor. Erik would turn off the water when he saw this; he wouldn't be able to resist. He'd better not be able to resist.

Kai left the sliding glass door open and went around to the crawlspace entrance, then contemplated the circuit panel for a long moment before flipping the breaker on. He went back inside to wait for Erik. If Erik stuck to his usual routine, he'd be back for lunch.

*"Kai?"*

The front door banged open. "Kai?"

From his hiding place in the laundry closet, Kai heard Erik curse. He peered through the crack between the sets of folding doors into the empty kitchen, his heart racing. Something scraped along the wall and clattered to the floor, then Erik stepped into view, cursing a blue streak, glaring at the faucet.

"You did this on purpose, didn't you?" He reached toward the faucet. "Because you—" As Erik's fingertips brushed the handle, there was a blinding flash. Erik was blown backward into the wall of cabinets. He landed on his feet, then tipped forward, his face slamming into the counter before he crumpled to the flooded tile floor. It wasn't what Kai had expected. He'd pictured Erik dancing like a marionette, unable to let go of the handle while the current flowed through him, seeking ground.

Then he noticed the lights had dimmed. He'd thought it was the aftereffects of the bright flash, but it wasn't—the lights in the kitchen were out, and so were the ones in the hallway. The circuit had blown.

In the kitchen, Erik groaned.

Kai stopped breathing, strained to see Erik in the dim light filtering through the living room windows.

Erik lifted his head. His normally flat, fishlike eyes were lit with astonishment. Kai felt a terrible, sinking dread as Erik pawed feebly at the wet floor. He looked as weak as a puppy, but he wouldn't stay that way. He'd get up, if Kai didn't stop him.

Kai burst from the closet, cast about for a weapon. He spotted the row of kitchen knives jutting from the block above the counter. He pulled out the biggest one with his good hand.

His heart was tripping, his breath coming in a wheeze as he splashed through the inch-deep water. Erik muttered something, rolled onto his back, raised an arm as Kai lunged. Kai knocked Erik's weakened arm away and stabbed him in the chest.

Erik hissed like he was filled with air and Kai had popped

him, but it was blood, not air, that spattered Kai's hands and face. He pulled the knife free and stabbed again, harder this time, horrified by the feel of it sinking into Erik's chest.

This time Erik screamed in pain and rage; his big fist came down on Kai's head, knocking him to the floor. Kai struggled to his knees, raised the knife, and stabbed again with all of his might as Erik howled.

Suddenly Kai was on his back. Lila was standing over him, her screams merging with Erik's.

"*What are you doing?*"

Kai stared up at her, gasping for breath, feeling like he'd been caught doing something unspeakable.

Lila knelt beside Erik, her knees in pink water.

Kai sat up. He watched Lila, who was sobbing and holding Erik's face. She looked back at him. "Where is Errol?"

"He's at Charlie's. He's safe."

"What happened? Did he attack you?"

"He would have," Kai said. He spotted an assault rifle lying on the floor along the wall. That's what he'd heard clatter to the floor after Erik barged in. Kai pointed at it. "He brought that with him."

"Lila," Erik said, his voice a deep gurgle.

Lila put her face close to Erik's. "I'm here."

In that moment Erik looked as human as Kai had ever seen him. His face was twisted in pain, or regret, or something, and spattered with blood. His forehead was a series of ripples. Kai wasn't sorry he'd done it, wasn't sorry Erik was dying, but he was sorry Erik was suffering. Kai knew what it felt like.

Outside, he heard the sound of gunfire, then the *boom* of a howitzer, or tank. It was starting.

"Are you sad to see me this way, Lila?" Erik asked.

450

"Yes, Erik, I am."

That seemed to console Erik. Kai watched as he shuddered and died in Lila's arms.

Lila stood, looked around the flooded kitchen, clearly trying to make sense of the scene. She looked at Kai. "What happened?"

Kai gestured toward Erik. "He was going to kill me. I could read it in his face this morning when he left. So I rigged a trap and killed him first."

Lila frowned. "You rigged a trap? What do you mean?"

"I ran an electrical current through the faucet."

"You ran..." Lila absorbed this for a moment, as outside, the booming and popping of battle intensified.

"Lila, don't blame me for being the one who's not dead."

Lila covered her eyes with her palm. "But you *stabbed* him. I saw you."

Kai stood slowly. He looked at his hands, caked with drying blood. The water was still running. He thrust them under the faucet; the chilly water turned light pink. Tendrils of deeper red carried up and out of the sink, over the counter.

Lila left the kitchen as he dried his hands on a towel hanging from the oven door. He could hear her in one of the bedrooms, opening and closing drawers.

Erik's assault rifle still lay on the floor in the living room. Kai went and picked it up. It weighed at least thirty pounds.

Lila reappeared carrying an oversized beige bedspread. She used it to cover Erik.

"I have to get out there and help," Kai said.

Lila looked at the rifle in his hands. "What? No. You're part of the command team. We need you."

A red stain had bloomed on the bedspread; it grew as Kai

watched. "No, you don't. I'm not CIA, or State Department, or a genetic engineer. I'm a poker player and a war veteran. I'd be more useful out there." He motioned toward the door with his head.

Lila reached up, grabbed his face with both hands, and turned it toward hers. He hadn't realized it, but he was avoiding her eyes. "You'll die out there. Please don't go."

Kai didn't answer.

"You're going out there to prove you didn't have anything against Erik personally. Forget what I said; I shouldn't have said it." She drew him into a hug. "This is all so fucked-up. Sometimes I'm not even sure whose side I'm on." She pressed her face into his shoulder.

"It's not that. Honestly." He wanted to explain why he felt the need to go out there, but he wasn't sure himself. He had to go for the same reason as everyone else. To fix their fucked-up world.

"You're still trying to live down *The Boy Who Betrayed the World*," Lila said. "You took four bullets. You've done your part, okay?"

Kai smiled sadly. "Everybody's done their part. There's no one who's coming fresh to this fight."

Lila inhaled to say something, then simply hugged him tighter. "I don't know what I'll do if you die out there."

He didn't want to make a promise that was outside his control. "Soon we'll be able to live a normal, boring life. You, me, and Errol." He lifted the rifle, turned toward the door. "I'll meet you at Oliver's apartment."

"That's another reason I wanted you to come," Lila called after him. "They kicked me out. I'm not being a team player."

"Be a team player. Just go, before things get too bad out there. They love you."

"Five doesn't love me."

Kai laughed. "Well no, Five doesn't."

"When will you meet me there?"

He looked back at her. "When I'm too tired to fight. Figure twenty-four hours."

# 86

## Kai Zhou

*January 18, 2048. Washington, D.C.*

As soon as Kai was outside, a Luyten was in his head.

*Head toward Lester Avenue. Eight blocks.*

When Kai reached for his keys, the Luyten added, *We're setting up roadblocks to slow the defenders' tanks. Go on foot. We can use that assault rifle. And congratulations on your kill. Sometimes Lila's past blinds her to some harsh realities; put her reaction out of your mind and focus on the fight at hand. She loves you. She's thinking about how much she loves you right now; she regrets the accusation she made.*

Kai was sure the Luyten speaking in his head was neither Five nor the crimson one, yet it spoke as if it were an old friend, or, better yet, his shrink. He hadn't realized they were offering soldiers psychological services as well as tactical direction.

He also hadn't realized he was letting the encounter with Lila bother him, but he'd take the Luyten's word for it. He willed himself to focus on the landscape, the smell of oily smoke, the sound of gunfire and, farther off, artillery fire. A defender fighter jet roared past overhead, flying close to the ground.

The streets were nearly empty. People appeared and disappeared, running bent at the waist, carrying axes or knives. They were men and women, young and old. Occasionally someone passed who looked to be flat-out fleeing. Kai wondered if some were refusing to follow the Luyten's directions.

*Some. About a third, although the number is dropping as they see others fight alongside us. You're highly social animals. Like us.*

As he approached Lester Avenue, the Luyten said, *Change of plans. Get inside the copy store up ahead. The red door.*

Kai saw the door it was talking about and hurried inside, his bad leg throbbing.

*There's a staircase in the back.*

It led him to an upstairs storage room with windows facing the street, instructed him to bust in the window with the nose of his rifle. He pushed a pallet of boxes filled with reams of paper into place to brace the butt of the rifle, got situated just as a defender trotted into view across the street. It was in full body armor.

Several dozen people advanced on it, surging toward cover behind parked vehicles, behind the corners of buildings. The defender raised his rifle, fired, hit a woman square in the chest. She fell backward, lay unmoving.

Kai didn't notice the Luyten on the roof above the defender until it leaped, dropping three stories, landing right on the defender's back. Somehow the defender stayed upright. He tried to angle his rifle to get a shot at the Luyten, while struggling to keep the butcher knife the Luyten was gripping away from his throat. The humans used the opportunity to charge. They closed on the defender from both sides, hacked at his thighs and feet with their makeshift weapons.

Howling in pain, the defender lashed out, slashing them with the blades on his legs and arms. Blood sprayed across the pavement as people suffered terrible wounds and dropped like sacks.

A second defender surged into view. Kai didn't need the Luyten to tell him what to do: He trained his sights on the defender and squeezed a quick burst from the rifle. It bucked violently. He gripped the rifle with his left hand, held it in place with all of his might, and squeezed off another round, then another, hitting the defender squarely in the chest and knocking it to the ground.

The defender's body armor meant the shots weren't lethal, but as soon as it was down, people attacked it, aiming for the face with their blades and bats.

A woman showed up holding a handgun like she knew how to use one, probably former police or military. She pushed into the crowd of assailants and put two slugs in the defender's face, point-blank.

Thirty seconds later, the street was deserted except for the dead. They were listening to the Luyten. And why not? It was working; the Luyten were coordinating them into an incredibly efficient force, using a million sets of eyes and ears to know what was happening everywhere, benefiting from brains that allowed them to think a dozen things at once, able to move their forces with a split second's notice. Kai hadn't realized just how lethal the combination of humans and Luyten would be.

*The defenders in your area are withdrawing. That means an air strike is coming. Move.*

Kai grabbed the rifle and bolted down the stairs and through the store, out into the street, his hip screaming from the exertion.

*Head west—to your left. Run. As fast as you can.*

Kai ran.

# 87

## *Oliver Bowen*

*January 18, 2048. Washington, D.C.*

"What are they doing?" Oliver's heart had been racing for so long, he was sure a heart attack was imminent. He watched as, on a half dozen of the feeds, the defenders hopped into transport vehicles, or ran, away from the fight.

*They're executing a retrograde action. A tactical retreat. We have an overwhelming advantage in troop numbers, so we're trying to take the fight close-in, to capitalize on that advantage. Their strength is their weaponry. They want to get their troops away from us, into tanks and bombers. This was one of the weaknesses your military strategists identified: The defenders have plenty of weapons, but most of their troops are embedded within human communities. If we can keep them from reaching those weapons, they can't use them.*

"How are we going to stop them?" Vanessa asked, watching the screen from behind Oliver. Oliver was acutely aware of her hand resting on his shoulder. He thought that maybe, finally, Vanessa was back in his life. This time, he wasn't going to lose her.

*Thanks to our defender "spies," we know most of their rendezvous points. We've been sending our troops to those places, to get between them and their weapons.*

"Yes, but Oliver said our troops are poorly armed. They'll be cut to pieces," Vanessa said.

*Remember all of those armed Luyten encampments we discussed? The ones that made Lila so angry?*

"Holy shit," Oliver said. "They're heading to these rendezvous points."

*Bingo.*

# 88

## Lila Easterlin

January 18, 2048. Washington, D.C.

It was Armageddon. No one was going to win. There would be nothing left by the time it was over, nothing but piles of rubble, and a few bloodied humans, mangled Luyten, and burned defenders, still fighting.

Lila hurried down Lester Avenue, past people carrying knives and machetes, past burning buildings. The *thump* of rounds hitting targets registered deep in her belly, reminding her of Australia. The rising chaos played out over flashbacks of Kai lifting and plunging that knife while Erik screamed. She would never have believed Kai capable of that kind of violence, even to save his own life.

But she was thinking of the prewar Kai, the one who hadn't fought the defenders, hadn't been shredded by their giant bullets. He wasn't the same Kai; she had to accept that, and love him just the same.

Up ahead, the road was blocked by a semi tipped on its side. It blocked the intersection so perfectly that Lila was sure it had been put there on purpose. She pulled her Lightfoot to the curb and stepped out. It was four blocks to Oliver's apartment. She took off at a brisk jog, thankful she'd sworn off heels in favor of jogging shoes since that fateful day in Australia.

*Defenders are headed your way. Duck inside—the white door just ahead on your left.* It was her old friend, the crimson Luyten. The door opened before Lila reached it; a plump old woman with dyed red hair waved her in.

"Thanks," Lila gasped as the woman swung the door closed. The apartment was small and cramped, the walls covered by paintings, all in the same style. "Are you an artist?"

"My daughter."

Lila nodded as she peered out the living room window. A phalanx of defenders rolled by in big, black troop transport vehicles. The streets were left utterly empty in their wake.

*All clear.*

"Thank you," Lila said to the woman as she slipped out. She took off at a run. Less than two blocks. She wondered how things were going. Maybe it was too early to tell. One thing was certain: There would be far fewer beings left alive when this was over. It was hard to believe that not long ago, there had been eight or nine billion humans on the planet. Assuming they won, would there be even one billion left?

Lila spotted Oliver's apartment less than a block away. She wondered if they'd be happy to see her. When she'd left she'd felt like an outsider, a gadfly. Maybe they needed a gadfly to stay on their guard—

An explosion knocked her to the ground. Chunks of stone and wood rained down, most of it landing short of Lila. The air was suddenly choked with gray smoke; some of the buildings ahead were missing, leaving a ragged gap.

A gap where Oliver's apartment building had been.

"*Oliver. Dominique.*" Lila scrambled to her feet, ran for the place where the bomb had hit, stumbling through increasingly thick rubble. She had to be wrong; the sudden devastation had disoriented her. That couldn't have been Oliver's building. Maybe it was the next block...

*It was, Lila. I'm sorry.*

"*No!*" Lila pushed through the rubble until she couldn't get any closer. She gripped a two-by-four, pulled it out of her way, trying to identify where she needed to dig, where Oliver's living room had been.

She stood, raised her arms toward the sky. "Where are you? *Help me. God damn it, help me find them.*"

*Dominique and Forrest are safe, at their apartment. But Oliver, I'm sorry, he's—*

"*Don't say it. Don't you dare say it.* You come here and help me." She brushed her hair out of her eyes; her fingers came away bloody. "Why didn't you warn them? Why didn't you get them out of there? You warned *me.*"

She spotted the crimson Luyten coming around the corner, bolting toward her on all seven limbs. *We didn't know. Your spies aren't everywhere; we only hear pieces of their plans. I'm sorry.*

"Get Kai. Tell him we need him."

*All right. We're telling him now.*

"Now help me find them."

The crimson Luyten joined her among the wreckage. It leaned in, grasped what seemed to be an entire wall tented onto a pile of bricks, and pushed it aside.

"Oliver?" Lila called. He couldn't be gone; Lila's mind clamped shut on the possibility. He just couldn't. "How far away is Kai?"

The crimson Luyten had been straining to lift a support beam; it let the beam drop. *They're going to firebomb the entire downtown.*

"What? When?"

*Humans and Luyten keep following their troops, staying close so they can't use their WMDs. They're not going to wait for the defenders to get out. We have to run.*

"Not until we find him." She dug at the wreckage. The jagged edge of a window frame sliced her palm as she pushed it aside. "*Oliver?* Was Vanessa with him?"

The Luyten rushed at Lila, getting far too close to her for comfort. Adrenaline coursed through her as it gripped her wrist and ankles with its cilia, hoisted her effortlessly.

She shrieked, thrashing with all of her might. Its skin was rough and lumpy, uncomfortably warm.

*We have to get out of here. Please stop struggling.* It took off, hurtling down the street, jostling her violently as it dodged and leaped over debris, sometimes moving on three appendages, sometimes four or five. Suddenly it cut toward the sidewalk, cut into a shaded, open-air mall, and ducked against the wall. It went motionless, not even breathing.

Lila heard defenders pass, their boots thumping.

When the noise receded, the Luyten released an enormous puff of air, then rose and bolted.

As the Luyten galloped, its cilia clenched and relaxed, clenched and relaxed, squeezing Lila. She felt like she was being crushed.

Then she suddenly remembered Kai. "Where is Kai? We have to get him."

*He's on a bicycle. I can't carry two.*

They turned a corner, where dozens of people were running, all in the same direction, away from the heart of the city. If Kai was still near Erik's house, he wouldn't have as far to run. If she lost Kai, too, she might as well race back into the heart of the city so she could die quickly.

She couldn't believe Oliver was gone. How could that be possible?

The streets were teeming with people now, all of them running, many clutching weapons. There was no screaming, though—no panic. Even women carrying children were saving all of their breath to run, to keep running. The crimson Luyten weaved left and right, surging past others.

As they crossed Key Bridge and ran along Lynn Street, the buzz of defender bombers rose. Lila couldn't see the horizon behind them because the Luyten blocked her view, but she could hear them growing louder. People around her found energy somewhere to run faster.

The sharp boom of explosions began, far off. They were bombing the downtown area into oblivion, although hopefully most of the people had heeded the Luyten call to flee. The old and infirm were probably still there, unable to run fast enough, or at all.

The sound of bomber engines grew louder, punctuated by bombs hitting their targets. It sounded like they were leveling the whole area.

The explosions were deafening; they sounded as if they were right behind her.

The wall of a nearby building exploded, spitting bricks and glass. The world flipped upside down, then righted itself, then flipped again. They were hurtling end over end; heat scorched Lila's face, flames, rooftops, screams closing in from all sides.

She hit the ground with a tooth-rattling jolt, and she and the Luyten lay still.

Lila tried to lift her head, but it dropped back to the pavement. Huge feet rushed by—a defender.

"Come on," she called to the Luyten. She was confused about what had happened, where they were. She closed her eyes for a moment, opened them again. The world came into better focus.

Two of the Luyten's appendages were gone. Its dark blood was pinwheeled across the pavement and up the side of a half-standing storefront. Puffs of hot air pushed past Lila as the Luyten's center rose and fell, rose and fell.

*That way. Under.* There was a sewer grate in the street ahead, swung open.

She scrabbled at the pavement, trying to pull free. One of the Luyten's remaining limbs was on top of her. She came out a few inches, then slid back. She pulled harder, groaning with effort, and felt the Luyten's muscles bunch as it struggled to raise the limb. She spilled onto the pavement.

"Thank you," she said. The Luyten was still, its center no longer puffing.

A woman lay close by, dead, her face caved in, her legs smoking.

There was no way for Lila to make sense of what she was feeling, so she didn't try. She wiped tears from her cheeks with the back of her hand, roughly, as if they had no business being there.

# 89

## Kai Zhou

*January 18, 2048. Washington, D.C.*

Kai let the mountain bike coast as close to the pile of debris as possible, then swung his good leg over and jumped off. Pain shot up his hip. Ignoring it, he lifted the bike over his shoulder and carried it through the piles of concrete blocking his path. As soon as he was clear he set the bike back on the street and took off, pedaling as hard as he could. He checked the crossing street; he was on Taylor Street. The train depot was less than a dozen blocks away. It looked like he might make it out.

What worried him wasn't so much *his* status; it was Lila and his dad's. His Luyten guardian angel had been silent since warning him about the impending firebombing and telling him to head for the King Street Station in Alexandria.

"How about it?" Kai said, huffing. "Are they okay?"

*Lila is safe.* It was a different Luyten.

"What about my father?"

*I'm sorry. Your father is gone.*

Front tire wobbling, Kai skidded to a stop. He buried his eyes in the crook of his elbow as a terrible, howling grief filled him. He was falling, with no one to catch him. "What happened?"

*The defenders bombed his house. A precision strike. We think they traced Forrest's laptop when he linked into their channel.*

The loss was hitting Kai so much harder than he ever would have guessed. He felt frozen; he wanted to go somewhere and cry under a blanket.

*We've all suffered terrible losses; we can't let it keep us from carrying on. Not now.*

Kai forced himself onto the bike. He pedaled. Maybe he could funnel his grief into rage. As he picked up speed, he became increasingly confident that he could.

The train car was so tightly packed, and moving so fast, there were moments when Kai was lifted off his feet by the bodies pressing on all sides. It was a mercifully short ride, but as soon as Kai stepped out, part of him wished he could climb right back in. There was no fighting in the area around the train station, but by the sounds—tank engines, mortar fire, gunshots—there was an awful battle raging nearby.

Luyten were handing out weapons from open cars on a freight train, but selectively. Kai guessed they were digging into people's minds, giving them only to war veterans who knew how to use them well.

*Follow the others into the woods across the highway*, a Luyten instructed. Kai trotted toward the highway, limping heavily on his bad side. *The defenders are trying to withdraw their forces into Fort Meade. Most of them have yet to arrive, because we've been harassing them, slowing their retreat.*

*We're placing you between them and Fort Meade. Your job is to hold them back until enough of them have arrived. Then we'll send our reinforcements in behind them.*

A pincer movement. The defenders used the same technique to devastating effect against the Luyten. "Won't they be expecting that?" Kai asked, as he climbed the rise beyond the highway and pushed into the underbrush, trying hard not to think of his father. He could do that later; right now he needed to stay focused.

*They don't know these reinforcements exist.*

"They're Luyten?"

*Well armed. Just keep as many defenders as possible from reaching their heavy weapons.*

Kai pushed on, his leg and hip burning fiercely. Others passed him, many looking downright eager to fight. He passed rows of dead bodies, lined up shoulder to shoulder, and grim-faced people dragging more toward the rows.

There was a break in the forest ahead. He reached a big winding road fringed with blood-soaked grass. People, along with a few Luyten, were crouched behind trees on either side. A dozen or so dead defenders were piled in the road, creating a makeshift roadblock.

*This is the primary route into and out of the base. Cross it and keep going, but hurry—another convoy of defenders is about to make a push to break through. I'm going to station you toward the back of the base, away from roads, and put you in charge of a platoon.*

"I don't want to be in charge of a platoon," Kai protested.

*I don't want to be in charge of ten thousand humans. We do what we have to, Boy Who Betrayed the World.*

Kai would have laughed at that, if he hadn't lost his

stepfather an hour earlier. What a strange, strange world he lived in, that he would be having this conversation.

He passed a bright orange sign, warning that he was trespassing near a defender military installation and would be shot on sight. "Tell me something I don't know," he muttered, nodding to two women who were hurriedly setting up a machine gun beside the bough of a big ironwood tree.

The air was saturated with the sound of gunfire. The woods thinned out and gave way to scorched open fields. Thousands of people dotted the landscape, some of them crouching or lying on their stomachs, pointing rifles. Others stood clutching bladed weapons. Many others were already dead—bloodied or blackened, dismembered and disemboweled. Kai counted five Luyten as well, two dead. Power lines supported on big steel towers hung overhead.

A dozen or so people, and one Luyten, were running toward Kai. *Your platoon. There's a lull right now, but the bombers the defenders have managed to get in the air are battering our positions, and in ten minutes a dozen defenders will attack.*

"Wonderful," Kai said.

*I positioned you where resistance was lightest, because of Five.*

If this was light, he couldn't imagine what the people defending the roads were facing. "How is Five doing?"

*Five is alive. He's fighting. He says he hopes to break bread with you when this is over.*

"Tell him I'd like that."

*He also sends his condolences. Despite their past, he had deep respect for your father.*

Kai blinked back tears. "Thanks. We've all lost a lot."

*Yes, we have.*

Kai turned to greet his platoon. "How many of you have guns? Hold them up." Three people raised weapons: two pathetic 1911A-1 pistols—standard twentieth-century US Army sidearms—and one M-4 carbine.

The growl of an enormous engine cut through the other battle sounds.

*Bomber*, a new Luyten voice warned. It took Kai a moment to realize the Luyten speaking to him now was the one who was part of his platoon.

There were no ditches, and the tree line was too far away, so their only defense was to lie flat on their stomachs.

The first bomb landed on the opposite end of the long, rectangular field. Each subsequent explosion shook the ground a little harder until one landed close enough that Kai felt a blast of scorching air on his left side. He clung to the ground, his face pressed into the dry wild grass.

The bomber roared out of sight over the trees. Kai jumped up, scanned the tree line where the defender infantrymen would appear soon. Kai waved his rifle in the air to get his platoon's attention. "As you can see, I have an awesome weapon. We're going to fuck up some defenders with it."

*A tank is coming. It will try to provide cover for the infantry trying to break through. They're desperate to get troops inside. They've got parking lots full of idle weapons.*

The crack of falling trees preceded the enormous tank, which broke into the field and immediately started firing, its turret swiveling left and right, its report deafening.

Kai led his platoon left, trying to get out of its range.

A dozen defender infantrymen broke from the trees close by. Kai dropped to the ground, bracing his rifle against the edge of a bomb crater. He chose a defender, pointed him out.

"That one's ours. Harass him. Draw him this way. As close to me as you can."

*Easy*, his Luyten platoon mate said. *They're engineered to hate me; I'm like a red cape to a bull.* The Luyten headed toward the defender.

The faces kept changing, but Kai always had twenty, as new troops poured into the battle faster than the defenders could kill the old ones. There had to be forty or fifty defenders firing from the trees. A dozen charged onto the field, trying to make it to the base.

Kai closed one eye, squeezed off a few rounds. He was almost out of ammunition, then he'd be nothing but a guy with a gimpy leg swinging a shovel or a butcher knife, whatever he could pry out of a corpse's hand. The people who had to get that close to a defender to hurt it died quickly.

There were bodies everywhere, just everywhere. So many wounded, dragging themselves through the dirt, or just lying there screaming. Kai could no longer hear them; his ears had stopped ringing an hour earlier. The explosions and gunfire now registered as nothing but thumps in his chest and gut; otherwise, the battlefield was blessedly silent. His foot throbbed; the toe of his boot was gone, and, Kai assumed from the pain, some of his toes with it. There was a bloody shrapnel wound in his good side; Kai had no idea how bad it was.

He was glad he hadn't promised Lila he wouldn't let himself get killed. Surely some of them would survive this, but not many.

More defenders broke from the trees, rifles blazing. An explosion threw Kai forward; razors of agony tore through his back. He struggled to his hands and knees, wiped dirt out of his mouth. It felt like there was something stuck in his back, near his left shoulder blade.

"Jesus, this is a slaughter!" Kai shouted into the air. "Where's the help you bastards promised?"

*Soon. Hold on. Hold them back.*

Kai wasn't sure he could stand. He found his rifle, dragged it toward him, wedged the butt into a long scar in the ground, thought of Oliver, and looked for a target.

The defender closest to him was cutting people to pieces with his assault rifle, turning and spinning to keep people from coming up behind him. But people just kept coming, even the ones who had nothing but knives.

*Look in the woods.*

Kai lifted his head, strained to see. Bright colors were moving around in there, and the wall of defenders that had been pummeling them from the edge was now facing the other way, some of them backing into the open field.

A Luyten in full battle gear burst from the trees. Kai let out a full-throated scream of joy. Two more appeared, then a third, swooping down from above the trees in a flight sleeve. It sped right at the defender Kai had been watching, leveled a heater at it. The defender's head and shoulders blackened; it collapsed to the ground, smoking.

Struggling to his feet, Kai limp-trotted toward the tree line, wanting to help. He made it halfway before he stumbled and fell hard, felt searing pain in his shoulder blade. He pressed the ground, got back on his feet. Thousands of people were storming the tree line, burying the defenders under a crush, hacking them with knives, machetes, axes. Kai desperately wanted to join them, but he fell again.

He stayed on the ground this time, content to watch the others cut every last defender down.

# 90

## *Lila Easterlin*

Lila dropped the shovel on top of the pathetic pile of dirt she'd managed to accumulate. She looked at her palms. There were blisters on the pads below each finger, plus the jagged cut in her left palm she'd gotten trying to move debris to get to Oliver. Surveying the eight-inch-deep rectangle she'd managed to carve out, Lila sighed, gave the handle of the shovel a kick. How could anyone dig a hole six feet deep?

Tongue jutting from the side of his mouth, Errol retrieved the shovel and gamely tried to pick up where Lila had left off. The shovel looked enormous in his little hands. Lila knew she should take Errol inside where they were relatively safe, but Erik was still in there.

Squatting on her haunches, she watched Errol. He was an even worse digger than she, but far more enthusiastic. He was oblivious to the rubber stink in the air, the rumble of far-away jets, the pop of distant bombs. At least the fighting had moved off to somewhere else.

473

Lila pulled a tissue from her pocket and wiped Errol's runny nose, then went to the fence. She swung the gate open and surveyed the street. Surely Kai knew to come here, when he found Oliver's house was gone. Surely Five would tell him where Lila was, even if he wasn't speaking to her.

If Five was still alive. If Kai was still alive.

She had no idea what she would do if Kai died. She'd have no one but Errol. She'd never been adept at making friends; most of their friends were Kai's poker friends. Most of his friends would be dead when this was over, in any case.

Out on the street, a Luyten bridged the rise, heading toward Lila. After a glance back at Errol, who was hard at work with the shovel, she went through the gate to meet Five halfway.

"I'm sorry," she said when she reached him.

*Come on.* Five led her back into the yard, sidled up beside Errol. Errol looked at Five, held up the shovel. Five accepted it and began to dig.

"I really am sorry."

*There's no need. I know what's in your mind, what's in your heart. I don't care about what you felt yesterday, only what you feel now. If you do lose Kai, you'll have one friend, at least.*

"He's still alive, then?" She'd been afraid to ask.

*Yes. He's wounded, but should survive.*

Lila broke down then. Out of relief, out of grief for Oliver, out of gratitude, out of despair. She hated crying, but too much had built up; there was no holding it back.

Errol came over and wrapped his little arms around her legs, and that made her cry harder. She knelt and squeezed Errol to her. "Tell him to get his ass home, right now. Why are you digging?"

The grave was three feet deep. The only thing slowing Five was the human-sized shovel; he carved through the hard-packed earth like he was digging on a beach.

*He's already on his way. So are Dominique and Forrest.*

Only then did it occur to her to ask the most obvious question.

*Yes,* Five answered before she could ask. *It will be weeks before the defenders realize they've lost—bloody weeks, awful weeks—but they're taking too many losses. Whatever brilliant military maneuver they attempt, we're always a step ahead of them, and they can't figure out why. Thanks to you.* Five climbed into the grave, because it was too deep to dig from ground level.

Only the top third of the Luyten was visible as dirt flew out of the grave. Errol was mesmerized.

"What will we do when it's over?"

*In theory, that's up to you, up to the human race. As we said, we'll accept any reasonable arrangement. So the question is, what kind of world do you want? Humans and Luyten can try to forge an integrated society, or we can go to Australia, where we're too far away to read your minds.*

"I want you to stay."

*You do, and I appreciate that. I know how hard a climb it's been for you to trust us.* Five pulled himself out of the hole. His movements were slightly awkward, because of his missing limb.

"You said, '*in theory,* it's up to us.' Why in theory?"

*Because we know what you'll decide.*

The answer startled her. "What will we decide?"

*You'll want us to go away. Australia won't be far enough, but if that's as far as we can go…*

Lila nodded. It wasn't what she felt—not anymore,

anyway—but she could understand why people would feel that way. "We're afraid of you."

*If it makes you feel any better, we're afraid of you, too.* Five headed toward the sliding glass doors in the back of the house. *Do you want to take Errol around front while I do this?*

Lila didn't bother answering aloud. Death was everywhere; there was no way to protect Errol from it. Better he see it like this first, rather than bulldozers and mass graves, or bodies in the streets.

Moments later, Five dragged Erik into the yard. He'd wrapped him in bedsheets, and as he approached the grave he slowed, took one single step at a time, as if he were a pallbearer. It made Lila smile. As Five eased him into the grave, Errol pulled his hand free from Lila's and took off.

"Daddy!"

Lila turned to find Kai limping toward them. She rushed over, took in the gash in his side, the bloody, ruined boot. Wrapping an arm around his waist, she led him toward the house.

"No," he said. He gestured toward the grave. "Let's finish first. I can wait."

They gathered at the edge of the grave in silence. Lila stared down at Erik, his form visible beneath the sheets, and remembered the day she'd discovered him walking beside her, wanting to be her friend.

Five picked up the shovel. *I can take it from here. Why don't you and Kai go inside so you can help him?*

Lila led Kai inside as Errol, fascinated by the filling of the hole, stayed behind with Five as the daylight began to fade.

# Epilogue

## *Lila Easterlin*

### March 9, 2050

"Can you see anything yet?" Kai moved his head left and right, trying to see past Lila and Errol, out the tiny window.

Lila tried to see past Errol, who had his face plastered to the window, his hands cupped around his eyes to reduce glare.

"I don't see anything," Errol said. "Just clouds."

Lila suspected they would hear from Five, or some Luyten official, before they saw Australia. She hoped it was Five; she'd feel more comfortable peppering him with questions, starting with the rumor the Luyten had begun construction on a new starship. If the Luyten picked up and left, it would present some serious problems for Lila and Kai, given they'd de facto renounced their citizenship.

"Do you think there'll be a reception committee on the tarmac to greet us, or just some Luyten holding a sign with our names on it at baggage claim?"

"I kind of doubt they have a baggage claim," Lila said laughing.

"What's a baggage claim?" Errol asked, turning from the window.

"It's where you pick up your suitcases," Lila answered.

"Why wouldn't they have one?" Errol asked.

"Because Luyten don't have many possessions, and humans don't visit Australia very often."

Errol thought about this for a moment, his big, dark eyebrows pinched. "If we're not traitors for coming here, how come not many people come?"

For the hundredth time, Lila wondered if they were making a terrible mistake. It was too late now; she might as well stop worrying about it. If they tried to go back to the United States, Willis would hang them for treason. "They're afraid, that's all."

"The whole damned country. Most of the *world*," Kai muttered.

Lila wondered if Kai muttered the words because he didn't want Errol to hear them, or out of habit. There was nothing General Willis and his henchmen could do now that they'd made it this far.

She wondered if the crimson Luyten's sacrifice had led her to swing too far in trusting the Luyten. Willis was a paranoid xenophobe, yes. But no one could deny the Luyten were manufacturing weapons, and had an active genetics program under way. Lila couldn't blame them, given the mistrust and hatred for Luyten that was resurfacing among humans. Still, Lila had no idea what the Luyten felt. No one did.

*We feel sad, but we haven't given up hope. Your decision to come here, to show the world that humans and Luyten can live together, keeps that hope alive.*

"Hello, Five."

At Lila's words, Kai sat up straighter in his seat, looked at Lila expectantly. Then he chuckled, evidently receiving a communication of his own. He went on chuckling softly, shaking his head.

"What did he say?" Lila asked.

"He said, 'Welcome, Boy Who Betrayed the World.'"

*Before you ask, there's no starship under construction. It's just wishful thinking on the part of humans.*

Lila was relieved, but also a little disappointed. It would make things a lot simpler if the Luyten left. "Why not? I mean, why stay on a planet with an intelligent species bearing a grudge?"

*Because the trip here was awful, and it took generations. The nearest potentially habitable planet from here is three times as far. And who's to say that one isn't inhabited?*

"Good point," Kai said.

*I'd like to say hello to Errol. Can you prepare him, so he won't be startled?*

"Errol, Five wants to say hello to you," Lila said. "Is that okay? It's a little scary at first."

Errol's eyes widened. He drew his legs up to his chin, clapped his palms tightly over his ears, then nodded eagerly. "Okay, go."

Watching Errol grin, and then answer Five with a string of "Yeses" and "Okays," Lila thought maybe everything would be okay. If they could just manage to get along for a generation or two, maybe this would all seem normal, and people would stop being afraid.

# Acknowledgments

Dr. Jim Pugh played a huge role in helping me map out this novel, on napkins at Moe's Southwest Grill in Statesboro, Georgia. I dedicate this novel to him with thanks for his help, and more important, his friendship.

I'm deeply grateful to my father, Brigadier General William F. McIntosh, for his assistance with the military aspects of *Defenders*. Before I began writing, I didn't know a platoon from a division, an M-16 from an M1918A-1. I do now.

Sincere thanks to Ian Creasey, a terrific writer and one of the most insightful critiquers on the planet, for providing invaluable feedback on the first draft.

Thank you to Jacob Robinson for reading the first section of this novel early on, and making a few very crucial suggestions. You spared me from a great deal of backtracking, Jacob! And special thanks to Jacob, Donald De Line, and Michael Prevett for their encouragement and support in this project.

# ACKNOWLEDGMENTS

I'm grateful to John Joseph Adams, who bought "Defenders," the short story, for *Lightspeed* magazine, and got the ball rolling.

Orbit Books took a chance on this novel before I'd written a word. I'm extremely grateful for their faith in me, and in *Defenders*.

As always, a shout-out to Clarion and Taos Toolbox, writing workshops that were crucial to my development as a writer.

Love and gratitude to my wife, Alison Scott, for her support and patience as I talked out plot and character over countless car rides and dinners.

Finally, thanks to my agent, Seth Fishman, who read the short story this novel is based on, and saw potential in it. *Defenders* would not exist if not for him.

# extras

orbit

www.orbitbooks.net

# about the author

Hugo Award-winner **Will McIntosh** lives in Williamsburg, Virginia, after recently leaving a career as a psychology professor in southeast Georgia to write full time. He still teaches as an adjunct professor at the College of William and Mary. His debut novel, *Soft Apocalypse*, was a finalist for both a Locus Award and the John W. Campbell Memorial Award. His novel *Love Minus Eighty* was published in 2013 by Orbit Books. *Defenders* is his fourth novel.

Find out more about Will McIntosh and other Orbit authors by registering for the free monthly newsletter at www.orbitbooks.net.

# if you enjoyed
## DEFENDERS

look out for

# ANCILLARY JUSTICE

by

## Ann Leckie

# 1

The body lay naked and facedown, a deathly gray, spatters of blood staining the snow around it. It was minus fifteen degrees Celsius and a storm had passed just hours before. The snow stretched smooth in the wan sunrise, only a few tracks leading into a nearby ice-block building. A tavern. Or what passed for a tavern in this town.

There was something itchingly familiar about that out-thrown arm, the line from shoulder down to hip. But it was hardly possible I knew this person. I didn't know anyone here. This was the icy back end of a cold and isolated planet, as far from Radchaai ideas of civilization as it was possible to be. I was only here, on this planet, in this town, because I had urgent business of my own. Bodies in the street were none of my concern.

Sometimes I don't know why I do the things I do. Even after all this time it's still a new thing for me not to know, not to have orders to follow from one moment to the next. So I can't explain to you why I stopped and with one foot lifted the naked shoulder so I could see the person's face.

Frozen, bruised, and bloody as she was, I knew her. Her name was Seivarden Vendaai, and a long time ago she had been one of my officers, a young lieutenant, eventually promoted to her own command, another ship. I had thought her a thousand years dead, but she was, undeniably, here. I crouched down and felt for a pulse, for the faintest stir of breath.

Still alive.

Seivarden Vendaai was no concern of mine anymore, wasn't my responsibility. And she had never been one of my favorite officers. I had obeyed her orders, of course, and she had never abused any ancillaries, never harmed any of my segments (as the occasional officer did). I had no reason to think badly of her. On the contrary, her manners were those of an educated, well-bred person of good family. Not toward me, of course—I wasn't a person, I was a piece of equipment, a part of the ship. But I had never particularly cared for her.

I rose and went into the tavern. The place was dark, the white of the ice walls long since covered over with grime or worse. The air smelled of alcohol and vomit. A barkeep stood behind a high bench. She was a native—short and fat, pale and wide-eyed. Three patrons sprawled in seats at a dirty table. Despite the cold they wore only trousers and quilted shirts—it was spring in this hemisphere of Nilt and they were enjoying the warm spell. They pretended not to see me, though they had certainly noticed me in the street and knew what motivated my entrance. Likely one or more of them had been involved; Seivarden hadn't been out there long, or she'd have been dead.

"I'll rent a sledge," I said, "and buy a hypothermia kit."

Behind me one of the patrons chuckled and said, voice mocking, "Aren't you a tough little girl."

I turned to look at her, to study her face. She was taller than most Nilters, but fat and pale as any of them. She outbulked me, but I was taller, and I was also considerably stronger than I looked. She didn't realize what she was playing with. She was probably male, to judge from the angular mazelike patterns quilting her shirt. I wasn't entirely certain. It wouldn't have mattered, if I had been in Radch space. Radchaai don't care much about gender, and the language they speak—my own first language—doesn't mark gender in any way. This language we were speaking now did, and I could make trouble for myself if I used the wrong forms. It didn't help that cues meant to distinguish gender changed from place to place, sometimes radically, and rarely made much sense to me.

I decided to say nothing. After a couple of seconds she suddenly found something interesting in the tabletop. I could have killed her, right there, without much effort. I found the idea attractive. But right now Seivarden was my first priority. I turned back to the barkeep.

Slouching negligently she said, as though there had been no interruption, "What kind of place you think this is?"

"The kind of place," I said, still safely in linguistic territory that needed no gender marking, "that will rent me a sledge and sell me a hypothermia kit. How much?"

"Two hundred shen." At least twice the going rate, I was sure. "For the sledge. Out back. You'll have to get it yourself. Another hundred for the kit."

"Complete," I said. "Not used."

She pulled one out from under the bench, and the seal looked undamaged. "Your buddy out there had a tab."

Maybe a lie. Maybe not. Either way the number would be pure fiction. "How much?"

"Three hundred fifty."

I could find a way to keep avoiding referring to the barkeep's gender. Or I could guess. It was, at worst, a fifty-fifty chance. "You're very trusting," I said, guessing *male*, "to let such an indigent"—I knew Seivarden was male, that one was easy—"run up such a debt." The barkeep said nothing. "Six hundred and fifty covers all of it?"

"Yeah," said the barkeep. "Pretty much."

"No, all of it. We will agree now. And if anyone comes after me later demanding more, or tries to rob me, they die."

Silence. Then the sound behind me of someone spitting. "Radchaai scum."

"I'm not Radchaai." Which was true. You have to be human to be Radchaai.

"*He* is," said the barkeep, with the smallest shrug toward the door. "You don't have the accent but you stink like Radchaai."

"That's the swill you serve your customers." Hoots from the patrons behind me. I reached into a pocket, pulled out a handful of chits, and tossed them on the bench. "Keep the change." I turned to leave.

"Your money better be good."

"Your sledge had better be out back where you said." And I left.

The hypothermia kit first. I rolled Seivarden over. Then I tore the seal on the kit, snapped an internal off the card, and pushed it into her bloody, half-frozen mouth. Once the indicator on the card showed green I unfolded the thin wrap, made sure of the charge, wound it around her, and switched it on. Then I went around back for the sledge.

No one was waiting for me, which was fortunate. I didn't want to leave bodies behind just yet, I hadn't come here to cause trouble. I towed the sledge around front, loaded Seivarden onto it, and considered taking my outer coat off and laying it on her, but in the end I decided it wouldn't be that much of an improvement over the hypothermia wrap alone. I powered up the sledge and was off.

I rented a room at the edge of town, one of a dozen two-meter cubes of grimy, gray-green prefab plastic. No bedding, and blankets cost extra, as did heat. I paid—I had already wasted a ridiculous amount of money bringing Seivarden out of the snow.

I cleaned the blood off her as best I could, checked her pulse (still there) and temperature (rising). Once I would have known her core temperature without even thinking, her heart rate, blood oxygen, hormone levels. I would have seen any and every injury merely by wishing it. Now I was blind. Clearly she'd been beaten—her face was swollen, her torso bruised.

The hypothermia kit came with a very basic corrective, but only one, and only suitable for first aid. Seivarden might have internal injuries or severe head trauma, and I was only capable of fixing cuts or sprains. With any luck, the cold and the bruises were all I had to deal with. But I didn't have much medical knowledge, not anymore. Any diagnosis I could make would be of the most basic sort.

I pushed another internal down her throat. Another check—her skin was no more chill than one would expect, considering, and she didn't seem clammy. Her color, given the bruises, was returning to a more normal brown. I brought in a container of snow to melt, set it in a corner where I hoped she wouldn't kick it over if she woke, and then went out, locking the door behind me.

The sun had risen higher in the sky, but the light was

hardly any stronger. By now more tracks marred the even snow of last night's storm, and one or two Nilters were about. I hauled the sledge back to the tavern, parked it behind. No one accosted me, no sounds came from the dark doorway. I headed for the center of town.

People were abroad, doing business. Fat, pale children in trousers and quilted shirts kicked snow at each other, and then stopped and stared with large surprised-looking eyes when they saw me. The adults pretended I didn't exist, but their eyes turned toward me as they passed. I went into a shop, going from what passed for daylight here to dimness, into a chill just barely five degrees warmer than outside.

A dozen people stood around talking, but instant silence descended as soon as I entered. I realized that I had no expression on my face, and set my facial muscles to something pleasant and noncommittal.

"What do you want?" growled the shopkeeper.

"Surely these others are before me." Hoping as I spoke that it was a mixed-gender group, as my sentence indicated. I received only silence in response. "I would like four loaves of bread and a slab of fat. Also two hypothermia kits and two general-purpose correctives, if such a thing is available."

"I've got tens, twenties, and thirties."

"Thirties, please."

She stacked my purchases on the counter. "Three hundred seventy-five." There was a cough from someone behind me— I was being overcharged again.

I paid and left. The children were still huddled, laughing, in the street. The adults still passed me as though I weren't there. I made one more stop—Seivarden would need clothes. Then I returned to the room.

Seivarden was still unconscious, and there were still no

signs of shock as far as I could see. The snow in the container had mostly melted, and I put half of one brick-hard loaf of bread in it to soak.

A head injury and internal organ damage were the most dangerous possibilities. I broke open the two correctives I'd just bought and lifted the blanket to lay one across Seivarden's abdomen, watched it puddle and stretch and then harden into a clear shell. The other I held to the side of her face that seemed the most bruised. When that one had hardened, I took off my outer coat and lay down and slept.

Slightly more than seven and a half hours later, Seivarden stirred and I woke. "Are you awake?" I asked. The corrective I'd applied held one eye closed, and one half of her mouth, but the bruising and the swelling all over her face was much reduced. I considered for a moment what would be the right facial expression, and made it. "I found you in the snow, in front of a tavern. You looked like you needed help." She gave a faint rasp of breath but didn't turn her head toward me. "Are you hungry?" No answer, just a vacant stare. "Did you hit your head?"

"No," she said, quiet, her face relaxed and slack.

"Are you hungry?"

"No."

"When did you eat last?"

"I don't know." Her voice was calm, without inflection.

I pulled her upright and propped her against the gray-green wall, gingerly, not wanting to cause more injury, wary of her slumping over. She stayed sitting, so I slowly spooned some bread-and-water mush into her mouth, working cautiously around the corrective. "Swallow," I said, and she did. I gave her half of what was in the bowl that way and then I ate the rest myself, and brought in another pan of snow.

She watched me put another half-loaf of hard bread in the pan, but said nothing, her face still placid. "What's your name?" I asked. No answer.

She'd taken kef, I guessed. Most people will tell you that kef suppresses emotion, which it does, but that's not all it does. There was a time when I could have explained exactly what kef does, and how, but I'm not what I once was.

As far as I knew, people took kef so they could stop feeling something. Or because they believed that, emotions out of the way, supreme rationality would result, utter logic, true enlightenment. But it doesn't work that way.

Pulling Seivarden out of the snow had cost me time and money that I could ill afford, and for what? Left to her own devices she would find herself another hit or three of kef, and she would find her way into another place like that grimy tavern and get herself well and truly killed. If that was what she wanted I had no right to prevent her. But if she had wanted to die, why hadn't she done the thing cleanly, registered her intention and gone to the medic as anyone would? I didn't understand.

There was a good deal I didn't understand, and nineteen years pretending to be human hadn't taught me as much as I'd thought.

# 2

Nineteen years, three months, and one week before I found Seivarden in the snow, I was a troop carrier orbiting the planet Shis'urna. Troop carriers are the most massive of Radchaai ships, sixteen decks stacked one on top of the other. Command, Administrative, Medical, Hydroponics, Engineering, Central Access, and a deck for each decade, living and working space for my officers, whose every breath, every twitch of every muscle, was known to me.

Troop carriers rarely move. I sat, as I had sat for most of my two-thousand-year existence in one system or another, feeling the bitter chill of vacuum outside my hull, the planet Shis'urna like a blue-and-white glass counter, its orbiting station coming and going around, a steady stream of ships arriving, docking, undocking, departing toward one or the other of the buoy- and beacon-surrounded gates. From my vantage the boundaries of Shis'urna's various nations and territories weren't visible, though on its night side the planet's cities glowed bright here and there, and webs of roads between them, where they'd been restored since the annexation.

I felt and heard—though didn't always see—the presence of my companion ships—the smaller, faster Swords and Mercies, and most numerous at that time, the Justices, troop carriers like me. The oldest of us was nearly three thousand years old. We had known each other for a long time, and by now we had little to say to each other that had not already been said many times. We were, by and large, companionably silent, not counting routine communications.

As I still had ancillaries, I could be in more than one place at a time. I was also on detached duty in the city of Ors, on the planet Shis'urna, under the command of Esk Decade Lieutenant Awn.

Ors sat half on waterlogged land, half in marshy lake, the lakeward side built on slabs atop foundations sunk deep in the marsh mud. Green slime grew in the canals and joints between slabs, along the lower edges of building columns, on anything stationary the water reached, which varied with the season. The constant stink of hydrogen sulfide only cleared occasionally, when summer storms made the lakeward half of the city tremble and shudder and walkways were knee-deep in water blown in from beyond the barrier islands. Occasionally. Usually the storms made the smell worse. They turned the air temporarily cooler, but the relief generally lasted no more than a few days. Otherwise, it was always humid and hot.

I couldn't see Ors from orbit. It was more village than city, though it had once sat at the mouth of a river, and been the capital of a country that stretched along the coastline. Trade had come up and down the river, and flat-bottomed boats had plied the coastal marsh, bringing people from one town to the next. The river had shifted away over the centuries, and now Ors was half ruins. What had once been miles of rectangular islands within a grid of channels was now a much smaller place, surrounded by and interspersed with broken, half-sunken slabs, sometimes with roofs and pillars, that emerged from the muddy green water in the dry season. It had once been home to millions. Only 6,318 people had lived here when Radchaai forces annexed Shis'urna five years earlier, and of course the annexation had reduced that number. In Ors less than in some other places: as soon as we had appeared—myself in the form of my Esk cohorts along with their decade lieutenants lined up in the streets of the town, armed and armored—the head priest of Ikkt had approached the most senior officer present—Lieutenant Awn, as I said—and offered immediate surrender. The head priest had told her followers what they needed to do to survive the annexation, and for the most part those followers did indeed survive. This wasn't as common as one might think—we always made it clear from the beginning that even breathing trouble during an annexation could mean death, and from the instant an annexation began we made demonstrations of just what that meant widely available, but there was always someone who couldn't resist trying us.

Still, the head priest's influence was impressive. The city's small size was to some degree deceptive—during pilgrimage season hundreds of thousands of visitors streamed through the plaza in front of the temple, camped on the slabs of abandoned streets. For worshippers of Ikkt this was the second holiest place on the planet, and the head priest a divine presence.

Usually a civilian police force was in place by the time an annexation was officially complete, something that often took fifty years or more. This annexation was different—citizenship had been granted to the surviving Shis'urnans much earlier than normal. No one in system administration quite trusted the idea of local civilians working security just yet, and military presence was still quite heavy. So when the annexation of Shis'urna was officially complete, most of *Justice of Toren* Esk went back to the ship, but Lieutenant Awn stayed, and I stayed with her as the twenty-ancillary unit *Justice of Toren* One Esk.

The head priest lived in a house near the temple, one of the few intact buildings from the days when Ors had been a city—four-storied, with a single-sloped roof and open on all sides, though dividers could be raised whenever an occupant wished privacy, and shutters could be rolled down on the outsides during storms. The head priest received Lieutenant Awn in a partition some five meters square, light peering in over the tops of the dark walls.

"You don't," said the priest, an old person with gray hair and a close-cut gray beard, "find serving in Ors a hardship?" Both she and Lieutenant Awn had settled onto cushions— damp, like everything in Ors, and fungal-smelling. The priest wore a length of yellow cloth twisted around her waist, her shoulders inked with shapes, some curling, some angular, that changed depending on the liturgical significance of the day. In deference to Radchaai propriety, she wore gloves.

"Of course not," said Lieutenant Awn, pleasantly—though, I thought, not entirely truthfully. She had dark brown eyes and close-clipped dark hair. Her skin was dark enough that she wouldn't be considered pale, but not so dark as to be fashionable—she could have changed it, hair and eyes as well, but she never had. Instead of her uniform—long brown coat with its scattering of jeweled pins, shirt and trousers, boots and gloves—she wore the same sort of skirt the head priest did, and a thin shirt and the lightest of gloves. Still, she was sweating. I stood at the entrance, silent and straight, as a junior priest laid cups and bowls in between Lieutenant Awn and the Divine.

I also stood some forty meters away, in the temple itself—an atypically enclosed space 43.5 meters high, 65.7 meters long, and 29.9 meters wide. At one end were doors nearly as tall as the roof was high, and at the other, towering over the people on the floor below, a representation of a mountainside cliff somewhere else on Shis'urna, worked in painstaking detail. At the foot of this sat a dais, wide steps leading down to a floor of gray-and-green stone. Light streamed in through dozens of green skylights, onto walls painted with scenes from the lives of the saints of the cult of Ikkt. It was unlike any other building in Ors. The architecture, like the cult of Ikkt itself, had been imported from elsewhere on Shis'urna. During pilgrimage season this space would be jammed tight with worshippers. There were other holy sites, but if an Orsian said "pilgrimage" she meant the annual pilgrimage to this place. But that was some weeks away. For now the air of the temple susurrated faintly in one corner with the whispered prayers of a dozen devotees.

The head priest laughed. "You are a diplomat, Lieutenant Awn."

"I am a soldier, Divine," answered Lieutenant Awn. They were speaking Radchaai, and she spoke slowly and precisely, careful of her accent. "I don't find my duty a hardship."

The head priest did not smile in response. In the brief silence that followed, the junior priest set down a lipped bowl of what Shis'urnans call tea, a thick liquid, lukewarm and sweet, that bears almost no relationship to the actual thing.

Outside the doors of the temple I also stood in the cyanophyte-stained plaza, watching people as they passed. Most wore the same simple, bright-colored skirting the head priest did, though only very small children and the very devout had much in the way of markings, and only a few wore gloves. Some of those passing were transplants, Radchaai assigned to jobs or given property here in Ors after the annexation. Most of them had adopted the simple skirt and added a light, loose shirt, as Lieutenant Awn had. Some stuck stubbornly to trousers and jacket, and sweated their way across the plaza. All wore the jewelry that few Radchaai would ever give up—gifts from friends or lovers, memorials to the dead, marks of family or clientage associations.

To the north, past a rectangular stretch of water called the Fore-Temple after the neighborhood it had once been, Ors rose slightly where the city sat on actual ground during the dry season, an area still called, politely, the upper city. I patrolled there as well. When I walked the edge of the water I could see myself standing in the plaza.

Boats poled slowly across the marshy lake, and up and down channels between groupings of slabs. The water was scummy with swaths of algae, here and there bristling with the tips of water-grasses. Away from the town, east and west, buoys marked prohibited stretches of water, and within their confines the iridescent wings of marshflies shimmered over the water weeds floating thick and tangled there. Around them larger boats floated, and the big dredgers, now silent and still, that before the annexation had hauled up the stinking mud that lay beneath the water.

The view to the south was similar, except for the barest hint on the horizon of the actual sea, past the soggy spit that bounded the swamp. I saw all of this, standing as I did at various points surrounding the temple, and walking the streets of the town itself. It was twenty-seven degrees C, and humid as always.

That accounted for almost half of my twenty bodies. The remainder slept or worked in the house Lieutenant Awn occupied—three-storied and spacious, it had once housed a large extended family and a boat rental. One side opened on a broad, muddy green canal, and the opposite onto the largest of local streets.

Three of the segments in the house were awake, performing administrative duties (I sat on a mat on a low platform in the center of the first floor of the house and listened to an Orsian complain to me about the allocation of fishing rights) and keeping watch. "You should bring this to the district magistrate, citizen," I told the Orsian, in the local dialect. Because I knew everyone here, I knew she was female, and a grandparent, both of which had to be acknowledged if I were to speak to her not only grammatically but also courteously.

"I don't know the district magistrate!" she protested, indignant. The magistrate was in a large, populous city well upriver from Ors and nearby Kould Ves. Far enough upriver that the air was often cool and dry, and things didn't smell of mildew all the time. "What does the district magistrate know about Ors? For all I know the district magistrate doesn't exist!" She continued, explaining to me the long history of her house's association with the buoy-enclosed area, which was off-limits and certainly closed to fishing for the next three years.

And as always, in the back of my mind, a constant awareness of being in orbit overhead.

"Come now, Lieutenant," said the head priest. "No one likes Ors except those of us unfortunate enough to be born here. Most Shis'urnans I know, let alone Radchaai, would rather be in a city, with dry land and actual seasons besides rainy and not rainy."

Lieutenant Awn, still sweating, accepted a cup of so-called tea, and drank without grimacing—a matter of practice and determination. "My superiors are asking for my return."

On the relatively dry northern edge of the town, two brown-uniformed soldiers passing in an open runabout saw me, raised hands in greeting. I raised my own, briefly. "One Esk!" one of them called. They were common soldiers, from *Justice of Ente*'s Seven Issa unit, under Lieutenant Skaaiat. They patrolled the stretch of land between Ors and the far southwestern edge of Kould Ves, the city that had grown up around the river's newer mouth. The *Justice of Ente* Seven Issas were human, and knew I was not. They always treated me with slightly guarded friendliness.

"I would prefer you stay," said the head priest, to Lieutenant Awn. Though Lieutenant Awn had already known that. We'd have been back on *Justice of Toren* two years before, but for the Divine's continued request that we stay.

"You understand," said Lieutenant Awn, "they would much prefer to replace One Esk with a human unit. Ancillaries can stay in suspension indefinitely. Humans..." She set down her tea, took a flat, yellow-brown cake. "Humans have families they want to see again, they have lives. They can't stay frozen for centuries, the way ancillaries sometimes do. It doesn't make sense to have ancillaries out of the holds doing work when there are human soldiers who could do it." Though Lieutenant Awn had been here five years, and routinely met with the head priest, it was the first time the topic had been broached so plainly. She frowned, and changes in her respiration and hormone levels told me she'd thought of something dismaying. "You haven't had problems with *Justice of Ente* Seven Issa, have you?"

"No," said the head priest. She looked at Lieutenant Awn

with a wry twist to her mouth. "I know you. I know One Esk. Whoever they'll send me—I won't know. Neither will my parishioners."

"Annexations are messy," said Lieutenant Awn. The head priest winced slightly at the word *annexation* and I thought I saw Lieutenant Awn notice, but she continued. "Seven Issa wasn't here for that. The *Justice of Ente* Issa battalions didn't do anything during that time that One Esk didn't also do."

"No, Lieutenant." The priest put down her own cup, seeming disturbed, but I didn't have access to any of her internal data and so could not be certain. "*Justice of Ente* Issa did many things One Esk did not. It's true, One Esk killed as many people as the soldiers of *Justice of Ente*'s Issa. Likely more." She looked at me, still standing silent by the enclosure's entrance. "No offense, but I think it was more."

"I take no offense, Divine," I replied. The head priest frequently spoke to me as though I were a person. "And you are correct."

"Divine," said Lieutenant Awn, worry clear in her voice. "If the soldiers of *Justice of Ente* Seven Issa—or anyone else—have been abusing citizens…"

"No, no!" protested the head priest, her voice bitter. "Radchaai are so very careful about how citizens are treated!"

Lieutenant Awn's face heated, her distress and anger plain to me. I couldn't read her mind, but I could read every twitch of her every muscle, so her emotions were as transparent to me as glass.